Soundings in the Dark

by

Brian Anderson

The Lyle Dahms Mysteries, Book Three

Cover Art by *Tina Lynn Stout*

The Wild Rose Press, Inc.
PO Box 708
Adams Basin, NY 14410-0708
Visit us at www.thewildrosepress.com

Publishing History
First Edition, 2024
Trade Paperback ISBN 978-1-5092-5514-6
Digital ISBN 978-1-5092-5515-3

The Lyle Dahms Mysteries, Book Three
Published in the United States of America

Dedication

To Sue. My wife, my rock, my life.

Chapter One

When I was seventeen years old, I knew everything. And one of the things I knew was that my friends would be my friends forever.

Greg Walsh was one of these friends. He and I had met those many years ago when I took a job at a pizza parlor in the Minneapolis suburb of Apple Valley. It was located in the same building as a bowling alley and a tavern, and the whole complex went under the stunningly generic moniker of Valley Place. But at the time it was *our* place. It was not only where we worked, but where we hung out, where we dreamt and philosophized, where we ogled girls, and where we read and, in Greg's case, wrote some of the worst poetry ever to deface a sheet of vellum. In short, we were everything young men are supposed to be—engaged, full of ourselves, and deathly earnest.

We also partied pretty earnestly. We had a coworker named Jimmy Dolan who was over the legal drinking age, a trait that made him invaluable to management since no one underage could serve alcohol. It was also a distinction that made him invaluable to us for not only could Jimmy buy us beer, but he also had his own apartment—the site of a party that started the day he moved in and, for a time, showed no signs of ending.

But, in truth, the party had ended long ago. It now raged on only in memory, a memory clouded by the passage of over twenty years. Twenty years since I'd seen Jimmy or Greg or any of my timeless comrades. But cloudy though it was, the memory of Jimmy Dolan's tiny studio apartment was with me as I pulled up in front of Greg Walsh's spacious "executive-style" home. Greg now lived in subdivision a few miles and a lifetime away from where Jimmy had lived. I parked my rust-pocked Ford next to a shiny Porsche 911 in the driveway and surveyed the Walsh residence.

The house tried to bring together different styles of architecture on a grand scale. At least that's what I figured the contractor told Greg to sell him on the thing. For the most part, it was a sprawling, Spanish-style home iced with white stucco and capped with burnt sienna roof tiles. Flowers sprouted from a series of large terracotta urns that squatted along the length of a fieldstone walkway leading from the driveway to the front door. Twin cantilevered balconies ringed in wrought iron flanked a huge leaded glass window positioned above the inset doorway. Single-story wings sprouted on either side of the two-story central portion of the house, angling back to form a spacious rear courtyard. But strangely, what appeared to be a rounded Victorian turret tower was grafted onto the elbow of one of the wings, topped with a spike that extended skyward like the upraised middle finger of some guy you cut off on the freeway. The effect was jarring—aggressively unharmonious.

I squinted as the summer sun reflected off the gleaming stucco and tried to imagine my old friend now in the latter half of his third decade. But I just couldn't do it. Instead, I remembered Greg at seventeen.

Specifically, I remembered the time Greg decided that we should all gather and cement our friendship with something like a ceremony. Always more spiritual than the rest of us, Greg suggested that we make a point of breaking bread together—an act that he felt would knit our individual souls into one strong, holy cloth. For my part I felt that getting together to drink beer and eat Double Stuf Oreos was sufficient, but I agreed to go along with Greg's plan. When the night arrived, Greg came into the party late. We had been drinking steadily and, since some ladies that we knew slightly had agreed to come by, the music was a little louder than usual and the machismo had shifted into overdrive. Greg carried a brown paper bag and set it on the kitchen table as he went to the fridge for a beer. He looked at me with sad eyes and tried to smile as he scanned the room. The music thumped loudly, and a couple of attendees were very close to passing out. He reached into the bag and drew out a loaf of sliced white bread.

I stared at the floor. I don't know who was hurt more, Greg or me. Even if the timing had been right, I thought, even if there had been candles and sensitive music playing softly in the background, even if we had gathered in darkness only to have our circle bathed from above by sudden ethereal light, the bread Greg had brought would have been wholly inadequate. What he needed was a crusty loaf of peasant bread. Bread of the earth. Bread that could be torn off in great hunks and chewed hard. Bread to nourish our souls.

I turned away. I don't remember much after that. I remember I didn't make it home. I remember waking up in the morning, curled up at the end of Jimmy's couch, watching bleary-eyed as Jimmy stood in the kitchen, making toast with Greg's poor, sad bread.

There must have been a pond nearby. As I

approached the front door, two large geese waddled out from around the corner of the house. They took turns squawking at me with what I imagined was goose menace. When I ignored them, they quieted and took turns pooping on the walkway. Stepping carefully, I reached the house and pressed the doorbell. The geese cocked their heads to listen to the muffled Westminster chimes that sounded within.

When Greg opened the door, it wasn't bread that he was holding. It was a cell phone. His hairline had perhaps receded a bit since the last time we'd seen each other and worry lines crowded around his eyes, giving him something of a pinched-off expression, but the blush of youth still lingered about him. He was trim and looked fit in a pair of khakis, a polo shirt, and a pair of brown loafers. He was too immersed in his phone call to greet me with words. Instead, he smiled, gave me a look of friendly exasperation, and made little pincer-like *talk, talk, talk* movements at the phone with his free hand. But he didn't allow my arrival to interrupt the phone conversation.

For the next couple of minutes, I shuffled in the expansive entryway of his home, while Greg talked intently about a production deadline, licensing requirements, and the possibility of pushing back a release date.

As he talked, I surveyed the interior of the house. The floor's gray flagstone extended from the entryway into a great room with an impossibly high, vaulted ceiling upheld by sturdy, rough-hewn beams. The center of the room was covered by an ivory area rug that glowed in the sunlight streaming in through huge windows. Identical recliners flanked a downy sofa, each covered in an almond-white fabric that shone with a soft luster. Built-in shelves took up nearly an entire wall opposite the furniture. Along with a television and carefully arranged groupings of books and knickknacks, the shelves were lined with photographs. Most were of a boy. He was blond, like Greg, with clear blue eyes, and the photographs documented his life from infancy to his teenage years.

I didn't hear Greg say goodbye. All at once the phone conversation was simply over and he was at my side. "Pretty nice, huh?" he asked me, his eyes glinting with pride. "We just had the place redecorated. You should have seen it before. What a dump."

I thought of my small room at the Bijou, the rooming house where I lived. A couple of weeks before, the tenant who lived above me had purchased a *Best of the Ramones* box set and after a solid week of solo slam dancing, he had managed to redecorate my place as well. But that had been limited to the ceiling when some of the plaster shook loose and rained down upon my bed.

"It's lovely," I told him.

Greg stared at me briefly, a half-smile playing about his lips. "You could at least greet me," he said at last, extending his hand.

I stepped in to shake his hand and Greg clasped me by the elbow, pulling me in for a hug. I'm not a big hugger, but I managed to stand still while he squeezed me and thumped my back. "Damn, it's great to see you, Lyle," he said. "Why the hell is it that we lose contact with the people we like best?"

I extricated myself from his embrace. "Great to see you too, man. How long's it been?"

"Too long. Too long. Don't just stand there. Come

in, have a seat. Make yourself at home. Evelyn has some coffee ready for us in the great room, but I've got a cold one if you prefer."

"Bit early for beer. But the coffee sounds good."

He reached back over and gave my arm a squeeze. "Come on in," he repeated.

In the living room, a black thermal carafe sat in the middle of a coffee table surrounded by three hand-thrown coffee cups and saucers, each accompanied by a silver spoon. I poured myself a cup of coffee and was about to take a seat when a woman entered the room.

They'd sent me an invitation to the wedding. I remembered receiving it. We were in our early twenties then. I hadn't seen Greg in a while and didn't recognize the name of the woman on the invitation. But it didn't surprise me that she wasn't the girl that Greg had dated in high school. Janet Kleiner had been the perfect companion for him at seventeen. He wanted to change the world. She was deeply needy and continually tested his resolve. It seemed that Greg had not been up to the challenge.

I hadn't gone to the wedding. I didn't even answer the invitation. Aside from some law enforcement courses, I hadn't gone to college, my flirtation with joining the police department had ended badly, and I was working day labor at the time. I figured that Greg had graduated college and started off on the computer career that he'd often talked about. The truth was, I just didn't want my old friends to know that I hadn't made it. But despite our never having met, Evelyn Walsh greeted me as an old friend. She kissed me lightly on the cheek, then took my hand and held it long after the formal introduction.

She was thin, with brown hair, pale almost translucent skin, and a smile as bright as the sunlight that filled the room. But there was something about her eyes. No light danced in her deep brown eyes. Instead, they simmered with something that wasn't quite sadness. More like weary dismay. It made her radiant smile seem brittle.

Then we sat. We sat and sipped the coffee in awkward silence, casting vacant glances at one another. "So, Greg," I ventured at last. "Do you still write poetry?"

He chuckled. "Heck no. I don't even write code anyone."

"Code?"

"Yeah. I started off as a programmer."

'That's right. And I guess you were pretty good at it," I said, glancing around the room.

"We've done all right. But I gotta admit, my real talent wasn't so much for programming as for hiring the right programmers."

I nodded. "What is it you guys do again?"

"We specialize in internet-based business applications."

I cocked an eyebrow. "I don't even know what that means."

"You want me to explain it?"

"Not really."

He smiled and let the conversation drop. Evelyn's spoon made clinking sounds as she stirred her coffee.

"Well, *you* look great," I told Greg.

"Thanks. You look great, too. Maybe a couple of pounds heavier. But then we both always liked to eat."

I grinned. "Not me, man. I force myself. I hear

chicks dig guys with a little extra meat on 'em."

I glanced at Evelyn Walsh. She was still smiling, but something in her expression suggested that I might be wrong about what chicks liked.

"So," Greg asked, "is there currently a chick digging that extra meat on you?"

"Come again?"

"Are you married?"

"Married? No. But I'm seeing someone pretty steady."

"Are those marriage bells I hear?"

I shifted in my seat. "We haven't discussed it."

"Well, get to it," Greg said, beaming. "Marriage was the best thing that ever happened to me." Greg looked over at Evelyn whose perfunctory smile did not warm.

"That your boy in those pictures over there?" I asked.

Greg nodded but instead of answering he began pulling imaginary threads from the seam of his slacks.

"Yes. That's our Tyler," Evelyn said, her smile tightening noticeably.

"Good looking boy."

"He's sixteen," she told me.

"About the same age Greg and I were when we first met."

They both nodded. We all sipped at our coffee. Somewhere in the house a clock chimed. The blades of a ceiling fan swooped high overhead.

"I was really glad you called, Greg," I said at last. "Glad, but a little surprised. It usually takes some kind of event to bring people together after this many years. I guess I figured you had something specific you wanted to talk about."

"You mean a guy can't just decide to rekindle an old friendship?"

"I don't mean that at all. It's just that most of the time there's a reason."

Greg drained the last of the coffee from his cup and set it down a little too hard. The cup clacked sharply against the saucer. Evelyn Walsh's eyes darted nervously toward her husband.

Greg grinned crookedly. "Okay," he admitted, "there is a reason. It's Tyler."

"He in some trouble?"

"Trouble? Why do you assume he's in trouble?"

I smiled. "You called me, Greg. After all these years. You know what I do for a living. People don't call in a private investigator unless there's some kind of trouble."

Greg nodded and sighed. "I didn't know who else to call, Lyle. It's not that I think Tyler's into anything criminal or dangerous or anything. It's just that…You remember when we were kids? Can you imagine what our folks must have thought about us? I'll bet their imaginations ran riot."

"Is your imagination running riot?"

"I hope so. I hope it's just my imagination."

"Tell me about it."

"Tyler's always been a great kid. You know, baseball, football, good grades. The whole nine yards. Then this last year, things start to change. His grades slip. He doesn't go out for football. He starts dressing like a punk. He dumps his girlfriend."

I shrugged. "They all dress like punks. We used to dress like punks, too."

"Yeah. But it's not the way he dresses. It's…I don't

know. You should see the guys he hangs out with."

"You remember Stan Johnson?" I asked. "Had hair down to his butt. Always wore that T-shirt with the ZigZag guy on it. I hear he's an aide to the governor now."

"It's not just how they look. It's…It's…"

"You think it's drugs? Something else?"

"I'm not so naïve as to think that Tyler's never been exposed to drugs. We've had the talk. He told me that he knows plenty of kids who smoke dope or do coke, but that he's never bothered with it."

"That's pretty much what we told our folks," I said. "Wasn't exactly true, remember?"

"I remember. And I'm sure Tyler's tried what he's tried. But it's not drugs I'm worried about it."

"What then?"

Greg drew a breath before answering. "It's Hitler."

"As in Adolf Hitler?"

Greg glanced at Evelyn, then nodded. "It's him and Goering and the whole fucking Reichstag. Suddenly the kid is fascinated by Nazis. He's got posters up there in his room. Books. Pamphlets. He's shaved his head, for God's sake."

"Shit," I muttered, sipping at my coffee. "It might just be his way of rebelling. I mean, maybe it's just the look. Has he expressed any racist attitudes? Has he—"

"He barely expresses anything," Greg interrupted. "We hardly speak. When we try to talk to him, it's like we're not even in the same room. But I've seen some of that shit he reads. I don't think it's just the look. I think it's the real thing. I think he's bought into the hate."

"But maybe—" I began.

Greg cut me off. "We did talk about it once. I sat

him down just like you're supposed to. I tried to approach it reasonably. I explained the futility, the ugliness, the soul-destroying stupidity of any philosophy that deems one group of people superior to another based on…Well, you know. Gender, race, religion, sexual preference. Whatever. You know what he said? He called me a nigger lover and a race traitor. He told me that soon there would be a…what did he call it? A 'blood cleansing,' and that me and all of my 'kike' puppet masters—he actually used the word 'kike'—would be swept away. Nice stuff coming from your kid, huh?"

Greg stared at his coffee cup and Evelyn stared across the room at the pictures of her son. I looked at them, too. There he was as a toddler in a little suit and tie. And a little older, kneeling in a boat holding a fish. And again, more recently, standing in front of a brilliantly blooming rose bush with his arm around a pretty, waif-like blonde girl. They beamed like newlyweds.

"I couldn't help myself," Greg continued. "He said that, and I let him have it. I slapped him. Hard. Christ, I'd never hit him. Not once. But I hit him that day. Since then, we've been farther apart than ever. My fault, I suppose. Now, I've just got to figure out a way to get to him. To get him away from those pricks. I've got to get him back."

I sighed. "What did you want me to do? I mean, I have no experience. I don't know how to…you know, connect with a kid. I don't know anything about being a parent."

Greg shrugged. "I thought you could maybe…I don't know, *watch him* or something. Maybe get some kind of information. Something we could use to scare him."

"You mean, what, like blackmail him or something?"

"No, no, no," Greg insisted. "Nothing like that. More like. I don't know. I was thinking maybe if you watched him, then I'd know for sure. *We'd* know for sure. We'd know if there's really something to worry about."

"Greg, you know there's something to worry about. Otherwise, you wouldn't have called me. But spying on the kid's not the answer. You lose the kid's trust, you'll never get it back."

"So, I should just let him do whatever? I shouldn't try to find out what he's up to? I shouldn't try to help him?"

"He's not going to think of it as help. *You* remember what it's like being a teenager. You want to do anything you can to prove that you don't need your folks. That you're not like them. Kids that age just break it off. They go off, they do what they do, and a few years later they come back. You raised him. You gave him the tools to do the right thing. You can only trust that he'll do it."

Greg stared at me. "You're right, Lyle. You don't know anything about being a parent. When you're a parent, you don't see your kid making a mess of his life and then get all philosophical and decide to do nothing about it. It's okay to let a kid make a few mistakes, get out of a few jams without your help, but you don't stand by and let him become a racist, a freaking white supremacist, and hope that he just comes out of it on his own."

"Okay, okay. Then get him away from these guys he's hanging with."

"How the hell do I do that?"

"You could move," I suggested.

"I can't just move. This is our home. Anyway, it's not this town. I grew up in this town. I'm not a racist. I mean, some of my best friends are—"

Greg stopped himself before he could finish the sentence. His eyes narrowed into a pained expression. "Who am I kidding? My best friends are all exactly like me. Christ, if there are more than a handful of black families living in this whole damn neighborhood, I'll eat my Porsche."

"Moving might not hurt, then."

"Moving's not an option," he said.

"Maybe you could get him involved in something else. Something that would serve as a counterpoint. Like an internship or some city-based sports league or something."

Greg chuckled. "You ever try to get a sixteen-year-old to do anything you want? Evelyn can't even get him to help with the dinner dishes. And a city-based league? Tyler's had no experience with the city. They'd eat him for lunch up there."

"Who'd eat him for lunch?"

"Will you help us?" Evelyn interrupted. All pretense of a smile was gone. Her voice was desperate. The dismay that I'd seen in her eyes had deepened into despair.

I felt vaguely queasy, like I'd done something wrong, but couldn't say exactly what. It took me a while to respond. "Spying on the kid isn't the answer. This kind of thing takes love, not a private investigator. Sorry guys, there's nothing I can do."

Evelyn's lower lip quivered, but she didn't cry. She

didn't say anything, either. She simply stood and left the room.

Greg sat on the sofa for some time, looking at everything except me. "I suppose you're right, Lyle," he said at last. "Sometimes it seems like doing something, even the wrong thing, is better than doing nothing at all. I appreciate your honesty. I'll think of something. Everything will turn out all right."

"I'm sure it will."

He led me to the door and shook my hand firmly. "I really do appreciate your coming by, Lyle."

"Will you keep in touch? Will you let me know how things turn out?" I asked him.

"You know I will, buddy."

The door closed and I went to my car. The geese had moved to the front lawn. They squawked victoriously at me as I drove away.

I didn't expect to ever hear from Greg Walsh again.

Chapter Two

"You owe me seventy-five dollars."

I was in my room at the Bijou, reading a book on radio comedy when Stephen Edgerton's lanky frame appeared in my doorway. Head down, his face was nearly covered by cascades of curly, red hair. He kicked a cardboard box through the open door. In one hand he clutched the handle of what looked like a thin, wire suitcase; in the other hand he held a leash and a small rubber bone that squeaked when he squeezed it.

My closest friend and fellow denizen of the University area rooming house, Edgerton had long since regarded himself as above such niceties as actually knocking before entering my room. I set my book aside and looked up at him. "Why do I owe you seventy-five dollars?"

Edgerton set the wire suitcase down next to my bed and narrowed his eyes. "You're not going to go stingy on me at this point, are you? I mean, the dog was free, but all of this stuff set me back nearly a hundred and fifty bucks. I figured we'd split it."

"What dog?"

"And it's not just this stuff," Edgerton continued. "There's puppy chow, those rawhide things—for chewing, you know—and the vet visit. He's healthy, by the way. Thanks for asking."

"What dog?" I repeated.

Edgerton stared at me with exasperation. "*Our* dog."

"I don't have a dog."

"Correction. Yesterday, you had no dog. Today," he paused. "Today, you have a dog.'

"Wait a minute, Stephen. I—"

"I figured we'd keep him in your room," he interrupted. "You've got more space in here. It's pretty cluttered in mine. I've really got to do something about that."

"Stephen," I said, straining to remain calm, "this is insane. I don't want—"

"Listen, you can just quit your grousing. It's a *fait accompli.*"

"What's a *fait accompli?*"

"The cockapoo."

"The cockapoo's a *fait accompli?*"

"Now you're getting it."

"I don't want a cockapoo. I don't know anything about cockapoos. I don't even like to *say* cockapoo. It makes me sound like a moron. I'm not interested in taking care of some mutt."

"He's not a mutt. He's a superior hybrid. Noted for his long life, absence of shedding, and wonderful disposition. Which, by the way, is more than I can say for you."

"You really got a dog?" I asked, sounding a woefully plaintive note.

Edgerton nodded.

"What are you? Possessed?"

Edgerton beamed. "Well, in a way. It's the damnedest thing. There's this guy that works with me at the copy center. Bill. His dog had puppies a few weeks ago and he's been bringing in pictures and everything.

And I said something like a puppy would be nice, or maybe it would be a good thing to have someone to greet me when I get home at night. Something. Anyway, today he asks if I'd like to see the puppies, so he drives me over to his place, and I got to tell you, you wouldn't believe it. I'm mean, you just can't help yourself."

"You be surprised what I can help."

"You want to see him? I'll go get him."

Edgerton scampered out of the room. I heard him pattering up and down the hallway a couple of times until he finally returned, a tiny, buff-colored, fur ball squirming in his arms.

"Eeek," I said. "Where's its tail?"

"They bobbed it. They do that. Isn't he beautiful?"

"What's all that crap around his eyes?"

"Oh, that stuff. Bill calls that stuff 'eye boogers.' Cockapoos can have watery eyes. It's the cocker spaniel in them. Or maybe the poodle. I forget."

"Seriously, Stephen. There's no way I'm going to—"

"I figured I'd let you name it."

"Name it? I don't want to name it. I want you to—"

"You know what I think would be a good name? Basil. You know, like Basil Rathbone. The silver screen's Sherlock Holmes."

"I know who Basil Rathbone is, Stephen. What I don't know is—"

"I thought with you being a private detective and all it was fitting."

"Absolutely *none* of this fits, Stephen. You're going to have to take this thing back."

Edgerton looked at his watch. "Christ!" he exclaimed. "Is that the time? I gotta be getting back to work. Watch after little Basil, will you? I left a bag of food in the hall. Make sure he has plenty of water. You'll have to take him out. The wire thing folds out into a kennel. It sounds cruel, but if you're going out, put him in the cage. He's not trained or anything. Bill says kennel training is best. Says that they are not apt to poop where they sleep and if you take them out a lot, they get the message that you're not going to let them poop all over your house. There's a pamphlet on training in the box. You might want to glance at it. I gotta go."

"Stephen!" I hollered, as he put the dog down and turned to leave. "I never agreed to any of this. I'm just not going to do it."

Edgerton turned and stared at me. "You and me, Lyle, we don't have much. We've got room in our lives for this little guy."

I started to protest, but there was a kind of melancholy in his eyes that I didn't want to argue with.

"Besides," he said, "your birthday's in a couple of days. Think of this as your present."

"Then why am I paying you seventy-five dollars?"

"Don't be an asshole. After all, it's the thought that counts."

"We'll talk about it when you get back."

"You're going to fall in love with him."

"Don't bet on it."

Edgerton closed the door behind him. The dog looked first at the closed door, then at me. He had the same look in his eyes as Edgerton.

"I suppose you're thirsty or something," I said to the dog.

The dog opened its mouth wide and panted.

"Okay, okay. But don't get used to it around here.

You're not staying."

I rummaged around in the cardboard box and found two small plastic dog dishes. One blue and one pink. I filled the pink one with water from the small sink in my room, then sat watching the dog lap happily for several seconds. Its thirst quenched, it looked up at me expectantly.

"What? Hungry, too?"

The dog opened its mouth wide again and made a squeaky sound.

I went out into the hall and found the bag of puppy chow. I filled the blue bowl and winced while the dog crunched noisily on the hard, brown pellets. After a couple of minutes, the dog stopped and looked back up at me.

"I'm all done here, pooch," I told him. "That exhausts my expertise."

The dog yawned, circled itself a couple of times, and lay down on my rug. I retrieved the book I'd been reading and lay down on the bed. Within a couple of minutes, the dog hopped up on the bed and rested its head against me.

"You poop on my bed, and I'll make a sandwich out of you," I warned.

He made his squeaky sound again, but otherwise didn't move.

I read for a while, but before long the book was on my chest and my eyes were closed. I don't know how long we'd been lying there when the door swung open again. "Looks like I've been replaced," a woman's voice sounded, rousing me from my slumber.

"What's that?" I muttered.

"There's a new woman in your life."

Naomi Miller and I had been seeing each other for about ten months. We'd met the previous fall when there'd been some trouble at the Midwest Renaissance Festival, and I got dragged into it. To my surprise, when the trouble ended, Naomi stayed—something for which I daily thanked the gods. She was tall—tall and round, yet firm and shapely; strong, yet incredibly gentle. She had the most amazing head of hair, more burnt orange than red, like the sun rising over a new day. Long hair that tumbled over her freckle-spattered shoulders like rivulets of water hugging the contours of a hill in paradise.

She tossed back her tresses and her small, bud-like lips spread into a knowing smile. "Who's the bitch?" she asked.

"Not a bitch," I told her. "Stephen assures me it's a male. You want to check for yourself?"

"I'll take his word for it."

"What brings you here?" I asked, rising. "I'm hoping it's because you're desperate for that brand of loving that you can only get from me."

Her smile broadened. "Best not to refer to desperate loving when you're in bed with a dog."

"Point taken."

"Whose is he, anyway?"

"Stephen's. But he's suffering under the delusion that the dog is in our joint custody. He calls it a birthday present."

"You realize that he's missing his tail?"

"I noticed that."

"And what's wrong with his eyes?"

"The technical term is *eye boogers*."

Naomi nodded. "As long as there's a technical

term."

"Seriously, what brings you around?"

"I thought you might like to take me to lunch."

"We could walk over to McCauley's," I suggested.

"Good. On the way, you can tell me what you *really* want for your birthday."

"Oh, I don't know. A loaf of bread, a jug of wine, and thou."

"Seriously, what would you like?"

"I *am* serious."

She smiled and kissed me. "You're going to have to be more help than that. This is the first time we've celebrated a birthday together. It's gotta be special."

"You're joining me for birthday dinner at my parents' house," I reminded her. "You've never met them. You've never experienced my mom's cooking."

"I know," she said, crinkling her eyes. "I'm a little nervous."

"We'll stop and get you something on the way over there. No one should have to face Mom's pot roast on an empty stomach."

"I'm nervous about meeting them. Not about the cooking."

"Only because you little know what evil lurks in Mom's kitchen."

I locked up my room and we went outside, stepping over a copy of that morning's *Star-Tribune* on our way out. I thought about bringing it with me but decided against it. Instead, I took Naomi's hand in mine and began the three-block walk over to McCauley's pub. We'd gone barely a block when she elbowed me lightly and asked, "So, what should I get you?"

"For my birthday? I don't know. I was just reading

about this radio show of the '30s and '40s called *Vic and Sade*. They called themselves 'Radio's Home Folks.' It was sponsored by Proctor and Gamble. Anyway, there were only four cast members in the thing—Vic, Sade, their son, Rush, and Uncle Fletcher. As a gift, every week Proctor and Gamble sent the cast three pounds of Crisco. Three pounds of Crisco every week. The show was on for like fourteen years. Three pounds of Crisco every week split among four cast members for fourteen years. Now, that's one heck of a lot of Crisco."

Naomi raised her eyebrows at me. "So, you're saying that I should give you shortening?"

"It really *is* only the thought that counts."

"Maybe Stephen will let me go in on the dog."

"Shit, the dog!" I exclaimed.

"What?"

"I was supposed to take him out or kennel him or something."

"Can we do it later?'

"I don't think so."

We'd only been gone a couple of minutes, but that was plenty of time for Basil. There was a delightful little puddle just inside the door and I slipped and nearly fell on my butt as I re-entered the room. I'd left my leather jacket slung across the back of a chair and Basil seemed so happy to see me that he stopped chewing on it almost immediately upon my return. Naomi laughed so hard you'd have thought she was having a seizure.

"You figure out that kennel thing," I grumbled, pointing to the folded suitcase. "I'll get something to clean up the mess."

I ran up the stairs to the kitchen on the second floor and found some paper towels. I got all the way back to my room before it occurred to me that I'd probably want to line the bottom of the kennel with newspaper. Or maybe Edgerton's comic book collection, I thought. Narrowly deciding on newspaper, I grabbed the edition I'd seen lying by the front door.

Naomi soon had the kennel set up, despite her inability to stifle her laughter as she watched me wipe up the puddle, and I was lining the kennel floor when I saw the headline.

Greg Walsh had been murdered.

Chapter Three

It's a funny thing about redballs—the high-profile cases that the media latch onto and turn a police chief's hair gray. They change things around a police station. It would be more than an understatement to say that most of the time when I visited Minneapolis police headquarters, the cops weren't exactly happy to see me. But that morning I approached the desk sergeant and told him I had something on the Walsh murder and damned if he didn't have me personally escorted upstairs to see the detectives. When we discovered that the detective in charge was busy, I was offered coffee, and more than one cop came over to tell me how much everyone appreciated my patience. I got the impression that if I'd asked for a Nut Goody, someone would have scurried off to the nearest vending machine. The unusually warm welcome could only mean that the cops were under major pressure to clear the Walsh case and that, thus far, they had nothing going.

Unfortunately, the convivial atmosphere was not to last. Not after I discovered that the detective in charge of the investigation was my old friend, Augie Tarkof. When he rounded the corner and laid eyes on me, he sighed painfully. "Jesus, Dahms, not you. Go on, run along. Ruin somebody else's day."

"I'm fine, Augie," I told him. "Thanks for asking."

Tarkof waved a dismissive hand at me, turned, and

headed down the hall to his desk without looking back.

"Augie," I called after him, "have you lost weight?"

Tarkof whirled around. There was real anger in his eyes. "You got some wiseass comment you want to make, Dahms?"

In the past, each time I'd seen Tarkof, he seemed shorter than he had the time before. I didn't think he was actually shrinking, I just figured that as his belt size got bigger one had to view Augie through a kind of forced perspective. Like a pixie who had swallowed a bowling ball, his middle loomed ever larger, and the rest of his body appeared scaled back by contrast. Now, I'm not saying that he was suddenly ready for a tryout with the Chippendale dancers, but that morning his slacks gapped noticeably at the waistband and his mustache clung to a face that seemed more angular than it had in years. "No, really, Augie," I said. "You've lost a ton of weight."

The anger in his eyes slowly drained away.

I stood and patted myself on the belly. "You'll have to tell me how you did it. I'm nearly the same size I was when I graduated high school, but back then my nickname was Lumpy."

Tarkof couldn't completely suppress a smile. "Okay. I guess flattery *will* get you something. In this case, about five minutes."

He turned and walked to his desk. I followed meekly.

Once seated, Tarkof leaned back and said, "The sarge said you got something on the Walsh murder. Let me say at the outset that you don't want to be fucking with me on this one."

"Believe me, Augie, neither of us want that."

"So why are you here?"

"Greg Walsh and I used to work together back when we were in high school."

"You didn't come in here to tell me that you and the dead guy went to the prom together, did you?"

"He got back in touch with me last week. He wanted to hire me."

A spark in Tarkof's eyes signaled interest. "What he want you for?"

"Can't tell you, Augie. That's privileged."

"You working for a lawyer?"

"Walsh software's got a lot of lawyers."

A vein in Tarkof's temple pulsed alarmingly. "You don't listen so good, Dahms. I told you already, you don't want to be fucking with me on this one."

"Believe me, I heard you. It's an image that will probably haunt me to my grave."

"So, you came all the way in here to tell me that you can't talk to me?"

"I figured we'd find a way to help each other without stepping all over my client's rights."

"If you're working for Walsh, he's your *former* client. He's dead, remember?"

"Tell me a little about that, Augie."

"You want to know about the murder, buy a newspaper."

"I'd rather hear it from you. You're such a strong stylist."

Tarkof sighed again.

"If you show me yours, I'll show you mine," I said.

He sighed one more time, then reached for a pile of papers perched on the corner of his desk. He plucked a folder off the top of the pile, opened it, and stared at the contents.

"I'll let the pictures tell the story, Dahms," he said, turning the open folder toward me.

The pictures told the story, all right. And there were a lot of pictures. But they all showed pretty much the same thing: my old friend had been sliced up. He'd had the misfortune of wearing a yellow pullover that day and the red blood against the yellow background had a startling effect. He'd been stabbed several times. Lack of blood around some of the puncture wounds made them look to me as if they'd been inflicted after he was dead. Two of the wounds almost certainly were, but they weren't puncture wounds. Someone had carved a pair of ragged swastikas into him—one on each of his cheeks, below each of his wide-open eyes.

"That's a lot of stab wounds," I noted.

"Forty-two," Tarkof replied, "according to the M.E.'s report."

"Just one killer?"

"Three different knives used. Most likely, three killers."

"Lousy way to die," I said, wiping something from thc corner of my eye.

Tarkof reached over and took the folder. "They found him in the parking lot of a Mexican Restaurant on Cedar Avenue about two a.m. the day before yesterday. His car was parked downtown at his office building. What's that, maybe five miles away? I doubt if he hoofed it."

"Somebody drove him there."

Tarkof nodded.

"You know if he was killed in the restaurant parking lot?"

"No. Looks like the slice and dice went down at the

Walsh building lot. We found some blood near Walsh's car. The killer'd tried to clean up some, but…" Tarkof let his voice trail off.

"Two in the morning's pretty late for him to be out," I noted.

"Yeah. We wondered about that. His wife told us that she was concerned when he didn't call, but that he often worked late, and she wasn't too worried. That's about all she's said. She's not really talking to us."

"What do you mean?"

"I mean, we got an initial interview from her, but then some lawyer showed up and told us his client was under too much strain to continue and led her off. Then we started getting the phone calls. The mayor's office. The chief's office. Every official from the governor down to the head of fucking garbage collection is calling me up telling me how to do my job. The latest is that Mrs. Walsh now refuses to talk to us."

"Yeah?"

"You know how it is, Dahms. The lawyers say that the family needs time to adjust to their loss and that they'll let us know when they will be available for questioning."

"You letting them get away with that?"

Tarkof reached into his desk drawer and produced a small, square, plastic food container. He pried off the lid, shook the contents, then extended it toward me. It was filled with peeled, baby carrots. I shook my head at his offer.

Chomping on a carrot, Tarkof continued. "I'm letting them get away with anything the Lieutenant tells me they get away with. I tell him I'm going to bring Mrs. Walsh and their kid in for questioning. He tells me to back off. I tell him I'd like to take a look around Walsh's office and home. He tells me to back off. That leaves me standing around in that restaurant parking lot sniffing the same ground over and over. Worse—the place makes its own corn tortillas, and you can smell the chorizo frying for nearly half a block. It's killing me." He sighed and chomped another carrot.

"So, Walsh had a lot of pull in this town?" I asked.

Tarkof smirked. "The way I hear it, a few years back Walsh was trying to decide whether to locate his company headquarters here or in some Arkansas backwater or other. The city offered Walsh everything they could think of to get him to build here. They bought and gave him the land. They closed down and bulldozed the existing buildings. They promised him massive tax breaks. Shit, the mayor did everything but bend over and tell him to have at."

I chuckled. "So, you haven't been to the house, then?"

Tarkof's eyes flashed. "No. Why do you ask?"

"Just wondering."

"Something there I need to know about?"

"Nothing springs to mind."

"What happened to 'I show you mine, you show me yours?'"

"The Nazi shit's gotta be a lead," I said.

"Yeah. We're checking out every hate group there is. You'd be surprised how many there are."

"Not too surprised. Why do you think Walsh would be on the wrong side of any of those guys?"

"Maybe you could tell me. He was your friend."

"We hadn't seen each other for a long time. He's not a member of a minority group. Unless having piles of money qualifies. Back when I knew him, he was pretty liberal, but he wasn't out there or anything. He was...I don't know. *Artistic*, I guess. Not very political."

Tarkof shook his head slightly. "People we talked to say that he donated to liberal causes. Rich folks always figure they gotta change the world, don't they? He tossed a fair amount of money around. He was big into the ACLU. He supported gun control, internships for inner city kids, college funds, stuff like that. Some of that made the paper."

"But he wasn't exactly in the vanguard of the coming worker's revolution?"

"Nah. The charity thing was probably a tax write-off."

"Then why would he be a target for some right-wing group?"

Tarkof shrugged. "Again, he was your friend. You tell me."

"I wish I knew, Augie."

Tarkof picked out another carrot, carefully closed the container, and stowed it back in his desk drawer. "You gonna tell me why Walsh wanted to hire you?"

"It was nothing related to this mess. It was...you know, personal."

"Not much more personal than getting killed."

I shrugged.

"If you got information you're not letting me in on, you might be protecting your pal's killers."

I nodded. "I got nothing."

Augie kept staring, but he didn't challenge me. I thanked him for his time and made my way toward the elevator.

The clock atop city hall struck noon as I emerged

from the building. It was sunny and warm, and a light breeze tickled through my hair. I headed across the street toward the Government center. A group of half a dozen women in business attire, each wearing a pair of dazzling white tennis shoes, came out and sat on a low wall that faced a little square of lawn. I watched as they opened their lunch bags, chatted, and laughed in the sunshine. I went inside and up to the skyway level.

There's a little soup and sandwich place tucked away in the skyway near Pillsbury Center. They've got a chicken and wild rice soup there that some men would kill for. When I got there, I grabbed a plastic tray and waited in line. After the guy behind the counter wordlessly ladled my soup into a throwaway bowl, I was lucky enough to nab a table in the adjacent food court. Most people must be outside enjoying the day, I decided.

I stirred at my soup. The only thing I'd learned from Tarkof about the murder that wasn't in the newspaper reports was that he'd been killed outside his office, then dumped at the restaurant. That and the fact that Tarkof didn't know about the kid. No doubt Evelyn and her lawyers were cleaning up his room, boxing up all the propaganda, replacing his SS posters with paintings of dogs playing poker. But it wouldn't work. Tarkof would know soon enough. And that was not going to be good for Tyler Walsh.

I wasn't sure why I hadn't just told Tarkof myself. The mutilation of the corpse made Tyler and his goose-stepping cronies the logical suspects for Daddy's murder. Greg had been my friend. Was I protecting his killers?

I lay down my spoon and picked up the warm roll that came with the soup. I realized that I'd forgotten to grab any butter. No matter, I thought, tearing the crusty roll in two.

No, I decided. I wasn't protecting anybody. Greg had asked me to help protect Tyler. I'd refused and now Greg was dead. I couldn't just feed the kid to the cops. But I had to do something. If not for Greg, then for myself.

I sat in silence, feeling older than I had in years, chewing hard on the roll. Once again, my mind was flooded with the image of Greg at seventeen as I sat there solo, finally performing the sacrament that we should have shared long ago.

Chapter Four

We had good weather for the funeral. The sun was high, and the sky was a pale blue, laced with wispy clouds that stretched out to eternity. The cemetery was taking no chances, however. They'd set up a large canopy next to the gravesite and dozens of people huddled underneath it. More spilled out into the sunshine. Many of them kept sneaking glances at those under cover as if they felt cheated not to have been granted one of the good spots.

Evelyn Walsh had the best spot. She was under the canopy in front sitting in an ornately carved chair that was upholstered in red velvet. I looked through the mist of many years and recognized Greg's mom sitting beside her. Greg had never come right out and told me, but it had been clear that she'd had a drinking problem when we were growing up. Now she'd be in her early sixties, and she looked every year of it, and then some. Her gray hair was pinned tightly back beneath a tiny, black hat trimmed in black lace. Her eyes were red-rimmed, and tears streaked her heavily rouged cheeks. Her nose was a network of burst capillaries. A man I didn't recognize sat next to her. I didn't see Greg's father. I scanned the crowd. I didn't see his son Tyler, either.

But I saw Augie. He was standing at the edge of the crowd, head bowed, a little notebook in his hand.

A minister stood next to the casket, said some

words, led us in a hymn, then closed his Bible and nodded to Evelyn. She rose shakily as a groundskeeper moved a switch that lowered the casket into a hole in the earth. In absolute silence, Evelyn dropped a single white rose on top of the casket. I shuddered as it landed, amazed that something so delicate could alight so loudly.

Evelyn turned away from the casket. There were no tears in her eyes, only emptiness.

About a dozen people dropped roses onto the casket as a murmur rose above the gravesite. Most of the discussion concerned who was driving over to the church for the funeral reception, but some were discussing how Greg's death was affecting the price of Walsh Software stock. "A momentary downturn," one of them said. Surely, it would quickly recover.

A camera crew from a local TV station stood at the edge of the crowd, moving forward as the gathering dispersed. A phalanx of mourners hovered protectively around Evelyn as she made her way from the gravesite. She was flanked on one side by Greg's mom and on the other by a tall woman with a stern face who wore a blazer with red checks against a vibrant yellow-green blouse and matching yellow-green pumps. I figured the woman in the clown suit for Evelyn's mother. The others were mostly young men and women, the young men looking uncomfortable in the suits and ties that were required wear at a funeral, but seldom worn in their more familiar business casual—or more likely, *casual* casual—work environment. More than one glared at me as I made my way through them toward the widow of their fallen boss and mentor. When I reached Evelyn, there was no recognition in her eyes.

"Lyle Dahms," I prompted.

"I remember," she said, although the expression in her eyes did not change.

"I just want you to know if there's anything I can do for you—"

"You're very kind," she said, automatically.

"No. I mean it," I pressed. "I feel…well, guilty. You asked for my help before, and I wasn't there for you. I'm there for you now."

She leveled a suspicious gaze at me.

"Really," I continued. "If I could do something, I might feel like I…" I paused. "You know, I'm not sure what I'm trying to say."

Her eyes softened, becoming thoughtful. She took me by the elbow and led me a couple of feet away from the others. "I know what you mean," she told me. "About feeling guilty. You know that you're not doing enough, but you really don't know what else to do. And you have no one to tell you what's appropriate."

"Things are pretty bleak now," I said, trying to sound comforting. "They'll get better."

A half-smirk appeared on Evelyn Walsh's face, then was gone. "That's what everyone tells me. That I'll be okay. But I can't even imagine it. You know what I think? I don't think you get over something like this. I think this just becomes what passes for normal. Maybe I'm supposed to feel like this. Like I should just wither away. Like nothing matters anymore. Maybe I *am* okay. Maybe this is normal for me now."

"Everybody finds their own way to grieve," I heard myself say.

"Yeah, maybe. But people keep asking me how I'm doing, and I don't know how to respond. I haven't any experience with this kind of hurt. Then I wonder, maybe they're asking me because they don't think I'm doing this right. Maybe they don't think I'm crying enough or maybe too much. I don't know. Maybe if I was handling this correctly, someone would come up and say, 'Good job! You got this down. Way to grieve, Evelyn.'"

This time I just stood there and watched as tears welled in her eyes. She seemed to shrink within herself. I started to get a little blurry too. Finally, I stepped in and wrapped my arms around her. I patted her gently on the back, then held her until her sobbing subsided. Then she pushed herself away from me but held onto my hand.

"Where's Tyler?" I asked.

Alarm crackled across her wide, brown eyes before she said, "He's at home."

I nodded. "It would have been better if he'd been able to come."

"What does that mean?"

I cocked my head and squinted in the direction of the departing mourners. "People will wonder, that's all. It would be better to keep people from wondering."

"What are you implying?" Evelyn asked, letting go of my hand.

I spotted Tarkof leaning against the trunk of a maple tree a few plots over. He was staring at us coldly. "The cops are here."

Evelyn's eyes darted back toward the grave.

"They don't know about Tyler's interests yet," I said. "But it's only a matter of time."

"How do you know that?" she asked, accusation joining the alarm in her eyes.

"I talked to them. I've got history with the cop in charge of the investigation."

"What did you tell him?"

"Relax. I didn't tell him anything."

"But…but, you probably drew his suspicion. He's going to—"

"It didn't make any difference, Evelyn. Cops are always suspicious. In fact, you're not talking to them is what's really going to draw their interest."

"But my lawyers—"

"Your lawyers are trying to protect you. And that's fine. But you're not going to get on the other side of this thing until you talk to the cops. And when you do, you gotta tell them everything."

"But Tyler. We have to protect Tyler. If the police find out they'll think—"

"Right now, it's not important what the cops think. What *you* think—*that's* important."

"What?"

"Do you think Tyler had anything to do with Greg's death?"

Her mouth gaped open, and she exhaled audibly. "How can you even suggest that? There's no way. If you saw him, then you'd know. This whole thing has nearly killed him. He won't talk. He can't eat. Even tears won't flow. I've had to take him to a counselor. Everyone agrees that talking to the police right now might force him over the edge."

"By not talking to the cops, you'll be making it worse. The cops are going to find out about Tyler's interest in…um, German history. The only lead they have right now is the swastikas found on the body."

Evelyn shuddered.

"When the cops find out about Tyler and neither of you have talked to them, well, it'll look like you were playing them. They won't like that. They'll be looking hard at Tyler."

"But his counselor said—"

"Have the counselor attend the interview," I interrupted. "With you there, the lawyers, the counselor…Talking to the cops isn't going to send him over the edge. His dad getting killed is what's hurting him. Talking to the cops is part of getting past it."

"But they told me—"

"Just think about, okay. Talk it over with everyone, then decide. But remember, you will have to talk to them eventually. And when you do, tell them everything. You don't and you're screwed. Count on it."

Evelyn nodded, but her eyes remained fixed on mine. "I need to look out for my son. He's all I have. Since the day he joined our family, he's been the center of my life. Can you understand that?"

I smiled reassuringly, able, I thought, to keep the puzzlement out of my expression. *Joined our family?* That seemed an odd way to put it. More like a merger than a birth. I kept the smile in place as Evelyn turned away.

I then became aware of a ruckus that had broken out on the far side of the grave plot. Two very large men in matching, ill-fitting, off-the-rack blue polyester suits—one with a shaved head, the other with long, stringy, blond hair—were scowling down at maybe a half dozen skinny young men with determined yet frightened expressions. I figured the young guys for more of Greg's employees, but they looked like preppy school children in contrast to the burly pair they'd faced off with.

But who really caught my interest was a man standing between the two bruisers. He was fairly short, maybe five foot six, with thinning blond hair that had been styled carefully to appear fuller. He was wearing an expertly tailored navy-blue suit that nearly succeeded in hiding his weight problem. He had an open, pudgy face and, despite the commotion, he wore a dreamy smile. But his eyes were proud, focused, and as hard and cold as sapphires.

I heard a couple of the techies shouting at the threesome. I distinctly made out the words "get out" and "racist asshole."

I moved a little closer and soon found myself leaning against that maple tree with Augie Tarkof. Augie's eyes sparkled and he wore a gleeful smirk. "Lookee what we have here," he said, nodding toward the men.

"Who are those guys?"

"I don't know who the two meatballs are," Tarkof said, "but the guy is the middle is Matty Beam, head of the Creator's Covenant Christian Church."

"That guy's some kind of priest?" I asked. "And those birds with him don't look much like clergymen. More like rentals from Goons 'R Us."

"I'm afraid Beam's church has a lot more to do with goons than God, Dahms."

"How's that?"

Tarkof stared at me for a second or two. "Matty's church is an offshoot of the Christian Identity movement. Basically, they think that white folks are made in God's image. Anybody with a splash of color on them is less than divine. Subhuman, really. Oh, and the Jews. They don't think much of them, either."

"No latkes at their Sunday potlucks, then?"

"They don't have Sunday services. Hell, they don't even have actual meetings. There's only a handful of members in the CCCC, Beam and a few gullible souls he's promised to take care of when he comes into his own. Matty's what? Thirty-two years old? Still lives at home. His little terror cell meets in his parents' basement. They get together, talk about how much they hate everybody, read a little *Mein Kampf*, get sloshed, and come up with ideas for these hate fliers they plaster all over town."

"What kind of hate fliers?

"You know, the usual crap. Jews run everything, the white race is under attack, Black guys just want to sleep with your sister. Whatever."

"If these guys are so insignificant, how come everyone here seems to know who this guy is?"

"Everybody but you," Tarkof pointed out. "Beam's been in the papers lately. Matty took off enough time from his proselytizing to get himself a law degree. But the State Bar won't admit him. They say he's unfit 'cause of his racism. The ACLU got itself involved. They say that although they find Beam and views repugnant, since Beam hasn't broken the law, the state Bar Association hasn't the right to deny him his law license. They're bringing suit on his behalf."

"That's mighty white of them," I said.

Tarkof grunted.

Several more mourners had joined the original group that had confronted Beam and his flunkies. Soon the crowd had swelled and the distance between them and the intrusive trio had narrowed. Anger replaced fear on the faces of those assembled against them. The eyes of the men flanking Beam simmered with hate. Beam remained expressionless—nary a ripple in his calm blue eyes. The crowd inched forward. Things were going to get ugly, I thought.

Tarkof slowly pushed himself away from the tree and loped over to the growing conflagration. He pulled out his badge and used it to stiff-arm his way through the crowd. I followed in his wake. When we reached Beam, Tarkof smiled broadly. "You're coming with me, Matty."

"Am I under arrest?" Beam asked, letting his eyes wander over the crowd.

"Call it protective custody."

"I appreciate the gesture, Detective, but I don't feel the need for protection."

Tarkof turned to look at the crowd. Emboldened by their number, a couple of mourners had actually picked up rocks and fallen branches.

Tarkof cocked an eyebrow. "You're shitting me, right?"

"I refuse to fear these deluded sheep," Beam said, puffing himself up. "As I refuse to accept the so-called 'protection' of the police. The truth will protect me and my fellows. A truth so resounding that even the Zionist news media cannot hide from the light."

The TV news crew I'd seen earlier had maneuvered close to us. Beam stuck his chin out as far as possible from his fleshy neck and turned his head directly toward the camera. A young woman with incredibly full hair stood next to the cameraman.

Tarkof rolled his eyes as the newswoman asked loudly, "What can you tell us about Greg Walsh's death, Mr. Beam?" She held a microphone out at arm's length and waited for the answer.

Beam edged toward the microphone. "I just came to pay my respects. As you probably know, Mr. Walsh was a great supporter of the American Civil Liberties Union. Like myself, Mr. Walsh believed that our civil rights— our rights to freely associate, to speak our minds without fear, and to practice our religion—are under attack by powers that seek to maintain the *status quo*. I felt a comradeship with the man but when I come to mourn his passing, these ZOG brainwashed zombies array themselves against me. It's truly sad."

"ZOG?"

"Zionist Occupational Government."

"Uh huh. Any comment on the swastikas that were found on the body?" the newswoman asked.

"Another truly sad element," Beam said. "The cross of our church should be used to unite Christians, not to desecrate the dead."

"The cross of your church, Mr. Beam?"

"Yes. As you probably know, the swastika is simply a redefined Greek cross. It is the symbol of the Creator's Covenant Christian Church and, I might add, several other like-minded organizations."

"Like the Nazi Party?"

Beam sighed. "Yes. But we are not Nazis. The Nazi party is a political organization. We are a religious group."

"A religious group that advocates hatred of Jews, African Americans, Latinos—"

"A religious group that advocates pride," Beam interrupted. "No matter your race. We believe that each of us should be proud of who we are. As a white man, I am proud of the accomplishments of the white race. I celebrate my forefathers and the stunning achievements that the white race has wrought throughout history."

"Like slavery, religious crusades, and the

Holocaust, Mr. Beam?" the newswoman asked, shouting to be heard.

"I prefer to be called 'Reverend' Beam," he said, a beatific smile on his face.

I stepped in front of the camera. "I like to call him 'Sphincterus Maximus' myself," I said, flashing a toothy grin.

Beam glared at me with equal parts anger and bewilderment.

"It's Latin," I added helpfully.

Beam turned to the newswoman. "You can edit that out, right?"

She chuckled and turned away.

"Is this man with you?" Beam asked Tarkof.

"If you mean, *is he a cop*? No."

"Who is he then?"

"Folks got a right to privacy, don't they Matty?"

Beam stared at me. "Lots of race traitors hide from the light. Even tubby here likely has a hole big enough to hide in."

"You saying he's got reason to hide, Matty?" Tarkof dared him. "You making some kind of threat here?"

Beam smiled. "No, Detective. I'm just saying that there are those that have reason to fear the truth and the people who speak it."

Beam and both of his cronies turned to face me. Their eyes seethed with malice. I reached into my back pocket and produced my wallet. I stepped forward, getting close enough that we stood eye-to-eye. "Here's my card, pal," I said. "Call me sometime."

Beam took the card and slipped it into his shirt pocket without looking at it. "I'll do that," he said, before turning his back on the crowd. Several people moved toward the departing trio, but Tarkof barred their way, holding up his shield and letting his coat open just enough that they could see his holstered gun. The angry mourners had to settle for tossing lame insults at them as they walked away.

I searched the crowd for Evelyn Walsh. She'd gone through enough without having some self-serving hatemonger crash her late husband's funeral, I thought. I didn't spot her, but on the edge of the crowd, too far away for me to be sure, I thought I saw someone else. Another figure from out of the past. I thought I saw Greg's old girlfriend, Janet Kleiner. She had her back to me, bending forward, putting something into the back seat of a battered, silver Toyota. She turned and I got a better look, but I still couldn't swear it was her. Too many years had gone by. I tried to make my way toward her, but before I could, whoever it was climbed into the car and drove away.

Chapter Five

My parents still lived in the suburban Burnsville rambler where my brother and I had grown up. Although he was younger, my brother Chuck had escaped the house before I had. After high school, I'd stuck around for a few years, working mostly warehouse jobs and trying to decide what to do with my life. Chuck didn't have much of a plan either, but it turned out he didn't need one. He had luck. He'd inherited the good looks that distinguished my father's side of the family with none of the weight problems that plagued my mother's. Barely out of high school, he'd started getting work as a model. It was nothing splashy at first. His image had appeared in a couple of catalogs and one of those glossy portfolios that hair stylists use to show off hot new haircuts. He was justifiably proud, but the work wasn't steady, and my dad kept after him to find something more regular.

Then he got the Call. A New York agency had seen one of his layouts and wanted to represent him. He was gone, off to Europe for a few years, then to the East Coast where he quit the fashion world, enrolled in college, and emerged with an MBA, a beautiful wife, and a six-figure salary. He'd done his dad proud. As for me, I'd graduated from day laborer to private investigator, which didn't pay quite as much and had the added advantage of being a profession my ex-cop old man held in complete disdain.

Naomi had insisted that I bring something to the birthday dinner. Stupidly, I'd thought that since it was *my* birthday, I didn't need to bring a present, but Naomi assured me that I was missing the point. So it was that I rang the doorbell to my parents' home with Naomi at my side and a five-liter box of White Grenache under my arm.

Waiting for the door to open, I glanced around the old homestead and noted that the lawn badly needed mowing. That was odd. Since his retirement, my father had devoted his life to his lawn. He would spend the winters readying his implements for the coming battle—sharpening the mower blades, oiling the drop spreader, adjusting and readjusting the length of line on the weed-whacker. Then, as soon as the snows of winter had melted and the ground was no longer spongy, he would be out there—mowing, weeding, fertilizing, and occasionally making sure the grass could breathe properly by perforating the ground with something called a "lawn corer." I was about to mention to Naomi the relative lack of lawn care when my mom opened the door.

Dad always liked Mom in dresses, so I was a bit surprised when she greeted us wearing a beige blouse stippled with light blue flowers tucked into a pair of wide, white slacks. Her short gray hair was sprayed stiff, and her smile nearly masked the apprehension in her eyes. "Happy Birthday, Lyle," she said, drawing out each syllable as if the words were oozing out of her. She gave my arm a squeeze, then extended her hand to Naomi. "It's *sooo* nice to meet you, dear" she gushed. "Lyle talks about you so much that I feel like I know you."

The truth is I'd talked to my mom on the phone only

a handful of times since I'd met Naomi and hadn't gone much beyond notifying her of Naomi's existence. But if there's one overriding principle that guides my mom it's that if you don't have something nice to say about someone, make something up.

"It's wonderful to meet you too, Mrs. Dahms," Naomi said. The corners of her mouth tightened as if she wanted to smile but her nerves were keeping her in check.

I peered past Mom. I heard the muffled sounds of a baseball game emanating from the living room beyond.

"Your father's got the game on," Mom told me. "But he promised to turn it off when you got here. Come on in."

I handed Mom the box of wine and took Naomi's hand. We made our way down the short hallway that led to the living room.

Mom had a roast in the oven and the aroma suffused the house, nearly masking another, more familiar bouquet. If a family lives in a house long enough, the place takes on a smell—a permanent fragrance that is peculiar to that family. Cooking odors compete, yet never quite conquer. Fresh flowers and Lysol augment yet are powerless to eliminate. It's the smell of a marriage. Of a family. It's as though as the years go by and all the joys, all the hurts, all the arguments, all the dull nights spent in silence settle about the house, giving off a particular scent—not altogether pleasant, but warmly familiar. The scent of home.

The décor hadn't changed much either since I lived there. The big screen TV was new, but the vinyl-covered recliner that sat directly opposite it was the same chair my dad had always sat in. As kids, Chuck and I would

47

vie with each other for the chance to sit in that chair whenever Dad was away. The sofa and matching loveseat also dated from my childhood but were now minus the clear plastic that had covered them until both of us boys were safely out of the house. Instead, slung across the back of the sofa was an afghan—yellow, green and orange against a black background—that my maternal grandmother had knitted in the dimly-remembered past. The sofa faced a large wooden coffee table edged in peeling, brass-colored plastic. Family photographs stood atop a round table at one end of the loveseat. There was a photo of Chuck and his wife, one of Chuck fishing, and another of Chuck holding his infant son. There was also a high school era photo of me with unruly hair, a wide collar, and a brown plaid sports coat. Against the opposite wall, to one side of the fireplace, was Dad's gun cabinet. Among his hunting rifles, shotgun, and handguns, I spotted his old revolver. A .38 Smith & Wesson. His old cop's gun. The same kind of gun I carried.

As we entered the living room, my dad looked up from his recliner, then at the television screen, then back at us. Despite the warmth of the July afternoon, he wore his customary flannel shirt, this time unbuttoned over a white T-shirt. Although getting on in years, he still exuded a sense of power. He'd put on some weight since I'd left home, but not much. He had a bench and a set of free weights in the basement to help keep him trim. A lock of his steely, gray-black hair had fallen across his forehead, and he nudged it aside as he turned his blue-gray eyes toward us. His face was impassive, until a tiny smile of resignation appeared, deepening the dimples that I'm sure had beguiled my mom back in their courting days. He slowly raised himself from his chair, a painful grimace replacing the smile.

"Hi, Dad," I said.

He didn't reply, instead he took a look a long look at Naomi, his eyes traveling the length of her in slow appraisal before coming to rest on her face. "So, you're the girl," he said. "You must be something. Lyle here has never brought a girl by before."

"Now, that's not true, Ray," Mom interjected. "Lyle's brought lots of girls here over the years."

"That's not how I remember it, Marjorie."

I managed an embarrassed chuckle.

"Come on into the living room," Mom told us. "Ray, you promised to turn that TV off when they got here. Naomi, sit over here next to me on the loveseat. I've got some appetizers on the coffee table there. I've got some cheddar cheese spread and I put out some of those tiny sausages you like, Ray. Lyle, put this lovely wine you brought into the fridge for me, will you? I just want to sit here for a few minutes and get acquainted with your lady friend."

I took the wine from Mom.

"What'ya bring that for?" Dad asked.

"She made me," I replied pointing at Naomi with a mock pout.

Dad nodded, then lowered himself back into his recliner. Another flash of pain registered on his face and his eyes darted briefly toward me. Then he absently rubbed his nose and reached for the remote.

I stepped toward the kitchen, then stopped. "You feeling all right, Dad?"

He pretended he didn't hear me as he muted the sound of the ballgame. Fixing his eyes on the silent screen, he said, "Get me a beer while you're in there, son. You can help yourself to one, too. That is, unless you'd rather have that *wine* you brought."

From that I gathered that he found blush wine a little too fey an accompaniment for baseball and canned cocktail wieners, so I put the wine away, and grabbed us a couple of Grain Belts.

Meanwhile, Mom rushed headlong into conversation with Naomi, speaking in a loud, shrill voice that I could hear clearly even from the kitchen. Naomi's hair was so beautiful. Wherever did she get it done? She worked in a restaurant? Well, they would just have to get out one of these next nights and come by to say hello. The food must be wonderful. Naomi and I met at the Renaissance Festival? What a fascinating place! She designed her own costume? She must be so talented.

I cringed as I listened, but at the same time I was grateful. Mom evidently felt as awkward as I did about Naomi's visit and was trying to put us at ease. She was trying too hard, but there was an earnestness underlying the artificial tone that I appreciated.

I returned to the living room and joined my dad watching the television in silence.

At the stretch, the Sox were leading the Twins four to nothing and Dad got up to get another beer from the fridge. Although he tried not to show it, he was obviously in pain whenever he moved. I caught Mom sneaking a glance at him as he crossed the room. When she noticed me staring, without breaking her conversation with Naomi, she nodded first at me, then at Dad. When I didn't respond, she nodded again, this time more forcefully.

Catching on, I dutifully followed my dad into the

kitchen. When I got there, I found him leaning heavily against the open refrigerator door. "You want another beer?" he asked.

"Sure, great. Uh, Dad, you sure you're feeling all right?"

He handed me the beer can without looking at me. "I'm a little tired is all," he said, sighing. "Say, I saw you on the tube last night."

"Yeah?"

"Yeah. You were getting into it with that Nazi guy, Beam."

"Yeah?"

"Yeah. At that funeral. By the way, I'm sorry to hear about that friend of yours dying like that. Don't I remember him coming around here a time or two back when you were in high school?"

"Yeah, he came by."

Dad nodded. "Anyway, I'm sorry." He began to make his way back into the living room, but stopped, turned around and frowned. "You know, you might want to leave guys like that up to the cops."

"Guys like who?"

"Guys like this Beam."

"I appreciate the concern, Dad, but I'm pretty sure he's not a threat. The way I hear it, he's just some loudmouth that still lives in his mommy's basement."

Dad cracked open his beer and stared at the little bit of foam that rose to the top of the can. "I saw you with him and I asked around. I still got some friends on the force and one of them works over in Apple Valley where this Beam lives. According to him, something's going on with this guy."

"Like what?"

"This Apple Valley cop says Beam's been making lots of friends lately."

I shrugged. "He had two guys with him at the funeral."

"No. This guy says Beam's been making lots of friends. A lot more than two."

"Like how many?"

"This guy doesn't say exactly, but a lot. Beam's been getting a lot of publicity lately and it's been drawing followers. That kind of thing can go to a guy's head. Oh, and they're following up on reports of weapons."

"Yeah?"

"Yeah. Informants have tipped them that Beam and his boys are stockpiling quite a little arsenal. The cops have tossed Beam's house a couple of times. Didn't find nothing, but that don't mean anything. Lots of places to hide things." Dad wriggled one side of his face, as though he was trying to scratch an itch without using his fingernails. "The whole thing's odd if you ask me. A bunch of white folks getting themselves all worked up about Jews and Blacks out here where we live. It's not like them people exactly been swarming down this way or anything."

"*Them* people?"

"Yeah. Them people. Anyway, like I say, he's probably somebody you want to stay away from."

"Did this friend of yours say if he thought Beam had anything to do with Greg Walsh's murder?"

Dad snapped his head up to look me in the eyes. "Now that's something you damn sure want to leave to the professionals," he said, his tone stiff with warning.

"You know Dad," I said, trying to keep my voice

light, "I *am* a professional. I've got a license and everything."

Dad shook his head. "You know what I mean."

I smiled weakly. "Yeah, Dad. I know exactly what you mean."

"Well, it ain't like you're on the force or anything."

"No," I agreed, my smile slipping, "it's not like I stuck it out like you wanted."

He took a swig of his beer and started fiddling with a meat thermometer that my mom had left on the kitchen counter. "Your mom and I only want the best for you children."

"I know."

"Like I say, I still got some friends. You bone up, you could take the exam again."

"I like what I do, Dad. But thanks."

"Whatever you decide," he said, setting the thermometer aside. "Just remember, as long as I'm around and have friends on the job, I can put a word in for you."

"I'll remember."

We returned to the living room where Mom appeared to be completely engrossed in Naomi's description of a computer class she'd been taking Wednesday nights at the Community College. Mom was literally at the edge of her seat as Naomi explained how spreadsheets are formatted. Dad surreptitiously nudged the volume up on the ballgame, and I sat back and wondered how long it would take for my ears to return to their natural color. Talking with my Dad about my job always made my ears redden. Mom sneaked a look at me. There was a question in her expression, but before I could ask her about it, she interrupted Naomi, asking her if she might help in the kitchen.

Naomi smiled apprehensively. I smiled back and the womenfolk disappeared into the kitchen while Dad and I watched the ballgame in silence. It was the bottom of the ninth when they called us in to dinner. The Sox were up six to zip and although the Twins had a man on second there were two outs and little hope for a rally. My Dad bumped the volume up a tad more and led the way to the kitchen table.

Mom placed the roast on the table. Looking at it, the one thing you could say for sure was that there was no doubt that it had been cooked enough. It had probably started off a plump three-pounder but had emerged from the oven a shriveled and blackened underachiever. Still, Dad carved it with an air of authority while Mom passed around an enormous bowl of potatoes that she gleefully told us Naomi had mashed for her.

"I tasted them already and I swear they're the best mashed potatoes I've ever had and I'm not just saying that."

Dad grunted, forked some meat onto his plate and waited for the gravy. If only Naomi had handled gravy duty, I thought. Mom just didn't get gravy. She'd read up on it. She had the theory, but somehow could never translate that theory into anything remotely edible. Dad peered into the gravy boat to find a lumpy brown residue submerged beneath maybe an inch of yellow-tinted grease. He scooped out some of the brown stuff and set it atop his mashed potatoes like a cairn marking the summit of a conquered mountain.

I was spreading margarine on my potatoes when Mom cleared her throat. "So, did he tell you?" she asked no one in particular.

"Tell who?" I asked.

"Tell *you*."

"Tell me what?"

"Ray," she said turning to her husband, "you said you were going to tell him."

"I didn't say that," he replied. "I said it was my business."

"Your health is everybody's business."

"Another time."

"We don't get together very often," Mom persisted.

"I said another time."

Mom didn't say anything else. Instead, all at once a great sob escaped her. Startled, she abruptly stood and quickly left the table. My father glared at me as if somehow it was my fault. I shrugged, turning my palms up in a gesture of helplessness. Still glaring, Dad followed Mom into the living room. Naomi raised both eyebrows at me. I shrugged at her too.

They didn't return for several minutes. Not sure whether we should go on eating or gather up our stuff and leave, Naomi and I merely remained at the table, trying not to listen to the muffled conversation that, merging with the sound of the post-game show, was coming in from the adjacent living room. When they did get back, my mom, her eyes rimmed with red and tears continuing to well, determinedly tried to change the subject.

She picked up her fork and poised it, unmoving, over her plate. "Is Naomi taking you anyplace special for your birthday, dear?" she asked, a tremor in her voice.

"You guys gonna tell me what's going on?" I asked.

Mom cast an inquiring gaze at Dad.

"Your mom's just being emotional is all," he said.

"It's no big deal, but she seems determined to blow it out of all possible proportion."

"Blow what out of proportion?"

"I've had some pain, is all. I went to the doctor. They checked it out. They ran a bunch of goddamned tests, and they still don't know what's wrong. They say they gotta run some more tests. Probably just gotta pay for all that expensive equipment. I've got insurance. I probably look like a good mark, is my take on all this."

"What kind of tests?"

"Every damned thing they can think of. Blood tests, urine tests, x-rays, the works. Now they say I gotta go in for one of those colonoscopies. You know, one of them tests where they run a camera up your backside and see what's shaking up there." Dad smirked. "You gotta know I'm just counting the minutes 'til they grease that sucker up for me."

"So, they don't have any idea what the problem is?"

"Oh, they got ideas. Lots and lots of ideas. But they say they want to be sure. I say I'm on rails. Once you're on board, you're stuck until you reach the end of the line. And it ain't no direct trip. That I can tell you. They run you down every spur line they got and there ain't no getting off."

"So, when's the colonoscopy?'

"Next week."

"You'll let us know how that comes out?"

A smile broke wide on his face. "I'll send you the freaking video tape if it'll get your mom off my case."

I laughed. "A phone call will do."

He hadn't exactly shared much, but my mom seemed satisfied that Dad had at least broached the subject, and the remainder of meal was markedly less tense. Mom went on to update me at length with news of Chuck and his family, as well as the latest from my various cousins in Iowa, most of whom I hadn't seen since my teens and wouldn't recognize if I was asked to pick them out of a lineup.

Dad, too, seemed cheerier than I'd seen him in a long time. Sitting next to Naomi, a couple of times he leaned over and whispered something closely to her. Each time Naomi erupted with genuine laughter.

Blessedly, Mom hadn't had time to bake, so after clearing the dinner plates she trotted out a supermarket carrot cake ablaze with candles. They'd also bought me a present. A sweater. A thick, burnt orange cardigan with a bulky rolled collar and brass buttons the size of half dollars all down the front. My dad didn't look up as I unwrapped the thing. But I told them it was lovely, even as I checked the tag to see which store I'd be returning it to.

As we prepared to leave, my mom hugged Naomi and gave me a conspiratorial little pat on the shoulder. I wasn't sure whether she was happy that I'd helped draw Dad out regarding his health concerns or if she was just relieved that she now had proof that I dated girls, but in either case I was glad I'd pleased her. I gave her a dweebish little smile and an awkward hug. Mom beamed at me.

I waved at Dad and was nearly out the door when he called me over to him. "She's got a great set of pins on her, that one. You keep her."

"I'll do my best."

He nodded.

"You call me about that test."

"Test? Oh, yeah. The test. Sure. And you remember

what I told you about that Beam."

"I still say he's a chump, but don't worry, I'll remember. I've got no plans that involve Matty Beam."

I pulled the door closed and Naomi squeezed my hand as we walked out to the car. "That was interesting," she said.

"Yeah?"

"Yeah. You're a lot like your dad, you know."

I smiled. "You take that back."

"No, I mean it. You've both got the sense of humor, the charm."

"Oh, yeah. That's what I remember most about my dad growing up—the charm. Like the time I was five and he was teaching me to ride a two-wheeler and I fell and hurt my arm. I'm all crying and shit and my charming father insists on my getting right back on the bike. When I told him I was hurt, he called me a wussy and said if I didn't get back on right away, he'd make me wear a dress and change my name to Lillian."

"He was probably just trying to get you to face your fear."

"I had a compound fracture for God's sake.

"That's a mistake in judgement. But even dads make mistakes."

"His boyhood nickname for me was Dufus."

"So, he had trouble showing his affection."

"There was this big kid picking on me in junior high. When my dad heard about it, he got the kid to come over and he made us both put on boxing gloves. He stood yelling at me while the kid beat the crap out of me. When it was over, he complained about how badly I'd embarrassed him."

"Okay, maybe that's a bit much."

"I broke curfew once and he made me sleep in the garage for three days."

"Okay, okay," Naomi conceded with a chuckle. "He was a jerk. Happy now?"

"Ecstatic," I said.

"Still, I gotta tell you. He's got something. You both do."

"Uh-huh. I noticed you two got pretty cozy there a time or two."

Naomi flashed a smile. "Do I detect a little jealousy?"

"As we were leaving, Dad made sure he let me know that he thinks you've got nice legs."

"That bother you?"

"Actually, yes. It pretty well creeps me out."

"The fact that I have nice legs?"

"No. In fact I'm quite glad you have nice legs. I've been known to make little sacrifices to the gods thanking them for the fact you've got nice legs."

"You're bothered that your father is even looking at your girlfriend's legs?"

"You're a quick study."

"I've been told that. But you gotta realize that your father noticing my legs is to be expected. The fact is that physical appearance is what men are most concerned with when they meet a woman. You know the first thing I thought when I met you?"

"Umm, umm. I gotta get me some of that?" I asked, hopefully.

Naomi paused. "Oddly, no. I thought you'd be fun to be with. I'll bet your mom thought the same thing when she first spotted your dad."

"Well, Dad *is* a barrel of laughs. I'm always saying

my childhood was just one big bacchanalia."

"You worried about him?" Naomi asked, becoming serious.

"Yeah, a little."

Her eyes narrowed. "But you don't want to show it?"

I shrugged. "I wouldn't want to embarrass him."

Chapter Six

Birthdays are a time for taking measure of your life's journey. An opportunity to check off the places you've been and note the destinations that still lie ahead. To pause and consider the people who are making the journey with you. That's what Edgerton had told me, anyway. So, he'd insisted that, although I'd already survived dinner with my parents, we should have friends over to the Bijou to further solemnize the occasion. He'd planned it for the late afternoon and not only promised to get out the invitations, but also to provide the beer and munchies. Of course, when the guests arrived, Edgerton was nowhere to be found, and I had to scrounge up what I could from the Bijou's meager pantry. Still, for a time at least, the half-bag of mini-marshmallows and two cans of energy drink that I'd brought out into the living room seemed to serve as adequate pogey bait. After all, there were only three of us there.

Every time Irving "the Milkman" Mulligan reached across for another marshmallow, the armchair that he'd squeezed himself into creaked loudly in protest. Mulligan was a six-foot-six nearly square block of solid bone and muscle. He had a big head with thick, unruly, reddish-blond hair sitting atop shoulders that were wide enough to land an airplane on. We'd met a couple of years back when I was working for the mob. Okay, I wasn't really working for the mob, but rather for a mobbed-up pornographer involved with a woman that Mulligan was sweet on. The big man and I didn't exactly hit it off when we first met. I was a little too pushy dealing with his inamorata and, even though I'm a pretty big guy myself, Mulligan felt compelled to grab me by the neck and hoist me off my feet. Some of the details of that encounter are still a little hazy, but I'd survived and had even gone on to become the imposing, ex-professional wrestler's friend.

To accompany his daunting physique, Mulligan had the biggest heart of anyone I'd ever known. During his ring days, he'd wrestled not only with an endless string of steroid cases, but with a panoply of personal demons. When his career in the squared circle was over, he cleaned himself up and thereafter dedicated himself to helping others. Never the sharpest pencil in the box, the Milkman didn't have the intellectual acumen to become a counselor or a teacher, but he helped out where he could. His full-time job was as the custodian of a community center that offered literacy and counseling programs, and he tackled the job with a missionary's zeal. The key, he once told me, is to contribute what you can and scraping gum from under desks and making sure that the bathrooms were clean was his part in the larger picture. In addition to his job, he volunteered all over— on a suicide prevention hotline, helping staff the summer parks department youth program, nursery duty at a local YMCA, and making coffee and stacking chairs at AA meetings. The guy was a rock.

Opposite Mulligan, sharing the sofa with me, was another big man. Dark-haired, tall, stout Max Wiseman was an insurance company middle manager and, despite his Jewish heritage, an enthusiast for all things Scottish.

I'd met him on the job as well, working the same Renaissance festival case on which I'd met Naomi. Unlike the rest of us, Wiseman was solidly middle-class—a family man with a wife and three kids. In spite of this, he fit in pretty well. He adored Edgerton and he put up with me. But it also kept him apart. Whenever he joined us at McCauley's Pub, our favorite haunt, he seemed to me a little like an anthropologist doing research. For example, he would occasionally make reference to what he termed "the Dinkytown underground," a subculture he defined as those lost souls who occupied the margins of the Minneapolis neighborhood adjacent to the University of Minnesota and who made McCauley's their unofficial hangout. It was a subculture that seemed to interest him in a clinical sort of way, but from which he clearly held himself separate. I often wondered how much of our friendship was based on the fact that Wiseman found me—a denizen of this "underground"—an interesting subject for study.

Wiseman and the Milkman were trying their best, but the party would definitely have been cheerier if Edgerton had managed to scrounge up a couple more people for the guest list. Still, we were getting by on forced smiles and awkward small talk until, about a half-hour after they'd arrived, I poured the last of the energy drink into Wiseman's glass and both he and Mulligan began to eye the remaining marshmallow.

Luckily, just then the front door banged closed, and Edgerton's voice rang out from the hallway. "Sorry I'm late, guys."

When he heard Edgerton, Basil, who had sniffed uncertainly a couple of times at Mulligan and Wiseman before retreating to my room, bounded down the hallway, yowling with delight. Edgerton entered the living room, knelt down, and began enthusiastically rubbing Basil's ears. The dog went limp and rolled over on his back.

"Who's a good boy?" Stephen crooned, drawing out each syllable while making a pouty face.

He then turned and smiled broadly at both Mulligan and Wiseman. The Milkman extracted himself from the armchair, crossed the room briskly, and enveloped Edgerton in a bear hug. Wiseman, too, rose to greet him with a handshake and a hearty clap on the back.

Edgerton turned to me and said, "I got a case of beer out there and some chips and stuff. Bring 'em on in, willya?"

"Why?" I asked. "Are your hands painted on?"

Wiseman glanced at me with irritation. "I'll get them," he said. As he left, Mulligan, ever eager to help, bounded after him.

Mulligan came in carrying a case of longnecks and Wiseman returned with a grocery bag brimming with cheese curls, pretzels, and kettle-cooked potato chips. They were laying the spread out on the coffee table when another familiar voice sounded quietly in the hallway. "Somebody say something about a party?"

In my experience, Skip, the bartender from McCauley's Pub, never found occasion to raise his voice. Whether he was asking you if you'd like another beer or informing a rowdy miscreant that his presence in the bar would no longer be tolerated, Skip always spoke calmly, which isn't to say that his voice was gentle. Rather, it was like bottled thunder—smooth but charged with an undertone of menace. He wasn't a big man, only a little better than medium height and tending toward skinny, but he had quick hands, clearly defined musculature, and a steely determination in his brown eyes.

When Edgerton had told me that he'd be inviting my friends over, I'd expected the Milkman and Wiseman, and maybe a few others, but I hadn't expected Skip. Skip and I simply weren't friendly. We got along fine, but I spent a lot of time in McCauley's, and I never got the impression that my company warmed him. Part of that could have been that since the bar drew mostly white, middle-class University students and Skip was normally the only Black guy to be found in there, he naturally tended to be a bit guarded. And part could have been the fact that his half-paralyzed face simply didn't register emotions the way others did. Whatever it was, I always felt vaguely edgy around him. But if ever I got into serious trouble, it was Skip, even more than massive Milkman Mulligan, I'd want at my side.

Edgerton turned to Skip and smiled. "You're late."

"I'm here," Skip replied.

"So's the beer," Wiseman said, handing one each to Skip, Edgerton and me as we reached out to him.

Then Wiseman motioned to Mulligan, who shook his head at the implied offer. "Don't drink no more," Mulligan said. "Had kinda a problem with it some years back. You guys go ahead, though."

We all nodded at Mulligan before taking small, furtive sips of our beers.

Skip took a seat opposite me at the end of the sofa and Wiseman was forced to scrunch in between us. Settling back, Wiseman twisted the cap off his beer bottle and said, "Hey, Lyle. I've been meaning to mention, I caught you on TV the other night."

I grunted. "Christ, didn't anybody miss that thing?"

Wiseman shrugged. "I thought you handled yourself pretty well."

"Thanks."

"You talking about that Nazi that Dahms squared off with the other day?" Skip asked.

"Yeah."

Skip gave me a thin half-smile. "Next time you decide to go up against him you can invite me."

"You got it."

Skip's smile remained, but behind the still surface of his eyes floated wisps of ire. "I mean it," he said.

"I know."

Wiseman cleared his throat. "I gotta say, though. I really wish the media would stop giving racists like that Beam a forum. It's reckless, if you ask me."

I smiled. "Reckless? I don't know, Max. I mean, those TV news types certainly pander a bit. They gotta come up with something hot to keep you from flippin' channels, but I don't see where exposing yahoos like Beam is reckless."

"These guys are looking for exposure," Wiseman said, a glint in his eyes warned that the conversation was threatening to turn serious. "Without it, they're nothing. I think it's better to ignore them than to allow them to broadcast their message to a mass audience." Wiseman turned to Skip. "You agree with me, don't you?"

"Why you asking me?" Skip said.

"I don't know. I guess if anyone here knows about racism it's likely you."

Skip stared at Wiseman for several seconds before replying. Then his thin smile broadened a bit and in an exaggerated Stepin Fetchit-Mammy's-making-chitlins patois, he said, "Well, thankee for noticin' that. We always *soo* glad when you white folks ask us 'bout racism."

Wiseman was clearly taken aback by the response. He paused, one eyebrow cocked, his mouth slightly open as he searched for a reply. "You saying I'm wrong?" he asked, at last.

"I'm saying it's not something I'm prepared to discuss with you," Skip said. Then he shrugged. "But I will say that guys like Beam aren't really the problem. At least they're honest about who they are."

Wiseman's eyes crinkled with bewilderment. Skip's smile had vanished, and his eyes shone like stones. They stared at each other quietly—the silence a frayed tether stretched tightly between them.

Finally, Skip grinned and looked away. He raised his beer bottle as if in salute. "Guess you got a right to ask, though. Nazis have always been more about hating Jews, anyway."

Wiseman nodded, but his eyes were dark with disappointment. "You know, I've got a photograph. I have it on the mantle back home. It's right there next to a picture of Vicki and me on our wedding day. It's black-and-white, taken in the early '30s back in Salzburg. My grandfather is standing in the middle. He's smiling. On his left are his two brothers. On the right is his sister. They have their arms around each other, mugging for the camera. They're young. Not one of them out of their twenties. Two of them didn't reach thirty." Wiseman paused. "I'm older now than my grandpa ever got to be. People claim it's all in the past. But when it's your family it doesn't seem so long ago."

We were all quiet for a moment. "Sorry, Max," was

all the response I could manage.

Wiseman knocked back the rest of his beer and smiled a forgiving smile. Basil, still lying in Edgerton's lap, let out a demanding whine. Edgerton began rubbing the puppy behind the ears, and Basil responded with a series of contented thumps with a forepaw.

Mulligan raised his head and after blinking several times more or less in sync with Basil's thumping, said, "So, Lyle, how's it feel to be a year older?"

I had to smile at the big man's attempt to steer the conversation in a cheerier direction. "About the same as before, Milkman," I said. "But I appreciate you guys coming by to mark the occasion with me."

"No problem." He grinned. "I went into work early at the center so's I could take off early. I was supposed to help out at the hotline tonight, but there's this guy there, another volunteer like me, who I did this favor for. He said he'd take my shift tonight, so it really wasn't a problem getting over here."

"That's quite a schedule you have there, Irv," Wiseman said, reaching for another beer.

"I like to keep busy," Mulligan replied. "But not so busy I couldn't say yes to an occasion like this one." He paused and rolled his eyes upward as though searching for something inside his skull. "What I said I will do, I will do," he said at last, "in the name of the friendship we've sworn."

"Sounds like a quote. That from *Njal's Saga*?" I asked, remembering the only book that Mulligan had ever mentioned reading to me. He'd told me that he read it over and over to "keep the words in my head."

Mulligan beamed. "Nope. It's from *Beowulf*. Stephen here lent it to me. He also lent me something called *Godel, Escher, Bach*, but I gotta tell ya, I haven't looked at that one yet." He glanced sheepishly at Edgerton. "But *Beowulf* rocks. Tough sloggin' in spots, but mostly really cool. Kinda like *Njal's Saga*, only with monsters."

"Speaking of monsters," I said, turning to Edgerton, "we're gonna have to discuss this dog thing."

"You mean your birthday present?"

"No. I mean the dog. I bought myself a birthday present."

"Do tell."

"I went out and got myself a new gun."

Wiseman winced. "What was wrong with your old gun?"

"Nothing. I just had an urge for modernity. I bought myself a 9mm Beretta. Very slick. Very expensive. I turned to Edgerton. "And speaking of expensive," I continued, pointing to the dog, "your four-footed friend there is costing me a fortune."

"I know you bought some more dog food," he said. "Glad to see you steppin' up."

"It's not just the dog food. Earlier today, he was in my room, and I had to go to the bathroom. I was only gone a minute. I mean, I didn't think I'd have to kennel him to take a pee. The little mutt ate my copy of *Aqualung*."

"He's not a mutt," Edgerton reminded me.

"Okay, then. The 'superior hybrid' ate my copy of *Aqualung*."

"He's still in training. You work with him, he'll stop doing that. Anyway, when was the last time you listened to Jethro Tull?"

"Probably high school. But that's not the point."

"The point is you should have kenneled him."

"The point is—" I began, my voice rising.

"Have another beer, Birthday Boy," Wiseman interrupted with a chuckle.

Grumbling, I stood up to get another beer. I was about to sit back down when Janet Kleiner walked in.

Unless I had indeed spied her at the funeral, I hadn't seen Greg Walsh's old girlfriend since the last time I listened to Jethro Tull. Back then, she was a pretty but very loud, blonde with an abrasive manner and an enticing gleam in her dark eyes. I didn't like her very much.

Greg changed when he was with her. Alone, he was a good-natured companion—fun-loving, with a ready laugh and a sympathetic ear. With Janet, he was edgy, his laughter seemed forced, his smile painted on by an artist with an unsteady hand. Janet was whiny and demanding and Greg was ever ready to serve—even, I thought, at the cost of making himself miserable. But Janet *had* something. There was something about the way she carried herself, something about the way her clothes clung to her shapely figure. She exuded an air of sensuality, of rock-your-world sexuality that was impossible for Greg to ignore.

He confessed that she had been his first and smiled shyly when he told me that he'd found something out of a storybook—a first love-true love relationship that would endure through the ages. I'd managed to keep quiet. I didn't tell him that I found her coarse and obvious. I didn't say that I worried that she sapped his enthusiasm. It wasn't my place, I told myself. Also, I was aware of a niggling little something inside me that said maybe I was intimidated. Maybe, when we were together, I found myself staring at her a little too much. Maybe I was jealous.

There wasn't much left to be jealous of, I thought, as she appeared at my door. The years had been less than kind. Deep bags sagged under her watery eyes and no amount of makeup could hide the wrinkles and liver spots that had overtaken her face. Her hair had been teased so much that it had fought back, coiling itself high atop her head like a nest of vipers ready to snap. She had thickened, and her skin seemed as leathery as the short black skirt she wore. High black boots and a stained silk blouse completed her outfit. It all labeled her more eloquently than words. Janet Kleiner was an aging hooker.

I didn't greet her. Instead, I stared at her, my mind making lazy turns as I tried to anticipate the reason for her visit. Greg had become very successful, I reminded myself. Now that he was dead there would be many enterprising hustlers stepping up to try to get their hands on some of what he left behind.

Janet glanced at the others in the room, then fixed her eyes on me. "Can I come in, Lyle?"

"Sure. Make yourself at home," I said, careful to keep my tone as emotionless as possible.

As she stepped into the room, both the Milkman and Wiseman half-rose from their seats. Janet flashed an automatic smile. But when she took a seat on the sofa, she was tight-lipped, and I saw the alluring glimmer that once danced in her eyes had been replaced by a glint that looked more like paranoia.

For a moment, everyone stared at me, waiting for me to speak.

"So, it's been a while," I said at last. "I mean, I saw

you at the funeral the other day, but I guess you didn't have time to talk. You weren't working, were you?"

Janet glared at the question, but then her eyes softened with comprehension. "So, that's the way it's going to be."

"Let's not kid each other, Janet. You didn't come here to revisit old times. You want something. With Greg dead, I figure it's money. There's no way I'm going to help you scam his family out of anything."

"I loved Greg."

"You using, Janet? You got that look about you. You're jonesing and you see in the paper that old Greg turned up dead and all his millions just lying around—"

"I'm not using."

I surveyed her bare arms for tracks and didn't see any. But that meant nothing. There are lots of ways to get high.

Edgerton stood. "Maybe we should leave you two alone."

I didn't turn from Janet, but my peripheral vision caught both the Milkman and Wiseman nodding. "No. Don't bother," I said. "This won't take long."

Edgerton stared at me narrowly. "I believe the lady would prefer to discuss things with you privately."

"Whatever," I said with a shrug, turning wordlessly to head down the hallway.

Janet began to follow but was stopped by Edgerton. "Nice to meet you…Janet, is it?"

She smiled appreciatively and nodded.

"Take care," he added.

Basil stirred from where he'd been lying and followed both Janet and me back to my room. Inside, he approached Janet gingerly, sniffing at her ankles. Janet glanced at my desk chair, the only chair in the small room, then looked at me as if asking permission to sit. Getting none, she shrugged, pulled it away from the desk, and sat down. Basil shook himself and approached her again. This time he lifted himself up and placed his front paws gently on her legs.

Janet reached down and rubbed the dog behind his ears. "At least your friend and your dog have manners," she said.

"Did I invite you here?"

"No, you didn't. Stupidly, I came because I'm in trouble. I thought you might be able to help me. I guess I thought wrong."

"I guess you did."

She patted the dog one last time, then stood. "Sorry you turned out so bitter, Lyle."

"Not bitter. Just wary."

"And smug," she added.

"Wow, that stings, Janet. I'll probably spend the rest of the day beating myself up."

"What did I ever do to you?" A reedy strain of anger surfaced in her voice.

"Nothing, Janet. You never did a damn thing. But I'm not going to let you do anything to the Walsh family, either. Greg was my friend. I owe him that much."

She was quiet for a moment, then turned to the door. She stepped forward but stopped. Then she shuddered, breathed deeply, and shuddered again. She wrapped her arms around herself as if to keep from shivering. Without turning to face me, she said, "If you were his friend, you'd at least listen to me. You'd be interested in seeing justice done."

"What kind of justice are we talking about, Janet?

The kind where the Walsh estate ponies up a cash settlement just 'cause you used to sleep with Greg? If he was just another john, you should have posted your prices at the time. It's a bit late now."

She turned, trembling uncontrollably. She tried to speak, but her words seemed to catch in her throat. The gleam in her eye that I'd dismissed as narcotic-related paranoia had widened into panic. Fear flickered in her blue eyes like neon about to go dark.

"Janet?" I called out to her.

She made no sound.

Suddenly, she was a lost teenager again. But Greg was no longer there to help her. I tried to ignore it, but my insides seemed to sink with the weight of inherited responsibility. I rose and barely touching her, led her back to the chair. "Can I get you something?" I asked. "A glass of water?"

She shook her head.

I sat down on the bed opposite her and watched as she tried to quiet the tremors that had overtaken her.

"They killed him," she said at last.

"They killed Greg?"

"Yes."

"Who killed him?"

"The same ones that are after me."

"Do you know who they are?"

Janet turned to face me. She nodded her head.

"Tell me."

She shook her head.

Sudden rage bubbled within me. "Dammit!" I shouted. "Tell me who they are!"

Janet burst into tears. "I can't!" she wailed. "I can't! They'll kill me. They'll kill—"

She stopped abruptly, slumped forward, and buried her face in her hands.

I stood up and stumped angrily about the room. "This is just great, Janet," I huffed. "Just fucking great. Well, hell, thanks for stopping by. You have a nice fucking day."

"Lyle," she said, raising her head. There was a wrenching plea in her voice, but I ignored it. "I don't care about myself. Not really. Not anymore. But…"

"Oh! What? It's Greg you care about? Your long-lost love? If you gave a shit about him, you'd let me know what's going on. I saw pictures of his body, Janet. I got to see how they carved him up. It wasn't a pretty image."

"It's not Greg," she said, sobbing.

"What do mean it's not Greg?"

"Well, it *is* Greg. And me too, I guess. In a way, it's both of us."

I sighed in exasperation. "Thanks for clearing that up."

Janet rubbed at her eyes with a balled hand, mixing her tears and mascara into an inky mess that framed the wild desperation that had joined the fear in her eyes. "Lyle," she gasped. "If you could do something to save Greg, would you do it?"

"Greg's past saving."

"But if you could?"

"I'd do anything for Greg. But I gotta be honest. I won't do anything for you."

"But you'd help Greg?"

"This is bullshit, Janet," I said, tossing my head back in disgust.

"Swear you'd help Greg," she entreated.

"Fuck this!" I spat the words at her. "I don't have to prove anything to you."

Janet leapt to her feet and threw herself at me. She latched on to my shirt with both hands and stared with frenzied passion into my eyes. "Swear it, goddammit!" she shrieked. "You fucking swear it!"

Janet was gone. Something terrifying had swept her away and an awful fury had taken control of her empty shell. It was sucking me in as I stared into the vortex of her eyes. "I swear!" I shouted. "I swear!"

Janet slumped, still grasping my shirt, still shaking, but less noticeably now as if whatever had possessed her was slipping away. "I'm going to hold you to it," she said weakly.

I didn't know what to say.

At last, she let go of my shirt and with a surprising dignity raised herself, adjusted her clothing, and stepped toward the door. She swallowed hard. "I'm going to hold you to it," she repeated as she left the room, closing the door behind her.

The dog looked up at me.

"What?" I asked in irritation.

Basil continued to stare.

"It's some kind of scam," I assured him. But my voice rang a little hollow in the quiet of the room.

Basil lay his head down across a foreleg and pretended to sleep. I wasn't real proud of myself, either.

I listened to Janet's rapid footsteps retreat down the hallway. I heard Edgerton call after her as the front door opened and closed. I picked up a magazine that was lying on my desk and briefly thumbed through the pages. I set the magazine back down, then slowly emerged from my room. Edgerton was standing at the end of the hallway, holding open the front door. The sound of a car pulling away from the front of the house echoed down the hall. Even after the car had long gone, Edgerton continued to stare at something at the front of the house.

"Lyle," he said finally in a quiet, but urgent voice. "You better get out here."

Skip, Mulligan, and Wiseman had all picked up on it, too. We all reached the door at more or less the same time. Edgerton stepped aside to reveal a child, maybe three-years-old, standing on the front porch. Her blonde curls appeared almost white in the slanting rays of the late afternoon sun. She was wearing an orange, short-sleeved, cotton jumper over a pair of maroon tights. Next to her was a shiny vinyl suitcase with Pooh Bear on it. She had a bright blue and yellow pacifier in her mouth. She'd been crying but had managed to stop the flow of tears.

She removed the pacifier and looked up at us with big, shimmering, blue eyes. "Mommy said I stay here now," she said, stoically. She picked up the suitcase with one hand and put the pacifier back in her mouth with the other, as if to muffle the sobs that then overtook her.

Chapter Seven

Her name was Ava and, for a half-hour or so, that's about all we got out of her. We led her into the living room where she stopped crying after the first ten minutes, then sat primly on the sofa looking at each of us with an impassive expression that I imagined masked disapproval. Her eyes only brightened when they lighted on the dog and then only slightly. All the while, the Milkman, Wiseman, Skip, Edgerton and I stood there, glancing at each other, then back to the little girl occasionally asking her if we could do something for her and nodding when she shook her head.

At last Edgerton motioned me into the hall and in hushed tones I told him all I knew about the girl and her mother. It didn't take long. I didn't know much. I didn't know where Janet had gone, when she would be back, or how to get in touch with her. Edgerton eyed me suspiciously but didn't question what I told him. Finally, he asked me what we were going to do with the kid.

"I don't know. Call the cops or child welfare or something."

Edgerton nodded deliberately. "Bad idea."

"Why's that?"

"This Janet trusted you. If she wanted the kid in some kinda foster home, she wouldn't have come to you. She wants the kid back when the trouble's over. You gotta keep her."

"I sure as hell don't have to keep her. That's insane. I'm already sharing my room with that canine clothes shredder you saddled me with. I'm not making room for some little girl I don't even know."

"She can probably hear us," Edgerton whispered.

I cringed.

"I'll help out," Edgerton assured me. "It'll be okay."

"It won't be okay. You can't just say it'll be okay and then magically everything's okay. It's probably not even legal."

"Babysitting's illegal? Shit, I gotta go to polls more."

I rolled my eyes. "The whole idea creeps me out. How will it look?"

"How will what look?"

"How will it look for two single guys to be looking after some little girl? What will people think?"

"You telling me you go in for the toddler set?"

"Fuck you. You know what I mean."

"You're looking after someone in need. It don't matter what people think."

"We don't even know how long Janet will be gone. It could be years for all we know."

Edgerton shrugged. "She could be back tomorrow. Anyway, she trusted you. You have to give her a chance."

"Look," I insisted, "kids need constant attention. We're just not here enough. There's no way that we can work it so that one of us can be with her all the time. We both have jobs, for Christ's sake."

"I'll cut back my hours."

"You do that, how you gonna pay your rent?"

"I'll manage."

"We can't do it. Between the two of us, we just can't do it."

"Okay then, we'll get help. I'm sure the guys inside will pitch in."

"What, Skip and the Milkman?"

"Yeah. Mulligan's great with kids. And what about Max and Vicki Wiseman? They've got experience."

"Come on, Stephen. They both work and they've got three kids of their own. They're not going to have the time."

"Okay, but if they both work, how do they do it?"

"Do what?"

"Who watches the kids when they're working."

"They got daycare, I suppose."

"Then we'll get daycare."

"Jesus, Stephen. We can't afford daycare."

"We still got the Milkman. He'll help us out for sure."

"You want to ask a three-hundred-pound, ex-professional wrestler to be your nanny?"

"Why not?"

"Well, he's got a job, too. On top of that, he volunteers all over the place, so he's got like no free time at all."

"What about Skip. I'm sure if I ask him, he'll—"

"Stephen," I said, lowering my voice to a near whisper, "Skip is pretty much the scariest guy I know. He's not exactly the nurturing type."

"You gotta give people more credit, Lyle. Anyway, we'll work it out. Think about it. We all waste time every day. If we waste less time, if everybody helps out just a little, we'll be okay. Trust me. It's the right thing to do."

Dust particles swirled like fireflies in and out of the

stream of light that sliced through the darkened hallway. Edgerton reached out his hand and dipped the tips of his fingers in the brilliant yellow beam.

"Why do you care, anyway?" I asked. "I didn't even know you liked kids."

"This isn't about liking kids. It's about opportunities. How often do people like us get an opportunity to have a positive effect on a child? Sending her off into some system filled with bureaucrats and desperate kids. It just don't seem right."

"They're professionals. They're equipped to deal with these situations. With us, it'd be amateur hour. We could screw up bad."

Edgerton shrugged again. "I think we could be good at it. I think we could make a difference."

"Well, I won't do it," I said.

"You won't?"

"No."

"Whatever," Edgerton said, and we went back into the living room. I was heading for the telephone when Edgerton cleared his throat. "You want to go get a hamburger, Ava?" he asked with a soft grin.

I turned and glared at him.

Ava smiled brightly behind the pacifier, then as quickly as it had appeared, the smile vanished and was replaced by a practiced glower. Then she said something that sounded like, "Mommy shed note go no way a whiff stwain chayos." The pacifier between her lips bobbed as she spoke. I cast Edgerton a bewildered look.

"She said her mommy told her not to go anywhere with strangers," he translated.

"For God's sake, kid—" I began, but Edgerton cut me off.

He knelt on the floor in front of Ava and looked her in the eyes. "My name's Stephen. That guy over there is Lyle. That's Skip, and Max, and the great big fella is Milkman Mulligan."

Each of the men grinned uncertainly at Ava.

"Your mommy knew you'd be safe with us," Edgerton continued. "She asked us to look after you. She'll be busy for a little while. She wouldn't mind if we take you out for a bite."

Ava took the pacifier from her mouth and set it on a nearby shelf. "Can I get a Kids Meow?" she asked, allowing a glimmer of excitement to peak out from behind her frown.

"A Kids Meal? Of course. Can I have one, too?"

"Kids Meows for kids," Ava told him.

Edgerton gasped in feigned shock. "You mean I'm not a kid?"

A chuckle escaped her. "No, you gwoan up. Gwoan ups eat big people food."

"Okay. A Kids Meal for you and something big for me."

Ava cast a wary glance in my direction. "He comin'?"

"I expect so."

"What's he ga have?"

"What do you think he should have?"

"Mommy says fat pee oh wheat sawad."

Edgerton laughed heartily.

"What did she say?" I asked.

"Her mommy says fat people eat salad." Then turning to the little girl, he said, "We'll get him a salad."

Edgerton turned to our trio of party guests. "You guys gonna come along?"

Skip uncrossed his legs and got slowly to his feet. "Sorry, Stephen. I got things to do. But you keep me informed. Let me know if you need anything. Let me know if the little one needs something, too.

"Thanks for the offer, Skip. I'll be taking you up on it."

Wiseman stood up beside Skip. "I think I'll be taking off, too. You guys have a nice time. But you'll be wanting to give this some thought, Stephen. Dahms has a point about the staff down at child protection services being professionals. This raising kids thing isn't as easy as it looks."

"I appreciate that, Max," Edgerton said. "But we won't be raising her. Just looking after her a couple of days."

The Milkman stood, shuffled a couple of times, then stared uncomfortably at us. "I'd better be going, too. And I'm sure Max is right, his being a daddy and all. But if she stays and you need help, you gotta know I'm there for you. You know that, right?"

Edgerton beamed. "Fuckin' A, Milkman," he said.

Mulligan's eyes darted to Ava with alarm. "Gotta be careful with the explicatives," he cautioned.

"Oops."

Mulligan smiled, clapped Edgerton on the shoulder, then knelt down in front of Ava. "You have fun. And I hope I see you again, sweetie."

Ava blinked a few times but said nothing.

After all the party guests had gone, Edgerton again knelt down to our little visitor. "Time to go, Ava," he told her. "I'll just go lock up my room."

"I go whiff chew," she offered.

Edgerton smiled as he shook his head. "I'll just be a

minute."

Ava turned to look at me again.

"Really," Edgerton assured her, "it'll be okay."

"Willwee?"

"Really."

Edgerton scampered comically from the room. Ava giggled, then stopped as she looked at me.

I sighed. We'd call the cops after we fed her, I decided.

I ran a hand through my hair and smiled at her. "So, what's it gonna be? Chicken nuggets or a hamburger?"

She looked at me like I was from another planet.

"Your Kids Meal?" I prompted.

Her little face started to crinkle up. Her eyes began to cloud over.

"Make it snappy, Stephen!" I hollered.

He returned before the floodgates opened.

We stepped into the hall, and I was locking the door to my room when Edgerton cleared his throat. "You've got money on you, right?"

I nodded.

"Don't forget the dog."

"The dog?"

"*Aqualung*," he reminded me.

"Oh. Yeah, right."

After chasing Basil around the room for a couple of minutes, I was able to coax him into his kennel and I locked the door to my room. We made it all the way to the front entrance before Ava said, "Mommy wote a note."

"She wrote a note?"

"Yeah. In my tootcase. A big note."

I looked at Edgerton. "So, why didn't we check the

suitcase?"

He smirked. "Hey, you're the detective."

I clopped back to my room. Basil started jumping up and down in the kennel, acting as if instead of thirty seconds, we'd been gone an eternity. But then, maybe it had been that long in puppy years. It took some effort, but I ignored him.

I placed Ava's suitcase on the bed and opened it. On top was a three-page letter written in blue ink on yellow legal paper. It was a list of instructions. I didn't examine it too closely just then, but it seemed pretty complete. There were headings for mealtimes, dressing, washing, going to the bathroom and the use of something called pull-ups, even notes on television shows and favorite bedtime stories. It was like Ava's personal owner's manual.

I rolled up the pages and stepped to the door. As I was locking up, I remembered what Janet had said about the guys that killed Greg coming after her. I wondered if I should get my new Beretta out of the lock box in the corner of my room. Stephen and Ava are waiting, I thought, dismissing the notion. Besides, what kind of guy brings a handgun to a fast-food joint?

Dinkytown was only a few blocks away from the Bijou, but Ava was pretty little, so I asked Stephen if he thought I should drive us over.

"You got a car seat?" he asked.

"Yeah. There are seats in the car. A steering wheel, too, and a gas pedal. All kinds of neat stuff."

"A child safety seat for the kid," Edgerton said. "They gotta use one until they are either four years old or weigh forty pounds. After that they recommend you put 'em in booster seats. I think you use a booster until they're eighty pounds. For most kids, that's like twelve."

I squinted at him. "How is it you know all that?"

"Do you have one?"

"No."

"Then we hoof it."

Outside, a single cloud drifted across the dark blue-sky dissolving into a lacy veil in the slanting sun. Because it was getting on toward evening and the University was not in regular session, we had the streets pretty much to ourselves. As we walked, a light breeze stirred through the trees, their leaves turning slowly like a chorus of lethargic strippers flashing us with reflected sunlight. Edgerton took Ava by the hand while I brought up the rear. He kept talking to her and pointing at things along the way. I couldn't clearly hear what they were saying, but I could see the shy smile on Ava's face and the light that, like the flickering sunlight on the leaves, shone in her eyes.

I was feeling kinda left out and when we passed my office building on the way to Dinkytown, I called out loudly to them. "That's where I work. Over there."

Ava looked at Stephen apprehensively as if to ask if she was required to respond. Edgerton patted her gently on the head and they went on talking to one another. I tucked Janet's childcare instructions under my arm, jammed my fists in my pockets, and pretended I wasn't with them.

Two large men sat in a faded brown Mercury sedan parked across from my office building. It took me a couple of seconds to recognize them. They'd traded the blue suits that I'm sure the Reverend Beam had insisted they wear to the funeral, for less formal attire. The first guy out of the car was the bigger of the two. He had to be six-foot-five and nearly as wide. Easing his bulk through the car door, he made the mid-sized sedan look like a clown car. Sunlight glinted off his shaved head and he hitched at his blue jeans a time or two but despite his effort they still rode dangerously low. He wore a plain black T-shirt tucked tightly into his jeans.

The second guy was slightly shorter, but more heavily muscled. He wore a baseball-type cap perched high on his head, embroidered with the name "Blauer Construction." Long blond hair hung down to his shoulders in greasy strands and his chin and upper lip were covered with sparse facial hair like wisps of mist clinging to a dewy hillside. He had a sloppy swastika tattooed on his right bicep. Too sloppy to be professional, I thought. Probably a prison tatt. As they came toward us, the one in the cap stopped a few feet distant, put an index finger along the side of his nose and deftly blew an acorn-sized glob of snot to the asphalt.

"Take Ava to the restaurant," I told Edgerton, handing him the note from Janet. "I'll catch up with you in a couple of minutes."

"Who are those guys?"

"Acolytcs."

Edgerton started to say something else, but I cut him off. "Get the kid out of here. She's not safe."

Out of the corner of my eye, I watched Edgerton pick up the little girl and carry her across the street as the two men reached me. I forced a smile. The bald guy rubbed his big hands together. His knuckles were huge and knobby, like they'd been battered flat and hardened by use.

"We come to talk to you," said the guy with the newly cleared sinuses. "We come to talk to you about calling Beam names in front of them TV people."

I sneaked a glance across the street. Edgerton never did listen to me. Instead of hightailing it with the kid, he'd stopped and was watching us from about a half a block away. I considered my options. They were definitely the kind of guys your mommy warned you not to play with, but neither looked like a professional. If it came to it, I figured I'd be able to handle myself.

Then I remembered the police photographs of Greg Walsh's body—all that blood on that yellow pullover. I felt my smile slip a bit. "What is it you guys think you can accomplish here?"

"We think we can kick your ass, funny man," Baldy explained. He crossed his beefy arms dramatically. He had tattoos on both—on the left arm, a skull with a snake curling through the empty eye socket; on the right, the legend, "Born to Fuck You Up."

"Is that how it was with Walsh?" I asked. "Did you just mean to kick his ass? Or did something go wrong?"

Baldy blinked a few times quite rapidly, before his eyes widened with surprise. "We never—" he began.

Snotty cut him off. "We didn't come to talk about Walsh." Baldy turned to his partner and blinked a couple more times. Snotty didn't look at him. He continued to stare icily at me.

"I hate to bore you, pal," I said, "but maybe you'd better be thinking about Walsh. His death's got a lot of people stirred up. The cops are under a lot of pressure to get the bad guys. And here you are, looking so right for the roasting. I'm an old friend of Walsh's. I've been talking to the cops. Suddenly you show up and bat me around. In broad daylight. In front of witnesses. Why don't you just hang an 'Arrest Me' sign around your necks and have done with it?"

Baldy's eyes went vacant, as if his brain was trying to engage, but was so frozen from disuse that it wouldn't catch the spark. He turned to his partner again, his forehead furrowed into a wordless question.

Snotty didn't take his eyes off me. "Walsh don't matter," he declared. "Matty said beat you."

Baldy's eyes refocused. That settled it. He started to move around in back of me, while Snotty reached into the front pocket of his jeans. Please God, don't let it be a knife, I prayed. Maybe God was watching. It wasn't a knife. Snotty slipped a roll of quarters into his right fist.

I dropped and went down so hard my tailbone *thunged* on the concrete. As I did, I kicked my right leg out at the same time. My foot caught Snotty hard in the shin. Not good enough. I'd been aiming for a disabling shot to his knee. He stumbled back momentarily, cursed, then, drawing back his clenched right hand, he advanced toward me.

Baldy moved in, coming at me from behind, waddling like some great bow-legged penguin. I let him get close enough to tower over me. Then I spun and drove a hard left directly to his groin. For an instant, his face was without expression. I glanced quickly at Snotty. His features were scrunched together in a mournful wince as he stared at his colleague. Baldy doubled over while I tried to scramble to my feet.

I nearly made it before Snotty nailed me in the temple with his quarter-fortified right. A multicolored mist exploded inside my skull. I shook my head to clear the Technicolor fog, but the air was suddenly knocked out of me. The colors faded to gray as my head slammed against the sidewalk. I tried to draw a breath but took a foot in the side. The fog was no longer gray. Things were going completely dark.

Then I got lucky. They stopped kicking me in the guts and started to pound on my back, enabling me to suck in enough air to keep from passing out. I got one leg under me and tried to push myself to my feet. They must have realized their mistake because something hit me hard in the solar plexus. As my breath rushed from me, I went down again.

This time I didn't try to get up. Thoughts of sleep began to drive everything else from my mind. Maybe if I just went to sleep, I thought, maybe when I woke up this would all be over. Maybe I was asleep now. Maybe I was dreaming. I began to disappear into the murk.

Somewhere far away I heard a voice cry out. It was Edgerton. "No!" he shouted. "Come back!"

I smiled in my head. That's nice, I thought, he doesn't want me to leave. Then I heard another voice. Quite near. Too near. It was Ava. Screaming a thin, shrill, little girl scream. "Weave him awone! Yow bad! Yow weave him awone!"

My eyes snapped open. I sucked in all the air I could and turned in time to see Snotty getting ready to swing on Ava. I flailed at his legs, but I was like a walrus flopping on a beach. With every ounce of energy I could muster, I made one last push toward him. It wasn't enough.

Then Baldy grabbed Snotty's upraised arm and pulled him off balance. Snotty whirled around, his face contorted with anger. "What the fuck!"

The groin shot had left Baldy a little wobbly and he didn't seem to be able to stand totally upright. But the look on his face as he held on to his partner's arm was one of calm defiance. "We don't hit no kids."

It was Snotty's turn to blink. He stared at his partner for several seconds, his eyes opening and closing slowly. Finally, he nodded, gave me one last boot to my shoulder and began to walk back to the car. Baldy followed meekly.

I let myself go and lay on the sidewalk listening to the squeal of tires on the roadway as they peeled away. After a minute or so, I managed to sit up.

Edgerton was sitting on the grass near me. Ava was in his arms, her face in his chest.

"I thought I told you to get the kid out of here," I muttered.

"They weren't after the kid," Edgerton said. "They were after you."

I nodded.

"You want to tell me about it?" he asked.

I didn't want to say anything in front of the kid about how they may have been the guys that that her mommy was running from. The same guys who may have killed Mommy's old boyfriend. "I think I pissed off their boss."

"How's that?"

"I sort of pointed out his uncanny resemblance to an anal orifice on local TV."

"That all?"

"So far."

Edgerton nodded. "You saying this isn't over?"

"That's what I'm saying."

Ava turned her head just enough to sneak a peek at me before reburying her face in Edgerton's embrace.

"Anyway," Edgerton said, giving the kid a squeeze and tousling her hair. "It's a good thing I didn't just head out like you asked. Without Ava here, who knows how it would have gone for you."

I glared at him. "She could have been hurt, Stephen. Sticking around was irresponsible."

"So, is this you taking responsibility?" he asked.

I lowered my head. When I looked up, I saw two sparrows take off from a nearby rooftop, racing toward a distant maple. The winner alighted in the lower branches while the loser circled lamely overhead. Seeing this, the faster bird left its perch and the two birds tussled briefly in the air before both settled on separate branches in uneasy alliance.

"What are we gonna do?" Edgerton asked.

"About the kid?"

"Yeah. Do you want to head back to Bijou and call the cops?"

"Let's get the kid a burger," I said.

"And after that?"

"We'll see."

Chapter Eight

Over lunch I listened to enough of Ava's conversation with Edgerton to start being able to understand her little kiddy argot more clearly. I wouldn't say I became fluent, but once I realized that the letters "R" and "L" were both pronounced as "W," that "V" was pronounced "B," and "Th" as "F," I felt I was on my way.

We also had the opportunity to read over Janet's child rearing instructions and, after we were finished eating, Edgerton suggested that he and Ava do a little shopping. It turned out there was a lot of stuff she was going to need that we didn't regularly stock. I walked with them to the convenience store on the corner of Fourteenth Avenue and Fifth Street, then crossed over to my office building. There was a message waiting for me.

A lawyer working for the Walsh family named Zebulon Pope had called and was wondering if I had time in my schedule to call him back. I stared for a few moments at a stack of bills I'd lovingly arranged on the corner of my desk and listened to the loud, measured ticking of the clock on the wall. I figured I had time.

I'm not fond of lawyers. I've worked for many over the years and have needed the services of several others, and on the whole, I'd have to say that I've had more laughs in a dentist's chair than in a lawyer's office. Of course, some of this is my own fault. Despite my best efforts to mask my dislike, some of these lawyers were astute enough to pick up on it and treat me accordingly.

I dialed the lawyer's phone number. "Pope!" he barked after my call was routed to his desk.

"Zeb!" I countered cheerfully. I find that calling a self-important prig by his first name is the quickest way to get on his good side. "Lyle Dahms, returning your call."

There was a brief silence as he struggled to remember who I was. "Oh, yeah," he said at last, "Dahms. The private detective. Evelyn Walsh told me about you. I thought we might like to get together and talk. I understand you knew Greg long ago. My firm is handling things for the Walshes."

"Your firm? You're not handling things yourself?"

"I…um. I only meant…" His voice took on a steely quality. "Yes, I'm handling affairs myself. I only meant that my associates are available in a supportive capacity."

"Well, if you need the help. What is it you want to talk about?"

"I understand that you've spoken with the authorities. We are readying both Evelyn and young Tyler for a police interview and I thought it might be enlightening to have your insight as to their current thinking."

"You mean do they consider young master Walsh a suspect?"

An audible sigh came over the line. "That's what I mean."

"If they don't now, they will soon. Are we done here?"

"Perhaps if we met face to face, we'd be able to discuss things in greater detail."

I listened to the clock ticking for a few seconds before answering. "What time were you thinking?"

"How about my office, say ten o'clock tomorrow morning?"

"I was thinking more like over a meal. Don't you find that having a little something to eat promotes the convivial exchange of ideas and information?"

Pope paused. I heard the sound of pages flipping back and forth. "It looks like I can arrange that Dahms. Yes. We'll call it breakfast tomorrow morning. Say nine o'clock? At Morey's downtown?"

"I'll clear my schedule, Zeb."

"I know that Evelyn would appreciate it. You spoke to her about trying to be of some help."

"I'll bring my best intentions. You bring a credit card."

What Pope had said about my promise to Evelyn actually hit home. I had told her that I would help if I could. I resolved to try to be a good boy when I talked to Pope the next day.

Helping Evelyn was a responsibility that I'd taken on freely. But responsibilities were suddenly sprouting like back hair. Edgerton had to work that evening and I was going to be stuck taking care of Ava until he returned. I was going to need some help myself. I called Naomi.

I wasn't exactly sure how to approach the subject, so I didn't tell her much. I just said that I was wondering if she could help me with something and asked if she would come over.

"You fishing for an early birthday present?" she asked, a wonderfully salacious note sounding in her voice.

"God, yes. But it'll have to wait until later."

"What do you mean?"

"I'll explain everything when you get here. I'm leaving the office. I'll meet you at the Bijou."

I got home and had time to take the dog out before Edgerton returned with Ava and three large grocery bags. Basil leapt repeatedly at Edgerton but, finding him too occupied, the dog turned his attention to Ava. Smiling, Ava bent down and awkwardly patted Basil on the head. The dog rolled over on its back. Ava, not knowing what was expected, looked up at Edgerton.

"You owe me seventy-five dollars," he told me.

The dog got up and, sniffing, meandered around the room. Ava stood and inched toward Edgerton.

"You've got to be kidding," I said.

"You got no idea how much this stuff costs. I mean we're looking at pull-ups and applesauce and yogurt and that canned pasta I remember from back in my childhood days. And macaroni and cheese—it's gotta be the blue box; Ava was very specific—squishy, white bread and peanut butter—it had to be creamy, and…and…Well, hell. Just look at all this stuff."

I looked at all the *stuff*. Then I peered around Edgerton and found Ava standing near the door looking as if she were about to bolt. I pasted a huge, artificial grin on my face. "I hate this."

Ava smiled at me. A worried little smile.

Edgerton stared at my face and winced. "Is there anything you can do about those bruises?" he asked, shaking his head. "You look ghastly."

I walked over to the mirror. The left side of my face, from forehead to cheekbone was puffy and mottled with several shades of purple. There was a slight cut on my lip that was sealed with a blotch of dried blood. I shuddered to think what my ribs looked like. "I guess I could clean up a little."

"Good," Edgerton replied. "Once you get yourself cleaned up, you can clean up this room, put these groceries away, figure out where you're going to sleep tonight, and all that. You don't have the luxury of living like a slob anymore. You've got Ava to think about now."

"I'm not a slob," I protested. "And what do you mean, 'figure out where I'm going to sleep tonight'?"

Edgerton looked around my tiny room. "You're right. You won't have to waste much time on that. The floor's your only option. You got a sleeping bag?"

"Why the hell am I sleeping on the floor?"

"Watch your language in front of the kid."

"Sorry."

"Do you?"

"Do I what?"

Edgerton rolled his eyes. "Do you have a sleeping bag?"

"No."

"I've got an extra one in the basement. I gotta warn you though; it might be a bit musty. But then I'm out of here. I'll be late for work."

"Why am I sleeping on the floor?" I asked again.

"Well, I assumed Ava would get the bed."

"Why can't she have your bed?"

"She could. But then you're sleeping on *my* floor. There's no way I'm letting her sleep alone in a strange room her first night with us. She's only three."

"Three and a half," Ava said proudly. "Almost."

Edgerton turned and squatted down in front of her.

"You're a very big girl."

"Why can't you sleep in there with her?" I asked.

Edgerton stood and nodded a couple of times. "I can. Only not before about one o'clock. I'm working late. Tell you what. We'll set her up in my room. You start off in there, and when I get home, you can come back over here."

"Why can't she sleep over there without me. I'm right next door."

Edgerton glared at me. "You got a baby monitor?"

"No."

"Then if she wakes up there's no guarantee that you'll hear her. You get a baby monitor, I'll think about it. Until then, you sleep on the floor next to her."

I started to protest, but Edgerton waved me off. "I don't want to hear about it. Maybe we can do things differently starting tomorrow, but tonight we do it my way."

He had that look. I just nodded in agreement.

Ava sat on the edge of my bed while Edgerton went downstairs to find the sleeping bag. I stepped over to the small sink in the corner of my room, ran some water, and dabbed at my bruised and battered face. I was nearly done when I heard Edgerton emerge from the basement.

"Here's a spare key to my room," he said. "I tossed the sleeping bag in there. Now I gotta get out of here. See ya in the wee, small hours."

I waved lamely at him as he left the house. I smiled at Ava, the same phony smile I'd used before. With Edgerton gone, she barely looked at me. Instead, she focused on the grocery bags that were still by the door.

"You just sit there for a minute, okay, sweetie?" I said in a syrupy voice that I wasn't sure was even my own. "I'll put this stuff away, then we can talk about what you want to do tonight."

Ava stayed silent. I ran around as quickly as I could, stowing the food in the cupboards in my room and Ava's personal items, including her Pooh Bear suitcase, in Edgerton's room. When I was finished, I returned to Ava and asked, "Well, what do you want to do next?"

She burst into tears. She sat bolt upright on the bed, her little hands folded neatly in her lap, her head raised, and her mouth wide open in a piteous wail. Tears chased each other down her enflamed cheeks. For a moment or two, I couldn't move. Her cries were so loud they actually hurt my ears. Then I remembered the other tenants of the Bijou. I thought of them knocking on the door. I thought of me trying to explain.

"You want some candy?" I asked desperately.

If possible, her bawling got even louder. I thought I heard footsteps coming from the room above me. A board on the stairway outside squeaked loudly.

I threw up my hands. "Shit, kid," I said, "how bad can it be?"

The stupidity of the remark immediately crashed down upon me. Ava was three years old. Her mom had just left her here. I was a stranger. She'd even seen me fighting. Hell, I almost started crying myself. But instead, I scooped her up and held her. She wrapped her arms tightly around my neck and her spindly legs enwreathed me with unexpected strength. I felt the dog clawing at my legs, cajoling me to do more to help her.

"I want my mommy!" Ava cried.

"How 'bout that thing you had in your mouth earlier?" I asked. "Where's that pacifier?"

"I want my Nuky!" she screeched.

"I'll find your Nuky!" I promised.

I twirled about the room; Ava clung to me like a shipwreck survivor to a wave-tossed buoy. I spotted the pacifier on my shelf and lunged for it. I brought Ava back over to the bed and slowly, gently, pried her off me. When I tried to put the pacifier in her mouth, she let it fall from her lips. She wailed incoherently.

Basil stood on his hind legs next to the bed and sniffed keenly at Ava. It took a while, but finally I smelled it too. "Do you need to go to the bathroom, Ava?"

She let out another howl.

"Did you already go to the bathroom?"

"I went poopy!" she cried with such anguish, such abject despair that I couldn't help myself. A chuckle escaped me. Hearing me laugh, Ava froze and glared at me. Then her tiny face scrunched back up and the tears started again. I picked her back up in my arms and paced with her, stroking her hair, mumbling apologies. It took some time, but her sobbing finally came to an end.

"Do you want to go in and change?" I asked.

She nodded.

"Do you need help?"

She nodded again.

I looked at the clock. Surely, Naomi should be here by now, I thought. I stared at the door. Nothing. I took Ava by the hand, stopped at Edgerton's room to get a clean pull-up and then took her upstairs to the bathroom. Before I was done, I'd had to run down to get another pull-up and washed my hands like four times. But I held it together.

I confess I tangled briefly with jolly Mr. Gag Reflex, but I gulped air and pushed through. I emerged from that bathroom with two new convictions. The first was that my mother, who had raised two boys and presumably dealt with similar situations thousands of times, was a saint. The second was that Ava needed to be potty trained immediately.

Ava was quiet as we returned to my room, but she reached up and took my hand on the stairway and when we arrived, she began playing with the dog contentedly. It was as if we'd reached some kind of agreement.

When the knock on the door sounded, Ava grabbed for Basil and pulled him close. He struggled to get away, but finally settled and even gave her a quick lick on the nose.

Naomi's eyes went wide when I opened the door to her. "Lyle," she exclaimed, "what happened?"

"Huh?"

Her eyes softened with tenderness. "Your poor face."

"Huh?"

"The bruises?"

"Oh, yeah. Uh. Yeah. Um…"

Naomi raised her eyebrows. The tenderness that had shone in her face dissolved and was replaced with disdain. "You've been fighting again."

"It's not my fault," I whimpered. "Two guys jumped me."

She put her hands on her hips. "Two guys jumped you for no reason?"

"Yeah. Well. Okay, I called their boss a name, but that's not reason enough to—"

"You should watch what you say to people," Naomi interrupted. "Your mouth is forever getting you into trouble."

"I know," I said, hanging my head dramatically.

A smile tickled the corners of her mouth, but she fought it back. "Let me in. I'll take a look at you."

"Before you come in, there's just one other thing."

All traces of the smile disappeared. "What is it?"

I pushed the door open wide. Ava was sitting on the floor, still clinging to the dog.

Naomi's face went blank. Her eyes darted first to me, then back to Ava. "Yours?" she asked, swiping at a tangle of red hair that had fallen across her face.

"No, no," I blurted, "nothing like that."

"Well, that's something. Why is she here?"

"I'm sort of babysitting."

"Babysitting?"

"Yeah."

"Go on."

"It's kind of a long story."

"I got time."

"Yeah, but," I motioned toward Ava, "it would be better if I gave you the details when we're alone."

Naomi nodded. "Okay," she said uncertainly. "Is she the reason you asked me over here?"

"Um, yeah."

Naomi nodded again. "So, I could help you babysit?"

A blush began to warm my cheeks. "Uh...Yeah, I guess."

Naomi was silent for what seemed like an eternity.

"Well, don't you want to...I don't know. Don't you want to nurture her or something?" I asked.

Naomi put her face in her hands. "How long will she be with you?" Her voice was fortified with hard-won patience.

"I honestly don't know. At least a couple of days, I figure."

"And you figure I'll take one look at her at get all motherly and want to take right over for you?"

"Uh…The thought had crossed my mind."

"Let it pass right on by, pal."

"You mean…"

Naomi eyes were blazing, but she kept her voice calm. "I mean that I find this incredibly insulting. I mean that it is frankly outrageous that you would assume that just because I have a uterus that I would come in here and bail you out of whatever you've got yourself into."

"Okay, I may not have fully considered—"

"Damn right, Lyle. You didn't fully consider anything. You made your assumptions, and you were—"

"Wrong!" I shouted. "I was wrong!"

"That's right."

"So, will you help me anyway?"

Naomi looked at Ava. She seemed a bit calmer. "Are you all by yourself in this?"

"Yes. Well, Stephen said he'd help out. But he's at work until one in the morning."

"So, it's just you and her for the next few hours."

"Yes."

Naomi smiled brightly at Ava, then turned to me. "Have a nice evening, Lyle," she said stepping toward the door.

"But…But…"

She turned around and walked over to Ava. She smiled once more and knelt down to look into her eyes. "It's not you, honey," Naomi told her. "It's him. You just gotta…You just gotta let them learn from their mistakes, that's all. You'll understand when you get older."

Ava nodded and, clutching the dog in one hand, reached up to touch Naomi's wild, red tresses with the delicate fingertips of the other. Before she stood, Naomi gently placed a palm against Ava's cheek.

"You can't be serious," I said as Naomi pushed past me. "I don't know anything about dealing with little girls."

"Or big ones," she said turning to face me. "You'll get through the night. If you find time tomorrow, give me a call." Her expression left no doubt. She wouldn't be staying.

I smiled wanly. "Does this mean you're still on my team in the playground?"

Her glare softened. She patted my shoulder. "Call me tomorrow," she said as she left the room.

I closed the door behind her and turned back to Ava. "She's my sweetie," I told her.

Ava let go of the dog and beamed. "She's got nice hair."

"Yes, she does. Now let's see about getting you some dinner."

Chapter Nine

Even though Morey's had opened only a few months earlier, the restaurant had a wonderful timeless feel. Located on the street level of the Brady building in downtown Minneapolis, it featured exposed redbrick walls, a series of high-backed booths upholstered in maroon leather, and tables that appeared etched by decades of long use but were probably "antiqued" by some designer with a length of chain. One side of the long room featured large windows that looked out on 2nd Avenue, the other a counter surfaced in marble and lined with swiveling stools. The place was dubbed "Morey's" in tribute to funnyman Morey Amsterdam, best known for his role on the old Dick Van Dyke show. A cello, Amsterdam's trademark, was displayed behind the counter, and photographs of Morey and his Van Dyke show colleagues covered the walls.

As I entered, soft music played, and I recognized the Andrews Sisters singing the chorus to Amsterdam's classic "Rum and Coca-Cola." Despite the care that had gone into the details of the place, I suspected the owners likely weren't huge fans of the comic, once nicknamed "the human joke machine." My bet was that instead they had chosen the old vaudevillian simply for the "kitsch" factor. But, as I'm sure a showman like Morey would have appreciated, kitsch puts keisters in the seats.

The place was crowded and a line of waiting

customers had formed in front of a podium set up just inside the door. As I approached, a slender brunette sporting an off-the-shoulder Laura Petrie bob, a short-sleeve cashmere top, and pink capri pants was arranging a stack of faux leather-bound menus. When I asked if someone named Zebulon Pope had left his name with her, she smiled and pointed toward one of the window booths. There a man in a gray suit sat facing a woman with her back to me. When I got close enough, I realized it was Evelyn Walsh.

Neither rose to greet me, but I smiled and bowed slightly to Evelyn. This morning I'd almost convinced myself that the bruises on my face might go unnoticed, but the look of concern on her face told me otherwise. I extended my hand and she placed hers weakly in mine. She nodded gently, her eyes staring steadily at the discolored side of my face.

I then held my hand out to Pope. He ignored me and took a sip of coffee. I tried to recover by raising my hand and passing it through my hair, but we all caught the slight. I slid in next to Evelyn and a balding waiter handed us each a menu. I glanced at the menu and smiled. Morey's may have been designed to look like a neighborhood diner, but the menu selections were decidedly upscale and featured expense-account prices. It was fine if Pope didn't shake my hand as long as he picked up my tab.

The lawyer looked to be in his mid-forties, with a well-trimmed mustache, a touch of gray at his temples, and a head like a coffee can. He had a square jaw, a low-profile nose, and his hair was cropped close on the sides of his head and rose to a flattop. The effect was distinctly Karloffian. I found myself sneaking peeks under his stiff, white collar to see if he had bolts sticking out of his neck.

Pope and Evelyn continued the conversation that they'd evidently been immersed in prior to my arrival. Well, at least Pope had been immersed in it. He kept droning on about stock prices, product commitments, customer loyalty, and someone named Tibbs who had been named interim CEO of Walsh Software. Evelyn didn't seem to be paying much attention. Occasionally Pope would ask Evelyn a question, but her responses seemed automatic, barely considered. Evelyn glanced at me a time or two, and Pope acted as if I wasn't there.

At a pause in their conversation, I managed to get Evelyn's attention. "How's Tyler?"

She glanced at her lawyer before answering. "Bearing up."

The waiter returned and Pope ordered a two-egg omelet with Muenster cheese and Portuguese sausage, while Evelyn ordered a dry English Muffin. I settled on the seared ahi benedict, an order of hash browns, and a caramel sticky bun. I briefly considered tacking on an order of chicken fried steak and eggs, if only to see how they got by with charging twenty-seven bucks for the thing but decided against it.

When the waiter departed, Pope cleared his throat. "Dahms," he began, "I understand from the comments you made to me on the phone yesterday and those you made to Mrs. Walsh at Greg's funeral that although you have spoken with the detective in charge of the investigation, you did not share with him all that you know of Tyler's interest in right-wing political causes. Is that correct?"

"You listen real good, counselor."

He raised an eyebrow at me, then leafed through a

legal pad that he had on the table in front of him. "I further understand that you have…How did you put it? That you have 'history' with this particular detective. Tarkof, I believe his name is."

"And you take good notes, too. Your mother must be very proud."

Pope leveled a stare at me. "Would this 'history' be of the friendly or unfriendly sort?"

"That's hard to say. Bit of both, I guess."

"But you have had dealings in the past?"

"Frequently."

"How is it that this detective allowed you to exit the interview without sharing this pivotal piece of information?"

"What are you driving at, Zeb?"

"I'm wondering, Mr. Dahms, if you lied to the authorities or are lying to us."

I gave him a half-smile. "Neither. I just didn't tell him. Augie didn't press because I suggested that I had been hired by one of the Walsh family lawyers and any information that I may have about the family was privileged."

Pope smirked in triumph. "You told the authorities that you were working for me?"

"Not in so many words, Zebby, but I left that impression. Yes."

Pope leaned back in the booth. "I don't know whether to be grateful or appalled, Mr. Dahms. We, of course, prefer to handle sensitive information like that about Tyler ourselves, yet it is disturbing that the authorities would actually believe that my firm would employ someone like you. I mean, I've never chased an ambulance and I don't advertise on late night TV."

Pope's eyes glinted. I noticed that the pupil of his left eye was slightly larger than that of his right. I wondered what that meant.

"You ever handle a criminal case, Pope?" I asked.

"I have a seasoned criminal litigator on my staff."

"But you've never tried a criminal case yourself?"

"No."

I turned to Evelyn Walsh. "Dump this prick."

Pope couldn't help himself. He gasped slightly, but Evelyn merely turned her head to look at me. "Come on, Evelyn, we're leaving," he declared, rising and tossing his napkin on the table.

She didn't move.

Pope stared at her for a few seconds before smoothing his trousers and resuming his seat. Evelyn kept her eyes on me the whole time, but they were glassy, her thoughts elsewhere.

"Why?" she asked at last.

"This guy is one of the corporation lawyers, right?"

"He's our chief counsel, yes. He's been with us since the beginning."

I nodded. "I'm sure he's heck in the boardroom, but this dweeb's probably never seen the inside of a courtroom, let alone had a client questioned by the murder police. He's out of his element. He knows it, but he's just too arrogant to admit that he's not the right man for the job. If he goes lumbering into that interview with you and Tyler, he's gonna do two things. First, he's gonna piss the cops off and that means that they won't be looking to cut you much slack. Second, he's gonna give you bad advice. He'll have you in there telling half-truths and making non-denial denials when giving the cops the straight story is the smart play. You follow his

109

advice, and the cops are gonna look at you all the harder."

Pope laughed, I thought a bit nervously. "You're forgetting several key pieces of the puzzle, Mr. Dahms. Unlike the lowlifes that I'm sure you are used to dealing with, Evelyn and Tyler are extremely well thought of in this town. And as for myself, the chief of police and the state's attorney general have both been guests at my club. This 'slack' you say they won't cut us, is guaranteed."

"See what I mean," I told Evelyn. "That kind of arrogance just doesn't cut it in a murder investigation. This guy could hurt you bad."

Pope started to say something, but Evelyn raised her hand to cut him off. "Lyle's point has some merit, Zebulon. Not the way he put it, but what he said. I would like an experienced hand in that interview with us. Your Mr. Finch is the expert in these matters, isn't he?"

"Yes, he is. If you would be more comfortable with Finch, Evelyn, then I'll assign him to you. Either way, you have nothing to worry about."

I grunted with satisfaction. Pope raised his coffee cup to his lips.

"One more thing," Evelyn added. "I'd like you to hire Lyle."

A pro like Morey would have done a better job, but old Zeb performed a pretty passable spit-take. "You're joking," he said, wiping coffee from his chin with a linen napkin.

Evelyn cocked her head. Her voice was even, but there was no mistaking how she felt. "My husband has been murdered. My son is a suspect. I am not joking."

Pope recovered, "I'm sorry. I misspoke. Of course, you're not joking. But really, Evelyn, despite whatever obligation you feel toward this…individual, despite the friendly feelings you may have for him as an old acquaintance of Greg's, we simply do not need him. It is *his* presence in this that suggests that we have something to hide."

Evelyn was firm. "I want him working for us."

Pope leaned forward. "I think he's involving himself in this out of greed. I think he's just another grifter looking to make some money off of Greg's death."

"That's precious," I said, "coming from a lawyer. Greg was my friend, Pope."

When Pope turned to face me, his eyes gleamed with malice. "I doubt that Mr. Dahms knows the meaning of the word 'friendship.' Perhaps, since he's such a friend of the family, he'd like to donate his services. I wouldn't want a paycheck from us to compromise his principles."

"You got it, counselor. I'll sign on for nothing. Of course, I'm assuming that you too are willing to handle this as a favor to the family."

"That would hardly be ethical," he said.

"Of course not." I smiled. "We've all got to mind our ethics. As for me, I'll send your office one of my standard contracts."

Pope chortled. "Standard? No doubt you'll hike your price substantially to take advantage of Mrs. Walsh's beneficence."

"Zeb," I said, staring hard into his eyes, "I'm afraid we've got off to a bad start. It's partially my fault, I know. It looks like we just don't understand each other, and this lack of understanding has made us suspicious of one another. Let me do what I can to clear this up. I want to assure you that I have Evelyn's best interests at heart. I want nothing more than to bring Greg's killers to justice." I paused. "And I assure you that if you question my allegiance or my integrity again, I'll whup you 'til you cry like a little girl."

Pope twitched a smile and started to reply but then he must have seen something in my eyes. He turned to Evelyn. "You see. This man is nothing more than a common thug."

"Yeah, Zeb," I told him. "But I'm *her* thug."

Evelyn shook her head. "I want him on the payroll, Zebulon."

Pope rose abruptly, nearly upsetting his coffee cup in the process. "You're making a serious mistake, Evelyn. As your lawyer, it's my duty to point that out to you. That being said, if it is your wish that this man work for you, so be it. If you say we have to pay him, I'll pay him, but I certainly don't have to eat with him."

Pope made a great show of gathering up his papers and closing his briefcase. I stood and bowed extravagantly to him as he pushed past me and toward the door. He'd started to push it open when he turned and approached the Mary Tyler Moore wannabe at the lobby podium. Mary spoke briefly to our waiter who pulled a guest check from the pocket in his apron. Pope opened his wallet and peeled off some bills, handing them to the waiter before departing.

I rose and repositioned myself in the booth opposite Evelyn. She didn't even look up as the waiter cleared Pope's coffee cup and returned almost immediately with our food. He set my benedict in front of me and Pope's omelet to the side. Evelyn nibbled at her English muffin silently as I tucked into my hash browns. They were perfect—crispy brown on the outside, moist and tender on the inside. But after a time, the silence began to get to me.

"I'm really sorry," I said at last. "I'm afraid I didn't handle your Mr. Pope very well."

Evelyn gave me a knowing look. "I think you handled him exactly the way you wanted. Why feel sorry now?"

"Okay," I admitted. "I didn't like him and wanted him to know it. But I didn't have to be such a jerk in front of you. I could have been a jerk later when Pope and I were alone."

A soft light appeared in Evelyn's smoky eyes. "Greg didn't like him much, either. But he's quite the cutthroat—a good man to have working on your side."

"He's not on *my* side."

"No. But you're both on mine."

"Why?"

"Excuse me?"

"I understand why you need Pope, Evelyn, but why me? The cops will find Greg's killer and Pope and company will protect your interests. What is there for me to do?"

She crinkled her brow. "I need somebody on my side who's not just doing their job. I need someone who cares."

I nodded but didn't say anything. Instead, I turned my attention to the benedict. Twin muffin halves were layered with a strip of seared, deeply red, barely warmed tuna, poached eggs, lemony hollandaise, and just a touch of light green wasabi. I cut off a small section and hummed with approval as each ingredient asserted its individual flavor in my mouth before melding into a scrumptious whole. The thing was heaven on a plate.

"I'll have to talk to him," I said, wiping up the last

bit of egg yolk and hollandaise with a final morsel of English muffin.

"Tyler?"

"Yeah."

"Of course. But I don't think he'll tell you anything."

"Probably not."

Evelyn's expression was equal parts hope and suspicion. "You don't think he had anything to do with Greg's death, do you?"

"I don't think anything at this point. I don't know the kid."

Evelyn sighed. "I'm not sure I do either. Not anymore." A warm smile appeared on her face. "If only you'd met him a year ago. Even less than that. He was a different kid then. My kid."

"Before he turned Nazi?"

Irritation flashed in her eyes. "He can't really believe that nonsense he's been spouting. He just can't. Someone put him up to it. There's something he's not telling us. Something he's hiding."

I grunted and picked up my sticky bun. It was as big as my head and delightfully gooey.

"You know," I said, eyeing the bun, "if Tyler didn't have anything to do with Greg's death, someone damn sure wants it to look as though he does." I took a bite and had to use a napkin to wipe the caramel off my nose.

Evelyn nodded but said nothing.

"Who knew about Tyler playing Nazi?" I asked.

"Unfortunately, my son didn't exactly keep it a secret. It was well known at school. One of the parents even spoke to me about it."

"Which parent?"

"Actually, it was his girlfriend's father. Charlie Blauer. Charlie told me that he had nothing against me or Greg but that he wouldn't allow his Megan to socialize with Tyler anymore."

"How long ago was that?"

"About six months ago."

"How did Tyler take it?"

"Well, this happened at a time when Tyler wasn't exactly talking to us about what was going on with him. We'd been trying and trying to get him to open up, but he was retreating farther and farther from us. Still, I got the impression that it didn't bother him much. At least he didn't let it show if it did."

"Like maybe they'd broke it off themselves before daddy stepped in?"

"That's possible."

"How were they before this?"

"Come again?"

"How did Tyler and Megan get along before Tyler started to change?"

"Oh, they were inseparable. For a while we were worried that they got along too well. You want your teenage boy to be happy, but you don't want him to become too deeply attached too young. We were afraid we'd be looking at a teenage wedding. Seems silly now."

"Still, there might have been bad blood between Tyler and this Charlie Blauer?"

"Possibly. But I don't think it's likely. Tyler just didn't seem interested in his old life anymore. It was like he'd given up everything that made him what he was to become something he knew everyone would hate."

I finished the sticky bun and began eyeing Pope's untouched omelet. "You want to split that?"

115

Evelyn shook her head.

The sausage was nicely smoky, but on the whole, I thought the omelet a little too dry. If I were to come back, I thought, I'd stick with the benedict. I was taking the last bite of the omelet when I asked, "What does Charlie Blauer do for a living?"

Evelyn looked at me curiously. "He's a general contractor. Why?"

"No reason," I said. But the image in my mind was of the guy that beat me. The one I called Snotty. The one wearing the "Blauer Construction" ball cap.

Chapter Ten

Evelyn agreed to let me meet with Tyler later that day. Both she and Pope had been insistent that he stick around the homestead until the investigation of Daddy's murder was completed and, according to Evelyn, he had thus far complied. She was pretty certain that he would be home to meet with me that afternoon.

Evelyn left me at the table, and I took a few minutes to consider my next move. I basically had two problems—the Ava problem and the Tyler problem. Ava herself was taken care of. Edgerton had told his cronies at the armory, where he worked during the day, that they would have to do without him for at least the rest of the week, so he was at the Bijou watching Ava. But I had to start trying to track down Janet. I didn't want the kid on my hands indefinitely. Still, the ball cap coincidence was just too much for me to leave alone. I decided to use the time I had before my meeting with Tyler to check out Blauer Construction.

I checked Google on my cell phone before leaving Morey's and found the address for Blauer's company. It was in St. Helena, a tiny township just south of Apple Valley. I cross-referenced on another site and found that Blauer's home address was the same as that of his company. I tossed a few dollars on the table in case Pope hadn't left enough of a tip, got in my car, and drove to the south suburbs.

Actually, that's not quite true. You couldn't really mistake St. Helena for a suburb. On County Road 9 heading out of Apple Valley, the corn and soybean fields that edge the road were momentarily broken by a couple of two-story houses that I'd guess dated from the 1920's. Next to one of the houses was a squat outbuilding, its red paint blistered and peeling. A hand-lettered sign that read "Antiques" was hanging beside a weathered whitewashed double door. Directly across the road were the remains of a long-closed Sinclair station, the outline of a green brontosaurus dimly visible on a badly listing signpost. And finally, next to the old gas station, stood a tiny, flat-roofed roadhouse that styled itself "Sully's Empire Room." I spotted a small sign next to the tavern as I drove past but was unable to slow in time to read it. I made a U-turn about a quarter of a mile down the road and returned to pull into the Empire Room's parking lot. The sign read "Welcome to St. Helena."

I got out of the car and looked around. There were some houses huddled together well off the road behind Sully's, but the tavern and its nearly empty parking lot seemed to be what passed for St. Helena's town square.

I figured I could either drive around looking for Blauer's or I could go into the roadhouse to ask for directions. Never one to pass up a visit to a bar, I decided to check out the Empire Room. I opened the door to a narrow, dimly lit room that smelled strongly of fried meat. A bar ran nearly the length of the place, perhaps a half dozen tables in front. A pool table was squeezed into a cramped alcove in the back. A sign above it read "Free Pool."

Good thing, I thought. Shooting pool in there would be like trying to make love in the rumble seat of an old roadster. You'd have to be a contortionist to get the job done.

The walls of the tavern were decorated for the most part with simply framed drawings of historic farm machinery—tractors, combines, and the like—that looked to have been clipped from magazines. But behind the bar was an ornately framed portrait of the Emperor Napoleon, his hand disappearing into his waistcoat. However, Napoleon's face had been neatly excised and replaced with that of a pudgy fellow in his mid-fifties with flushed cheeks and wispy gray hair. A small brass plate was affixed to the frame reading "Frank Sullivan, Proprietor."

But the person that greeted me from behind the bar as I entered was neither "the Little Corporal" nor the usurper in the portrait. A large woman wearing a white apron over a blue-checked housedress smiled brightly as I closed the door behind me. She too was on the high side of fifty and looked remarkably like the man in the portrait except for a full head of hair dyed a shade of brown that I was pretty sure couldn't be found in nature.

The only customers in the roadhouse were two kids, probably still in high school, both wearing baseball caps and plain white T-shirts. They glanced up at me as I entered, then returned immediately to drinking their coffee in silence.

"What can I get ya, mister?" the woman said cheerfully.

I sat down at one of the stools in front of the bar and returned her smile. "Just a little direction, ma'am. I'm looking for Blauer Construction."

She stared at me for a moment, her gaze lingering on the bruised side of my face. She may have been too polite, or perhaps facial contusions just weren't that unusual among her clientele. In either case she made no comment. Instead, her small eyes twinkled merrily. "Little town like this and you can't find Charlie Blauer's place?" she scolded me.

I smiled. "Just hopeless, I guess."

"Well, nothing I can do but write it all down for you I suppose."

"I'd appreciate it."

"Now, while I'm doing that, you think maybe I could talk you into a little something for breakfast. There's fresh blueberries in my blueberry pancakes."

"I'm afraid I had rather a large breakfast earlier."

"Just a cup of coffee and a piece of pie, then?"

"No thanks."

"Fresh blueberry pie? Made it myself. Now, when was the last time you had homemade blueberry pie?"

It dawned on me that she was suggesting the pie to cover the cost of her trouble, so I smiled a bit broader. "Come to think on it, I don't reckon I can pass up that pie after all." It bothered me a little that my voice no longer seemed to belong to me, but rather to Chester on *Gunsmoke*.

"Now you're talking.". She turned and hustled through a door behind the bar. At each step her bulk shivered like ripples through a great mound of gelatin.

She returned and the slice of pie she placed before me was beautiful—glossy blueberries peered through a lightly browned lattice crust. My hostess stepped back and watched carefully as I took my first bite. I did what was expected. I made an overblown yummy face at her as I struggled to down the gluey crust and a blueberry filling that was tart and unpleasantly grassy.

"Don't tell me I don't know nothing about pie," she said laughing and jiggling.

I didn't. I just picked at the pie while she wrote the directions out for me on the back of a guest check.

"You looking to have some work done?" she asked, handing me the directions. "Some construction work, I mean."

"I'm thinking about it," I said, nodding. "But I'm only at the planning stage."

Her eyes lit up. "Good thing. Charlie gets all backed up this time of year. I remember a couple a summers back, Sully and me, we needed Charlie to rebuild our deck. Now we've known Charlie since he's a little kid, right? Darned if we didn't have to wait until nearly the first snowfall before he got to us. Sully'd like to have had conniptions. Just ain't summer for Sully if he can't spend it on his deck."

"Is Sully your husband?"

"Gracious no." She chuckled. "Sully's my brother. My name was Sullivan too before I got married. Name's Johnson now. Prudence Johnson. Everybody calls me Prude. Kinda a little joke, you might say. Sully says that's probably why my old man left me, 'cause I was such a prude. But that wasn't it. No, sir. That man had problems that would fill a book with the telling."

"How did the deck turn out?"

"Pardon?"

"The deck that Mr. Blauer rebuilt for you."

"Oh, it's a thing of beauty. If want, I'll write down our address for you. You can go by the house and take a look for yourself. That what you want Charlie to do for you? Build you a deck?"

"I don't know yet. Maybe something a little grander.

I'm still getting ideas."

"That's good. That's good 'cause Charlie hasn't been taking on little jobs like decks lately on account of all the bigger jobs been coming his way. He only did the deck for us 'cause we've been friends so long, you know? That and he does most of his drinking in here. Wouldn't do him no good to get on the bad side of the folks that pull him his beers."

"I don't suppose it would," I said, rising and removing my wallet. "I guess I'd better be going to talk to him myself, now. Thanks for everything, Ms. Johnson."

"Now, you can call me Prude. Everyone does. That 'Ms. Johnson' stuff makes me feel like an old lady."

"Thanks again, Prude."

I got all the way to the door before she called out. "Hey, you didn't finish your pie."

I smiled. "Afraid my eyes were bigger than my stomach, Prude."

"I'll let you get by this time." She laughed. "But next time come hungry."

"I will," I promised, hurrying out the door.

As I was climbing into my car, I noticed that the two high schoolers had finished their coffee and were also leaving Sully's. They got into what looked like a brand-new, forest green Dodge pickup truck. They took their time before driving away, sitting in the cab of the truck, probably debating what to do next. If they were locals, I thought, they'd head out of town. Drinking coffee at Sully's likely exhausted their list of things to do in St. Helena.

I pulled out and began following Prude's remarkably detailed directions. I headed back out on the county road and, as instructed, turned at a large willow tree about three-quarters of a mile away from the tavern. There, a gravel road bisected a field of ripening corn and ran past a farmstead that sat atop a low rise. At the edge of yet another cornfield sat the rusting hulk of an old Chevy pickup truck. Next to the truck, at the end of a gravel driveway, stood a mailbox with a flock of ducks painted on it. The mailbox read "The Blauers." A chain link gate barred the driveway.

I parked my car and got out. There were no buildings visible from the road and the gate was secured with a heavy padlock. I looked around for a call box or bell or something that a potential customer could use to signal the house. Nothing. The gate was tied into a barbed wire fence that appeared to enclose the property. About fifty yards from the gate, the driveway curved lazily into a stand of trees. Blauer's house would have to be behind the trees, I thought. I checked the padlock. It wasn't much. It wouldn't take me more than a minute to pick the thing. But why? There was no reason that I could think of to break in just to find that Blauer was out on a job and had the good sense to lock up after himself. I'd just have to call, make an appointment, and come back out to see him. There was nothing I could do.

I returned to my car and was just about to pull away when a vehicle came down the drive. It was an older Dodge pickup—gray with a rumpled white topper covering the cargo bed. Stenciled in blue calligraphic letters on the side of the truck were the words "Blauer Construction." The pickup stopped at the end of the drive and a short man wearing a white ball cap, blue jeans, and a green pocket T-shirt climbed out from behind the wheel. The man cast a glance my way before unreeling a large key ring from his belt and unlocking the gate.

I got out of my car and called to him. The man turned toward me and adjusted his cap. He looked to be about my age, but he'd worked harder, and it showed. Deeply etched wrinkles surrounded his eyes and the skin covering his prominent cheekbones was ruddy with windburn. His legs bowed slightly at the knees and his hands were callused claws with thick, yellowed fingernails. As I approached him, he took a deep breath, puffing out his chest like a territorial rooster.

"Charlie Blauer?" I asked.

"Who's asking?" he said, in a tone that managed to be both cheerful and suspicious.

"You don't know me, Mr. Blauer. My name's Lyle Dahms. I'm a friend of Greg Walsh."

I stuck out my hand and he shook it automatically, but he also searched my face minutely. "What can I do for you, Mr. Dahms?" he asked in the same pleasant yet guarded tone.

"Evelyn Walsh has asked me to look into her husband's death. I'm sure you can imagine just how hard this has been on her and Tyler."

"Of course. But isn't investigating Walsh's murder a job for the police?"

"It is," I agreed. "But I'm a private investigator. You see, Mrs. Walsh thought it might be a good idea to have someone around concentrating exclusively on Greg's death and her family's safety. The police, with their limited resources, must divide their time among so many different cases, so many different crimes."

Blauer smiled. "You say you're working for her?"

"Yes."

"Minute ago, you said you were Walsh's friend.

Which one is it?"

Since it was working for him, I tried a smile myself. "I'm a friend who happens to be a private investigator. Greg and I went way back. Back to high school. We used to work together at the old Valley Pizza."

"The one that used to be in Valley Place?"

"That's the one."

"That was a while ago," Blauer said. "Used to go in there myself back then. And I got a vague memory of Walsh working there. We weren't exactly friends, but I knew who he was since we went to the same high school. Don't remember you, though."

I chuckled. "Well, I was there. Still have burn marks from those pizza ovens on my arms to prove it. But I didn't go to Apple Valley High. I grew up in Burnsville."

Blauer stared at me some more before glancing briefly up the driveway toward his unseen house. "Okay, so how can I help you, Mr. Dahms?"

"You can start by calling me, Lyle."

"Uh-huh."

"I was wondering if you could tell me something about a guy I ran into. Long blond hair, pretty big, pretty tough looking. He's got a swastika tattooed on his right arm. When I met him, he was wearing one of your gimme caps."

Blauer made some motions with his mouth like he was chewing gum, but he didn't appear to actually have any. "Sounds like Albert Grogan," he said at last.

"So, you know him. Does he work for you?"

"Used to. Had to let him go."

"What happened?"

"Didn't like him is what happened. That and he lied to me. Asks right on the job application if you've ever done time. He writes down that he hasn't then turns around and starts bragging about what a big deal he was in the joint. Didn't get along with the other guys on the crew, neither. One guy—Corky—he's been with me like five years. He's a Black fellow. Or African American, or whatever. Anyway, this Grogan spends more time trying to get Corky's goat than he does working. So, I got rid of him. What's he got to do with Walsh's murder, anyway?"

"Maybe nothing. But he showed up at Walsh's funeral with Matty Beam. You know who Beam is?"

Blauer nodded. "Fat little fuck's been spouting his mouth off, making all of us down this way look like rubes. It don't surprise me, Grogan hooking up with him. You think Beam had something to do with Walsh getting killed? I mean with the swastikas on the corpse and all."

"It's at least worth looking into."

"Uh-huh. Mind if I ask how you got them bruises?"

"Bruises?"

Blauer pointed to the side of my face.

"Oh, well, coincidentally I got some of these from Grogan. He and this enormous bald guy took a run at me outside my office."

"Don't sound like coincidence to me," Blauer said, letting out a little grunt-like chortle.

"Okay. So maybe not."

Blauer chuckled again, then looked at his watch. "It's getting late. I really should be getting to work. Just came home for lunch."

"Oh, just came home to eat with Megan, huh?"

The smile fell from Blauer's face. "What business is she of yours?"

"Hey, don't get the wrong idea. Evelyn just

126

mentioned that you had a daughter named Megan. In fact, I think I've seen her photograph." I paused as I conjured up the memory of the photograph in the Walsh living room of Tyler with a fragilely beautiful girl with blonde hair. "Evelyn said she used to go out with Tyler."

Blauer nodded.

"Evelyn said Tyler and Megan broke it off kind of suddenly. She said you spoke to her about Tyler."

Blauer nodded again.

"Did you and your wife ask Megan to stop seeing Tyler because of all that Nazi stuff?"

"Megan's mother's no longer in the picture," Blauer said. "It's just Megan and me now."

I didn't know what to say to that, so I repeated myself. "Was it Tyler being a Nazi that made you ask Megan to stop seeing him?"

"Among other things."

"Don't get me wrong here," I told him. "I'd have done the same thing. No matter who his dad was, no matter how big a deal Walsh was, no way I'd let my daughter see his goose-stepping son."

"I'm glad you understand," Blauer said, the tension growing in his voice. "So did Mrs. Walsh. At least that's what she told me."

"And Greg?"

"What?"

"Did you talk to Greg about it?"

"Why should I?"

"Just wondering."

Blauer pushed his cap back on his head and eyed me narrowly.

"The cops have been by, right?" I asked. "They ask you the same thing?"

"You think I'm just some stupid farm boy, don't you, Dahms?"

"'Fraid I don't know what you're talking about, Mr. Blauer."

"The hell you don't. You come down here knowing that this Grogan worked for me, knowing that Walsh's kid went out with mine, knowing I talked to Mrs. Walsh about it. You figure you can come down here and trick me into saying something makes me look guilty. That it?"

"I'm just looking for the truth, Mr. Blauer."

"Well, you can quit looking around here. You want the truth, you check with the Walshes. You find out why I seen Greg Walsh and Albert Grogan sitting together in a booth over at Sully's. The week before he was killed, no less. You ask that kid of his why all of a sudden he's got to start spouting bullshit around my daughter, telling her his old man's gonna pay for the things he's done. You want to know who killed Greg Walsh? Go ask somebody who cares. I don't want anything to do with any of it. Didn't then, don't now." He glanced down the driveway. "I got work to do, Mr. Dahms."

"I'm sorry we seem to have gotten off on the wrong foot here, Mr. Blauer. Maybe if we just—"

"Am I going to have call the cops?" he snapped. "Or are you going to get the hell out of here?"

Blauer's voice shook with tightly controlled anger. He stood still, but his whole being seemed charged with motion. We stared at each other for a moment or two. Then he allowed himself another quick glance up the driveway toward the house.

"You're worried about Megan," I said. "Cops coming by. Now me. Beam and his guys are out there someplace. I don't blame you looking out for your own."

Blauer said nothing, but the skin tightened at the corners of his now shimmering eyes.

"I'm sorry to have bothered you, Mr. Blauer," I said, turning and walking to my car.

By the time I reached it, Blauer was inside his pickup and was driving it through the gate. Then he hopped out and locked the gate behind him. He stood beside his truck, the gate key clutched tightly in his hand, as he watched me drive out of sight.

Chapter Eleven

The way I'd left Blauer bothered me, but I had managed to learn a couple of things. I now had a name for one of the guys who beat on me outside my office, and I'd found out that this Albert Grogan had some kind of relationship with Greg Walsh. They'd been seen together at that roadhouse in St. Helena. Sully's didn't strike me as a place that Greg Walsh would have chosen for a casual drink with a friend. And Grogan wasn't exactly the kind of guy with whom Greg would normally drink. Something had been going on between those two. Something that probably involved Tyler. I definitely needed to find out more.

But while driving through Apple Valley, I turned my attention to my other problem. There was a kid waiting for me at home—a kid I wanted off my hands. And to get rid of the kid, I had to find her mom. The logical place to start looking was her home, but Janet Kleiner hadn't left me an address. Although I didn't know where she was living now, it occurred to me that I did know where she used to live. When we were young, Janet lived in Apple Valley. My memory was that her parents moved out of state when she was a senior in high school. She'd wanted to graduate with her class and arranged to stay with an aunt in town until school let out. Maybe the aunt still lived there. If she did, she might be able to help me locate her niece.

For nostalgia's sake, I pulled into the parking lot of Valley Place, parking outside the front entrance to the old pizza parlor where Greg Walsh and I worked so long ago. Except, it had vanished in the interim. I stepped inside and found that the walls that once separated the old pizza parlor from the original bar had evidently been knocked out to make way for a larger watering hole, now called "Humphrey's"

I went back out to my car and pulled out my cell phone to check for addresses. I found two Kleiners listed in town. I dialed up the first number but hung up when I got an answering machine. The second number was for an M. Kleiner, and I listened to the phone ring maybe four times before an elderly, female voice answered.

"Excuse me, ma'am," I began, "might I speak with Ms. Kleiner?"

"I don't want to listen to someone trying to sell me something," the voice replied tartly.

"I'm not selling anything, ma'am. I've got some information concerning a Janet Kleiner and I'm trying to locate her family."

There was a silence, then the voice said, "I don't take sales calls."

"Would you be Janet's aunt, ma'am?"

Another silence.

"It's really quite important," I assured her.

"If Janet's in some kind of trouble, I'm sorry, but that doesn't concern me."

"There's no trouble, ma'am. And I'll only take a moment of your time. Please, if you could just spare—"

The line went dead. I stared at the phone for a moment then started the car. Driving away I cast one last glance back at the building where I'd spent so many nights so long ago. Getting misty at the sight of suburban bowling alley left me feeling pretty stupid.

I remembered enough of Apple Valley to find the Kleiner house without any trouble. It was a split entry painted a light green with dark green trim and a lawn brightly speckled with yellow dandelions. I parked in front of the house, walked up, and rang the bell. When I didn't get an answer, I knocked loudly.

It took some time, but finally the same elderly voice called down, "You might as well leave now. I've called the police."

"Please Ms. Kleiner," I said, stepping back from the door. Looking up, I saw movement in the bay window above me. I smoothed out my hair and smiled—winsomely, I hoped.

"Go away!" she called out harshly.

"It's not just about Janet," I entreated. "It's really about Ava."

There was no reply—nothing at all, not even her footsteps on the stairway. But all at once the door drew open.

She was a frail looking woman in her seventies with curly gray hair pinned up into a tight bun at the back of her head and faded brown eyes set deep in a network of wrinkles. She inspected me carefully, pausing to scrutinize the bruises on my face. Then, with a look of beleaguered resignation, she stepped away from the door, waving me in with a bony arm.

I led the way into the living room. The old woman followed silently, drifting past me to take a seat at the far end of a sofa upholstered in a blue floral pattern. "Did you really call the police?" I asked, sitting opposite the sofa in a similarly upholstered armchair.

She turned away, barely shaking her head.

I smiled softly. "What's the 'M' stand for?"

Momentarily puzzled, she stared at me, then replied, "Mavis."

I nodded.

The scent of flowers filled the room. I looked around, but the only flora visible was a dusty arrangement of plastic gladiolas erupting from a tall vase in a corner. An upright piano sat against the far wall and atop the piano was a photograph of a much younger Mavis Kleiner, her head tilted toward that of a young man in a military uniform. The colors of the photograph had been muted by time. Next to the photo of the man I assumed was Mavis' husband was a picture of Janet and Ava. The photograph was recent, judging from how little Ava had changed since it was taken. Both Janet and her daughter were smiling untroubled smiles. There was no trace of paranoia in Janet's eyes, only the sweet, steady gaze of a mother's love.

"Is there a Mr. Kleiner?" I asked pointing at the picture of the man in uniform.

"There was."

"Sorry."

She turned her palms upward and shrugged her shoulders. "What can you do?" she asked, casting a glance at the ceiling.

"I see you've got Janet's picture up there, too. Are you and Janet close? I seem to recall that she stayed with you her last year of high school."

Mavis leaned forward. The faded brown of her eyes seemed to glow momentarily. "You've known Janet for a while?"

"Back in high school I used to work at Valley Place.

133

With Greg Walsh."

The corner of her mouth twitched slightly when I mentioned the dead man's name. "Janet used to go out with Greg," I added.

Mavis nodded several times. "You said something about Ava."

"I don't know if you're aware of this. But Janet's disappeared. I'm trying to find her."

Mavis sighed. "I suppose you'll be threatening me next."

"Why would anyone threaten you, Mavis?"

"You're looking for her. I suppose you'll try to force me to help you find her."

"No, ma'am."

"A pimp with manners," she said, shrugging again.

I smiled patiently and took one of my cards out of my wallet and handed it to her. "I'm not Janet's pimp. I'm a private investigator looking into Greg Walsh's murder. But that's not primarily why I'm here. I recently took on a whole new line of work. Now I'm also running a day care center."

"What's that supposed to mean?"

"I hadn't seen Janet in years before she turned up at Greg's funeral the other day. Then she shows up at my door and leaves Ava with me. Seems she trusts me. Maybe you could, too."

The old woman exhaled slowly and lay a skinny arm across the delicate cage of her chest. She settled back and for a moment was as still as a corpse. "I've really been all she's had since her parents moved to Phoenix," she said at last. "What kind of parents move away and leave their teenage daughter behind? It was shameful. They said it was because she wouldn't leave her friends. That she was nearly grown. But that wasn't it. Janet's always been difficult. Hard to know. After seventeen years, my brother and her mother…they just gave up. I'd call them. Asking for their help. They'd tell me things. Finally, they said to just let her go. I tried a little longer. She got into more trouble. After a while I took their advice. I let her go."

"Sounds like you did all you could."

"Bullshit!" she exclaimed with surprising intensity. "I just got tired. I told myself that there was nothing I could do. That she wasn't mine. That I wasn't responsible. We all have something that we'll have to answer for when we pass. Giving up on Janet, that's mine."

"Do you know where she is now?"

She didn't seem to have heard me. "I'll tell you what was almost as bad," she continued. "Almost as bad as her folks leaving her. When she broke off with that Walsh, that was almost as bad. She was better when she was with him. She had friends. She stayed in school. They could have made it work. But Janet just couldn't be happy. She said it was because they were too different. You know what I think? I think she just wouldn't let herself be happy. She said it was because she was Jewish, and he wasn't and that they just didn't fit together. But I know better."

"I didn't know she was Jewish," I said.

Mavis straightened and raised her eyebrows. "How could you not?"

I cringed. I knew that I'd said something that I shouldn't have. "I guess that sort of thing just doesn't make much difference to me."

Mavis' eyes hardened. "This is what you tell me,"

she said, her voice for the first time, showing traces of long-abandoned accent, "that what a person *is* makes no difference to you? Shame on you."

A blush warmed my cheeks. "I didn't mean any disrespect, ma'am."

"Of course not," the old woman said sharply. "Never mind. Never mind. You say you have Ava?"

"Yes, ma'am," I replied, hoping to hide my growing uneasiness behind a smile.

"I suppose you'll be wanting me to take over for you."

"Actually, I hadn't thought of that. But, hey, that would be great if you want to."

"I don't want to," Mavis snapped. "I'm an old woman. There are days I can barely take care of myself. If I had anybody close who cared about me, they'd probably insist I move into one of those nursing homes. I can't take care of a baby. It's not like Janet even acts like family. I've never even met the child. Janet's mentioned her. She calls every month or so, but we only talk for a moment or two and then we go on leading our own lives. Janet will just have to take care of that child on her own."

"When was the last time you talked?"

"Couple of weeks ago, I think."

I leaned forward. "Janet's disappeared," I repeated. "She told me she was afraid. Afraid of the same people who may have killed Greg Walsh. Has she mentioned any of this to you?"

Mavis shook her head. A tendril of gray hair slipped out of the pin that held her bun together and fell to her scrawny shoulders. "Janet knew I disapproved of her. She knew that I didn't like having a…a harlot in the family. But she *is* family. I took her calls, but all we ever really talked about was the weather. And the baby."

"Did she sound scared the last time you talked? Did she give you any indication at all that something was wrong?"

"She said she was fine. The baby was fine. The weather was fine."

"But how did she sound?"

The old woman sighed. "She sounded like she always does. Sad. Sad, but hiding it behind a lot of prattle. I suppose I sounded the same way."

Mavis gave me the address where Janet and Ava had been living. I asked her to call me if Janet got in touch. Then I made my excuses and prepared to leave.

She stopped me at the door. "I've never actually seen the child," she said again. "What's she like?"

I couldn't help smiling. "A lot like her picture," I said, pointing. "She's a runty little thing with pudgy cheeks and rings of hair so blonde you have to squint to look at them."

Mavis allowed herself a soft smile. "The hair must come from the father. Janet's hair's always been brown and straight."

"She been blonde since I've known her," I said.

"Hair can be any color you want it to be anymore. But without a bottle of dye and a curling iron, Janet's hair would be brown and straight." Mavis paused. "I suppose the curly blonde look brings in more customers," she added, her voice taking on a bitter edge.

I gave her a noncommittal nod. "Who is the father?",

"Janet never told me." Mavis paused. "Supposing she knows."

I turned toward the door, but Mavis stopped me

again. "If Janet doesn't turn up, you give me a call. Janet's folks don't want anything to do with her and I can't be raising the child, but maybe I could talk to some folks at temple. Maybe find a nice Jewish couple that will raise her right. Might even be a blessing, her being with her people and all."

Something about that rankled me. "You might be right, Mavis," I replied, surprising myself with the bitterness in my voice. "And let me apologize for not being the right kind of person to be looking after her."

Mavis picked up on my irritation, but instead of apologizing, she held my gaze. "I don't know anything about the kind of person you are," she said.

We stared at each other for another moment before I made my way out to the car. I sat behind the wheel for a while, pretending to make notes on a little yellow pad I keep in the glove compartment. But really, I was steaming. It's not that I considered myself the ideal candidate for raising little Ava, nor was I thinking of volunteering for the job. But it wasn't like I couldn't do it if I had to. Janet trusted me, I thought, didn't that mean I was the right kind of person for the child's mother?

I was pulling away from the curb when I noticed a green Dodge pickup parked about a half-block behind me. It looked like it might have been the same pickup I'd seen back in the parking lot at Sully's. I drove around Mavis Kleiner's neighborhood for the next few minutes. Just long enough to assure myself that it was the same truck and that it was indeed following me.

Chapter Twelve

The two high school kids in the pickup tailed me to the Walsh home. They weren't real good at it. At one point they lost me at a red light on Country Road 42 and I had to pull into the parking lot of a convenience store to wait for them.

After I reached the Walsh home, I rang the bell and Evelyn showed me into the great room. She told me that Tyler was still in his bedroom but would be out shortly. She smiled a nervous smile as her eyes darted down the adjacent hallway leading to the south wing of the house.

"I could talk to him in his room," I suggested.

"No," she said, shaking her head. "Tyler doesn't let very many people in his room."

I nodded.

"You can talk out on the patio if you like. It's a lovely day."

I nodded again and she led me to the back of the house and out into the spacious courtyard. I took a seat on a padded wrought-iron chair at a glass-topped patio table as Evelyn stepped toward the house to fetch Tyler. When she got to the glass door, she paused and cleared her throat softly. "There's something I found out," she said. "Something that Zeb Pope told me not to mention to you."

"Ever the trusting soul, isn't he?"

Evelyn hesitated.

"I appreciate your confidence," I told her.

She nodded. "There's money missing."

"Money? From the business?"

"No. From one of our accounts. One of Greg's and mine. Our accountant knew about it. Greg had told him it was private, but he hadn't said anything to me."

"How much money?"

"Not much at first. This has been going on awhile. For the first two, two and a half years just a couple of thousand a month. But just a couple of days ago, a lot more."

"How much more?"

"Nearly ten thousand."

"Dollars?"

Evelyn nodded, then lowered her eyes.

"And your accountant has no idea what Greg was spending the money on?"

"No, but..." She let her voice trail off.

"But what?"

"You know. What do well-to-do, married men spend that kind of money on?"

"You think he was keeping a mistress?"

Evelyn raised her head slightly in a meager gesture of defiance. "I didn't until now."

We stared at each other in silence. Her eyes held mine in a tenuous, shimmering grasp.

"If I find out," I said, "do you want to know?"

She closed her eyes and a tear escaped to trace a line down her cheek. "I think so. I think I'd like to know." She turned and in a voice I could barely hear said, "I'll go get Tyler. Can I offer you some iced tea? It's quite a warm day."

"Thank you."

Alone on the deck, I watched a couple of young Latino men pulling weeds from flower beds that ran along a tall privacy fence that bordered the expansive backyard. The two geese that I'd noted on my first visit watched them, too. Watched and squawked menacingly from the edge of a small pond at the open rear of the property. One of the young men raised his arms, yelled, and took a couple of steps toward the geese. They fluttered off to the safety of the pond where they craned their necks and honked loud jeers at the gardener.

I let my mind run through the facts, as I understood them. Greg had been spending money on something or someone for years and didn't want his wife to know about it. This was almost certainly Janet. At least the earlier, smaller installments. But what about the ten grand? When Janet came to me, she'd said that the men that killed Greg were also after her. Then she'd made me swear that I'd help Greg. Maybe, since Greg was dead, she meant that by helping her—Greg's "special friend"—I'd actually be helping him. But if Greg had just given her ten thousand dollars, why had she come to me at all? Why hadn't she just packed up Ava and skipped town? She'd have had plenty of money to set up elsewhere.

Then there were Grogan and Matty Beam. I assumed that Greg had met with Grogan to see if there was some way he could keep Tyler away from them. If the ten grand hadn't gone to Janet, had it gone to them? In the days before his death, had Greg tried to buy his son out from under their influence?

Then there was the big question. Who killed Greg? Augie had told me that three different knives had been used. Now I had two kids waiting outside and another...I really didn't want to think about that. I didn't want to believe that Greg's son could have been involved in his dad's murder.

And the swastikas on the corpse? What kind of sense did they make? Greg wasn't a member of a minority group. He supported some liberal causes, but he didn't seem to be doing anything that would provoke the ire of a hate group. Even if Tyler and the boys in the truck were racist pinheads looking to do violence, why pick Greg? Were the swastikas a diversion? Were they carved on the corpse to throw suspicion onto Tyler and his pals and away from the real murderer? Or did the boys just get so whipped up thinking about hurting people that they just picked somebody close by, killed him, then carved their twisted cross on the corpse?

Evelyn reappeared carrying a tall glass of iced tea. Tyler slunk out onto the patio behind her. I stood and thanked Evelyn for the tea before retaking my seat. In answer to the question in her eyes, I told her that I'd prefer to speak with Tyler alone. The boy sniffed loudly as his mother disappeared into the house.

"Have a seat Tyler," I said.

"I'll stand," he replied, crossing his arms defiantly. He was wearing an oversized T-shirt with the insignia of some rock band I'd never heard of over a pair of field shorts that reached below his knees. His hair was shaved close to his scalp except for a little blond tail that hung down at the back of his head. He kept his eyelids half-closed in a manner that I'm sure he meant to appear inscrutable, but actually made him look like he was about to nod off. Sparse facial hair several shades darker than his little ponytail sprouted around the cleft of his chin like threads that had loosened from a poorly stitched seam. He had moderate acne that had probably flared up under the recent stress. A pimple, white and ready to burst, bulged along the side of his nose.

"Suit yourself," I told him and took a sip of tea and watched the geese creep out of the pond and back onto the lawn. The gardeners, who'd gone back to their work, didn't seem to notice. "Did you kill your dad, Tyler?" I asked. I tried to keep my voice as flat and unemotional as possible.

"Hell, no," he replied in a voice as dispassionate as my own.

"No? You sure? You threatened him."

"No way I threatened him."

"Sure, you did. Your dad told me all about it. You told him that there would be a 'bloodletting' and that he would be swept away."

"That wasn't a threat. Just a prediction."

"Sounds like a threat to me."

Tyler shrugged.

"You know a guy named Albert Grogan?"

Tyler's jaw went slack. "Uh, no. Somebody say I did or something?"

"He used to work at Blauer Construction. You went out with Charlie Blauer's daughter, didn't you? What's her name?"

"Megan. But that's been over for a while. What's this got to do with anything anyway? I thought my mom hired you to find out who killed my dad. If you can't do the job, I'll have her can your ass and find someone who can."

I smiled. "You figure you got any say in anything that's going to happen to you in all of this?"

He nodded and stuck his jaw out again. "Damn

right."

"Think again."

Tyler snorted. "You don't know what you're talking about, man. My dad had lots of friends. Important friends. People will look out for me."

"Your dad did have lots of friends. I'm one of them. And let me tell you, if it looks like you had anything to do with his death, I'm damn sure *not* going to look out for you."

Tyler tried to keep up the tough guy act, but his eyes got noticeably wider. "I didn't have anything to do with it. Anyway, I got friends of my own."

"Matty Beam one of your friends?"

"I've heard of him."

"Any of your friends drive a new, forest green Dodge pickup?"

"No," he answered, moving his head slowly from side to side. "Not that I recall."

"You're not much of a liar," I told him.

Tyler inhaled deeply, puffing up his chest and slowly releasing the breath through his nose. "What you think don't matter to me."

"Your lawyer and your mommy tell me you'll be talking to the cops soon. Maybe it'll matter what *they* think."

"I don't have to tell them nothing. I got rights."

"You're sixteen. You've got fewer rights than you think."

I looked away, took a long sip of iced tea, set the glass down, and drummed my fingertips on the tabletop. After a couple of moments, I looked back up at the boy. "Your dad meant something to me, Tyler. For his sake and your mom's, I've decided to try to help you. But I gotta tell ya, I don't like you. And if you don't come out of this, I'm not going to shed any tears for you. I'll feel bad for your mom, but only for a little while. She'll go on. She'll make up little care packages of cookies and fresh fruit and bring them to you in the penitentiary. It won't be too bad."

"You're trying to scare me."

"Sorry, pal, but I'd have to give a shit about you to bother with trying to scare you. No, the more I think about it, the more I figure the best thing that can happen is for you to go away."

Tyler shifted and looped a thumb in his belt, one corner of his mouth curling into a sneer. "What do you think, I'm just some stupid kid? That I don't know how things work? I'm not going to jail. You think the son of someone with my dad's clout is going to do time for something he didn't even do? No way, man. There's just no way."

"Your dad's dead," I reminded him. "Oh, and by the way your heartbreak over the loss of your father is truly pitiable. I'm sure that's the first thing the cops will pick up on when you try this act out on them."

"Screw them and screw you."

"Whatever, pal. Like I said, it's probably for the best. All I can say is don't make any long-term plans."

Tyler kept his arms crossed, but his eyes went soft. Something about his eyes struck me. I could see a resemblance to his father in his soft, blue eyes. "I told you I didn't do nothing," he said, some of the defiance now missing from his tone.

I shook my head. "If you didn't, then you either know or suspect who did. You protect them, you still do time."

"I don't know anything about it. How many times do I have to tell you?"

"You don't have to tell me anything, junior. But you'll be talking to the cops. Probably for hours. And you'll be telling them things. First, you'll tell them over and over how you don't know anything. Then you'll tell them over and over again. Eventually, it will dawn on you that the innocent act just ain't working. Then you'll try out some version of the truth. But by then they'll know you're a liar. They'll know what you are, and they won't let you walk out of this. Your life is over, kid."

"You think you're so smart."

"Smarter than those friends of yours in the pickup. They're sitting out front right now wondering what you're telling me. Wondering if you're giving them up. Don't worry, I'll square it with them. I'll tell them you stuck to your guns. I'll tell them you wouldn't talk to me. But the cops? That's another story. I wonder if your pals out there are willing to bet their lives that you won't talk to the cops. What do you think?"

"I don't know what you're talking about. I don't know anything about a pickup and my friends had nothing to do with my dad's death."

"You want to do this on your own, fine. Like I say, I don't really care." I finished the iced tea and set the glass down on the tabletop with a loud clink and made sure I didn't look directly at Tyler as I passed him and began to open the sliding door.

"That's right. Get out of here," Tyler said. He probably wanted it to sound like an order, but the words came out with an underlying sigh that made me turn around. I looked at him and I couldn't help myself. The thing I hate most about dealing with kids is that they're young and no matter how screwed up they are, you figure you might still have time to reach them.

"Are you really this big an asshole, Tyler? Or do you think this is the way real men are supposed to act?"

"What do you mean?"

"I mean, your father's dead. If you're not lying and you didn't have anything to do with his death, then that's gotta hurt. Even if you weren't on the best of terms with him—hell, even if you hated his guts, he was your father. Him cashing out, especially all carved up like he was, that's gotta be eating you up. You think hiding the hurt is what a real man's supposed to do?"

"Beats crying like a pussy, don't it?"

"Nope. Denying who you are and what you feel, now that's acting like a pussy."

Tyler flushed. He uncrossed his arms and let them fall to his sides. He struggled against them but couldn't keep tears from welling up in his eyes. "You don't know anything about who I am," he said. "No one does."

I nodded. "Tyler, everyone—I mean, *everyone*—feels exactly that way. You open up, you talk to people about it, you'll find that out."

"No," he said, hanging his head, "this is different. No one knows about me. Not Mom. Not my friends. You sure as shit don't. Dad knew, but he hid it from everyone. Even from me."

"Hid what? What did your dad hide?"

A couple of tears escaped and ran down his cheeks. Tyler wiped at them with the back of his hand. He shook his head, wiped at his cheeks again, then turned to stare out into the yard. The two gardeners had stopped their work and I caught them sneaking furtive glances at us. The geese waddled past them, unconcerned.

147

"I don't have to tell you anything," Tyler murmured.

"No. You don't. But I'm going to find out anyway. When someone's murdered, it all comes out. Pretty soon everyone's gonna know."

Tyler turned back to face me. He swallowed hard. "That happens and maybe I'm the one that ends up dead."

Anger rose bright red within me. "I don't have time for games, Tyler," I said, more loudly than I'd intended. "Just tell me what the fuck's going on."

Tyler glanced at the glass patio door and slowly walked toward it. Evelyn stood on the other side, staring anxiously at us. Wordlessly, he pulled the door slowly open, slipped inside past his mother, and disappeared.

Evelyn shuddered slightly. "I heard shouting."

"Yeah."

"Is he all right?"

"No."

Evelyn continued to stare at me. "You aren't giving up, are you?"

"No."

"What do you do now?"

I thought for a moment. "Do all of your neighbors' backyards open up onto the pond?"

"Uh, yes."

"I gotta go out the back."

"Why? I don't understand. Why do you have to—"

"It's just something I gotta do, Evelyn. Don't worry. I'll be in touch."

I stepped off the patio onto the lawn and made my way down to the pond with both the gardeners and the geese staring at me. I went around the fence and into the adjacent yard. I didn't figure that was far enough, so I went down two more houses. The tricky bit was going to be finding a way back up to the street in front without arousing a lot of suspicion. With my luck, I thought, I'd trip some neighbor's perimeter alarm. But I needn't have worried. The third house down was owned by an egalitarian type that didn't believe in privacy fences. That made it pretty easy for me for me to return to the street well behind where the pickup was waiting for me.

I didn't have much of a plan. I just wanted to sneak up on the two kids that had tailed me. Scare them, make them feel vulnerable, maybe get something out of them. I slipped my shiny new 9mm out of my shoulder holster. The Beretta, unlike my old .38, was equipped with a safety and I checked to be certain that it was on. Then I headed for the pickup in a brisk, hunkered down, Groucho Marx walk. I was feeling quite proud of myself when I reached the truck and heard no sound of alarm. I burst into view alongside the driver's side window with the gun in my hand. Even then there was no sound from my quarry. There also wasn't anyone in the truck.

My first thought was that the two kids must have decided to approach the house, maybe get close enough to hear our conversation. It was a pretty stupid play with little hope of working, but these were kids. My second thought was that maybe they'd decided on a confrontation. I don't know what my next thought was going to be. It was interrupted when the sound of a gunshot split the quiet of the street.

The shot came from the Walsh home. I hunkered back down and ran for all I was worth. I stumbled a bit where the front lawn met the flagstone walkway but managed to stay on my feet as I reached the open front door. I hesitated for just a moment before bursting through the door and into the huge great room. It was frighteningly empty.

Hallways on either side of the great room led to the two wings of the house. A gunman could be on either side, I thought. Then again, there were two kids, maybe two guns. They could be on both sides. I knew Tyler's room was in the south wing. If they were friends of his, they'd know that too. I plunged into the hallway to my left.

Another shot rang out somewhere in front of me. Then another, but this one from behind. A dimple appeared in the wall behind me with a snap and a white puff of sheetrock dust. I was caught in the middle. I gulped some air, got down low, and dove through the open door to Tyler's bedroom.

A bullet cracked the doorframe behind me as I hit the floor. I rolled over and spotted Tyler on the floor in front of me. He had a bloody gash on his forehead and more blood was flowing from between his fingers where he held his left arm, but he was whimpering, so he wasn't dead. There was a bed in the middle of the room and Tyler was trying to crawl under it, but he was too big. Standing on the opposite side of the bed holding a long-barreled .22 target pistol was one of the high school kids. As he shifted the barrel of the gun toward me, I aimed my 9mm. and pulled the trigger. Nothing happened. I'd left the goddamned safety on.

I rolled just in time. The bullet caught me in the side, tracing a searing path along my rib cage. The pain jolted me to my knees and, fumbling, I managed to click the safety off my gun. I pulled the trigger on my Beretta before the kid could fire again. My bullet hit him square in the chest sending him sprawling backwards to the floor.

I scrambled to my feet, the pain in my side growing ever more insistent. I picked up the kid's pistol from where it had fallen, took a deep breath, and stood listening intently. At first all I could hear was my heart pounding in the hollow of my chest and Tyler moaning on the floor. "Stay down," I whispered to the prostrate boy.

I heard an indistinct gasp coming from the great room. It sounded like Evelyn. Then an unfamiliar voice called down the hallway, "Did you get him, Toby?"

I let the silence answer him.

I knew the second kid had a gun and I figured he'd be waiting for me to come back down the hallway, probably using Evelyn as a shield. I also figured that I'd used up all my luck diving through the door of the bedroom. I wasn't going back into the hall.

The wound on my side was on fire and the muscles of my face had hardened into a wince so tight I was afraid it might shatter my cheekbones. The acrid smell of gunpowder had filled the bedroom and I felt a sneeze working its way forward from the back of my sinuses. An icy drop of perspiration was dangling precariously from the very tip of my nose. I wiped it away and fought back the mounting sneeze. I glanced up and saw a set of blinds closed over a bedroom window that looked into the back courtyard. I raised the blinds and tried to slide the window open quietly. It wouldn't budge. I turned the locks on the side of the window and tried again. It still wouldn't go. It was probably fixed in place with another lock or a length of doweling or something, but I didn't bother to find out. I knew I didn't have much time.

The second kid would eventually find the courage to

come into the bedroom and I didn't want to take one in the back while wrestling with a goddamned window. I put two slugs into the thing and the glass shattered spectacularly. Trying to keep an eye on the bedroom door, I tore off my shirt, wrapped it around my left hand and quickly knocked the jagged remains of glass out of the window frame. Then I pushed myself through the window and out into the yard. I slowly made my way toward the patio and the glass doors that led back into the great room. The gardeners had taken off, but the geese, heads cocked, stood a few yards from the edge of the patio.

I flattened myself against the house when I heard the patio door slide open.

The gun was the first thing that emerged from the house. The second kid held it way out in front of him as he stepped outside. Like the one I'd taken off his pal, it was a .22. Next came Evelyn, held closely by the kid with the gun. He was a skinny thing with a dopey mixture of fear and intensity on his pockmarked face. He'd turned his baseball cap backwards.

I was afraid to breathe, afraid to make any sound at all. It paid off. He didn't spot me right away. His first glance was in the wrong direction, and he wasted precious seconds studying a clump of bushes on that side. I took aim carefully, but Evelyn was too close. I waited, hoping he'd turn his back to me. In the quiet, I distinctly heard both Evelyn and the gunman's individual breathing. I wondered why they couldn't hear mine.

Then, I sneezed. A loud, juicy sneeze that came out of nowhere and instantly caused my eyes to water. The gunman turned toward me, Evelyn in front of him. For a startled second, the boy did nothing. Then he tightened his grip on Evelyn and raised his gun. Through a filmy haze I watched as first Evelyn's eyes shifted uneasily, but then fixed with determination. She brought her leg up, then drove her heel down hard on top of the kid's foot. She broke free as he yelped in pain, his gun hand swinging wildly.

He tried to make a grab for her, then remembered me. He turned his gun toward me, but his finger tightened on the trigger before he could aim properly. He didn't do badly, though—his bullet splintered the siding inches in front of me. The impact shook me enough to throw my aim off, too. Instead of hitting him dead center, as I'd intended, my bullet went high, catching the boy in the jaw and bursting wide out the back of his head. He fell and was still making some sounds when I reached him. But there wasn't enough mouth or tongue left for him to be articulate. Then the sounds stopped altogether.

I reached down and checked for a pulse in his neck. Finding none, I turned to Evelyn, who was shuddering in wordless horror. A silence settled over us, only to be rent by the piercing squawk of a goose. A shrill bugle sounding over a still battlefield.

Chapter Thirteen

They weren't high school kids. Both eighteen-year-old Toby Hollenbeck and his pal, seventeen-year-old Sam Segulia, had dropped out of high school. That little tidbit was provided by the officer who took my statement, a particularly chatty Apple Valley cop named Davidson. It turned out that Davidson was the cop whom my dad had spoken to about Matty Beam. He was only too happy to look after Ray Dahms' kid. I felt so special.

The cops had files on both boys. They were suspects in a rash of petty burglaries and were once briefly arrested when pulled over driving a car that had been reported stolen. But once the car was returned, its owner declined to press charges. The garrulous Davidson was only too happy to give me the name of the guy whose car they'd stolen. Charlie Blauer.

Considering I'd capped two kids, my interview with the cops went surprisingly well. It didn't hurt that I was the son of an ex-cop, but the main reason they took it easy on me was their assumption that they now knew who had killed the town's most famous resident and they weren't eager to ask any questions that might upset their settlement of the Walsh murder case. The theory was that the two boys had decided to rob Greg, had waited for him at his downtown office building. When Greg put up a fight, they killed him and dumped the body in the restaurant parking lot to divert suspicion. The cops figured that Hollenbeck and Segulia were afraid that I was onto them, so they followed me to the Walsh home and decided to take us all out. When I asked Davidson why he figured the boys had carved swastikas into the corpse, he shrugged and suggested that it could have been something the lads had seen in a movie.

After a couple of hours, they told me that they'd have to keep my brand-new gun as evidence until after the coroner's inquest, but that I was free to leave. I was nearly out the door when Augie Tarkof showed up.

Although the cops had run me by an emergency room before taking me to the police station, the wound in my side still hurt like hell and I yelped a little when Augie hauled me back into the station. He pointed at an empty chair and told me to wait. I was in the chair for another half an hour before he reappeared, crooked his finger at me, and showed me back into an interview room.

Since I'd ruined my own shirt during the gunfight, Evelyn had lent me an old T-shirt of Greg's that didn't come close to fitting me. When I sat down, the shirt rode up on me at the waist, indelicately exposing my bulging waistline.

As I tugged at the hem, again, Tarkof grunted. "Low fat, high fiber, Dahms. That's how I'm losing the weight."

"I've never been big on tofu and brown rice, Augie."

He grunted again and rustled some papers he was holding in his hand. "You're not big on details either. I've been reading this statement you gave the cops down here."

"I just answered the questions they asked."

"I've got a few more."

"Go ahead. I'll tell you what I can."

Tarkof nodded a couple of times, his eyes fixed on mine. "According to this, Segulia and Hollenbeck followed you from a restaurant in St. Helena to the Walsh place?" He checked his notes. "A roadhouse called Sully's Empire Room?"

"Yeah."

"What were you doing there?"

"Eating really bad pie."

"They didn't follow you because you've got no taste in pastries," Tarkof said.

"No," I admitted, "I was poking around down there. The kids overheard me asking about a guy named Charlie Blauer. When I drove back to the Walsh place, they were behind me."

"Who's Blauer?"

I chuckled. Augie had been investigating Greg's murder for days. He knew who Blauer was. "He's a guy whose name keeps popping up," I said, playing along. "Tyler Walsh went out with his daughter, and it turns out these two kids—what are their names?"

"Segulia and Hollenbeck."

"Segulia and Hollenbeck boosted Blauer's car some months back. When the car was returned, Blauer declined to press charges."

"You think Blauer's involved?"

"I don't know. But he's probably worth another look. I told the woman at the restaurant that I was looking to have some work done. Blauer owns a construction company, so why'd they follow me? What was it they didn't want me find out?"

"Maybe it didn't have anything to do with Blauer," Tarkof suggested. "Could be they just recognized you."

"How so? They stopped running my underwear commercials years ago."

"You were on TV this week. Remember."

I stared blankly at him.

"The funeral?" Tarkof prodded. "Matty Beam?"

"Oh, yeah."

"If they went after you because they recognized you, could be Beam is involved in all this."

"You hope."

"I'd like to see him go down for something."

I nodded. "I just might have something for you."

Tarkof perked up. "What?"

"The day after the funeral, Beam sent a couple of guys to rough me up. One of them was wearing a cap that said 'Blauer Construction' on it."

"This was yesterday?"

"Yeah."

"Helpful of you to tell us that."

"I don't need you guys to look out for me, Augie. I can do that for myself."

Tarkof pointed to the side of my face, still puffy and off-color from my run-in with Beam's goons. "That you taking care of yourself?"

I shrugged.

"So, you figure this Blauer is a Nazi like your dead pal's kid?"

I kept my face as emotionless as a ball bearing. "Oh, you know about Tyler?"

"Wasn't much of a secret."

"I suppose not. Do you know if Tyler Walsh and the two shooters palled around?"

"Several of little Tyler's classmates say they did."

"And there were three knives used on Tyler's dad."

"I was thinking the same thing. Did you talk to Blauer? Or his daughter?"

"Him, yeah. Didn't get much out of him, though. Just that this guy that came after me wearing one of his ball caps did work for him briefly. That guy's name is Albert Grogan."

Tarkof made a note.

"When you check, you'll find that he did time," I said.

"Yeah?"

"Yeah. Blauer told me that the guy lied about it on his job application. When Blauer found out, he canned him."

"He don't like ex-cons?"

I shook my head. "I got the impression he just didn't like Grogan. Grogan was making trouble. He didn't get along with other guys on the crew. Especially one that happens to be African American."

Tarkof smirked. "Big surprise there."

"Blauer also told me that he had his daughter call it off with Tyler Walsh after the boy started spouting off all that racial crap. Didn't want his daughter exposed to that kind of thing, I guess."

"So, you're telling me that this Blauer probably isn't involved with Matty Beam?"

I shrugged. "I don't know. He could have been lying. I don't think so, though."

"Supposing that all three of these guys—Blauer, Segulia, and Hollenbeck—can all be tied to Beam, it'd explain why Blauer let the two kids off the hook when they boosted his car."

"It would," I agreed. "But if they were all such great buds, why did they boost it in the first place? My guess is that stealing the car was intimidation. Blauer's got a kid of his own, and Beam's got some pretty scary people hanging around him. Grogan's pissed about getting canned so he asks a couple of members of Beam's Hitler Youth group to steal his former employer's car. Their way of telling Blauer they could get at him. And his daughter. He didn't press charges because he was afraid."

"Could be," Augie said.

"And there's another thing Blauer told me that could get him into trouble with Beam and the boys."

"What's that?"

"He told me that he spotted Greg Walsh, the week before he died, having a drink with Grogan at Sully's, that roadhouse in St. Helena."

Tarkof made a little humming sound as he wrote this down. "You got any idea what that was all about?" he asked.

"I'd only be guessing, And I gotta be careful here. I'm working for the Walshes, remember. I've got privilege to consider. Evelyn Walsh's lawyer—a serious shit named Zebulon Pope—he's gonna be mighty put out I talked to you at all without him being present."

"This ain't a good time for you to get coy, Dahms."

I shrugged. "What can I tell you, Augie? I gotta play by the rules. But you guys got the manpower. Get out there and find someone who can tell you what you need to know."

"Like those two dead kids? We had their names, you know. We were going to pull them in for questioning. Things might be a little clearer if you hadn't killed off two of my chief suspects."

"So, you think those kids killed Greg?"

Tarkof scooped up his notes and rolled the papers tightly in his hand. "The cops down here sure think so. The question is, was anyone else involved?"

"I gotta think there was. But how do we prove it?"

"*We* don't," Tarkof growled. "You're staying out of this."

"I gotta look out for my client's interests, Augie."

Tarkof's eyes gleamed. "I'll be having a talk with Evelyn Walsh, Dahms. It might just occur to her that it wasn't in her best interest for you to lead two gunmen to her door."

I flushed. "I may have underestimated them."

Tarkof chortled as he walked out of the interview room.

I sat alone in there for a few minutes before I remembered that the Apple Valley police had already released me. Even so, I felt vaguely guilty as I exited.

The evening sun was low in the sky when I pulled up in front of the Bijou. Although I hadn't eaten since the Empire Room and my stomach was grumbling, I wanted nothing more than to go to my room, clean up, and get some sleep. That, unfortunately, was not to be. Inside the house, I found the door to my room wide open and my television blaring. Edgerton was sitting cross-legged on my bed with little Ava in his lap.

She was wearing a nightie trimmed in lace at the collar with tiny pictures of ducklings all over it. On the TV screen, one head of a two-headed cartoon dragon was playing a trumpet. The other head didn't seem real happy about it. Neither Edgerton nor Ava bothered to look up as I came in. Basil, however, was delighted to see me. He yelped, scratched with both paws at my legs and went into a dance that had him twisting back and forth with such excitement I was afraid he'd put an eye out with his stub of a tail.

I reached down to scratch the dog behind the ear and looked at my watch. "They got kid's shows on this late, now?"

Edgerton finally looked up at me. "It's a DVD. Ava and I stopped by the library." He paused. "Did you find you-know-who?"

"Come again?"

Edgerton motioned toward Ava and mouthed the word "mom."

I shook my head.

He gave Ava a little squeeze. The child continued to stare at the screen.

I pointed at the TV. "Must be a heck of a show."

"It's her favorite. Of course, every show we watched today was her favorite."

"You guys didn't spend the whole day in here watching *Scooby-Doo*, did you?"

Edgerton glared. "You think I'd let Ava watch anything but educational TV? And no, we did not watch TV all day. We took the dog for a walk. We went to the park. We played on the swings, went down the slide, and we saw a rabbit. Basil loved the rabbit. Didn't he, Ava?"

Ava was too immersed in her show to respond.

I glanced back at the TV. A pudgy blue dragon joined the two-headed dragon on the screen and soon several dragons and a couple of children were performing a tuneless ditty on a variety of instruments.

I crossed the room to my sink and peeled off Greg's T-shirt.

"Shit!" Edgerton exclaimed, seeing the bandages that were wrapped around my ribs. "What happened to you?"

"Language," I said.

He glanced at Ava. "Oops. But hey, what gives with the Amenhotep routine?"

"You mean the bandages?"

"Well, yeah."

"I got shot."

For the first time, Ava turned to look at me. Her eyes went wide even as her little face scrunched up. "That's a really bad ouchie," she said, her voice quavering.

"It'll be okay," I assured her. "The doctor gave me some medicine."

"Did you fall down?" Ava asked, her expression wavering between sorrow and panic.

"No, honey. Some bad men were doing some bad things and I had to stop them."

Ava nodded. Edgerton's eyes narrowed.

"There were two of them," I said, forcing a smile and trying to keep my tone light. "They didn't make it."

Edgerton had been through this with me once before. That guy had also been trying to kill me. He didn't make it, either. I'd told Edgerton over and over that I was okay with it, but he also knew that sometimes I still saw the guy's face in my dreams.

"We'll talk later," he said.

I shook my head. "I'm fine with it, really."

"I know. But we'll talk anyway."

"Yeah. Okay."

Ava kept looking at me. Thankfully, sleepiness was mingling with the concern in her eyes. I tried not to wince as I pulled on a fresh T-shirt. I looked at my watch again. "Just about your bedtime."

"I brushed my teeth," Ava said, breaking into a grin.

"Stephen said I could sleep in his room tonight. Can Basil sleep with me?"

"I think that's a great idea."

"I go to bed now?"

"I'll take her into bed," Edgerton said. "The dog, too."

"Thanks."

They turned for the door.

"Goodnight, honey," I said.

Ava rubbed her eyes with a closed fist. "Night-night."

"Oh, by the way," Edgerton remembered as they entered the hallway. "Your mom called. She wanted you to call her back."

"I wonder if she heard about me on the news. If she did, she'll be pretty worried."

"She sounded calm," Edgerton told me. "Not happy, but calm. You call her. I'll be back for the dog in minute."

When they'd gone, I called my mom. She hadn't heard about the shootings on the news. She hadn't turned on the TV. She and Dad had been busy all evening. He'd had the colonoscopy that afternoon. The preliminary diagnosis was colon cancer.

Chapter Fourteen

I wanted to rush right over, but Mom said that Dad didn't want to deal with any "relatives" just then. I told her that I'd come by first thing in the morning, but she asked me to wait. He'd have to have a couple of days to himself with this thing, she said. I knew this was bullshit, but I also knew he had to have his way. Mom told me she would call me back early next week.

With Ava asleep in his room and a baby monitor to his ear, Edgerton returned with a six pack of pale ale. He spent half the night sitting up with me, listening to me claim that neither killing two kids, nor my dad's cancer diagnosis was "any big deal." I awoke the next morning still fully clothed, lying on top of my bed covers, unable to remember either falling asleep or Edgerton leaving.

My curtains were drawn, but the sun shone through a gap in the center, splitting my bedroom with a blade of light but leaving most of the room in shadow. Through sleep-bleary eyes I noticed that my door was open. Then I heard a movement at the foot of my bed. I sat up, expecting to find the dog prowling about, but instead a shadowy figure, tall and topped with a marvelous tangle of untamed tresses stood at the foot of my bed.

"I'm dreaming," I murmured.

"Good morning, Lyle," Naomi said. "How are you feeling?"

"Hmm. Better now that you're here."

I couldn't see her smile in the darkened room, but I imagined that I could feel it radiating against my skin.

"Stephen called. He told me about the shooting," she said in a whisper dusted with concern. "He also told me about your dad."

"I'm okay, babe. Really. And my old man's too much of a bastard to let this cancer thing get him. No doubt he'll beat it, then spend the next couple of decades using his victory to prove what a wussy I am by comparison."

Naomi didn't answer, but she moved alongside of the bed and placed a warm palm on my forehead.

"What time is it?" I asked.

"Just after nine."

"Shouldn't you be at work?"

"Yes."

"But you took off just for me? Must be true love."

"Yes, Lyle," she said, chuckling. "I gave up a couple hours of waitressing just to be with you. And all you had to do was get shot and have your father come down with cancer."

"When you put it that way, it sounds like you're kinda demanding."

"Nobody told you I was a pushover."

"No, ma'am," I said, reaching for her hand and kissing it. Naomi hummed softly.

"You want some coffee?" she asked.

"All this and room service, too?"

"You'd be getting more than coffee if you hadn't just been to the emergency room." I could sense that smile again.

"Well, I'd hate to ruin any plans you might have made. Maybe we could—"

"I don't think so, tough guy. That'll have to wait for you to start healing."

"Who knows? It could be therapeutic."

She patted me gently on the cheek. "Not gonna happen."

"Nuts. Just the coffee then."

She turned on her heel. "That I can give you," she said briskly before going out the open door.

I snuggled back into the warm softness of my pillow. My eyelids were still heavy with sleep and I must have dozed off for a few seconds before I heard footsteps reenter the room.

"You sure you haven't changed your mind about the…you, know?" I asked, without opening my eyes.

There was no answer. I took my face out of the pillow and glanced toward the foot of the bed. A figure loomed indistinctly before me. No curves, no cascading tresses. It wasn't Naomi.

It was a man. I couldn't make out his features in the dim light, only the fact that he was enormous. My first thought was that it was Baldy, Albert Grogan's large accomplice, but this man was even larger and had hair. Whoever it was stood absolutely still, both hands high in front of him, holding something long and wide. It took another second or so before it occurred to me that it didn't matter who the hell it was, I shouldn't be just lying there.

"Yeeahh!" I cried, rolling off the bed and landing face first onto the floor. The big man jerked at my cry, jostling whatever he was holding. There was a distinct clinking sound.

"Jeez, Lyle!" he exclaimed. "You almost made me spill the coffee."

It took a moment for me to recognize the voice. "Milkman?" I rolled over and watched as he stepped into the shaft of sunlight.

Milkman Mulligan smiled down at me. I could see now that he was carrying a large tray with two mismatched china cups in the center. On the wide tray, against the background of his broad chest, the cups looked like they were from some little girl's dolly tea service.

"How do you take it?" he asked me, smiling broadly, his eyes splashed with pride.

"Take what?"

"Your coffee."

I blinked rapidly. "You scared the shit out of me, man. What are you doing here?"

The pride in his eyes was replaced by puzzlement. "I'm bringing you coffee," he said, evidently feeling that this was all the explanation needed.

He set the tray down on my desk and came over to give me a hand up. He helped me to my feet and put a coffee cup in my hand. I went over and pulled open the curtains, filling the room with bright yellow light. Then Basil bounded in, took a moment to sniff at Mulligan, then ran over to me and began doing repeated vertical jumps, trying to plant a kiss on me.

I gave the dog a quick scratch behind the ear. "Where's Naomi?"

"She's helping Ava with something."

I listened carefully and I could hear their voices coming from Edgerton's room. Ava was excitedly relating something, her words racing, occasionally tripping over themselves. Naomi's tone was reserved.

"Where's Stephen?"

"Had to go to work," Mulligan said. "They had some kind of crisis with some copy machine or other. Stephen said he was the only one trained on the thing."

His expression became suddenly serious. "Stephen told me about the day you had yesterday. Then he asked if I could come by and help look after the little one." His eyes brightened and his smile returned. "She's a peach, ain't she."

Basil finally realized that he wouldn't be getting any more attention just then. He trotted over to a blanket that I'd tossed in the corner for him, and he lay down, keeping his eyes on me lest I change my mind and feel an urge to pet him some more.

I took a sip of the coffee, then raised the cup toward Mulligan as if in a toast. "Sorry you had to come by, Milkman. Just let me get a shower and I'll take over. You probably got things to do."

"No, no, no," Mulligan insisted. "I'm happy to do it."

I smiled at him but went ahead and started getting ready for the shower. I was peeling off my shirt when Naomi's voice called out from the hallway. "Lyle," she said, "if you're not going to be needing me, I should probably go in to work."

"You didn't tell me that the Milkman was here," I called to her.

"Sorry. But it's great 'cause now I know somebody's with you."

"No offense to the Milkman here, but I'd rather it were you."

Mulligan grinned and shuffled his huge feet.

Naomi was smiling as she stuck her head in the door. The smile slowly faded as she saw me, my face bruised, shirtless and swathed in bandages. "Oh, Lyle," she moaned. "Look at what you've done to yourself."

"Makes you want to nurse me back to health doesn't it?"

Naomi tried to smile, but just couldn't manage it. She approached me, touched me lightly on the chest, then kissed me gently. Then she shook her head and turned away. "I really should be going," she said.

"But you'll be back?"

"I really…I…"

"Meet me for dinner. Tonight. We'll go to McCauley's, have some beers, relax. What do you say?"

She turned back to me. Her expression was sympathetic, but sad, and maybe a little disappointed. "Okay, Lyle," she said, sighing. "Okay. See you tonight."

"Say six o'clock?"

"Make it six-thirty," she said as she headed out the door. I watched her leave. Mulligan had been there, I told myself. And Ava. That's why she'd left so soon. We weren't free to talk. Still, I had the distinct impression that dinner with me was not the thing she most wanted to do that evening. I'd have to remind myself to be extra charming.

"I better check in with Ava," the Milkman said, startling me slightly. "Why don't you grab that shower?"

"Thanks, Irv."

In the shower I tried unsuccessfully to clean and deodorize myself without getting my bandages all wet. I was back in my room trying to undo the damage with some tape and gauze when the door opened, and Basil came bounding back in. As usual when I'd been out of his sight for more than a few seconds, the dog began squeaking and yelping. Then he tried to scale my leg and, when he discovered that he couldn't get his claws in deep enough to actually climb me, he began to spring skyward on his rear legs, his jaws snapping in loud, wet smacks. Holding a length of gauze in one hand, I stooped to stroke the dog with the other. He must have thought it was a game because as I stooped, he snatched ahold of the loose end of the bandage and began an impromptu tug-of-war. Basil was doing a victory lap around the room, the gauze streaming behind him, when Ava came in. I quickly slipped into a T-shirt to cover up the bandages. Unlike the dog, she entered timidly, inching toward me with a tight little grimace on her face and her hands held behind her back.

"Good morning, sweetie," I said, stuffing the leftover gauze into a cupboard. "How are you? Did you sleep well?"

Mulligan came into the room behind her. "Go ahead and tell him, Ava. Tell him about your surprise."

Ava glanced back at the Milkman, then turned to me and lowered her head in silence.

"Tell him what you made for him," the Milkman prompted.

Ava remained with her head lowered for a few more seconds, then drew her hands from behind her back. With both hands she handed me a sheet of paper, then stepped away. It was a drawing. Using a great many markers, she had produced a multi-colored swirl with a couple of dots and a crooked line in the middle. Her fingers were blotched with ink. Her mouth remained tightly drawn, but light danced in her eyes.

"It was all her idea," Mulligan said, beaming.

I turned the drawing over a few times examining it

intently. "It's uh…It's beautiful, honey," I said. "Look at all the colors. It's like a…It's like a rainbow."

The light faded from her eyes. Mulligan gave me a doleful, disappointed look. I felt my bottom lip start to quiver. I'd said something terribly wrong.

"It's you," Ava said. "I drawed a picture of you."

I looked at the riot of tumbling colors. "Ah, um, ah…Of *course*, you did sweetie," I stammered. "It uh…it looks just like me. I only meant…"

Mulligan stepped forward. "He only meant that all them colors you used reminded him of a rainbow."

"That's it!" I exclaimed. "And what beautiful colors. They're…They're…"

Mulligan tapped lightly on the drawing. "See, there's your eyes and your mouth and these are…What are these again, Ava?"

"Those are your cheeks," Ava said, a proud smile finally appearing on her face. "And this is your hair," she said, her little finger swirling over the drawing.

"This is so great," I said. "I going to put it up on my wall right away."

"It's for your ouchie," Ava told me.

"That's right," Mulligan explained. "Ava said that a picture would make you feel better."

"You better now?" Ava asked.

"Absolutely. This thing fixed me right up. Thanks."

I placed the picture on my crowded desk and Ava retreated into a corner to play with the dog. Mulligan crooked a finger at me and stepped into the hallway. I followed.

"You know, I've been thinking," Mulligan began in what I'm sure he meant to be a whisper, but which was loud and harsh enough to scrape paint from the walls.

"You probably got things to do, and me and Ava have been getting along real good, and I was thinking about taking her with me to the 'Y.'"

I smirked. "She's a bit young for a workout, don't you think?"

Mulligan became flustered. "No, no, no," he repeated. "I didn't mean that. It's only that, you know, I'm supposed to be there right now. I called a couple of the other gals but couldn't get no one to cover for me this morning. Marcia'll be there all by herself. It ain't so bad until about ten o'clock. Folks like to sleep in on Saturdays, you know. But after ten, it can get pretty hairy. Marcia's gonna need my help."

"With what?"

"With the kids."

"What kids?"

"At the 'Y.' The 'Y' kids."

"Oh yeah," I said, remembering. "You work at the nursery at the YMCA on Saturday mornings."

"Yeah."

I sighed. "Ah, Irv, you got enough to do. You don't need another kid down there. You run along. I'll watch after Ava. At least until Edgerton gets back."

Mulligan was crestfallen. "Uh," he began, "uh, it's like this Lyle, uh…I kinda already mentioned to Ava that we'd be going. I told her there'd be other kids there. And like I said, we've been getting along real good. Now, I'll do whatever you think is best. I mean, if you was planning to spend the morning with her and everything…" He let his voice trail off, but fixed me with a look that was sad, yet hopeful.

I couldn't help but smile. "I suppose I could find something else to do."

Mulligan fairly quivered with glee but strained to appear thoughtful. "Maybe that would be the best way to go then," he said, nodding his head and stroking his chin.

"I think so."

"I'd have her back by one o'clock. Two o'clock if we stop for lunch. If you and Stephen ain't here, I could let myself in. Stephen gave me a key."

"I don't have a car seat for her," I told him.

"Oh, that's okay. Stephen borrowed one from Max Wiseman. Oh, and Stephen said to tell you that the Wisemans would be willing to help out with the tot if we need it."

I nodded. "Sounds like a plan then, Milkman."

"Golly!" the big man exclaimed, glancing at my alarm clock. "We gotta get going."

Mulligan held out a hand to Ava, who gave the dog one last clumsy pat on the head before reaching up and putting a tiny hand into Mulligan's huge mitt.

Watching them leave felt strange, as if I were avoiding a responsibility. But I forced a smile and said to Ava, "Bye-bye now. You and the Milkman have a real nice time. I'll see you later today, okay?"

Ava stared up silently at me for a moment, her eyes wide and soulful. "That girl," she said, "that girl that was here before, why doesn't she like me?"

"Naomi? What do you mean, honey? Of course, she likes you. Everyone likes you."

"That girl doesn't," Ava said.

"I'm pretty sure she does, Ava."

"She doesn't seem like she does."

I knelt down and looked into her clear blue eyes. She didn't seem sad or upset, just curious. "Well, sweetie, she might not seem like she does because she not real happy with me right now."

"Because you were fighting again?"

"Yes, honey."

"People shouldn't fight."

"No, they shouldn't."

"So, you really like my picture?" Ava asked, an ephemeral twinkle flashing in her eye.

"It's beautiful, sweetie."

"It *is* beautiful," she said.

"You're beautiful, too," I told her.

"Oh, I know that," she said, finally breaking into a smile

I turned to the Milkman. "Thanks for everything, Irv."

With a hand large enough to swallow her entire head, Mulligan gently tousled Ava's hair. Then his eyes went a little vacant, as if he was trying to remember something. "What I did," he said at last, "my heart helped my hands to perform."

"Huh?"

"It's from *Beowulf*."

"That book with the monsters?" I intoned dramatically. "Don't go scaring those children now, Milkman."

Mulligan gasped. "I didn't mean...I mean, I wouldn't—"

I grinned at him. "I'm just kiddin.' You guys have a great morning."

Mulligan blushed, looked first at me, then at Ava, then returned the grin. "We will, Lyle. Don't you worry about nothing."

"I know she's in good hands."

After they'd gone, the house seemed awfully quiet.

There was a little coffee left in the cup that Mulligan had brought me, and I sipped at it. It was cold, but I drank it anyway.

I didn't want to dwell too much on the events of the day before, but neither did I want to think about the events of that morning. Naomi's departure had me thinking. I mean, she'd done the girlfriendly thing. When she'd heard that I'd been hurt, she'd come to my side. But she'd left so quickly. And there was something about her expression as she was leaving. Something thoughtful and dispirited. She hadn't said anything, but maybe she was wondering what I was wondering—what kind of guy works a job where sometimes you gotta kill people?

I glanced over at the picture Ava had drawn for me. The images of those two teenagers I'd shot flashed before me, then faded, and were slowly replaced by Ava's picture. Ava shouldn't be here, I thought. She shouldn't be here, in this house, with me.

I grabbed my keys and headed out the door. Before getting in the car, I checked my wallet and found the slip of paper that Mavis Kleiner had given me. The one with the last-known address of her niece Janet, Ava's mother.

Chapter Fifteen

The Midway neighborhood in St. Paul is one of those parts of town that could go either way. Located at the midpoint between downtown St. Paul and downtown Minneapolis, it has a lot to offer—convenient commutes, lots of shopping, schools, and plenty of affordable, charming, craftsman-style homes. But it's also suffered its share of problems. Drug dealers worked the playgrounds, there'd been shootings, and as some of the landlords had elected to simply collect rent while letting their properties fall into disrepair, many of the homes had a less than charming appearance. But at its core, it's a neighborhood of solid, working people who do what they can to make it a good place to call home.

Janet Kleiner called an apartment on Midway's Sherburne Avenue home. It had a brick exterior and a wide front stoop that led to an arched, inset doorway. Just outside the door was a row of mailboxes and on the box for unit 3A were the names Kleiner/Hanson. Before entering, I glanced to my right and spotted a toddler-sized, red and blue plastic slide crouched in the shade of a large pine tree. It was covered in needles and speckled with bird droppings. I wondered if it was Ava's.

The front door to the building was unlocked and I made my way up to the third floor and stood outside unit 3A long enough to convince myself that someone was inside before knocking. There was a creak, then some rustling, then the light in the peephole went dark. I cocked my head and smiled a confident little smile. The light reappeared in the peephole and there was more rustling, but the door remained closed. I knocked again. Still no response.

"Excuse me!" I called out in what I hoped would sound like a friendly voice. "I'm trying to reach Janet Kleiner."

Whoever was inside still didn't answer.

"I know someone's home," I continued. "Could you please come to the door? It's really important."

"Janet's not here," a woman's voice finally sounded from within.

"Do you know where I can find her? I got something she needs."

The woman inside responded with a clipped chuckle. "All you guys are just so damn sure of that, aren't ya?"

"Come again?"

"She don't need what you got," the voice declared. "And you guys are supposed to know better than to come by here. You want to get your rocks off, drive into Frogtown. Lots of girls working up there. Just get away from my door."

"Um, ah…" I stammered, realizing that this woman assumed that I was one of Janet's clients. "I didn't come by to, uh…transact any business with Janet. I'm actually an old friend of hers and I really do have something important to her. Could you open the door so we can talk?" I shuffled in the hallway for a moment before adding, "It's not just about Janet. It's about Ava."

The door abruptly flew open. Framed in the doorway stood a woman in her late twenties with shoulder-length blonde hair wearing a pair of blue jeans and a T-shirt with a drawing of a couple of stick figures running. Below them a legend read, "The Race for the Cure." She was trim, with chipmunk cheeks, and her blue eyes were glaring at me from behind a pair of wire-rimmed eyeglasses. Arm raised over her head, she gripped a tennis racket. "What's this about Ava?" she demanded.

"You must be Hanson," I said.

Her eyes went wide, and a shiver of shock passed over her as if I'd suddenly asked her for a hand-job. "The mailbox," I explained. "It was on the mailbox. Two names, Hanson and Kleiner."

Anger returned to her eyes. "You don't need to know my name, mister. Just tell me what you meant about Ava?"

I smiled. I couldn't help myself. I always smile when someone calls me "mister." "She's with me," I told her. "Janet came by my place the other day with a wild story and her little girl. I haven't seen Janet since. But Ava's still with me."

"Who are you?" she asked, still holding the tennis racket aloft, but her grip slackening so that it looked like she was about to return a lazy lob.

When I reached for my wallet, her grip on the racket tightened. I handed her one of my cards and she stared at it in silence.

"I knew Janet a long time ago, Ms. Hanson. I hadn't seen her in years. Then all of sudden she asks me to watch after her kid. I'm starting to wonder when she's going to come back and get her."

She stood her ground in the doorway, refusing to actually let me enter the apartment, but she lowered the racket until it hung limply at her side. She turned my card around so that it faced me. "This doesn't mean anything. This stuff about you being a private investigator. Anybody could print these up. It doesn't mean anything."

"I'm not saying it means anything, Ms. Hanson. It's just who I am. And what I do doesn't change the fact that I'm an old friend of Janet's or the fact that I'm watching her kid. I just think it's time for Janet to pick Ava up and I'm trying to let her know that."

"Or you'll what?" the blonde asked.

"Or I'll what, what?"

"If Janet doesn't come by and get Ava, what are you going to do?"

"Why wouldn't she come get her? I got the impression she loved the kid. She's maybe not the best role model, but she's the kid's mom."

The blonde stiffened. "You don't have the right to judge her. Janet's doing what she can. This society doesn't exactly make things easy for a single woman trying to raise her child."

I allowed myself a soft smile. "What's your name?"

She smirked. "You just told me you knew my name."

"Well nana-nana-boo-boo, Ms. Hanson. I guess you've got me there." I waited for the smirk to fade from her face. "I meant your first name."

"It's Lilly."

"Pretty."

"Like I care what you think."

"But you care about the kid?"

"How do you know what I care about?"

"If you didn't care, you wouldn't have opened the

door."

"Maybe I just—"

"Lilly," I interrupted, "I'm sure we could spar like this all day long, but that wouldn't help Janet any. Wouldn't help Ava, either."

"Is Ava all right?" she asked. She tried to keep her voice rigid, but behind the toughness, I detected genuine concern.

"She's fine," I assured her. "She's had to make do staying with two single guys in a rooming house, but she's eating well, and she's made great friends with our dog. But she needs her mom."

Lilly nodded. "You said Janet told you a wild story. What did she say?"

I stared at her for a moment. "How long have you two known each other?"

"About a year."

"You two just roommates?"

"What do you mean by that?"

"I mean is Janet more to you than just half the rent?"

"I thought you were implying…Oh, never mind. If you're asking me do I care about her and Ava, yes, I do. Very much."

I nodded. "Do you know who Greg Walsh is?"

Lilly tensed visibly. "I've heard of him."

"You know he was murdered?"

"Yes," she replied carefully, making the word more than one syllable.

"Janet told me that she was afraid that the same people who killed Walsh were after her."

"Did she?"

"Look, Lilly. I'm not one of the bad guys, if that's what you're thinking. I told you who I am. If you want, before talking to me, you could call the better business bureau or whatever and check me out. But the bottom line is, I need to find out what's going on. I need to decide if I continue watching Ava or hand her over to child protection services."

"Oh, don't do that!" she exclaimed, alarm flashing in her eyes.

"I'm thinking that Janet gave her to me not only because she trusted me, but also so that she could get Ava back when the trouble blows over. She may not have been sure that the courts would do that. I need you to trust me, too."

"Do you think the trouble's blown over?" Lilly asked, her voice still tentative.

"I don't know. Maybe. The Apple Valley cops think they know who killed Walsh."

"You mean those two guys that died yesterday. I read about that in the paper."

"Yeah," I said. "And they didn't just die. I killed them."

I don't know why I told her. Maybe I was trying to be completely honest. Maybe I had a subconscious need to confess to somebody. It doesn't really matter. Whatever the reason, I immediately regretted it. I winced, bracing myself for Lilly to slam the door in my face. Instead, she remained rooted before me, a series of emotions flickering across her face, like frames on a strip of celluloid—shock, fear, disgust, and finally, something that I took for empathy.

"I read in the newspaper they were armed," she said. "I read they were trying to kill the rest of the Walsh family. It said a family friend protected them. That was you?"

I nodded.

"Were any of you hurt?"

"Not seriously."

"And you really have Ava?"

"Really."

"Why don't you come in and take a seat, uh…" She glanced down at my card in her hand. "…Lyle."

"Thanks."

Lilly ushered me inside and motioned me toward a lumpy-looking sofa, a beige terrycloth bedspread tucked into its curves. "You want some coffee?"

"No thanks," I answered, taking a seat.

Lilly closed the door and stood for a moment, not looking at me, but rather at the business card I'd given her. The sofa I was sitting on faced the kitchen. There, atop a sturdy pine table, were several open textbooks and a notebook with pages covered with tight blue script. "You a student?" I asked, pointing at the evidence.

"Yeah."

"What's your major?"

She thought a moment before answering. "I've got a bachelor's in social work. Right now, I'm a divinity student at Luther Seminary."

"Really," I said, smiling. "That probably means you're not hooking."

Her eyes flashed with momentary anger, then softened. "You're a quick study," she replied with her own smile.

"It also explains why you let me in."

"How's that?" she asked, some of her former toughness re-entering her voice.

I shrugged. "Most people hear you've just killed someone, they don't ask you in for coffee. You figure

I'm a lost soul in need of saving?"

"You want to talk about that?"

I chuckled. "Some other time, padre."

Lilly took a seat in an armchair opposite me. "You sure?"

There was real compassion in her eyes.

"Yeah. I got it covered."

We stared at each other for a moment.

"I came here hoping that you could tell me where Janet is," I said at last.

"You said she was afraid. Is she all right?"

"I really don't know."

She continued to stare at me, her lower lip trembling barely perceptively. Then she sighed—a resigned, little sigh. "I wish I help could you. But I really don't know where she is."

"You sure? I know it's hard, but you can trust me. I'm not looking to hurt her."

"I believe you. God help me if I'm making a mistake, but I really do believe you."

"You're not making a mistake, Lilly. So, Janet left you no clue as to where she went?"

"No. I came home and found the place empty and some of her stuff was gone. She left her half of the next month's rent in an envelope there on the kitchen table. There was a note, but all it said was that she'd be away for a few days. She didn't say where she was going or for how long."

"How had she been acting? You know, before she left."

"She was edgy," Lilly said. "Janet was trying to hide it. Probably didn't want it to show around Ava. But she was clearly jumpy. Had been ever since she'd heard about Greg Walsh."

"You know much about her and Walsh?"

"No. I really only saw him once. This Porsche would come by to pick her up from time to time. Janet would be ready, looking out the window, and this car would drive up. I knew the guy was special. Janet didn't work out of this apartment. I mean, she knew a lot of guys, but they didn't come by here to get her. Only this one. I wouldn't even have known it was Walsh if I hadn't seen him once get out of the car to open the back door for Ava."

"You sure it was Walsh?"

"Yeah. I'd seen his picture in the paper a few times. He was a pretty big deal in the business section. It was him."

"And you say that Ava went with them?'

"Not all the time. Most of the time she'd be at a sitter's. But a couple of times. Yeah."

"What did Janet say about her relationship with him?"

"She was pretty closed mouthed about it, to tell the truth. I asked her about him a couple of times, but all she said was that he was a friend helping her out. I could tell it was more than that, though."

"Yeah?"

"Yeah. In the first place, there was the fact that she let Ava near him. She loves that kid more than anything and she's really protective. She wouldn't let Ava near anyone she wasn't absolutely sure of." Lilly flashed me a knowing glance. "Like you, I guess."

I grunted.

"There's something else," Lilly continued. "I don't know if I should say this. I mean, I don't know for sure or anything, but I always kinda thought that Ava looked a lot like Walsh."

I leaned forward.

"Like I say, I don't know for sure. I never asked. I cared about Janet, but she was my roommate, you know. I needed rent that I could afford, and I just answered an ad. Janet was always my roommate first, not my friend. There were lines I got the impression she didn't want me to cross."

"But you think maybe Walsh was Ava's father?"

Lilly nodded. "You should have seen the way she reacted when she heard that he'd died. She was beside herself. For the first time since I moved in, she asked me to take Ava. She shoved some money in my hands and asked me to take Ava out for ice cream or something. Then she went into her room. She tried to keep it down, but she was sobbing uncontrollably. Ava and I were gone for nearly two hours. When we got back, Janet was still in her room, still crying."

"Anybody else come by here for her?" I asked. "Do you know anyone who maybe she'd go to or who might know where she's gone?"

"Janet had a couple of sitters she used for Ava sometimes. Janet mostly worked during the day when Ava was in daycare. That way she could be with Ava at night. But sometimes…you know."

"You think these sitters might know where she's gone?"

Lilly shook her head. "No. I really don't. I think she just answered their ads in the paper. They aren't friends or anything."

"Anybody else? Anybody you can think of that she'd go to?"

"She has an aunt," Lilly said hopefully.

I shook my head. "I've already talked to her."

"I can't really think of anybody else. There were these two kids who came by once. But that was months ago."

"Two kids? Tell me about them."

"There's not really much to tell," Lilly said. "Maybe six or eight months back there was this knock on our door. I opened it and there were these two teenagers standing there. A boy and a girl. Well-scrubbed, clean-cut types. Janet wasn't expecting them. I could tell that. But you should have seen the look on her face when she saw them. She was so excited. There was something…I don't know, something almost magical about her expression. It was like her soul opened, lighting up the whole room. The kids were really taken aback. They were very stiff and formal. They called her Ms. Kleiner and seemed really anxious. I didn't want to meddle, so I went into my room. They talked in here for maybe a half-hour or so. Quietly. The walls aren't real thick and I could tell they were out here, but I couldn't actually hear what they were saying. Then, Janet knocks on my bedroom door. She's got a camera and wants me to take their picture. The kids didn't seem too thrilled about it, but Janet was just beaming. She sat Ava on the couch next to the boy, then took a seat next to him, between him and the girl. I took a couple of pictures, then they left. A couple of days later Janet showed me one of the pictures. It was okay, I guess, but Janet acted like it was a Rembrandt or something. She framed the picture and put it on her bedside table. She never did tell me who they were and, like I say, I didn't think it was my place to ask. All I know is they were very important to her."

"Do you think I could see the picture?"

Lilly's eyes narrowed. "I guess it would be okay. It's in her room."

We stood and she showed me down the hallway to Janet's room. Lilly watched me closely as I entered. A queen-sized bed draped with a poofy comforter in a pink floral pattern took up most of the small bedroom. Four large pillows encased in matching shams trimmed in beige lace were propped against the wall at the head of the bed. On the floor against one wall sat maybe a dozen stuffed animals—an elephant, a moose, several bunnies and bears—all in a line like sentries keeping watch. A wide, low dresser against the opposite wall was topped with a wooden jewelry case, some books—mostly children's picture books—and lots of framed photographs. Most were photos of Ava, although a snapshot of a smiling Greg Walsh stood within the pictorial thicket. A blue plastic laundry basket filled with all varieties of toys sat lonely in a corner.

"It's on the bedside table," Lilly said, pointing.

I circled the bed and amid even more pictures of Ava, I found the photo that Lilly had taken. Ava was at the end of the couch, a smile on her face, but distracted and not looking at the camera. Janet sat in the middle, smiling widely, red spots like bull's-eyes shining from her pupils. She was flanked on either side by the two teens. One I recognized only from the photograph I'd seen in the Walsh living room.

It was Megan Blauer. The boy was Tyler Walsh.

Chapter Sixteen

Lilly promised to call me if she heard from Janet, and she let me take the photograph with me after extracting a promise from me that I return it. She was careful with Janet's things. It got me wondering. Why hadn't Janet asked her roommate to watch Ava when she went into hiding?

Lilly had told me that she and Janet weren't really friends, but she obviously cared. Before I left, she made sure to ask me if I needed anything, any clothes or toys for Ava. But pointedly, she hadn't offered to care for Ava herself. Lilly was sure to be busy with school and other commitments and finding the time to watch after Ava would have been difficult for her. But it was no less so for me. Why had Janet chosen someone she'd never been close to, someone she hadn't even seen for years, over a divinity student with a degree in social work?

What did I have that she thought Ava needed?

It was already early afternoon when I pulled into a parking spot behind my office building. Although it was only two blocks away, I'd elected to call the Bijou, rather than drop by. I figured a little distance might help get me out of any babysitting chores that Edgerton might have had lined up for me.

I had several telephone messages waiting for me at the office. Every local news outfit that I'd ever heard of and several that I hadn't had called me asking for an interview. The cops had made my name public, and everyone wanted to know how I felt about killing those two kids at the Walsh home. I erased the messages, then dialed Edgerton's number.

I was a little surprised to find that Edgerton was home, but Ava wasn't. "Where's the kid?"

"Ava?"

"No. Some other kid."

"I don't know about the other one, but our little Ava is playing over at Max and Vicki Wiseman's."

"Why isn't she with you?"

"I got delayed at work and the Milkman had to help set up for some AA meeting over in Kenwood. I asked him to drop Ava at the Wiseman's."

"She's sure getting shuttled around a lot today."

Edgerton's voice took on a disagreeable, defiant edge. "Is there something wrong with that?"

"I don't know. It's not real…I don't know. It's not a really *settled* lifestyle."

"It's not a lifestyle at all, for Christ's sake. I had to go into work. And I figured after the day you had yesterday, you could use a break. Forgive me. Next time, I'll just leave her with you and have done with it. Besides, it's not like other families don't have other people watch their kids when something comes up."

"We're not her real family, Stephen."

"You know what I mean. And we all know you want to get rid of the kid. You can stop mentioning it every chance you get."

"I do not want to 'get rid' of her. I want what's best for her."

"Uh huh." He paused. "You going to be home for

dinner? I'll probably feed Ava around six. I think she'd like you to join us."

"I'm hoping to have dinner with Naomi tonight."

"Hmm, well, I hope Ava won't be too disappointed," Edgerton said before the line clicked off.

I hung up the phone with a renewed resolve to find Janet Kleiner as soon as possible. Bickering with Edgerton like we were an old married couple was not something I planned to continue doing. The trouble was, I really didn't know where else to look for Janet. I thought about contacting Mavis Kleiner again, but I was pretty sure that she'd have called me if she'd heard anything. The only clue I had to go on was Janet's curiouser and curiouser relationship with the Walsh family. If Lilly was right, and Ava was Greg Walsh's daughter, then when Tyler Walsh had gone to visit Janet, he'd met not only with his dad's mistress, but also with his half-sister. I wondered if Janet had told Tyler that.

I also wondered how Tyler had come to know about Janet in the first place. Even if he'd suspected, for one reason or another, that his old man was having an affair, how did he know where she lived? Had Janet contacted him? Had Greg told him? And the timing of the visit was interesting. The meeting had taken place several months before, back when Tyler was still dating Megan Blauer, presumably before Tyler had taken up with Matty Beam and his jackbooted Defamation League. Did little Tyler's conversion from high school sports hero and scholar to anti-Semite have anything to do with his dad's relationship with the Jewish Janet Kleiner?

It was clear that I would have to have another conversation with Tyler, so I picked up the phone and dialed the Walsh home. A woman with an almost impenetrable accent answered. She told me that the Walshes were not at home. When I asked if I might leave a message, she politely informed me that she did not know when they would be back. I pressed for more information, but the woman refused to tell me anything further. Hoping to draw her out, I told her—feeling pretty important—that I was the guy who had saved her employers the day before.

There was a brief silence before she lit into me. I didn't catch everything she said, but it's safe to say that she was not my greatest fan. She took me to task for ever having been born, for endangering Evelyn and Tyler, for taking the lives of the two young gunmen, and—this seemed to be of particular importance—for all of the broken glass, cracked plaster, and stained carpets that were now her responsibility to deal with. She concluded by informing me that she would pray for my immortal soul, before hanging up with such force that the impact made my fillings rattle.

I then called Zebulon Pope. Evelyn's lawyer was not in the office, but, according to his assistant, he had left specific instructions that I was not to be told anything about Evelyn and Tyler Walsh. I asked the assistant to have Pope call me at his earliest convenience. She didn't actually laugh out loud, but I got the distinct impression that it would be a while before I heard from him.

That left the girlfriend. If I wanted to find out more about Tyler's meeting with Janet, I was going to have to talk to Megan Blauer. But Charlie Blauer had been pretty protective of her when I'd spoken with him the previous day. And that was before I'd blown away two of her former schoolmates. I called the Blauer home anyway and was surprised when a quiet, fragile-sounding voice answered.

"Megan?" I asked.

There was quite a pause. "Who is this?"

"You don't know me," I said. "My name's Lyle Dahms."

She gasped. "You're the one who—"

"Yeah," I interrupted, "I guess you've seen the news. I'm the one who saved your boyfriend's life yesterday."

"You killed those two boys. You shot them."

"They were going to kill Tyler and his mom. I had no other choice."

She paused again. "Why are you calling here? What do you want with us?"

"I'm hoping you can help me make some sense of all of this, Megan."

"I can't tell you anything!" she blurted out. "I don't have anything to do with Tyler anymore."

"I know, Megan. I'm sorry about that. And I'm sorry to have to bother you, but there is something you can help me with. Do you remember that visit a few months back when you and Tyler went to see a woman named Janet Kleiner?"

"I don't know what you're talking about!" she insisted. "I don't know anyone by that name."

"Megan," I said softly, "I have the picture."

"What picture?"

"The picture of you and Tyler sitting with Janet. Remember, her roommate took a picture."

Megan's breathing had quickened, growing louder and more rapid as I waited for her to respond. Finally, she said, "I don't have to talk to you."

"No," I agreed, "you don't. But this woman…this

Janet, she's got something to do with all of this. People are dead, Megan. Greg Walsh is dead. Those two kids you used to go to school with are dead. If you don't want to talk to me, that's fine. But I'll be talking to the police. And believe me, Megan, you'll have to talk to them."

As Megan mulled this over, I heard her father's voice in the background. "Who is it, Megan?" he asked. "Who are you talking to?"

"No one, Daddy," she said, her voice trembling.

"Give me the phone," Blauer said.

"Really, Daddy. It's just—"

Blauer didn't say anything else to his daughter. He simply grabbed the phone away from her and demanded, "Who is this?"

"It's Lyle Dahms, Mr. Blauer."

"We don't want nothing to do with you, Dahms!" he exclaimed. "We're decent people. You call us again and I'll have the law on you."

"You go right ahead and make the call, Mr. Blauer. It'll save me the trouble. If I don't go straight to the cops with what I know about your daughter's involvement in Greg Walsh's murder, they'll make things very unpleasant for me. I just thought I'd call you as a courtesy before I talk to them."

"What do you mean 'my daughter's involvement?' She has nothing to do with any of this and you know it."

"Ask her about going with Tyler to visit that woman."

"What woman?"

"Just ask her."

Blauer put his hand over the mouthpiece, muffling the sound. I waited. After a few minutes, he came back on the phone. "So, Tyler Walsh dragged her along to see his dad's floozy. So what?"

"Did she share that with the cops?"

"Cops? What cops?"

"Augie Tarkof, for one."

Blauer made a little hissing sound. "Never heard of him."

"Come off it, Blauer. I spoke with Augie yesterday. He was asking about you. No way he hasn't come out to interview you. No way."

"You got no right to be talking with the police about me. No right."

"You got a problem, Mr. Blauer. When the cops ask you a direct question, you're supposed to give them an answer. Seems you and your daughter are more inclined to hide things."

"You don't know nothing about us!" he thundered. "People like you, snooping around, trying to ruin good people."

"I'm investigating a murder, Mr. Blauer. During the course of this investigation, two teenagers tried to kill me. I had to shoot them. Then I find out that you not only knew them, you let them off when they boosted your car some time back. Now I find out that your daughter's been hiding things from the cops. Tell me again about 'good people.'"

"Them two stealing my truck ain't no secret. And the cops didn't ask Megan about some whore Greg Walsh was keeping. How's she supposed to know what to tell them if they don't ask?"

"Nice try, Mr. Blauer. But that kind of reasoning isn't gonna cut it. Not with the people you're going to be dealing with. The way I see it, you got the cops on one side and Matty Beam and his boys on the other with you in the middle. Could be I can help you with both of them. But you gotta level with me. Suppose you and Megan meet me somewhere. We can talk. Maybe set things right. What do you say?"

Before he hung up, Charlie Blauer told me, in graphic terms, exactly what he thought of my proposal.

I didn't know what my next move should be, and I spent the next couple of hours at my desk making notes but mostly staring at nonsense on the Internet. I was about to head home when the office phone rang.

"I've decided to talk with you, Mr. Dahms," Megan Blauer said in a hushed voice. "You still want to know about that woman? The one Tyler took me to see?"

"Very much."

"I can't talk now. Not on the phone. Dad's gone out, but…"

"Do you want to get together?" I asked, doubting that she'd take me up on it.

"Okay," she said. "Um, you know where the Empire Room is? Down here in St. Helena?"

"I do. But I don't think that's a very good place for us to meet. I've been told that's one of your dad's haunts and that's where those two boys spotted me the last time I was down your way. Someplace else would be better. Maybe in Apple Valley?"

"No," she insisted. "It's got to be Sully's. I won't meet you anywhere else."

I felt a tickling sensation, as if a platoon of tiny spiders were marching up the back of my neck. "Why's that?"

"I uh…um…. I feel comfortable there, is all," she stammered. "I'm nervous enough. Will you come?"

"Absolutely," I told her. "What time?"

"Come right away."

"I will, Megan. You sound a little desperate. Are you all right?"

"I will be after you get here," she said, hanging up.

I took a moment to check the load of the .38 I was carrying in the holster under my arm, as well as the .22 I had strapped to my ankle. Then I slipped on a light windbreaker and made my way down the stairs to the parking lot.

When I reached the freeway onramp, I switched on the radio and listened to the "Good 'N' Country" show on KFAI. The signal faded before I reached St. Helena, but by then, it didn't matter. By then, my mind was otherwise occupied with wondering why Megan Blauer had decided to set me up.

Chapter Seventeen

It was nearly three in the afternoon when I reached Sully's. There were only two other cars in the lot, and they were both parked along the side of the roadhouse near the door that led into the back. Gravel crunched under my tennis shoes as I made my way from the car to the front door. When I opened it, a little bell tinkled a welcome.

Just inside the door was a rack for those ubiquitous free newspapers that have maybe three articles and ten pages of ads. On the rack, beside the stack of papers, were some brochures for a local real estate agent, and next to those was a small pile of pamphlets printed on vivid red paper. I picked up one of the pamphlets. In jagged, Gothic type the headline read, "The Jew is the Anti-Christ! Read this Study!" I folded the pamphlet and slipped it into my pocket.

Since it was really too late for lunch and too early for dinner, I shouldn't have been surprised to find there were no customers in the place. In fact, the room was completely empty as the door closed behind me. The only movement inside was the lazy waving of a set of lace curtains partially blocking an open window by the pool table.

Then, Prudence Johnson flounced through the doors that led back to the kitchen. A wide grin pushed aside her chubby cheeks. "Blueberry pie!" she called out happily, but then her expression dropped as precipitously as a sparrow felled by a mid-flight heart attack. "Oh, but I hope you're not back for more," she moaned. "I'm all out of the blueberry, but I tell ya what. I got a slice of lemon meringue right here in the cooler if that'll do ya."

"Maybe later, Ms. Johnson," I said. "I'll just take a cup of coffee to start. I'm meeting someone."

"The coffee's coming right up," she said brightly. Then with a mock frown she added, "And it's Prude. I told you about that 'Ms. Johnson' stuff."

I made a little clicky noise with my tongue. "That's right, Prude. I'll remember next time."

She flashed me an alarmingly coquettish smile and hurried after my coffee, taking tiny steps that sent her bulk wobbling.

I took a seat at the end of the bar with my back to the pool table so I could face the front door.

"Did you get to talk to Charlie Blauer?" Prude asked, returning to set the coffee before me.

"I did. Thanks."

"You guys all settled then? With that work you wanted done, I mean."

I sipped at the coffee. "You know how it is. These kinds of projects can be a little open ended."

"Don't I know it," Prude said, chuckling. "When my brother Sully had Charlie build that deck a couple of years back, they got to talking and pretty soon they were thinking about maybe ripping out a wall and expanding the garage. Then they talked about those…whatchacallem? Dormers? They wanted to maybe make the upstairs bedrooms bigger by putting in these dormers. I had to draw the line there, let me tell ya. I told them that my bedroom's plenty big enough as it is." She leaned over the bar toward me and lowered her voice conspiratorially. "Big enough until I add a man to my life, if you know what I'm saying." She reared back, her chin disappearing completely into the fleshy folds of her neck and peeled off an eardrum-piercing giggle.

"What's all the hubbub out there, Prude?" a man's voice sounded from the kitchen.

The door squeaked open and a tall, portly man with thinning hair and ruddy cheeks emerged. He had on blue jeans, a white T-shirt stained yellow under the arms, and a frayed white apron so swiped with grease and sauce that it looked like a preschooler's finger-painting. He appeared a few years older than he did in the photo used in the portrait that hung behind the bar, but there was no question that this was Sully, master of the house.

"Just joking with the customers, Sully," Prude said. "Gotta keep 'em coming back for something. It's not like they're swarming in here 'cause of your cooking."

Sully gave his sister a good-natured grimace as Prude continued to laugh well past the point warranted by her little joke. There was a sense of boredom in his eyes that I took to mean that he and his sister had played out this particular routine many times before.

"You'll have to forgive my sister," Sully said. "She's got a peculiar sense of humor."

"You only say that 'cause I'm always laughing at you," Prude countered, nearly collapsing in a paroxysm of laughter.

Sully rolled his eyes but smiled amiably. "Did Lucille Ball here offer you anything to eat? Or is she just using you to try out material?"

"She asked. But I'm waiting for someone."

"Ah!" he exclaimed as though I'd said something

significant. "Anybody I know?"

"You know the governor?"

Sully's eyes grew wide. "Sure do!"

"Somebody else," I said.

Sully grunted out a chuckle. "Jeez, now I got two of 'em."

Prude, of course, found this hilarious. When she regained control of herself, Sully gave his hand a cursory wipe on his apron, then thrust it over the bar toward me. "Frank Sullivan," he said. "I own this place. He pumped my hand firmly. "I guess you know Prude," he said, without waiting for my name.

"We met yesterday."

"Ah! A return customer. Maybe my cooking's not so bad after all."

Prude, who, with effort, had managed to resume breathing normally, said, "Now, don't get no sprain patting yourself on the back, Sully. Only thing he had in here yesterday was a slice of my homemade blueberry pie."

"That and a helping of your infectious personality, Prude," I said.

Prude beamed, the yellow of her teeth contending with the rosy blush that enflamed her cheeks. "Now isn't that a nice thing to say."

I smiled and turned to Sully. He smiled too and his eyes twinkled, but, I thought, not so much with mirth than with a kind of icy intelligence.

"Now you're gonna just have to leave off the compliments," Sully said, still smiling. "Can't be letting 'em go to Prude's head. They'll be no living with her."

"I'm sure she's no stranger to flattery."

"You're not from around here, are you?" Sully

quipped, allowing himself another cough-like chuckle. Prude tapped him playfully on the shoulder.

"No, I'm not."

"And who did you say you were waiting for?" Sully asked.

"I didn't."

Sully glanced first at me, then at the bar in front of him. "I don't mean to be nosy, mister. It's just that…Well, I like to run my place the way I like to run it and we've been having some trouble down here lately."

I picked up my coffee cup and sipped lightly. "What kind of trouble?"

He picked up the bar rag and began wiping at something that wasn't there. "We've just been getting some outsiders down here,"

"I'm starting to feel unwanted, Mr. Sullivan."

"No, I didn't mean that. I'm sure you're not the sort I'm talking about."

"What sort is that?"

Sully eyed me again before responding. "Then again, you're a pretty big guy. The kinda guy they'd be looking for."

"Who are *they*, Mr. Sullivan?"

"Got them bruises, too."

Reflexively, my hand went to my face, and I lightly fingered the bruises that Beam's men had given me two days before.

He dropped the rag and met my eyes with an unwavering stare. "You know who Matty Beam is?"

"I've heard of him," I said, careful not to turn away.

"You down here to meet up with him?"

"'Fraid he's not my type."

Sully's eyes softened and a small, but seemingly

genuine smile spread over his face. He nodded a couple of times. "I'm sorry for the third degree, mister. It's just, like I said, we've been getting some folks coming through here. Folks I'd frankly rather not serve."

"It's your place, Mr. Sullivan. Serve who you want."

Sully nodded again. "You sure we can't get you something to go with that coffee?"

Prude perked up, raising both eyebrows expectantly.

"You know, Prude," I said, "maybe I will have that slice of pie you were talking about."

"I knew we could tempt you," she said gleefully. "I knew it."

Prude brought out the pie, an extra-large slice of lemon meringue. I smiled my thanks as I looked down at it. The topping had split open, forming a sluiceway for the weeping meringue to run down to the plate where it pooled around the preternaturally stiff lemon filling. "Looks mighty good, Prude," I said, hoping she didn't catch the tenor of dread in my voice.

Both Sully and Prude watched me intently as I took the first bite. The meringue was merely bland, but I swear the lemon filling had to have been something like Lysol thickened with cornstarch.

I swallowed a second forkful of pie and looked up at Sully. "So, this Beam guy is a major pain in the shorts, huh?"

"Shit, brother, you don't know the half of it."

"I suppose it brings in the wrong element. Rough guys looking for trouble, that sort of thing?"

He ran his hand over his head again. "Yeah. There's some of that. I don't usually have much trouble taking care of that sort of thing, though. I've been running this place a while and sometimes you just have to crack heads to keep things peaceable. Folks around here, they remember that kind of thing."

"I'll bet."

"Not that we have a crime problem. Some small-town kids' stuff every once in a while. Like hijinks, you know. But all in all, until Beam set up shop down here, your criminal element pretty much stayed away. Heck, we don't have probably no more than a handful of Blacks within twenty-five miles of here."

"That keep crime down, does it?" I asked. I tried to sound indifferent.

Flinty suspicion sparked in Sully's eyes. "Now, I don't think it's a prejudice thing, Leastways not before Beam started getting all that attention a while back. They just don't seem to like it down here."

"Probably prefer being with their own kind," I suggested.

Sully eyed me momentarily before responding. "Something like that, yeah. And why not? It's a free country, ain't it?"

I nodded. "I noticed some pamphlets when I came in."

Sully looked puzzled, then his eyes darted toward the front door.

"Are those darn things back again?" he asked, frowning and shaking his head. "I keep tossing 'em away and they keep coming right on back. Guess I'll have to keep a better eye out. That kind of thing can put people off, you know. Make ya think this isn't a friendly place."

"Might just," I agreed.

While we'd been talking, I'd heard the crunching of tires out in the parking lot. It sounded like two different vehicles had pulled up outside the roadhouse. Sully had started moving down along the bar, intending to go retrieve the offending pamphlets, I suppose. I never did find out for certain. Before he was out from behind the bar, the front door opened, and a group of men walked in. I didn't recognize the first two, but in their wake came Al Grogan and his bald buddy. Matty Beam brought up the rear.

The first two moved around me to the left and took up positions by the pool table. They were both in their mid-to-late twenties, tall, thin, scruffy, one wearing a Harley Davidson T-shirt, the other wearing a T-shirt with a trout leaping over the words "Doug & Mike's Bait Shop." The one with the trout shirt had a very full mustache and washed-out blue eyes. The one with the Harley shirt was clean-shaven and had eyes so dark that at first I thought his sockets were empty. Grogan and Baldy stopped about four feet in front of me, just enough room between them to allow for Beam.

"Well, if it ain't our pal, Killer," Beam said, smiling thinly. "How's it going, Killer?"

I glanced to my left as the two skinny guys each picked up pool cues. Sully and Prude were still standing behind the bar, eyes flickering nervously. I hoped it might occur to one of them to reach for the phone, maybe call the cops, but both were as motionless as statuary. Grogan and Baldy crossed their arms imposingly showing me their badass tattoos. Beam stood with both hands in the pockets of his khakis. He bit his lip slightly as he waited for my reply.

"Didn't you hear me, Dahms?" Beam said loudly. "I asked you, how's it going?"

"Well, I'll be," Sully said quietly behind me.

"How's that, Sully?" Beam asked.

"This here's the guy they mentioned on the news. The guy that shot the Hollenbeck and Segulia boys?"

"In the flesh," I said.

"Didn't know that when you came in," Sully told me, his voice shot through with betrayal. Prude, too, looked like I'd led her on.

I shrugged.

"So, what brings you down here, Dahms?" Matty pressed. "It's not enough you kill a couple of citizens, you gotta come down here and brag about it, too?"

"Not at all, Matty," I said, settling back on my barstool. "I'm here for two reasons. First, for the pie. And second, I came down hoping to see you."

Beam pulled his hands out of his pockets and began to closely examine a cuticle. "That so? You got business with me?"

"Uh-huh." I nodded. "Ever since we met at Greg Walsh's funeral, I've been thinking about it. And you know, I've finally decided to take the plunge. How does one go about joining your church, Reverend?"

Beam raised both eyebrows. "You want to join my church?"

"Yeah. Like I say, it took some thought. I gotta admit, I'm not the most religious guy. But I've been asking around and, you know, a lot of people join churches even though they're not particularly religious. Many join just for the social aspects."

"The social aspects?"

"Yeah, you know, the feeling of community, the potential job contacts, the cookouts."

"Listen!" one of the guys by the pool table piped up, "We don't want you joining no—"

"I wasn't sure what to bring," I interrupted. "I

205

figured you guys could provide the wooden crosses and the kerosene, but I got some sheets in my car, and I brought my own Zippo."

"Very funny, Dahms," Beam said, his smile tightening. "It's nice to see you didn't lose your sense of humor after that unfortunate encounter the other day with my two friends here." He spread his hands, palms upward, pointing toward the men flanking him like he was offering a kind of blessing.

"I'm not kidding, Matty," I said. "Your group's combination of sophistication and breeding really appeals to me. I've always wanted to be part of a social club where every other guy's name is Hickey."

The guy with the trout shirt looked at me first with a kind of awe, as if I'd mystically hit upon some great secret of his. Then, blinking, his face hardened as he realized that I might be making fun of him.

"Let's hope you still have your sparkle after my guys are through with you today," Beam said.

"Bring it on," I told him.

Grogan and Baldy both uncrossed their arms and out of the corner of my eye I caught the two guys with pool cues advancing toward me. I didn't let them get very far before I reached under my jacket and pulled out my .38. Everyone stopped as I leveled it directly at Beam. There was a clatter behind me as if the guys back there had dropped their pool cues. A quick glance over my shoulder told me that both men had pulled guns of their own.

"You can go ahead and shoot me, fellas," I told them, my eyes fixed on Beam. "But there's no way I don't bring down the Reverend Matty here before you get me."

I had to give Beam credit. Just the merest shiver of alarm passed over his features. He was about to say something when Sully stepped out from behind the bar. "God dammit!" he shouted. "There ain't gonna be no shooting in my place! You all just put those damn things away and get the hell out of here. My place ain't gonna be on no TV news with chalk outlines on my nice clean floor."

I kept the gun steady as Beam turned toward the men behind me and nodded slowly. Beam had trained them well. They both lowered their weapons.

"Let's go, boys," Beam said, a smile returning to his face. "If Sully don't want us here, we'd best be leaving."

Hickey and Dark Eyes circled behind Beam and out the door, followed by Grogan and Baldy. Grogan stared coldly at me before turning away.

"Hope to see you both again real soon," Beam said as he was leaving. "I'd love to resume our little discussion. Take care, now."

I probably looked pretty ridiculous, but I kept my gun leveled at the door long after I heard the sound of two sets of tires pull out of the parking lot. When I lowered the gun, Sully looked at me and shook his head.

"Thanks, pal," he said. "Thanks a lot. This is just what I need, trouble with that bunch."

I slipped the gun back into my shoulder holster, stood, and squinted at Sully. "You know, I've had a really bad week. Not just one of your run-of-the-mill bad weeks, mind you. It's like the gods have especially singled me out. An old friend was killed, I got beat up by white supremacists, my dad gets cancer, I shot a couple of kids, I got shot myself, and I've had to babysit. So, I want you to know how much I appreciate you guys trying to take my mind off my troubles with this little piece of community theater."

Sully was aghast. "What are you talking about?"

"And you guys weren't bad," I continued. "You all hit your marks, you remembered your lines, and there was real emotion in your voice when you said…What was it? Oh yeah, that bit about the chalk lines and the TV news. It really was my favorite part. You should be proud."

"Why don't you just come out and say what you're trying to say," Sully said, his voice now taut with menace.

"I'm sorry, weren't you listening? I'm just thanking you for going to all the trouble. And don't worry about any of the little glitches. You guys run through that a couple more times and I'm sure folks'll be convinced you and Beam aren't really mixed up together."

"I don't know what you're talking about," Sully said. His voice was leaden, as though he'd suddenly turned to stone.

I nodded, crossed the room to the front door, turned, and winked at him. "Of course not."

Chapter Eighteen

When I got back to the Bijou, I found a note on my door from Stephen. It said that he and Ava would be having dinner at McCauley's that evening and invited me to join them. Dinner was out of the question. Not only had Naomi agreed to have dinner with me later, but I suspected that Stephen had invited me largely with the hope that I would pick up the tab. On the other hand, it was happy hour, and I figured a beer would go a ways towards washing away the memory of Prude's pie. But the wound in my side had been giving me trouble and the ER doc had prescribed some pain medication, so first I went into my room to fetch it.

Inside, my footsteps echoed eerily and the numbers on my alarm clock turned over with an audible flip. No one was watching kids shows on my television; there was no one to greet me with art projects; no one needed help brushing their teeth or putting on their jammies. I found it oddly unsettling.

I crossed to my bedside table. Next to the little bottle of pain pills, the message light on my telephone answering machine pulsed in a set of bright, annoying blips. I hit the button and listened to my messages. There were several calls from various news operations requesting interviews. One guy went on at length about how devastated I must be having killed two such young and vital individuals and suggested that I use an

209

interview with him as an opportunity for "cathartic release." If only he was within arm's reach, I thought. Squeezing his neck until his eyeballs popped might be another nice stress reducer for me.

One of the messages, however, was welcome. Evidently, the Walsh housekeeper, after tearing me a new one during our phone conversation earlier that day, had delivered my message to her employer after all. Evelyn Walsh had returned my call and would be home that evening should I want to try and reach her.

I dialed up the Walsh residence. The housekeeper answered and a sullen silence greeted me when I gave her my name. Finally, she said that she would inform Mrs. Walsh and within a couple of minutes I had Evelyn on the line.

"I'm going to need to talk to Tyler again," I informed her.

Evelyn paused before responding. "I could ask him to come on the line, but I can't imagine he'd talk to you. He hasn't talked to anyone since those boys broke into our home. There was even a homicide detective here. A man named Tarkof. But Tyler barely said a word. He's too…I think he's too wrapped up in his grief. He's…Maybe he's beginning to wonder if some of the things that have happened to us could have been prevented. It's possible he's blaming himself and I just don't want that."

"Like it or not, Evelyn," I said, "Greg's death, the shootout at your home…Well, there's no way Tyler can divorce himself from it. He was definitely involved with putting all of this in motion."

Evelyn's voice became stony. "Do you have proof that Tyler was directly involved in Greg's death?"

"No, I don't."

"Have you proof of anyone else's involvement?"

"No, but I'm getting close."

"I spoke with Zebulon Pope earlier today and he thought you might need to be reminded that you are working for us. As a part of our investigative team any information you uncover must be reported only to him. Pope is responsible for determining what information is to be shared with the police. You are clear on that, aren't you, Lyle?"

"Yeah, Evelyn, I'm clear. But I trust that you understand that when I determine the extent of Tyler's involvement, I'm not going to hide it from you. You need to prepare yourself. No way you don't get hurt here."

"I understand."

"Now, I do need to talk to Tyler. You're probably right, I wouldn't get much on the phone. Maybe I can come by tomorrow?" I paused. "You can sit in if you want."

"Let's wait till Monday, Lyle. Call me then. We'll set something up."

"Two days is a long time, Evelyn."

"We need it," she said.

Before I let her click off, I asked, "What can you tell me about Megan Blauer?"

"Nothing I haven't already told you. She was Tyler's girlfriend. Her father made them break it off."

"Her father protective of her?"

"Oh, yes. Very much so."

"So, you don't think he'd use her to get to me?"

"I…ah, no. No, I don't. Do you suspect the Blauers in all of this?"

"I'm just asking questions, Evelyn. Talk to you

Monday."

I placed the receiver in its cradle and reached for the bottle of pain pills. I was choking a couple down when the stillness of the room was broken by a loud metallic rattle. I whirled around, reaching for the gun under my jacket, when I remembered the dog.

Basil had been sitting patiently inside the kennel the whole time I'd been on the phone but when I squeaked open the kennel door, he bolted free, nearly running into the bed. He barked twice, then ran to me, mouth open, his butt waggling furiously. He made a couple of wet smacks in the general direction of my face then raced over to the door to my room, planted himself before it, and stared at it intently. It took a moment, but it dawned on me that little Basil likely needed to heed nature's call.

Taking the dog out was developing into something of a sore spot between Edgerton and me. Stephen had been insisting that he was very busy with Ava and, besides, Basil was my dog. I was equally adamant that not only was he not my dog, but that I was conducting a murder investigation and didn't see why Ava couldn't color quietly or watch TV by herself while he occasionally took the dog out to make water and boom-booms. The result was that our dispute had been over-testing the dog's bladder.

I rubbed Basil behind an ear as I snapped the leash onto his collar and led him out of my room. The Bijou had a pretty large backyard, but nearly the entire area was taken up by parked cars, most of which hadn't been moved since Walter Mondale was considered a serious contender for the Presidency. I set Basil down and led him past the cars and over to the small grassy area up against the house that we'd staked out for him to do his business. Some ten minutes later the dog had finally completed his mission, I'd locked him back up in his kennel, and was heading for McCauley's.

McCauley's is actually two operations—a pub downstairs and a restaurant above. Since the entire menu was available in the pub as well as the restaurant, Edgerton and I rarely frequented the upstairs dining room. But since good form would dictate dining with Ava upstairs, I checked out that first. Edgerton never was much on form. When I didn't spot them, I crossed to the door that led down to the pub.

As usual, the jukebox downstairs was playing some atonal guitar anthem, but the volume seemed to have been set a bit more softly than normal. The pub was only about one-third full, but nonetheless, I didn't see Edgerton right away. I passed a regular we called the Pirate, the brim of his black leather cowboy hat pinned up in front Gabby Hayes style, as he gesticulated wildly at a drinking companion only he could see. There was a table of young men drinking beer and occasionally glancing toward a table of young ladies, who were, I thought, making calculated efforts to avoid said glances. Edgerton was in the back in the last booth along the wall nearest the rear game room. I had nearly reached the table before I saw that Max Wiseman was with him. It's not that Wiseman is hard to spot; he's nearly as big as me. But he was sitting beside the Milkman, and Irv's big enough that you could prop him up in front of a herd of Guernseys and never know you were in dairy land. There was a half-full pitcher of dark beer on the table. Both Wiseman and Edgerton had glasses before them. Mulligan was drinking coffee.

"Where's Ava?" I asked when I'd reached them.

Edgerton pointed toward the bar. "With Skip."

I turned and saw the top of Ava's head just visible behind the bar. Caught in the beam of a recessed spotlight, her flaxen curls glowed like the spray of a solar flare. Skip was standing beside her, and he reached down as if handing something to the mostly hidden toddler. After a moment, a tiny hand clutching a white terrycloth rag appeared and began to buff the surface of the bar. Skip grinned broadly. Broadly for him, anyway. Since the paralyzed half of his face remained grimly fixed, even his most heartfelt smiles were seasoned with what appeared to be barely concealed ill will. But light danced in his eyes. When he spotted me, he took Ava's tiny pink hand in his large brown one and led her over to the table.

"Teaching Ava to tend bar?" I asked.

"She was just giving me a hand," Skip said, setting an empty glass down on the table. "And doing a fine job, I might add."

Ava beamed up at Skip, who gave her hand a little squeeze. "Listen, honey, I've got to be getting back to work now," he said. "Thanks for all your help."

"I could help more," Ava said, her eyes wide.

"I know, honey. But later. Besides, I can't afford to cut you in on the tips. Not serving these tightwads, anyway."

"I could show you that video game you asked about," Mulligan piped up. "The one with all the flashing lights."

Ava nodded and I was afraid the Milkman was going to injure himself in his excitement to wrestle his bulk out of the booth.

Skip lingered as I took a seat and fingered the empty glass he'd brought over. We all watched Ava dash toward the video game, Mulligan actually breaking into a trot to keep up.

"You find her mom, yet?" Skip asked.

I shook my head.

"Stephen said her mom was in trouble."

"Yeah. She was pretty scared when she left Ava with us."

Skip nodded. "She'd have to be to let that one go. She's a charmer."

I nodded back.

"Her mom? Is she running from Beam and those guys down in St. Helena?"

I smiled at his question. "You do keep up."

"Stephen told me some. And some of this has been on the news, you know? Millionaire killed. Racists involved. You shooting up the dead guy's home. Stuff like that."

"Yeah. I'm becoming quite the media darling."

"Well…" Skip prompted. "Is she running from them Nazis?"

"It's possible."

"The little one in trouble?"

"That's possible, too."

Skip's eyes went as cold as the marble of a headstone. "You need me, you let me know."

"I will," I promised.

He held my gaze for a moment before turning back to the bar.

Wiseman lifted the pitcher and poured me a glass of beer, eyeing Skip warily as he walked away. "That guy scares me," he said. He tried to keep his tone light but was unable to keep the anxiety out of his eyes.

"He should," I told him.

"You gonna need him?" Edgerton asked.

I shrugged. "I don't know. Maybe things'll calm down now. All this recent gunplay's been generating too much attention for a guy like Beam. It's a fine line. He can't survive without publicity but too much of the wrong kind and his supporters retreat and the cops move in. If Beam wants to stay in business, he's gonna have to keep his nose clean until the whole Walsh thing shakes out."

"You saying you don't think Beam killed Walsh?" Wiseman asked.

"I don't think Beam's got the *huevos*. But he's certainly got guys on his team that do. He could have ordered it done. That's harder to prove. A lawyer-type like Beam would be sure to provide himself with some kind of plausible deniability to hide behind."

"Sounds familiar," Wiseman said.

"How's that?"

"Like the Germans after the war denying that they knew what was going on in the death camps or the modern-day hate groups that claim they can prove that the Holocaust never happened."

"I got something like that right here," I told him, remembering and reaching into my pocket for the pamphlet I'd picked up at Sully's. Dropping it on the table, I said, "I found this at a roadhouse down in St. Helena. There was a whole stack of 'em."

Wiseman reached out a couple of fingers and pulled the pamphlet cautiously toward him as if he was afraid he might catch something.

"I glanced at it," I told him. "It's some pretty bizarre shit. Like you said, the Holocaust never happened. You Jews own the government. The usual. Then it gets really strange. One of those articles is all about how these Anglo types are the real Jews. Turns out these guys are so screwed up they can't decide if they hate you guys or want to be you."

Edgerton reached across the table and took the pamphlet from in front of Wiseman. He looked at it for a moment, then tossed it back on the table. "It's called Anglo-Israelism. It goes back a ways. Puritans have long viewed themselves as the spiritual descendants of the ancient Israelites, but 'long about the mid-1800s, groups started to proclaim that the Brits, and by extension white Americans, Canadians and the like, are the actual descendants of God's chosen people."

"Sounds like crap to me."

Edgerton shook his head. "Not crap. It's a way of co-opting the opposition."

"What's that supposed to mean?"

"Demonizing your enemy only goes so far. Every group possesses qualities that are difficult to deny. Take, for example, the Jews. According to Scripture, Jews are the *Chosen People*. Well, these white-is-right types can't let that stand. They got to figure out a way to claim that designation for themselves."

I picked the pamphlet up off the table, folded it, and returned it to my jacket pocket. "I still don't get it. It's tough to see why anybody would be attracted to this crap."

Wiseman took a sip of beer. "Well, look at what you're dealing with. It's safe to say that the people that follow a guy like Beam aren't exactly qualified to hold seminars on successful life strategies. These guys are losers. They've been losers from way back. They look around and they see all these people driving sports cars and buying expensive homes. They see there's this party going on and nobody invited them. Then along comes Beam. *He* knows who's to blame. It's affirmative action that kept them from getting that job at the plant. It's all the illegal aliens flocking into their country willing to work for next to nothing. It's the Jew bankers conspiring to keep them down. It's gay men looking to make 'em their boy toys. Everybody's responsible for their problems. Everybody but themselves. Beam gives these guys their focus. He tells them God is on their side. God intended all the races to remain separate. God hates fags. Those who refuse to accept Christ as their savior are the enemy. By invoking the name of God in their campaigns, they make hate holy."

"Okay," I said. "But these guys gotta eat. How does a guy like Beam survive?"

"There's a website listed on that pamphlet," Edgerton said. "You check that out, I'll bet you find they not only solicit donations, but I'll bet they take both Visa and Mastercard."

"But who'd give 'em any money?"

Edgerton snorted. "A lot of people out there figure it's worth a few bucks to have God on your side. You run things right, hate can be quite the money-making enterprise."

Wiseman poured the last of the beer into each of our glasses. Edgerton looked back toward the game room, hoping, I thought, to catch a glimpse of Ava.

"Anyway, I wish I could do more to help," Wiseman said.

"Getting rid of Beam and his bunch?"

"No." Wiseman shook his head. "I mean, help with the kid."

"You are helping," Edgerton assured him. "When the Milkman got busy today, you and Vicki jumped right in to watch her."

"Yeah. And we'd be glad to do it again if we can, but there's really something else that needs doing."

"What?"

Wiseman didn't meet Edgerton's eyes. "How much longer do you think she'll be with you?"

"I honestly don't know," I said. "But It's worth a conversation."

"She'll be with us until her mom can come back for her," Edgerton said. "What's to talk about?"

Wiseman took another sip of his beer. "Don't get me wrong, Stephen. You're great guys and I'm sure you're doing a great job. But that little girl needs a family."

"Her mom's her family. When she's back, Ava'll have what she needs."

Wiseman scratched his head. "Vicki and I were talking. The truth is, we're a little concerned about how she's getting on with all the…uh, rotating caregivers."

"She's getting along great. She's even got used to Lyle here and that's no easy task."

I grinned.

"Yeah,' Wiseman continued. "A little *too* great. That's really what's bothering us."

"You'd rather she was throwing hissy fits?"

"In a way. Yes."

"I'm not following."

"The kid's what, three years-old?"

"Three-and-a half," Edgerton and I said simultaneously.

Wiseman smiled. "Three-and-a-half? Well, three-and-a-half-year-olds are emotional whirlwinds. I

219

know—I've shepherded a couple of kids through it. It's just not normal for Ava to be so accepting of this situation. Her mom abandoned her for chrisssake. Can you even imagine how devastating—"

"Her mom didn't abandon her, Max," Edgerton interrupted. "She told Lyle she's coming back."

Wiseman shrugged. "She's a kid, Stephen. In her mind, her mom left. She abandoned her."

"So, she's coping. That's a good thing."

"Yes and no. How is she coping? It looks like she's coping by being equally accepting of anyone who comes along. The normal intensity of her emotions seems…I don't know, dampened. She shouldn't be so accepting of strangers. She should be expressing her resentment. Her rage. Her tantrums should be the terrors of the earth. Instead…" He let his voice trail away. "It's not normal. Unless she can find a way to deal with all the stuff that's got to be churning inside her, it could cause real problems for her later in life."

Edgerton was about to respond, but I spoke first. "What do you suggest, Max?"

"I think she should be in foster care. I think she needs a stable family to focus on."

Edgerton glared. "That's no better. What happens when her mom comes back? If she's bonded to a foster family, like you say, that'll cause its own problems. We're just babysitting for God's sake. A couple of weeks of babysitting never hurt anyone. I used to spend two weeks with my grandparents every summer. It didn't cause any emotional scarring."

"I don't mean to butt in where I don't belong, Stephen," Wiseman said. "Vicki and I were just talking is all."

Edgerton's expression softened. "You're helping out, Max. And I appreciate it. I appreciate hearing what you think, too."

Both men sipped at their beers.

Edgerton smiled. "Anyway, it's like Lyle said. Things may be calming down now. They do, her mom'll be back real soon."

"I hope you're right," Wiseman said. "But one thing you learn dealing with kids. When it seems calm, that's probably just the surface. Underneath, other things are still going on. Remember, Stephen, beneath even the most placid seas, serpents roil."

Chapter Nineteen

Ava and the Milkman rejoined us just as Naomi arrived at McCauley's for our dinner date. It occurred to me that she might be less than pleased to find me surrounded by my cronies, and I was about to offer an explanation, but she ignored me. She nodded a cursory greeting to the boys, then kneeled down in front of Ava. "How you getting on, sweetie?" she asked, perhaps a little too intently.

Ava's eyes lost all expression; her mouth became a pensive bow. "Fine."

Naomi reached out and took both of Ava's hands in her own. "I'm sorry we haven't had more time together."

"It's okay. You busy. I know 'bout busy. Mommy's busy sometimes."

Naomi glanced at me, her expression glum. Turning back to the child, she said, "Maybe we could have some time together now. Lyle and I are going to get something to eat. You want to get something with us? To eat, I mean."

Ava glanced uncertainly at Edgerton. "We already ate," she said.

I cast a puzzled look at Edgerton. He shrugged. "Skip fed us on the house."

I frowned. "He's never picked up a meal for me."

Edgerton smiled. "Well, Skip *likes* me."

Still kneeling in front of the toddler, Naomi said,

"Okay, since you've eaten, maybe we could do something else."

Ava looked to Edgerton again. We all watched her closely for a moment. Real apprehension welled in her blue eyes.

Before Ava could answer, Edgerton broke in. "Sorry, guys. I just remembered. I promised Ava we'd go back to the Bijou. We got a couple more DVDs we picked up at the library. One's got a cartoon aardvark. She was really looking forward to it. 'Fraid we'll have to break this up."

Naomi gave Ava's hands a little squeeze before she stood up. "Okay. You two have your aardvark," she said, her voice ever so slightly strained. "Lyle and I'll get some dinner."

It took a few awkward minutes for Edgerton, Ava, Mulligan, and Wiseman to gather their things, say goodbye, and get out of there. Meanwhile I stood by with an insincere smile pasted on my face, trying to pretend I didn't see the disappointment, then the irritation in Naomi's expression. When at last they'd gone, we took seats in the booth, and I reached both hands out to her. She patted but did not take them. "How's your dad?" she asked.

"We haven't talked yet."

Naomi studied my face.

I shrugged. "They told me to stay away a couple of days. I'll stay away."

We grew quiet. "I don't think she likes me," Naomi said at last.

"Ava?"

Naomi nodded.

"She doesn't know you."

"Maybe she does."

Just then Skip came by with our menus. I ordered another beer and Naomi ordered a glass of red wine. When he'd gone, I asked, "What do you mean by 'maybe she does?'"

"Oh, I don't know. It's just that…It's just that I've been doing some thinking lately."

"That doesn't sound good for my side," I said, forcing a chuckle.

"We need to talk," she told me. She wasn't smiling.

"That *really* doesn't sound good for my side."

Thankfully, Skip came back to get our food orders. Naomi ordered a cheeseburger and fries. I ordered lasagna, a salad with French dressing, and an order of garlic bread. I didn't like the way Naomi was looking at me and I figured a condemned man should have a satisfying last meal.

Skip lingered for a moment by the table, staring at us intently. There appeared to be something he wanted to say. But instead, he turned, and left us alone.

I looked up at Naomi. There was regret in her eyes but also grim determination. I set a soft smile on my face and waited for the worst.

"Do you want kids, Lyle?"

"What? Uh, like right now?"

"No. Not right now. I mean someday. Do you want to have kids someday?"

"I don't know. I haven't really given it much thought."

"But if you were to think about it, what do you think the answer would be?"

I sipped at my beer. "I don't know. I guess I always sort of assumed I'd have kids someday. It just never seemed like the day, you know?"

Naomi nodded. "Until recently I hadn't thought much about it either. But the last couple of days. I don't know. I guess I've been thinking about it a lot."

"Come to any conclusions?"

She reached out her hands and I took them loosely in mine. "Yes. Like you, I've always assumed that I'd have kids. Only every time I'm confronted with a kid, I go all…I don't know, all moogly. You saw the way Ava looked at me. That's my fault. The first couple of times we met all I could think was when's this kid gonna go home? I didn't even try. So, tonight I figured I'd try. Helluva job, wouldn't you say?"

"It doesn't mean a thing," I assured her. "You have a kid of your own, all that, uh…moogliness disappears."

Naomi grew very quiet. "A kid of my own," she said, at last. "I've been thinking about that, too."

I nodded. "But then maybe you'll decide that kids aren't for you. Lots of people decide that. It's okay, you know."

She looked me deeply in the eyes as if searching there for her own thoughts. "It's not that. I'm pretty sure that I really do want kids someday. And I don't want you to take this the wrong way, Lyle, but I'm…I'm pretty sure that I don't want to have kids with you."

A weighty silence dropped down around us. After a moment, I leaned forward, brought her hands to my lips and kissed them gently. "How could anybody take that the wrong way?"

"Don't joke, Lyle. You don't know how hard this was for me to tell you."

"Probably as hard as it was for me to hear." I paused. "So, does this mean you're breaking up with me?"

I cringed as I said it. It sounded so Frankie and Annette. So Gidget and Moon Doggie.

"No," she said, a quaver in her voice. "I love being with you. You're warm and funny and we're good together. At least up to a point."

"And that point is making a family together."

Naomi turned away, glancing toward the bar as if summoning help. Skip noticed and did a head bob in our direction. She shook her head and turned back to face me. "Don't get me wrong, Lyle. It's not like I'm looking to start a family any time soon. And it's not that I don't think you'd be a wonderful father—"

"That's not really true, is it?" I interrupted. "You don't think I'd be much of a dad."

Naomi took a fortifying sip of wine before continuing. "It's just that…Let's face it. This job you do. It's not exactly conducive to a stable home life. The people you deal with. You come home beat up. All kinds of things. I mean, suppose we had a parent-teacher conference, and you didn't show up and I had to come up with some way of telling Junior's teacher that you couldn't make it because the cops were questioning you after you'd capped somebody."

"That's not likely to happen."

"Lyle, it just did."

I swallowed hard. "Okay. Suppose I find other employment. Even I know that I can't do this job forever. I could work security. Hell, I could even get an office job. Maybe answer phones somewhere."

Naomi chuckled. "Yeah, you could do telephone solicitations. I'd love to see how you'd handle trying to get some homeowner to buy replacement windows or switch his wireless phone plan."

"I could do that."

"Lyle, you wouldn't last a week before somebody brought charges against you. You've got something of a temper, you know."

"I can control it. You know that. Have I ever even raised my voice to you?"

Naomi reached over and stroked my cheek. I tingled at her touch. "No. Not one time. You love me. I know that. And I love you. And I don't want to leave you. I want to go right on seeing you. I want us to be together until…" She let her voice trail away.

"Until it's time for you to move on."

She tried to respond, but the words caught in her throat. She sniffed loudly. Tears shimmered in her eyes, brimmed, then trickled down her cheeks.

I glanced to the bar. Our dinner order was sitting over there. Skip had placed our plates on a large cork lined serving tray and set the tray on the bar. But he was no longer even looking in our direction.

All at once, Naomi stood. "I'm really not hungry, Lyle,' she said, her voice tight with suppressed emotion. "I hope that's all right. I mean…" She couldn't tell me what she meant. A sob got in the way. She leaned down and hugged me tightly. When she released me, my face was damp with her tears. "Call me," she said.

"I will."

I started to get up, but she grabbed her bag and, without so much as a backward glance, walked quickly to the door.

Skip let me sit there for a minute or two before he brought the tray over. I looked at all the food we'd ordered.

"You want a cheeseburger?" I asked him.

"She's not coming back then?"

"Not tonight."

Skip nodded, then placed my order on the table in front of me. I picked at it in silence for some fifteen minutes before giving up. I stood and walked up to the bar, pulling my wallet out of the back pocket of my jeans.

Skip glanced at me. "No charge."

Something heavy seemed to be pressing behind my eyes. I tried to smile. "And here I just told Stephen you'd never bought me a meal."

Skip pointed at the food I'd left on the table. "Still haven't. You didn't eat it."

"I guess you're right. Maybe another time."

"You could stay. I'm off in a little while. We could talk, if you want."

I shook my head. "No thanks, man. I'm okay."

"Tough guy," Skip said.

Walking home, the shadows had lengthened, but the mid-summer sun, though bowing, had yet to quit the field. She said to call, I reminded myself. She said we were good together.

Back at the Bijou, Edgerton and Ava were in his room. I could hear them laughing in there. There was still some beer left in the fridge from my ill-fated birthday party earlier that week. I don't how many I had that night. But I remember lining up the empties on my desk. I remember them standing over me like sentries when I finally nodded off to sleep.

Chapter Twenty

My mouth was notably furry when I awoke the next morning. I was brushing my teeth for the second time when Edgerton knocked on the door and came in carrying two cups of coffee.

"What's this?" I asked. "Since when are you bringing me coffee in the morning?"

He handed me one of the cups. "You probably don't want to get used to it."

"Seriously, what gives?"

Edgerton shrugged. "Skip called me last night, is all. No big deal."

I tried to think of a reply. No luck.

"Where's the kid?" I asked at last.

"My room. She's reading."

"Reading?"

"Okay. I picked up some kid's books. She's looking at the pictures."

"What do you two have planned for today?"

"We got a big day planned."

"Yeah?"

"Yeah. Let me go get the little one and we can talk about it."

I shook my head. "Let me get a shower in first, willya?"

Edgerton shrugged and went back to his room to check on Ava while I went down to the shower. When I returned, they were both in my room, a pile of children's books on my unmade bed and Ava was snuggled into Edgerton's lap hearing all about making room for ducklings.

She looked up at me. "How's your ouchie?"

"It stings a little, but it'll be okay."

"Stephen says we go to the zoo today," Ava said.

"He did?"

"To see giraffes and tigers and ride on the merry-go-round."

"I'm sure you guys will have a wonderful time."

"Oh, you're going, too," Edgerton informed me.

"I don't think so. Thanks anyway."

"You gotta go. You're driving."

"It's not my fault you never learned to drive, Stephen."

"I know how to drive. I just don't have a driver's license."

"You could take the bus."

"Too much hassle with the little one."

"I'd really rather just stick around the house this afternoon. Besides, what if you-know-who comes by? Someone should be here."

"Who?"

I nodded toward Ava.

Edgerton remembered Ava's mom and nodded back. "We'll leave word with Jansrud or one of the other guys who lives here. If she comes by looking, they can have her call us."

"You're going to make me do this, aren't you?"

"Uh-huh."

"What about lunch?"

"We'll have corndogs at the zoo. Bring your wallet."

I was about to protest again, but Ava looked over at me with those dancing eyes. "You drive us. Okay, Lyle?"

There was something indefinably precious about the way she said my name. My insides fell to the floor. "My pleasure, sweetie."

Edgerton ushered Ava off to the bathroom, I took Basil outside before confining him to his kennel. Then, at last, we piled into my Ford and took off for the zoo. Edgerton sat in back with Ava, beaming as he stared at the toddler, who looked out the window, watching as the world whirled by. And before long, I actually started to warm to the idea of the excursion. For a moment or two, I was even able to make believe that we were a typical family on a typical family outing. But the illusion just couldn't hold up.

The truth was that instead of Mom, Dad and baby, our family consisted of a hooker's kid being looked after by two middle-aged strangers, one of whom had a .38 revolver under his jacket.

Ozzie and Harriet we were not.

Chapter Twenty-one

It's only about a fifteen-minute drive from our place in Dinkytown to the St. Paul Zoo. I pulled into the parking lot on the northwest side of the zoo grounds and although the clear, warm, summer day had brought people out in droves, we got lucky and managed to grab a spot from someone just pulling out. I hadn't been to the zoo since I was a kid, and I was pleasantly surprised to find that much of it had been updated in the ensuing decades. The cramped cages that had once housed the lions and tigers still fronted the pale orange main zoo building, but now they were empty. The tigers occupied a large, open environment complete with a tiny stream that trickled into a pool and lots of trees and brush in which to hide from the prying eyes of their human visitors.

Next to the tigers, lions slept in the shade of their own outdoor habitat and both the king of beasts, and his Siberian neighbors had access to indoor facilities that would become necessary as summer faded and the chill of the Minnesota winter approached. There was a new primate house for gorillas, orangutans, and various small species of monkeys. The polar bear and aquatic animal exhibits had been vastly improved, and there was an enlarged food court. But some things remained the same. Harbor seals and sea lions still swam in the moat surrounding Seal Island, and people still lined up at the little booth nearby to purchase Dixie cups filled with raw fish chunks to feed to the squawking, gape-mouthed panhandlers. Next to Seal Island, the seats of a small-scale amphitheater descended to a stage adjacent to a semi-circular pool of blue water. A sign there announced the times of the Spunky the Seal show—something I remembered fondly from my boyhood—although I suspected that it was one of the descendants of the original Spunky who carried on the family business. Little Ava took it all in with wide-eyed wonder and Edgerton, walking with her hand in his, seemed equally enthralled.

We ate our corndogs and after we'd made a circuit and had peeked into most of the animal exhibits, Ava announced she was ready for a ride.

Edgerton led us across to the southeast side of the zoo grounds where two structures anchored opposite ends of a large parking lot. The first, I remembered from when I was a kid. It was the majestic multi-paned St. Paul Conservatory—its center cupola rising over sixty feet skyward and measuring some one hundred feet in diameter. The other was newer. A six-sided bronze and brick pavilion stood there—its glass doors open wide. A crowd ringed the building—mostly parents wearing polo shirts and shorts, rings of white along the cuff lines accentuating wince-inducing sunburns. Beyond the photosensitive throng, the inside of the pavilion was blurry with motion.

"What's that?" I asked.

"That," Edgerton replied, "is bit of restored history."

"Huh?"

Ignoring me, he bent down to Ava saying, "It's a really special merry-go-round."

Ava beamed as Edgerton launched into the history of what he told us was the oldest carousel in continuous operation in the state. Built in 1914, it had become increasingly dilapidated until it was finally removed from its original location. Consigned to the auction block, where each of its hand-carved horses would have been sold individually to collectors, it was saved and ultimately restored by a community that refused to allow one of its cherished, childhood memories to be sold to strangers. For some years, the carousel was housed in a downtown shopping mall. Unfortunately, ridership there was abysmal and before long it was once again mothballed. But carousel aficionados are a pugnacious bunch and after a determined campaign, sufficient funding was raised to build a new home for the beleaguered merry-go-round at the zoo. Following the move to the zoo, Edgerton assured us, ridership had increased markedly.

As if to prove his point, there was a pretty long line when we got there. Edgerton said he would hold a place for me while I got the tickets. He insisted that I buy three of them—one each for him and Ava, and another for myself.

Not about to let me sit this out, he challenged, "How often do you have the opportunity to ride history?"

When I rejoined them, a middle-aged woman in white slacks and a blue polo shirt stepped forward with a microphone to describe the carousel and some of its main features. There were sixty-eight horses, she told us, each hand-painted to their original 1914 richness and no two alike. A Wurlitzer organ provided the music and the ride peaked at a respectable eight miles an hour. Edgerton listened attentively, while Ava gawked at the lights and the horses, and I checked out the admirable backside of a young mother in line in front of us. When a toddler blocked my view, I too began to examine the horses. Although the ride had not yet started, the horses already seemed to be in motion. All had their hooves in the air, some with heads reared back, others with their heads thrust determinedly forward, flashing bared teeth and fiery eyes as they raced toward the finish. The carving of each horse was intricately detailed. Some sported blankets with tassels and golden saddles, others animal skins, embossed shields, elaborate buckles and sashes. I had to agree with Edgerton. The restored carousel was pretty special.

Despite the number of people in line, we only had to wait through one ride cycle before it was our turn. The lady in the white slacks stepped forward to give her spiel again and then began taking tickets from the anxious patrons. We climbed aboard and Edgerton placed Ava on a horse directly behind the mom with the nice backside. Ava's smile was as bright as the lights that flashed all around us. Edgerton took his place beside her, but his attention was held more by the workmanship of the horses around him than our golden-haired charge. He was lightly fingering the horse next to him—a black and white pinto with a tiger skin instead of a saddle carved in relief across its back—when I cleared my throat and nodded at him.

"You gonna saddle up, pard?" I asked.

He shook his head. "Someone should stand next to Ava."

"I'll do it," I told him. "After all, how often do you get the chance to ride history?"

He shrugged but climbed onto the pinto's back with

a tiny, but appreciative smile. I stood next to Ava, shifting into a position from which I could keep an eye on both her and the attractive mother in front of us. A bell rang, the organ whirred to life, and the carousel moved smoothly forward.

As it began to take on speed, I had to grab onto Ava's horse to retain my balance. Before long the forward motion combined with the rising and falling of Ava's horse had me feeling a bit queasy. The faces of the people standing in the ring surrounding the twirling carousel became indistinct, blurring into one another. The flashing of cameras competed with the flashing of the lights mounted inside the carousel, all swirling and racing, leaving brilliant contrails in their wakes. The organ music was loud, but not loud enough to drown out the squeals of glee as the horses bobbed up and down and kids clutched onto their reins. I swallowed hard and patted Ava's leg. She looked down at me with eyes near bursting with delight. All at once I realized that it wasn't just queasiness that I was feeling. There was something else. Something peculiar. It took a moment for me to realize what it was. This might be something that Ava would carry with her. This moment, this fleeting instant in this child's life, might be something she'd remember. And if she did, perhaps the memory would include me.

I turned away and looked around at the other children. Aboard their racing steeds, those riding alone waved happily as they spotted Mommy, Daddy or Grandma waving at them from the crowd of spectators that ringed the perimeter. A voice from the crowd began to puncture the general din of elated shrieks and blaring organ music. I caught sight of a man standing alongside the carousel holding a .35 mm SLR with an almost comically long lens attached. He was yelling at someone named Bobby to look his way. But the kid, who I assume was his son, must have been too caught up in the excitement of the ride to pay him any heed. With each circle of the carousel, the man with the camera shouted, but no one turned toward him. As the ride went on, the man's frustration grew and soon his shouts became tinged with anger.

I tried to ignore him, returning my attention to Ava. Directly across from us, on the inside of the carousel, was a mirror ringed with small lights. I found that if I stood in a certain spot the mirror captured our reflection—an image of Ava and me together, sharing the moment.

But too quickly the moment was lost. The man with the camera continued to shout more insistently with each turn. The young mom I'd been admiring turned around with a wince. Her eyes met mine and her expression softened. There was a plea in her eyes that bade me do something about the belligerent photog. Ever chivalrous, I shot him one of my best glares as we passed, but if he noticed, he didn't care. When we came around again, I took a half step away from Ava's horse, my hand still resting on its blue-gray mane. I took a deep breath, prepared to tell him off but before I could, I caught a glimpse of a tall man with long, stringy blond hair wearing a ball cap standing nearby. Al Grogan, I realized.

Alarm crackled inside my skull. I scanned the crowd for his partner, Baldy, but I didn't spot him. As we circled back to where he was standing, Grogan raised his arm. Something glinted in his hand.

The mirror opposite us shattered before I heard the

gunshot. I pulled Ava down from her horse and forced her to the floor. It glittered with diamond shards of broken glass. I crawled to Edgerton's horse, reached up, and hauled him down as well. "Cover her!" I ordered.

"What the hell?" Edgerton exclaimed.

"Just do it!" I demanded, getting up into a crouch.

The rest of the riders hadn't reacted as quickly as I had, but by the time I'd made it to my feet a panic had set in. Hysterical parents aboard the carousel grabbed at their children as the spectators that ringed the outside of the ride surged forward to reach theirs. Both groups struggled for balance and space as the now seriously overcrowded merry-go-round continued to whirl. I pushed through, elbowing my way to the edge. I leapt from the carousel, stumbling when I hit the ground, turning my ankle slightly. It was painful, but I tried not to let it slow me down. I got into the open, pulled my revolver from my shoulder holster and broke into a trot, not knowing which direction to go, unable to spot Grogan. I'd made nearly a complete circuit around the pavilion when I thought to look behind me. Sure enough, there he was, gun in hand, chasing me.

Fear is a wonderful motivator and the sight of Grogan on my tail helped to dramatically pick up my speed. I cut to my right, raced into the adjacent parking lot, and took refuge behind a big, black SUV. Grogan saw me duck behind the truck and fired. His bullet first skipped across the truck's hood and pinged into the driver's side door of a blue sedan next to me. I heard a frightened scream. Behind the wheel, inside the sedan, a young woman was frantically grabbing at something in the seat behind her—a toddler helplessly strapped into a car seat.

Another bullet cracked into the SUV, this one shattering the windshield. Another anguished cry sounded from the sedan next to me. I had to get away from them.

Hampered by deepening pain in my ankle and a pinching from the wound in my side, I took off running across the parking lot, not bothering to get down low. I had to get Grogan to chase me. It's hard to hit a moving target while on the run. If he ran after me, I thought, I'd be okay. If he stopped and took careful aim, I was in trouble.

I sucked in air and ran for all I was worth. Halfway across the parking lot, nearing the Conservatory, I managed a quick glance behind me. Grogan was there, closing in fast. I raced for the nearest entrance to the Conservatory—an onion-shaped porch with double doors surrounded by a low wall that led to a wing attached to the center dome. I was about to hop the wall when I saw the sign. "Use Main Entrance," it read, "Emergency Exit Only."

Shit, the damn thing's gonna be locked. For an instant I thought about trying it anyway. Maybe if I knocked or something. But there was a guy with a gun chasing me and I really didn't have time to wait for somebody to happen by and let me in.

Instead, I cut to my left. Not a great move, I found. A tall wrought iron fence topped with ornamental spikes loomed before me. There was no way I was going to be able to get over that and I was forced to turn around and run back toward the parking lot to bypass it. When I turned, Grogan was directly in front of me, a crooked grin on his face. I stopped, planted my feet firmly, raised my gun with both hands, and fired.

My shot went wide, but a startled Grogan threw himself to the ground. He had the presence of mind, however, to raise his gun immediately and as he did, I took off again. I felt his bullet tug harmlessly at the sleeve of my jacket.

I raced along the fence back toward the zoo grounds, hoping to find some cover from which to ambush Grogan. To my right a formal flower garden blazed with color. In the center of the garden stood a sculpture of a running Indian brave, his faithful wolf companion striding beside him. Three white-haired old ladies also stood there, admiring the flowers as well as the scantily clad young warrior. I hurtled past them into the zoo.

I rounded a corner and ran into a sidewalk densely crowded with zoo patrons—elderly couples holding hands, young couples with tiny children in tow, and other figures that were merely a blur. I knew that I had to get out of there. I couldn't risk the lives of these people, but I couldn't go back the way that I'd come. My breath now came only in labored gasps and my heart thumped alarmingly in my chest. Streams of perspiration raced down from my hairline and the burning from the day-old wound in my side had re-ignited. I wasn't going to be able to keep it up much longer.

I took off again, scrambling through the crowd. Just before I reached the empty cages that fronted the main zoo building, I spotted an vacant patch of lawn that led back toward the Conservatory. I plunged toward it, turned a corner, and was elated to find a small wooden door that led into a windowless rear annex to the huge, glass structure. If only it was unlocked, I thought.

I tried the doorknob, but it wouldn't turn. I threw myself, shoulder first, into the door. There was a slight cracking sound, but the door didn't give. I took a step back and kicked hard directly beneath the doorknob. There was another cracking sound, this one louder than the first, but the door still didn't budge. I glanced behind me. Grogan was maybe twenty yards away, running hard. I booted the door again. The wooden doorframe splintered, and the door finally swung open.

Uselessly, I slammed the door behind me. I found myself in a darkened hallway. To my right, I could hear voices coming down another hallway that led to an adjacent room. To my left was a silent entryway. I raced through it as Grogan burst into the building behind me.

I was in a long, narrow room with frosted windows filled with a multitude of ferns. The air was thick with humidity and pungent with decay, making it even more difficult for my spent lungs to draw breath. There was a rough stone wall on my left and a wrought-iron fence to my right that separated me from a lower level. I turned toward the sound of water trickling and spotted a little grotto below me. It would have been a great spot from which to ambush my pursuer, but I didn't think I'd have the time to get down there. Instead, I raced ahead.

I emerged from the fern room through a set of double doors and into the main part of the Conservatory. Impossibly tall palm trees reached upward toward the magnificent glass dome. In the very center of the palms a circular fountain gurgled. Perched joyfully atop the fountain was a statue of a naked girl standing on one leg, one hand raised skyward, the other covering her small breasts. Several children crowded around the pool, tossing coins into the rippling water. Again, I glanced to my rear, through the glass of the fern room doors. Grogan was right behind me. I'd have a shot as he came through the doors, I thought. But I'd have to make it count. If he got a shot off and missed, he might hit one of the kids. No good, I decided. I'd have to keep going.

Not sure which way to go, I cut to the left, along the walkway, toward another set of doors. There a sign read "North Garden." I pulled open one of the doors and ran smack into an old lady. She was maybe five feet tall and despite the warmth of the day and the fact that she was visiting a greenhouse, she had a pearly beige sweater draped over her narrow shoulders. I had to grab her to keep her from going down. I mumbled an apology and ran past her down the flagstone walkway toward the rear of the rectangular room. There was a door down there that appeared to lead back outside.

Grogan came barreling in behind me. He, too, collided with the unfortunate grandma. As she cried out, I turned around and watched Grogan viciously push her to the ground. There was a stone bench next to where the woman had been standing and I hadn't noticed an elderly man in a wool suit with a wooden cane sitting there in the shade of a papaya tree. Before Grogan could continue after me, the old man calmly reached out with crook of the cane and hooked him by the ankle. Grogan fell face first with a sickening squish. Unfortunately, he fell too close to the prostrate old lady and I didn't trust my aim enough to take a shot. Then he looked up, saw me, and fired wildly. A windowpane behind me shattered. The old lady on the ground screamed and the old man let go of his cane and began to pull the woman away from Grogan. I took aim and shot Grogan in the shoulder. He yelped but managed to sit up, raising his gun. I heard the shot as I dove for cover behind the bulbous trunk of a nearby fig tree, splashing belly first into a pool that had been hidden from my view.

Startled by the cold water, I dropped my gun. I stood and, disbelieving, stared for a moment at my empty hand. Stooping, I desperately began to search the murky pool for my revolver. Something white and yellow flashed in the water beside me. I drew my hand back involuntarily. Something else, red and black, darted past. Goldfish, I realized.

Then there was a rustling in the brush in front of me. Grogan appeared, listing to one side, his shirt soaked in blood. He smiled through his pain as he took aim. To his left, I noticed another statue, the figure of a monk, standing at the water's edge. His hands were raised in supplication; his eyes strangely cold as if he knew his prayers were in vain. Exhausted and unarmed, I let my arms fall limp at my sides, closed my eyes, and waited to be shot.

Instead, there was a thud, like the hollow thump of a melon being tested for ripeness. My eyes snapped open. The old man was standing behind Grogan. He'd picked up his cane and had swung on Grogan, thwacking him hard on the back of the head. The gunman pitched forward into the water, scattering more fish as he splashed face down.

For a moment, all I could do was stare. Grogan lay with his face in the water, twitching convulsively, large bubbles rising to the surface around his head. I began to wade toward him but stopped when I heard the old man's raspy voice. "What was that on his arm?" he asked.

I looked up at the old man. He had a deeply lined face and deathly pale lips, but there was no emotion in his eyes.

"What?" I asked.

"On his arm. What was that? The tattoo?"

"A swastika," I told him.

"That's what I thought." Then he turned and leaning only slightly on his cane, walked slowly over to the bench where the old woman was now sitting.

I turned back to Grogan. The water was still around him; no more bubbles rising. I splashed toward him, rolled him over, and pulled his lifeless body out of the water and into a patch of sunshine beneath a pimento tree near the statue of the monk. I probably imagined it, but it seemed to me that the monk's eyes had warmed a little. His aspect seemed meeker, more grateful, as though he too had been the recipient of an unexpectedly answered prayer.

Chapter Twenty-two

Mickey Aronofsky had always been a lady's man. The fact that he was in his eighties had, perhaps, slowed him down a bit, but Mickey still lived for the hunt. Wilma Phelps was a widowed, retired nurse who had moved into the "assisted living community" where Mickey had been staying since the death of his spouse. It hadn't taken long for Wilma to catch his eye. Mickey invested several months carefully working toward a relationship with Wilma. He'd wasted countless hours pretending to enjoy putting together enormous jigsaw puzzles, watching bad daytime TV, and sitting through truly awful group sing-a-longs, all with the aim of impressing the widow Wilma.

He'd even joined a senior aerobics class—which he dubbed "Sweating with the Oldies"—hoping that she'd be impressed with his spry, octogenarian physique. And it was paying off too, he told me. When the retirement home organized a trip to the zoo, Wilma and Mickey sat next to each other in the bus holding hands. Once there, they'd stolen away from the group, ducking into the conservatory with an eye towards some major spooning. Then Grogan and I busted in on them.

"You know what pissed me off the most?" Mickey asked me as we sat together in St. Paul's Western Precinct house. "It was the goddamned tattoo. Sure, I was plenty steamed that you guys barged in just as I was

245

making my move, and I damn sure wasn't happy when that punk pushed Wilma to the ground, but you get old, you gotta take fewer chances. I probably would have just grabbed up Wilma and got out of there if it wasn't for the tattoo.

Mickey twisted absently at a plain gold band he wore on the ring finger of his left hand. "I've tried not to be one of them angry Jews, you know. I'm not exactly religious, so most of the time I don't think about it. I'm just a regular American. No more Jewish than you are Norwegian or Czech or whatever the heck your ancestors were. But there's always some schmo out there wants to make something out of it. I tell ya, when I was in the army it was the same way. Always some sonofabitch thinking he's too good to share a roof with you. But when you're deep in the bush in 'Nam. waiting in the heat and humidity with the bugs crawling and who knows what slithering past, waiting for some guy in black pajamas to rise up out of nowhere and blow your ass away…Well, when those bullets start flying, they don't stop to check was there a yarmulke under a guy's helmet. Them guys lying face down in the bush didn't have no religion. They didn't worry was the guy lying there next to them the wrong race. They were just dead."

Mickey cast a wistful glance across the room. "But you know, it's the same thing with the female sex. Most of the time it don't matter that a guy's a Jew but sometimes it does. I remember when I was kid growing up. Back in the forties. Once we got too old for the sandbox, some of the Gentile girls didn't want nothing to do with a Jewish boy. Others did. But it was the damnedest thing. They'd ask me to meet them in secret. Didn't amount to much, you understand. They'd maybe steal a kiss or two, not much more, though at that age I thought it was a pretty big deal. But most of them dropped me right quick and then wouldn't admit they'd seen me in the first place. It turned out they were just interested, you know. They'd heard these stories about Jews. Like, did we have tails and all that? We were supposed to be like the Devil's children or something. Guess that's what their folks told 'em. So, they'd check it out for themselves. They'd find out what they wanted to find out, then move on, find Gentile boyfriends, get married and go on to treat Jews the same as their asshole husbands did. But they'd have this secret, you know. They'd been…I don't know, *naughty* I guess you'd call it."

Mickey chuckled. "It was that way with Wilma, maybe. I could tell she was kinda interested but it was taking a lot of work. You'd think at our age that stuff wouldn't matter no more, but it does. It was looking like I'd got past all that with Wilma, though. 'Course, I'd know for sure if you fellas hadn't a ruined things for me back there in that greenhouse."

"I take it that Wilma isn't Jewish."

A shiver of suspicion passed over Mickey's features. "No, she isn't. That make any difference to you?"

"No, man. Sorry, I was just wondering. And I'm sorry that I busted in on you like that. But the guy *was* trying to kill me. Thanks for keeping him from doing that, by the way."

Mickey smiled slightly. "Don't sweat it, junior."

I smiled back. "Thanks for calling me 'junior.' I've been feeling kinda old lately."

Mickey snorted. "Just wait 'til you're in your

eighties. You don't know what old is yet."

"I don't know, it sounds like you're doing all right."

Mickey gave a little shrug. "Who was that guy, anyway?"

"The guy with the tattoo? Name's Grogan. He worked for a guy named Matty Beam. Beam's this führer wannabe who's been in the news lately."

"I've heard of him."

"Anyway, I pissed Beam off. And evidently, he's the sensitive type. Looks like he holds a grudge. I've been told he's got plenty more guys working for him. Grogan getting killed? Beam's most likely going to blame that on me. You're probably out of it. But I don't know for sure. You're going to want to keep an eye out."

Mickey smiled and tightened his grip on his cane until his bony fingers were absolutely bloodless. "Junior, if they come after me, it's them that need to look out."

Mickey got to go home before I did. The cops took my statement, then kept me waiting alone in a little, windowless interview room for several hours. At least they had to decency to leave me with a full pot of coffee and the answers to a couple of questions. Most importantly, they told me that no one except Grogan had been injured at the zoo. Stephen and Ava were fine, and a squad car had taken them home. One of the cops added that Ava had seemed pretty shaken up when they first saw her, but that she'd calmed down considerably before they'd sent her back to the Bijou. And even though they were pretty ticked off at me for being at least partially responsible for shooting up a St. Paul cultural icon, the cops were generous enough to share some of what they'd learned about the guy who'd tried to kill me.

Al Grogan had done hard time in Illinois for armed

robbery and had only been out for a couple of months. It seems that once he'd been released, he made a beeline for the Twin Cities and Matty Beam. The speculation was that that he'd buddied up with the clique of hardcore racists that exists in every prison population, and he'd got the word at the time of his release that Beam was looking for new members for his organization. The cops had a line on the guy I'd been calling Baldy, as well. His name was Harvey Deason, and he was listed as one of Grogan's "known associates."

Deason had served time with Grogan, but not for armed robbery. Deason, it turned out, was a pedophile. He'd been convicted of the kidnap and sexual molestation of an eight-year-old girl in a Chicago suburb. He was the chief suspect in several other incidents, but for reasons that the report didn't make clear, he'd not been charged in the others.

I'll admit that Deason being a sex offender surprised me a bit. He was the one who'd protected Ava from Grogan when the child had intervened on my behalf. I wouldn't have thought that someone who preyed on children would have bothered to protect her like that, but, thankfully, I've never been able to get inside the head of someone like Deason.

It was early evening before Augie Tarkof came by. He spoke at length with the St. Paul cops in charge of investigating Grogan's death, then only briefly with me. He asked me to go over the shooting with him but asked few questions. When I was finished, he ran a hand roughly over his straggly mustache, smiled unpleasantly, and asked if after two shootings in two days I was maybe considering an out-of-town vacation.

"I appreciate the concern, Augie, But I think I better

stick around here. I'd kinda like to see what I can do about getting these guys to stop trying to kill me."

Tarkof nodded. "Sticking around's the surest way to get them to stop trying. They won't have to keep at it after they succeed."

"Your faith in me is overwhelming."

He shrugged. "I talked to the Apple Valley cops. They searched the homes of those two guys you shot. Segulia and Hollenbeck? They found two knives in the Hollenbeck kid's garage. They were wiped clean, so no prints, but they look to be good for the Walsh murder."

"Just two knives?"

"Yeah."

"Any sign of the third?"

Tarkof shook his head. "We searched like three blocks around the crime scene. Didn't come up with it. After that incident at the Walsh home, the cops were able to give that a good looking over as well. Nothing." He paused. "Maybe the Walsh kid was the only one with sense enough not to keep a souvenir."

"If I get anything, Augie, anything at all that leads to Tyler Walsh having killed his father, I'll wrap the little bastard up in it and bring him to you personally."

"I thought you were working for him," Tarkof said.

"I'm working for his dad."

Tarkof paused again, pretending to look around the small interview room. "So, who's the kid?"

"The kid?"

"Yeah, the little girl."

I blinked. "It's a friend's kid. She's out of town. Stephen and I are babysitting."

Tarkof's eyes narrowed. "Not the greatest time for anybody to be hanging out with you. When's this friend coming back?"

"Any time now," I lied.

"This kid got someone else, some family or something, she could stay with?"

"Not really."

"Find someone."

"I'll do that, Augie. I really will."

"Good. In the meantime, watch your ass."

"I'll do that too."

After he'd gone, the St. Paul cops announced that they were ready to let me go. But they weren't gonna make watching my ass any easier on me. When I approached the desk sergeant and asked for my gun, he told me they'd be keeping it until they concluded their investigation.

"But the Apple Valley cops have my other piece," I whined. "If you keep the .38, all I got is a teeny, little .22. Come on, there are bad guys after me."

The sarge shook his head. "Look at this as an opportunity, Dahms. Maybe it's time to reevaluate your line of work."

"You haven't been talking with my dad, have you?"

The sergeant waved me away.

I caught a bus back to the zoo parking lot where I'd left my car and, for the second day in a row, night was falling as I got home. A chorus of crickets had begun their lazy chirping, undercut occasionally by the piercing rasp of an insistent grasshopper. A bright, three-quarter moon hung low in the sky and Stephen and Ava were sitting on the front steps. As I got out of the car, a low, white blur streaked across the lawn toward me. The dog leapt as he reached me, hurtling himself, front paws extended, at my chest. Unfortunately, he was unable to get the necessary altitude and instead of my chest he banged hard into my upper thighs.

"Jeez, Stephen," I said, straightening up. "That smarts. If that dog had hit me any higher, you'd have had to call for a medevac unit. Can't you keep this mutt on a leash?"

"He's not a mutt," Edgerton replied. "Besides, I have him under voice command."

"Voice command?"

"Sure."

"Color me doubtful."

"Hey, I'm not the one with dog issues," Edgerton said, lightly smacking his forearm. "But if you want, we can bring him in. The mosquitoes are getting bad anyway."

"More moon, Stephen?" Ava implored.

"It'll be back tomorrow night, sweetie," Edgerton told her. "I don't want you to get bit up."

"Just a little more moon?"

"What's going on?" I asked, taking a seat on the steps beside them. "You showing Ava the man in the moon?"

Ava stared at me.

"Actually," Edgerton said, "I was explaining lunar maria." He turned toward Ava. "Remember what I told you, honey? Why are there smooth places on the surface of the moon?"

Ava perked up. "Really hot rock cooled off all smooth."

Edgerton hugged her lightly. "That's right, molten rock solidified on the moon's surface between three and four billion years ago. Now where did the moon come from?"

Ava's face scrunched up. "They don't know," she replied timidly.

Edgerton beamed. "That's right. There are several competing theories, but scientists just don't know for sure."

Ava puffed up with pride.

Basil, who'd gone off sniffing behind some bushes, suddenly felt a need for company. He abruptly rushed toward the steps, bypassed Edgerton and Ava, and climbed into my lap where he made loud smacking noises into my face and tried desperately to slip his tongue into my mouth.

"Eeww!" I exclaimed, grasping the dog's head with both hands to fend off his affectionate assault. "He's got some kind of puppy breath."

Ava giggled and reached over to stroke the dog. Then she looked at me and her expression clouded immediately over. "You knocked me down," she said. There was awful accusation in her voice.

It took me a moment to remember. "I'm sorry kid," I told her. "I had to pull you off that horse. Bad things were happening. I didn't want you to get hurt. I was trying to protect you."

"I know," she said. "Stephen told me."

"Then do you forgive me?"

She didn't reply, but she did reach up and pat me lightly on the arm.

"Come on," Edgerton said. "Let's get inside. It's time for a little girl I know to brush her teeth."

Ava smiled brightly at me. "Yeah. Gotta brush my teeth. I got puppy breath."

I went to my room while Edgerton went about getting Ava ready for bed. I left my door open in case they needed anything from me, grabbed a cold bottle of beer, and went over to open the window on the far side of the room. My room had become so overcrowded with dog and kid paraphernalia I could barely get to it. I got the window open, then sat down at my desk, leaned back in my chair, and closed my eyes. Before long I heard footsteps descending the stairs and Ava's tiny voice called, "Goodnight, Lyle," from out in the hall. I wished her goodnight but didn't bother to get out of the chair. I was fantastically, otherworldly, tired.

From Edgerton's room, I soon heard Ava softly saying her bedtime prayers. I had to smile. As an avowed atheist, you'd have thought that Edgerton might have a problem with prayers issued from within his sanctum sanctorum. But there he was, in his own room, watching over a three-year-old as she murmured prayers to his enemy god.

Like most children's prayers, Ava's sounded like something she'd been taught to recite from memory—an unchanging speech that could be repeated nightly without thought. "Now I lay me down to sleep. I pray the Lord my soul to keep. May angels watch me through the night and wake me with the morning light." Then she paused and I heard a little sigh before she resumed. "God bless Mommy and make her come home soon. And God bless Grandma and Grandpa and all my relatives and…and God, bless Stephen and Lyle for making me safe. Amen."

I couldn't remember anyone praying for me by name before. It made me flush. I felt warm and protected. It felt like an embrace. I heard the door to Edgerton's room close and suddenly Basil bounded into mine. The dog was in my lap as I opened my eyes and Edgerton came in. "I know you had another rough day, but it would be best if the dog could sleep in here with you. He's started this licking thing at night. It can get pretty loud. I don't want him to wake up the kid."

"That's mighty considerate of you, Stephen."

He smirked. "Well, it doesn't look like there's much chance he'll keep you up. You're a wreck."

"Yeah, I got to get some sleep. I'm too tired tonight, but tomorrow…Tomorrow, we'll have to talk."

"About what?" he asked, avoiding my glance.

"I think you know."

Edgerton shook his head.

"She can't stay any longer. You know that. We're going to have to find someplace for her. I talked to her aunt. She's too old to take her herself, but she said she might know some people at her temple. She said—"

"You shopping around behind my back, Lyle?" Edgerton asked. His tone was sharp with betrayal.

"She's the kid's family, Stephen. She's got a say."

"The kid's mom left her here."

"Come on, Stephen, it's over. You know it. She's not safe anymore. She's not safe around *me*. Hell, neither are you. People keep trying to kill me. *I've* killed three people in two days. This is the worst place for her, and you know it."

Edgerton's eyes went wide. "Then *you* leave!" he shouted. "They're after you, not her."

It was as though he'd stabbed me with an icicle. He was right. I had no business in the house. Not after what had happened at the zoo. But it simply hadn't occurred to me that I shouldn't go home. I was overtired, not thinking, and making mistakes. Potentially big mistakes. Not a good situation, I thought.

"Shit," I said. "You're right. I'll get out of here. I'll crash somewhere else. But that doesn't solve the problem. They know where I live. They take a run at me, and it might not matter whether I'm here. They shoot up the house, no one's safe."

"We'll all go, then. You go wherever you're going. I'll pack up Ava. I'm sure Max and Vicki will take us in."

"That's really not a solution, Stephen."

"Listen to yourself, Lyle. You just tell me that we're all in danger and all you do is keep carping about giving the kid away. Our immediate concern is tonight. Tomorrow will take care of itself."

Edgerton stormed from the room without another word. I was too tired to argue further. Instead, I started to toss a few necessities in a gym bag and tried to think of a place where I could stay. Naomi and I were having too many problems and, besides, if someone was going to come after me, the last place I wanted to be was with her. I couldn't go to my parents for the same reason. A motel looked like my only option. I'd become too much of a danger to be close to anyone I cared about.

I took my little .22 out of the lock box, loaded it, and put some additional ammunition into the gym bag with my undies and shaving stuff. I went to the closet to find the ankle holster that I usually use for the .22, but the closet was a mess and my eyes kept threatening to bang shut, so I gave up without much of an effort. Instead, I slipped the gun into a pocket of my windbreaker and tossed the coat on my bed next to the gym bag. I grabbed an extra pair of jeans and a couple of T-shirts and was zipping up the bag when Basil let out a little yelp and hopped away from in front of the window where he'd been laying.

Although that side of the room was mostly dark, I thought I caught a glimpse of movement outside the window. Startled, I ducked down low and peeped at the window. The curtain waved lazily in a light breeze that was blowing into the room. I stared for several moments until I convinced myself that nothing was wrong.

Turning around, I chastised the dog. "Jeez, it's just the wind."

A noise sounded down the hall from Edgerton's room. Basil barked and I went into the hall to see what the matter was. Hearing nothing further, I stepped back into my room. That's when I saw the guy by the window. He was in shadow, but I could tell that he was big, had a shaved head, and was carrying what looked like a shotgun with a shortened barrel. I didn't stop to drink in all the details. Instead, I dropped to the ground and rolled out of the way as the gunman directed both barrels at where I'd been standing. The blast in the small room was deafening.

I got my feet under me and threw myself headfirst toward the gunman. He saw me coming and managed to clip me on the side of the head with the stock of the gun as I plowed into his midsection. The blow dizzied me a bit, but I distinctly heard the *whoosh* of the gunman's breath rushing from his lungs. Before he had a chance to suck in air, I drove a hard right into his belly, just beneath his ribcage. As he doubled over, I grabbed his sandpaper skull with both hands and drove it into my upraised knee. I lifted his head, stared for an instant into his vacant eyes, and rammed his head into my knee again. I pushed him backwards, grabbing hold of the shotgun as he fell, wrenching it from his hands. The man spilled out onto the floor with a groan. I hit him squarely in the head with the gunstock and he stopped moaning.

Edgerton's panicked voice sounded in the hallway. "Dahms! Are you all right in there!"

He appeared at my door, his eyes darting from my face to the shotgun in my hand, then to the opposite end of the room where my would-be assassin lay still on the floor. He opened his mouth to speak, but no words came forth.

"Okay!" I roared. "Now, I'm pissed!

Chapter Twenty-three

Max and Vicki Wiseman were happy to take in Edgerton and Ava, but Vicki drew the line at the dog. So, Basil was in the car with me when I pulled up in front of my parents' house about ten o'clock the next morning. I took a long look up and down the street. I was pretty sure no one had followed me, and I didn't see any bad guys lying in wait. Still, I knew that being there at all was risky and I shouldn't have come, but I really needed something, and I'd decided to chance it.

A gentle rain had begun to fall, and Basil seemed a bit skittish when I clipped the leash to his collar and tried to lead him to the house. He'd take a few steps, then stop to look up at me with blame-filled eyes, holding me responsible for the rain.

When we finally got to the door, I was feeling a little skittish myself. The recent attempts on my life had been all over the news and I knew that if my mom had heard about them, she'd be pretty worried.

I took another look up and down the street and into the bushes that fronted the house. I couldn't help but notice that the lawn hadn't yet been mowed, and although my father had always been an early riser, the morning paper was still lying on the front steps. I picked up the paper and rang the doorbell again.

"Oh my God, Lyle, are you all right!" my mom shrieked as she opened the door. "I heard all about it on

259

the news this morning. I tried to call but you didn't pick up your cell phone and there was no answer at your apartment."

I stepped into the entryway. "It's not an apartment," I grumbled. "It's a room. And anyway, I'm not sure I live there anymore."

Mom stared at me for a moment, not sure how to respond. "Well, I'm certainly glad you came to us," she said finally, her expression brightening. "I can have your old room ready in just a few minutes. I've got my sewing stuff in there right now, but it won't take me any time to get it all straightened up for you. There's coffee in the kitchen. You get yourself a cup. Have you had breakfast? Your dad hasn't eaten yet either. I'll make extra. I've got some lovely ruby red grapefruit. They're from Texas. And I've got eggs, maybe some sausage, and I could make—"

"I won't be staying, Mom," I interrupted. "I just came to—"

"Won't be staying? Nonsense. I won't hear that. Tell you what, let's put breakfast on hold for a couple of minutes. I'll just go get the room ready. Say, who's this little guy?"

I glanced down at the dog. "That's Basil. Didn't I tell you about him?"

"No, but that's fine. He'll be needing a place to stay too, won't he? It's been quite a while since we've had a dog around here. Remember Champy? Back when you and your brother were just little? He never did come back. I kept hoping, but some things just aren't meant to be, are they?"

"I'd appreciate your looking after the dog, Mom. But I can't stay. It's just not safe."

"Safe? Your own home's not safe? Since when is it not safe?"

"Since people started trying to kill me, Mom. It's not safe to be around me right now. I just came by to ask Dad for something. How is he, anyway?"

Her eyes darted to the interior of the house. "Ornery as ever. What'dya expect?"

"Nothing less. Can I talk to him?"

Mom hesitated. "I'm not sure he's up yet. He's been a little tired lately. He's not sleeping much in the nights."

"It's kinda important."

She smiled. "Well, let's go check, then, shall we? If he's not up, you and I can have a nice cup of coffee while we wait. Come on in. I'll go check on your father. There's coffee brewed in the kitchen. Pour us a couple of cups, okay, honey?"

I unclipped Basil from the leash, and he bounded inside, nose to the ground. I tucked the newspaper under my arm and went into the kitchen to pour two large mugs of coffee. I carried the coffee into the living room, set them down, and paced around looking at the newspaper headlines. A blurb on the front page read "Participant in Carousel Shootout Finds Intruder in Room." At least I made the front page.

I rolled up the paper and crossed the room to Dad's gun cabinet. I was taking inventory when he entered the room. "I hear I'm supposed to watch your dog now," he said.

"For a couple of days. If you don't mind."

He nodded. "That my paper?"

I crossed the room and handed it to him. "One of those mine?" he asked, pointing at the coffee mugs.

I shrugged.

He picked up one of the mugs, carried it over to his recliner and slowly eased himself into the chair. The effort registered alarmingly on his face. The dog went over to sniff at his ankles, but wisely did not attempt to jump into his lap.

"How you feeling, Dad?"

He squinted at me. An icy shimmer passed over his blue-gray eyes, like a ribbon of wind-blown snow rippling across a frozen lake. "Just fuckin' peachy."

"You look like you're in some pain."

He smirked. "My son the detective."

I started to respond, but he interrupted. "It's what they call 'referred pain'. Hurts all over. They gave me some pills."

"What else they planning to do? Besides the pills, I mean."

He lowered his eyes and stared at the paper for quite a while before answering. "Starting both radiation and chemo next week."

"Yeah?"

"Yeah. They say they need to shrink the tumor before they go in after it."

"They say that works pretty good?"

Dad fussed with the paper a bit. "They got whole teams working overtime blowing sunshine up my ass. Anytime anybody mentions anything even remotely negative, they spend the next twenty minutes telling me about the wonderful success rate they have with all this shit they want to do to me. Don't want me to get depressed, I guess."

"What kind of negatives we talking here?"

He looked up and flashed a mirthless grin. "Well, I could die."

"There's that."

He looked back down at the paper. "The therapies are gonna wipe me out. There's gonna be pain. With surgery there's even more pain and the possibility that they'll have to do a colostomy. Oh, and it might make me impotent. So, worst case scenario, I'm dead. If I'm lucky, I do my business into a plastic bag and I can't get it up."

"They say the surgery will absolutely result in this colostomy and impotence?"

"Shit no. Like I said, they tell you the risks and then insist it probably won't happen to you."

"So, cheery fellow that you are, you figure there's no sense hoping for the best when you can get right down to expecting the worst."

"What I always tell ya, Lyle? You expect the worst, you're never disappointed. And there's always the chance of being pleasantly surprised."

I grunted.

Dad continued to leaf through his paper. When he returned to the front page, I studied him, wondering if he might register something as he scanned the article about me. He didn't seem to. After a few minutes, he set the newspaper on his lap and looked up at me. "You didn't come by here just to check on me, did you, son?"

"Not really, no. I need a favor."

"No shit."

"What do you mean?"

He tapped a finger against the newspaper on his lap. "I mean, I told you not to go on pissing off this Beam guy and the next thing I know you nearly get yourself killed."

I shrugged. "Things happened."

"No shit," Dad repeated. "Says here you left one of them alive."

"The one that broke into my room yesterday. He's in custody. Name's Simpkins. Cops say they got a file on him. Say he's part of Beam's organization."

"He rat out Beam?"

"So far he's relying on his constitutionally protected right to keep his mouth shut."

Dad winced and stared off toward the front doorway. "He'll start bragging soon enough. They all do. So, what's this favor?"

I motioned toward the gun cabinet in the opposite corner. "The Apple Valley cops got my new 9mm and the St. Paul cops got my .38. My backup .22 is back at my place. Be a couple days before I can get at it. My room's a crime scene."

Dad nodded. "They come at you again, that .22's not gonna do the job anyway."

"That's what I was thinking."

"So, you figured you'd come by here and load up on firepower?"

"That and ditch the dog. Yeah."

"Bad idea, son."

"You'll get used to Basil. He grows on you."

"You remember what I told you about how the Apple Valley PD's been checking out reports that these guys are stockpiling weapons?"

"You also told me that they tossed Beam's place and didn't find any."

"That where you thinking of going?"

I shrugged.

"Bad idea, son," he said again. "Guys like this always got a piece on them."

I grinned. "I know. It's so cliched."

Dad ignored me. "Tell you what. You crash with us for a few days. I'll talk to the cops out here and get them to put the squeeze on Beam and his outfit. They're probably doing that anyway. We can get them to keep a close eye on the house here too. If these guys take another run at you, they'll run into a wall of blue. Between the job and the two of us, we should be able to either get this guy to back off or maybe shut him down completely. Beats the hell out of you going off playing the Lone Stranger."

I shook my head. "Can't do it, Dad. If these guys decide to take another run at me, I can't let it happen here. You and Mom might get hurt."

Dad didn't like anyone suggesting that he couldn't handle any situation he found himself in. He particularly didn't like hearing it from me. His eyes smoldered as he stared at me. I kept my eyes fixed on him, careful not to allow any emotion to register, equally careful not to look away. We kept up the standoff for a few uncomfortable seconds.

Finally, Dad closed his eyes. "Yeah," he said, "maybe you're right. Better send your mom off for a few days. She and your Aunt Agnes have been making noise about going someplace up in Northern Wisconsin. What's the name of that place? Bayfield? Supposed to be the gateway to the Apostle Islands. Like that's some big deal selling point. Anyway, they been wanting me to drive them up there, but you gotta know there's no way I'm going. Could probably talk Aggie into taking your mom up there, though."

I shook my head again. "No way I can stay, Dad. You've got enough to worry about. You'd be at too much risk."

"I can take care of myself, boy." He raised a balled-up fist. "Take care of you too, if you catch my drift."

I smiled. "Any other time, I'd agree with you, Dad. But not this week. Not with radiation and the chemotherapy. You wouldn't be at the top of your game."

"I'll be fine," he growled. "Besides, they'll come here anyway. Don't matter if you're here or not, if they're looking for you, they'll look for you here."

"I was thinking maybe I'd save them the trouble of looking. I know where they are. I know where Beam is, anyway. I figured I'd pay him a visit."

Dad shook his head. "You gotta know the cops are talking with him. No reason for you to stick your nose into their business."

"It's *my* business, Dad. These guys tried to kill me."

"And they did a damn sloppy job of it, too. The cops aren't gonna have any problem putting these guys away. They've been making too many mistakes. You sit tight, you'll be out of this in no time."

"You expect me to just sit it out? Is that what you'd do?"

"Yeah. That's what I'd do."

I forced a chuckle. "And all those stories you told us growing up? About how when you were on the force and somebody or other would get out of line, how you'd make damn sure they never mess with a cop again?"

"That was different. That's part of the job. If you don't respect the man, you still respect the uniform. That's how it works. You ain't no cop."

"Bullshit, Dad. You and I know better. You being a cop might have made it easier, but if you'd been a garbage man or the guy who mans the Slurpee machine at the 7-11 it wouldn't have made any difference. If someone fucks with you, you fuck 'em back. That's maybe the only lesson you bothered to teach me growing up."

Dad rose from his chair. He tried mightily, but he couldn't keep the pain from contorting his face. "I can't help it if you didn't bother to listen. It's not my fault that you always had to have things your way. You wouldn't be in this mess if you'd have done things the way I wanted you to do them."

"How do figure that?"

"You'd have backup, dufus. If you'd a joined the cops like I wanted, you'd have a big, blue shield around you. There wouldn't be anybody trying to take you out. You and I wouldn't be sitting here discussing sending your mom out of harm's way."

"Well, sorry to disappoint you again, Dad. I guess if one of these assholes puts a bullet in me, you can always say that you were right. I got what I deserve for not doing what Ray Dahms told me to do."

Silence silted down around us. I heard the soft sounds of my mom moving around in the back of the house. She'd have been listening, I thought. Never mind. It's nothing she hadn't heard before. Finally, Dad sighed and shuffled across the room toward me. I flinched a little as he passed me on his way to the gun cabinet. Wincing, he reached up high and patted around on top of the cabinet until he found the key. He unlocked it and let the doors swing open wide.

He turned to face me and frowned. "You talk to Naomi about any of this? She's gotta be worried."

"I called her from the station first thing this

morning. I think she's more pissed than worried."

He nodded. "She's worried. She might not be showing it, but she's worried. Everybody shows it in a different way." He turned toward the gun cabinet. "I think you're being a damned fool, but if you want to borrow something, go on ahead."

I reached in and removed the .38.

"My old service revolver? Don't you want something with a little more firepower?"

"It's what I'm used to, Dad. Might as well take that .22, as well."

He nodded. "Okay, but you gotta take a look at this."

He opened a wide drawer fitted beneath the main part of the cabinet. Inside was a hard, black case, about a foot long, trimmed in silver. He opened the case slowly.

"Jesus Christ!"

A soft light seemed to flash momentarily in my father's eyes. "Ever use one of these bad boys?"

"What'dya get that for? You going elephant hunting this summer?"

He coughed up a chuckle, reached into the case, and brought out the biggest pistol I'd ever laid eyes on.

"It's a Mark XIX Desert Eagle," he said. "A .357 Magnum with a six-inch barrel. Holds nine rounds. They make 'em bigger. Almost went with the .50 A.E with a ten-inch barrel, but you gotta hold the line somewhere. Besides, this thing'll bring down anybody or anything I'd be likely to run into out here."

I held the heavy gun loosely in my hand. "You could take out a bull rhino high on angel dust with this thing."

I studied his face again. His expression hadn't exactly softened, but there was less iron in his eyes. "You shoulda heard the trouble your mom gave me over my buying it. But in the end, I just had to have it."

"A man's gotta do," I said.

"So, do you want it?"

I shook my head. "Bit showy for me."

"That's sorta the point, Lyle. You pull out something like this and most guys get to wishing they were carrying a roll of Charmin. Go on, take it with you."

"Just the .38, thanks. Oh, and if you've a holster for it as well…"

The disappointment in his face surprised me. "Suit yourself, son," he said, his voice becoming abrasive. He took the weapon from me and returned it to its case. "It's just as well. I don't think you'll be needing it. Nor the .38 neither. Like I said, the cops'll handle this thing for you. You're probably best just going off and smoothing things over with your girlfriend."

I bristled. "You telling me to go hide with the womenfolk until this mess blows over?"

"That's not what I meant, and you know it. But hell, believe what you want." He didn't say anything further. He just locked the gun away, crossed the room, lowered himself into his recliner, and resumed reading his paper.

I gave the dog one last stroke behind the ear and hurried out of there before my mom had a chance to stop me. I had quite a few things to do. I was definitely going to have to talk with Tyler Walsh. But first, I had to do something about Matty Beam.

Chapter Twenty-four

I don't know what I was expecting. I knew Beam lived in his parents' house in Apple Valley, but I'd imagined the place would be some barbed-wire-encircled compound and guarded by brown-shirted security and snarling rottweilers.

Instead, the Beam home was a split-entry with sea-foam green vinyl siding edged by junipers, barberry, and a couple of stunted lilacs. Overall, I thought, it was not unlike Mavis Kleiner's home only a couple of miles away. There was an unmarked police car parked across the street, but that was the only sign that marked this as different from any other house in the neighborhood.

The rain continued to fall lightly, more of a drizzle really, but enough that cops had to clear their windshield with a lazy swipe of the wipers as I got out of my car. They stiffened as I approached the house but didn't try to keep me from ringing the doorbell.

The weight of my dad's .38 nestled under my arm helped assuage the heavy feeling of dread that sank into my belly as the door opened and I faced my old friend Baldy, a.k.a. Harvey Deason. It was the first time I'd seen him since he and the late Albert Grogan beat me down outside my office. Deason seemed even larger than he had before.

Deason didn't say anything, but his eyes slitted and through them I could just make out a shimmer like water on the verge of boiling. He knotted his hands into fists and stared down at me for some seconds before Beam's voice called out. "Harvey! Be polite. Invite our guest in to join us."

Deason slowly removed his bulk from the entrance, and I peered inside. From the upper level of the house three more men stared down at me. Two of them were the guys with the pool cues from the other day at Sully's—Dark Eyes and Hickey. The other guy I didn't recognize.

"Come on up, Dahms," Beam insisted. "I got a beer if you want one."

I stepped into the entryway and tried not to react when I heard the bolt lock behind me. "Bit early for me, thanks," I said to my still unseen host.

"Come on," he urged, "it's after noon *somewhere*."

I made my way up the stairs. When I got to the top, the men stood their ground, refusing to allow me passage. We stared at each other for a moment before they parted just enough to let me pass.

On one side of the room, Beam sat in a leather-upholstered recliner, a can of beer in his hand. Opposite the recliner was a sofa with what looked like a brown corduroy bedspread tucked into its contours serving as a slipcover. A stack of brightly colored pamphlets spilled across the coffee table facing it. Several beer cans surrounded the pamphlets. A couple of the empties lay on their sides. Beam was wearing a solid navy-blue dress shirt and a pair of khakis. Around his paunchy midsection, the buttons gaped, revealing a stark white undershirt.

"Nice that Mommy and Daddy let you have so many playmates over, Matty," I said. "Are they around? Your parents, I mean. I'd love to meet 'em."

"Sorry, Dahms," Beam said. "They're on vacation. Maybe some other time."

They let me take one more step before they moved in on me. Deason and Dark Eyes each grabbed an arm, while old Hickey unzipped my jacket and removed the gun from under my arm. Keeping my dad's gun in his right hand, he drove his left into my midsection. I doubled over and watched a few of droplets of spit sail toward the middle of the room as my breath whooshed from me. Then they tossed me into a seated position on the sofa.

Beam smiled. It was a thin smile. "So, what is it you came here for, Dahms?" he asked. "You brought a gun. You didn't come here to hurt us, did you? I mean, we're not going to have to defend ourselves, are we? 'Cause that would be a damned shame."

It took another moment for me to be able to draw a deep enough breath, but finally I was able to croak out, "I came to end this thing between us."

Judging from their laughter, this was the single funniest thing any of them had ever heard. Hickey laughed so hard I swear he pulled something.

"Now, I'm going to have to ask you to stop talking like that," Beam said. "Folks'll get the wrong idea about us."

When this brought renewed peals of laughter from his men, Beam stopped laughing, shifted in his chair, and exchanged a significant glance with Deason. Deason pointed at Dark Eyes and the guy I didn't know, and they immediately moved into flanking positions on either side of Beam. Deason and Hickey moved to opposite sides of me.

"The cops got you staked out," I said, trying to sound dispassionate. "They saw me come in here. Might look a bit suspicious if I don't come back out."

Beam chuckled. "You afraid maybe you walked into something you won't be able to get out of?"

"I wouldn't say *afraid*, Matty."

Beam smiled his tight little smile. "A man of less limited intelligence would likely admit that he's afraid. That man might realize that the cops outside offer no protection against someone coming in here with a gun. If you end up injured or, God forbid, killed…Well, a man's gotta protect his home."

I shrugged. "You know, Matty, speaking of protection, I wouldn't count too much on your boys here protecting you. Let's face it, you've sent guys like this after me more than once. They haven't exactly been models of success."

Dark Eyes took a step toward me, but Beam waggled a finger at him, and he stepped back. "I read about your troubles," Beam said, "but they've nothing to do with me. Neither myself nor anyone from my church sent anyone after you. Our church was established to promote brotherhood. Violence, except in the case of self-defense, is not something that we condone."

I picked up one of the pamphlets from the coffee table in front of me. It was the same one I'd found at the Empire Room. "This you promoting brotherhood, Matty?"

"I wouldn't expect you to understand."

"You're a preacher. Enlighten me."

Beam stared at me for a moment, then leaned back in his chair. "We promote the brotherhood of the white race," he said, his voice taking on a professorial air. "We seek to heal the fractures that have riven us. To mend the damage done to us by outside forces that seek to maintain their stranglehold on true democracy."

"Uh huh."

Beam went on. "It is a travesty and a tragedy that a country that once shone like a beacon to the entire world has been corrupted by an avaricious, power-hungry minority that renders the common man a mere slave in the land that his forefathers purchased at the cost of their blood, toil, and tears."

"Golly, Matty. That's pretty neat the way you said all that in one breath. Do you practice in front of the mirror?"

Beam leaned forward in his chair. "The truth is hate to those who hate the truth," he declared.

"Hey, that's good too. Now I've got one for you—*I slit a sheet. A sheet I slit. Upon a slitted sheet I sit*. Feel free to use it if you'd like."

"Scoff if you want, Dahms. But the truth of how our government, in league with the Jews, has disenfranchised and systematically denied the white majority of this country their birthright is not something that I find amusing."

"So, you're uh…you're taking steps?

"Yes."

"But you're not advocating violence?"

"Certainly not. But we are ever mindful of our duty to practice Christian forgiveness to our over-zealous brethren."

I laughed. "Now there you go getting all lawyerly on me, Matty. You send your guys out to do your dirty work. They can die, go to jail, whatever, and you get to just sit here knocking back brewskies and forgiving them for their over-zealous behavior. That's real smart. Wussy, but smart. Unless, of course, they turn on you. You gotta ask yourself how much you can count on the loyalty of a bunch of thieves and pedophiles."

Deason visibly tensed at the word "pedophile."

"We've a strong bond, Dahms," Beam told me. "We stand together. We stand *for* something. That's a rare thing in this world. Something maybe you wouldn't understand."

"That guy in my room last night. Simpkins? He one of those people standing with you?"

Beam nodded. "He's someone who has visited us from time to time, yes."

"So, you'll be bustin' your ass forgiving him, but you're not about to take responsibility for his trying to kill me?"

"Honestly, why would I bother with trying to have you killed?"

"I don't know, Matty. How 'bout, the fact I'm trying to nail you for Walsh's murder?"

Beam smirked. "I'm not exactly staying up at night worried about your investigatory prowess."

"Okay, then, how 'bout payback for Segulia and Hollenbeck?"

"I'll admit that their deaths distress me. But equally distressing is the notion that you—and, more importantly, the police—would believe me stupid enough to send those two after the Walshes."

"We sorta figure you were trying to clean up the loose ends left over from your first bonehead move—killing Greg Walsh."

Beam grunted. "Sorry to disappoint, but there is simply no connection between myself and the late Mr.

Walsh."

"There's Tyler."

"Come again."

"Tyler Walsh. He'd joined you over here on the dark side, hadn't he?"

Beam shrugged. "Tyler had expressed some desire to seek the truth, yes. But, although an invitation had been extended for him to join us, he had yet to begin attending services."

"Uh huh. I suppose you're going to deny that you ever contacted Greg Walsh about his son's conversion to your whole whiteness *über alles* fantasy?"

"Why would I have done that?

"I can think of ten thousand reasons."

Living at home, I figured Beam had logged a lot of TV time and had turned into a pretty fair actor. He did seem *perplexed* as well as anybody I've ever seen. His eyes crinkled, his forehead furrowed, and his head began to shake slightly but rapidly from side to side, as though he'd suddenly contracted Parkinson's.

"Ten thousand *dollars*," I explained. "That's how much money Greg Walsh withdrew from his personal account in the days before his death. No one's been able to say what he needed it for or what he spent it on. But you know what I think? I think he gave it to you."

Beam smiled. "And why would Mr. Walsh want to endow us with such a sum?"

"To buy his kid out from under your clutches."

Beam snickered. "Now that's a fantasy."

"I agree," I told him. "It was a fantasy. But Greg was desperate. When you approached him with the proposal, I'll bet he jumped at it. You probably could have gotten more. You maybe even planned to touch him again later.

That would have been smart. Much smarter than killing him."

"I really must hand it to you, Dahms. You've quite the imagination. But really, you're doing your friend a disservice. By focusing your efforts on me, you and the police are allowing the real killers to get away. I neither blackmailed nor killed Greg Walsh. I know nothing about this supposed ten thousand dollars."

"You gonna deny knowing Albert Grogan, too? That'd be pretty harsh. The guy gets killed doing a job for you and you just shrug and ask, 'Al Who?'"

All four of Beam's men stirred, grunting, shuffling, and flexing. "Al was a dear friend," Beam assured me. "And his death is something that we will address in time."

"Well, that's good to hear," I said. "But, you know, now I'm confused. I got a witness that can testify that your good friend Grogan met with Greg Walsh at your other pal Sully's roadhouse. This was just days before Walsh was murdered. The cops are wondering what brought those two together. Probably wasn't the pie."

Beam went into his perplexed act again, this time throwing in an inquisitive glance at Harvey Deason. For his part, Deason wouldn't meet Beam's eyes. Instead, he glared at me.

"And then there's Al's relationship with Charlie Blauer," I continued. "Oh, and Megan Blauer's strange insistence that I meet her at Sully's. And we already mentioned those two kids, Segulia and Hollenbeck. Does everybody who works for you have to hang out at the Empire Room? I mean, is that some kind of group requirement?"

"I don't know what you're talking about but you're

277

beginning to bore me."

"And what about you and Sully? You know, that really was amateur hour the other day. You can't hope to hide your relationship with someone by drawing attention to it."

"You're fishing, Dahms."

I ignored him. "You and Sullivan are definitely into something together. The cops start hauling you guys in, people are going to be looking to protect themselves. It'll be tough for you to know who your friends are."

"Let's pause there for a moment, Dahms," Beam said, rising. "Let's talk about *your* friends."

Beam slowly walked across to the adjacent dining room. There, on a large oak table, lay a manila envelope. He picked it up, undid the clasp dramatically, and approached me.

"These are for you," he said.

I started to stand, but Deason shoved me roughly back onto the sofa.

"Oh, don't get up," Beam said, handing me the open envelope.

I reached inside and pulled out half a dozen black and white photographs. They were taken two nights previously at McCauley's. There was a particularly unflattering shot of me standing by the table, hiking my pants up, eyes closed, mouth wide, talking with Wiseman, Edgerton, and the Milkman. Naomi fared better. Her head was cocked slightly, her mouth set in a soft smile, a melancholic whisper in her eyes. The last shot was of Skip and Ava holding hands.

"I'm not trying to tell you how to live your life," Beam said, pointing to the photograph, "but if I was responsible for caring for such an angelic creature, I don't think I'd expose her to that kind of element. You wouldn't want anything to happen to her."

I stared into his eyes. The arrogance in them infuriated me, but I kept my voice calm. "Who took the pictures?"

"Oh, just some private investigator I found online. Does it matter? I mean, you dangle a few bills in front of one of those guys and they'll do anything. Right?"

"You having these pictures taken supposed to scare me, Matty?"

"Not at all. It's just that you've so busied yourself with my affairs lately, I thought a reminder was in order. You have concerns of your own to think about."

"You know, Matty. A fella might interpret that as a threat."

"Interpret it as you will. It's no concern of mine."

I smiled. I planted a big, sloppy, toothsome grin on my face, slipped the photographs into the envelope, and handed it back up to Beam. When he reached out for it, I grabbed his wrist with my left hand, pulled myself to my feet, and spun around in back of him. Beam dropped the envelope and the photographs spilled noisily out onto the floor. With my right hand I reached for the small of my back where, beneath my jacket and T-shirt, I'd taped my dad's .22. It stung like hell when I ripped it loose.

I jammed the barrel of the gun into the back of Beam's head and together we took a step back toward the stairs leading down to the front door. Beam's men moved in to form a semi-circle before us. Hickey seemed content with my dad's .38, but the other three all drew weapons of their own.

I chuckled. "Seems we're repeating ourselves, Matty. Didn't we just do this?"

Beam didn't answer. Instead, he turned his head to his men. "Kill him."

They had each taken shooting stances, feet apart, both hands on their guns, but none could get off a shot that wouldn't also risk taking out the boss. They looked to their leader, uncertainty in their eyes.

As if reading their minds, Beam said, "It doesn't matter. No way he gets away with this."

I pressed the barrel of the little gun even harder against his skull. "This ain't about getting away, Matty. You killed my friend. You sent others to kill me. You threatened the people I care about and you're planning to hide behind the law. I don't care about getting away. I care about taking you with me."

I moved the .22 behind Beam's right ear so that it formed a flap over the barrel of the gun. "Tell them to lower their weapons."

"If you're going to shoot, then shoot," Beam said.

I pulled the trigger. I held on tightly to Beam as his ear exploded in pieces that scattered spectacularly across the room. There wasn't much blood at first, but what there was sprayed in tiny droplets like the mist from an atomizer. Beam shrieked and tried to wrench himself from my grasp, but I held firm. Then a lot more blood began to flow, gushing from what was left of his ear.

Behind me, there was a loud crack as the front door frame splintered and someone burst in. "Nobody move!" a voice bellowed.

I glanced quickly to my rear. The two cops that had been sitting out front had booted the door open and stood on the landing below us, guns drawn. "Drop your weapons!" one of them yelled. "Now!"

"I will if they will," I shouted.

"Now!" the cop repeated.

Flinty hate shone in the eyes of Beam's men, except Hickey's, whose eyes crackled with panic. At last, Beam, whimpering, nodded his head and the men each slowly stooped to set their guns on the floor. Still clutching onto Beam with my left arm, I handed the .22 back toward the cops. One of them snatched the gun from me and rushed past to scoop up the other men's weapons.

We were all ordered to the floor, face down, our hands clasped behind our heads. One of the cops took a brief look at Beam's ear but declared that he'd be okay until the paramedics arrived. We lay there until the quiet street outside filled with the whirl of sirens and the squawk of radio traffic. While we waited, I found myself staring at Beam, only an arm's length away. His ear was a mess of ragged cartilage and blood. He moaned quietly and an occasional tear escaped his red-rimmed eyes, but all in all, he held himself together pretty well.

He caught me staring. "You die, Dahms," he said in a voice that struck me as comically loud.

I grinned at him. I was pretty sure he wouldn't be able to hear me, but I said it anyway. "Bring it, asshole."

Chapter Twenty-five

Cop coffee sucks. Not only do they start with inferior, canned, supermarket coffee, but it usually sits around on a hot burner for hours and hours, becoming ever thicker and more acrid. Subjected to that kind of coffee day after day, it's little wonder why cops are so cranky. Augie Tarkof was particularly cranky.

We were sitting in yet another interview room down at the Apple Valley public safety building—me, Augie, my dad's old friend on the force Davidson, and another guy with a video recorder. Augie was drinking coffee. And he was getting crankier and crankier.

"Let's go over it again, Dahms," he said. "Why did you go to the house?"

"I told you, Augie. I went there to interview Beam."

Tarkof shot a glance at the video camera taping the proceedings. "That's Detective Tarkof, Dahms," he snapped. "Now, tell us exactly what happened."

I nodded deferentially at him. "Things didn't go as well as I'd hoped."

"You shot the man's ear off," Davidson noted.

"Well, that's sorta where things broke down."

Tarkof glared. "Why'd ya want to talk to him in the first place?"

"I wondered if perhaps he had anything to do with the recent attempts on my life."

"You come to any conclusions?"

"I'd have to say that it's possible that he was involved."

Rubbing his temples, Tarkof leaned back in his chair. It creaked under him. "Have you proof of Beam's involvement?"

"Plenty of circumstantial evidence but nothing definitive. Not yet."

"Okay. Tell us everything you know. Everything. We'll decide what's important."

"I told you everything I knew the last time we did this," I insisted.

Tarkof stared at me. "Like hell. You've been withholding evidence from the very beginning. People are getting killed because of your games. That shit ends now. Let's start with the Walsh kid. Did he help kill his old man?"

"I really don't know, Augie."

Tarkof slammed on open palm down hard on the table. The sound echoed nicely in the small room. "God dammit, I said no more games!"

"I *really* don't know, Detective. Neither do you. We've both talked to him. Why would you think I got something out of him that you couldn't? What am I, the Amazing Kreskin?"

"Just tell us everything he told you."

I shook my head. "You know I can't do that. I'm working for the Walshs' attorney. That makes those privileged communications. I yap too much, and the guy'll have my license."

"You don't and I'll have your ass for a hat," Augie warned. Then, he remembered the video camera. "Turn that thing off," he ordered.

The cameraman, who worked for the Apple Valley

PD and didn't know how to react to an order from a Minneapolis detective, elected to get keep taping, but took a half step back from the camera.

"Let's momentarily suspend the taped portion of this interview," Davidson said. "I think we could all use a break."

The cameraman said something that I couldn't quite make out into the camera's microphone, then shut it down with a click. "You guys mind if I step out for a smoke?" he asked.

"Not at all," Davidson said. "We'll let you know when we need you again."

When the cameraman had gone, Tarkof leaned forward, his warm, dark-roasted breath crossing the table like an advance guard. "Visiting Beam was one fuckin' stupid play, Dahms. You really did it this time. You dove headfirst into a pool of dung without so much as a hairnet."

"That's a colorful image, Augie. Incomprehensible, but colorful. And I appreciate the concern, but I can look after myself."

"We've just seen how you take care of yourself, pal. If them cops hadn't a busted in there, you'd be dead."

I shrugged. "Maybe."

"What do you mean *maybe*? You're facing what? Four guns? No matter what you do with Beam, you're not looking at an open casket."

"Maybe," I repeated. "But the whole thing struck me as strange—"

"The whole thing strikes me as idiotic."

"You know, if I hadn't lost my temper—"

"Like that was a possibility."

"If I hadn't lost my temper," I persisted, "I think he

was going to let me walk out of there."

Tarkof grunted. "Smitten by your charms, I suppose?"

"More likely he wanted to use me as a patsy."

"Imagine that."

I grinned. "I think he wanted me around in case he was charged. He'd have his lawyer call me to testify that I busted in on poor innocent Matty, was disarmed, reasoned with, and let go. That might be useful in persuading a jury that even when provoked, he's not the violent type."

"Damn nice of you to hand him that option."

"He tried to kill me. What would you have had me do?"

"I'd have had you sit tight, shithead. This isn't a job for some blundering wannabe. We're looking at this guy for one of the highest profile murders been done in decades and you're making our case against him damn near impossible. Are you trying to fuck things up? I'm trying to nab the guy who murdered your friend Walsh. You stop carin' about that?"

"You know better, Augie. But I got other things to care about. I got other friends."

"What's that supposed to mean?"

I shrugged. "Beam made references to some people I know."

"Did he threaten them?"

"No. Not directly."

Tarkof cast a weary, exasperated glance at Davidson and sighed. I sighed. Davidson sighed.

Tossing a yellow legal pad across the table at me, Tarkof said, "Better give me their names. I can't promise much. Without a direct threat, there's no way I can authorize the manpower to baby-sit everyone you know."

"Forget it, Augie," I said. "I'll take care of it."

"Give me the fucking names!" Tarkof thundered.

Davidson handed me a pen. I'd finished writing when there was a knock on the door. I figured it was the cameraman back from his smoke, but instead a uniformed cop stuck her head in the room. "His lawyer's here," she announced.

Tarkof glared.

"I didn't call a lawyer," I protested, as a man entered the room. He was about five-foot-five, but solidly built, wearing pleated, charcoal gray slacks, a striped dress shirt, and a yellow tie with the sun, a crescent moon, and a few shimmering stars printed on it. I wondered if it was a Father's Day present. He was in his late twenties with dark brown hair slicked straight back, a receding chin, and an upturned nose that gave his face an unpleasant, insolent look. "You Dahms?" he asked as he entered the interview room.

I nodded.

He handed me a card that read Eugene Finch. Criminal Litigation. Pope, Dante & Osterman Associates. Turning to the two cops he said, "this interview is at an end."

"I didn't call a lawyer," I repeated.

Finch ignored me, noted the video camera, and said, "I hope you know that any statements made prior to arrival of counsel will be challenged."

Tarkof stood and looked down at the much shorter Finch. "*Challenged?* You got me quaking in my boots, counselor."

Finch and Tarkof locked eyes. "Is that some kind of

passive aggressive threat, Detective?" Finch replied.

Tarkof chuckled. "You nailed it, son. I'm the passive type. Ask anybody."

The stare down continued for another moment. Finch looked away first. "I'm going to need some privacy while I consult with my client," he announced to no one in particular. "Gentlemen, if you'd be kind enough to leave us now."

Tarkof shrugged, walked over, and tapped the video camera. "We got what we need for now, counselor," he said. He smiled again and led Davidson from the room.

"I'll need to know everything you told them prior to my arrival," Finch said, clicking open his briefcase.

"I didn't call a lawyer," I said again.

Finch cast me a puzzled look. "Evelyn Walsh heard of your predicament. She asked that we represent you."

"Nice of her. A bit presumptuous, but nice."

It wasn't obvious from his expression that Finch had even heard me. "I talked to the Chief down here," he said, looking down to leaf through some papers in his briefcase. "They're not prepared to charge you at this time. That works out for our side. And with no complainant, I think the worst you'll be looking at is unlawful discharge of a weapon within city limits. You'll likely end up with community service. Are there any charitable organizations or causes for which you are currently doing work? We might be able to get you credited for hours you've already put in."

"What do you mean, no complainant?"

Finch looked up. "I'm sorry?"

"You said there was no complainant."

"That's right. Mr. Beam has told the police that he has no intention of lodging a criminal complaint against you."

"Did he say why not?"

"No."

"I blew the guy's ear off."

Finch's eyes flashed with caution. "Allegedly."

"There were witnesses."

"As I understand it, the other people in the house at the time of the incident gave inconclusive statements."

"Huh?"

"They claim not to have actually seen the incident."

"You're kidding me."

"That's what I've been told."

I shook my head.

"Now, did you admit to any wrongdoing during the course of the interview that was conducted prior to my arrival?"

"Not in so many words."

Finch studied me minutely. "Are you sure?"

"Pretty sure. But then, some of this is rather obvious. I mean, they have my gun. It's got ear all over it."

Finch inhaled deeply and paused before replying. "Nothing is obvious. Not in a court of law."

I looked down at my shirt and smirked. It was stained with Beam's blood. "You got a pencil. I gotta write that down."

Finch continued to ignore me. After he'd shuffled through his papers a while longer, he closed the briefcase and announced that he needed to speak to the Chief again. He told me to remain in the room and, above all, to talk to no one. It wasn't hard. For the next half-hour or so I was completely alone.

At first, I occupied myself by trying to remember all the lyrics to the Harold Arlen/ Johnny Mercer classic

"Blues in the Night." I bogged down a little during the bridge—the part about the breeze that starts the trees to cryin'. But it was fun making train noises in the small, closed room. *A whoo-ee, duh whoo-ee.* And it helped keep my mind off the fact that Beam and his men didn't want the law to punish me because they wanted to do that themselves.

Then there were the photographs. Easiest thing in the world for Beam to reach out and touch everyone I cared about. I began to feel grateful to Evelyn for bringing in Finch. I had to get out of there as soon as possible.

Finally, Finch came back with the news that I'd been released. Then he informed me that his boss, Zebulon Pope, wanted to see me immediately.

"No can do, counselor."

"Mr. Pope told me that I could expect that kind of an answer. He asked me to remind you that you are working for him, and as his employee, he demands that you make an immediate accounting."

"Tell Pope I quit."

"He said that I could expect that response from you as well."

"Maybe *he's* the Amazing Kreskin," I said.

"What?"

"Never mind. Tell your boss I've got things to do."

"What kind of things?"

I glared at Finch. "Aren't you keepin' up, Eugene? I got bad guys coming after me. Worse, they may be coming after my friends or my family. I gotta do something about that. I can't waste my time chatting with lawyers."

"If it wasn't for us, you likely would not have been

released."

"If you're worried about your bill, I'm sure Evelyn Walsh is good for it."

Finch raised both eyebrows and shook his head slowly. "You may not believe this, but you *are* my client. I'm worried about you."

"Stop. I'm getting all misty."

"Do you have a car?"

"Uh, no. I mean, yes, but it's parked over at Beam's. Might not be a great idea for me to wander over to pick it up right now."

"I'll have a tow truck sent. Where do you want it dropped?"

"My office, I guess."

"Jot down the address. What else do you need?"

"A change of clothes would be nice."

"I'll drive you home."

"If they'll let me in. Last I heard it was a crime scene."

"I'll check. What else?"

"I need to contact my friends. Beam threatened them. Not overtly, of course. But by implication."

"You can call them on your cell while I drive you home. Do you mind if I ask you exactly how Beam delivered this threat?"

"I was with some people I knew a couple of days ago in this pub. Beam hired a P.I. The guy musta followed me. He took pictures. Beam showed me the pictures. He was too smart to say anything directly. He's a lawyer, after all."

"Actually," Finch said, "he's not a lawyer. He's not been admitted to the bar."

I started to reply, but Finch interrupted. "You say

that these photographs were taken a couple of days ago?"

"Yes."

"Before…what's his name? Grogan? Before his man Grogan shot at you at the zoo? Before the other man Simpkins broke into your home?"

"Yeah. What's your point?" I asked. I was impressed that he remembered their names.

Finch stared keenly at me. The insolence that I had originally noted in his face now seemed more like intelligence. "It's just odd is all," he said. "Presumably, Beam had the photographs taken to intimidate you."

"Yes."

"But then before he had a chance to use them against you, one of his men tried to kill you. Doesn't make sense."

I shrugged. "So, he changed his mind. He sent in Grogan and Simpkins and when they failed, he reverted back to his original plan."

Finch nodded. "Could be. But there are other possibilities. You know for sure that these two men were part of Beam's organization?"

"Yes. For sure."

"Maybe Mr. Beam is not as firmly in control of his members as he would like."

I remembered Beam's expression when I told him about Greg Walsh withdrawing the ten grand. He acted like he didn't know what I was talking about. And again, when I told him that I knew about Greg and Al Grogan's meeting at Sully's Empire Room. He pretended that was news to him, as well. What if it wasn't an act? What if he didn't know about it?

I suddenly realized that I'd been staring at Finch for some time. "Shall we go?" he asked.

"I'm going to need my gun."

"They'll keep the .22 at least until they run ballistics on it. Probably longer. I might be able to get you the other."

"Please try."

Finch blinked a couple of times, then crossed the room toward me. He reached out and gave my shoulder a little squeeze. "We'll get everybody out of this thing."

I smiled a grateful smile. I was going to need all the help I could get.

Chapter Twenty-six

I called Max Wiseman as we drove to the Bijou. To his credit, although his replies were somewhat terse, when I told Max that he and his family might be targets of armed skinheads, he didn't rail against me. It was enough that we both knew I was to blame.

When I informed him that the police wouldn't be able to do much in the way of protecting them, Max decided that he'd take his family to stay with his father for a few days. Since daddy was a district court judge, Max figured they'd be safer there. He also told me that Stephen and Ava would be welcome to join them, but that Stephen was at work and the Milkman had taken Ava off sightseeing. Max said that he'd send Vicki and the kids off right away, but that he'd contact Stephen and Skip, then wait at home for the Milkman and Ava to return. When he asked me what my plans were, I had to admit that I didn't have any. After he hung up, I tried to call my parents. I let it ring a long time but there was no answer. That was a bit worrisome, but they'd been so busy with doctors' appointments it was hardly unexpected. I'd have to try back again later.

We got to the Bijou, and I asked Finch to wait out in the car while I went in for some clothes. The door to my room was still strung with yellow cop tape, but there were no cops around. I crawled through the tape and grabbed up the gym bag I'd packed the night before.

Then I sat down on the bed and called Naomi at home. She listened quietly to everything I had to say—about the shootout at the carousel, the intruder in my bedroom, my visit to Beam's place, and most importantly, about the photographs he'd shown me of everyone who'd been at McCauley's with me earlier in the week.

"Are Stephen and the baby safe?" she asked when I'd finished.

"Yes. Well, they will be. Max is seeing to it. Right now, Stephen is at work and Ava's with the Milkman. But everybody's being warned."

"This is something you're taking seriously?"

"Very seriously."

"Are you calling to tell me that I'm in danger?"

"You may be. Yes."

Naomi sighed. "What am I supposed to do, Lyle?" There was a sorrowful edge to her voice. I'd have preferred anger.

"You should probably get out of town. For a while at least."

She sighed again. "Where?"

"Maybe someplace nice. I hear good things about Bayfield, Wisconsin. Supposed to be the gateway to the Apostle Islands."

"I'll go stay with my parents in Anoka. Will that be okay?"

"That should be fine. I really don't think you're in danger. But we can't risk it. I…I can't let anything happen to you. I…I…you know."

I waited a long time for her reply. "I know," she said at last. "Call me when it's over."

She hung up before I could say any more.

I changed clothes and about half an hour later, we—

Finch, me, and my gym bag crammed full of clothes and ammunition—were sitting in Zebulon Pope's spacious downtown Minneapolis office. To my surprise, both Evelyn and Tyler Walsh were also in attendance. Evelyn sat up perfectly straight in her chair. There was a small purse in her lap; her hands were clasped on top of the purse. She held her head cocked slightly, like a bird perched on a telephone wire eyeing an uncertain horizon. Tyler slouched in his chair, the crotch of his baggy cargo pants at his knees, a sullen look on his pockmarked face.

Pope sat behind an oak desk in a high-backed leather chair, his fingertips together, and his lips pursed in a smug pout. "You've been quite a busy little beaver, Mr. Dahms."

"Yeah, Zeb," I admitted. "It has been an event-filled couple of days."

"Indeed. In fact, your recent actions have been truly alarming, if not actually criminal. And, as I was unfortunate enough to have acquiesced when Mrs. Walsh here insisted that we hire you, it now falls to me to see if this firm shares any liability with regard to those actions."

"I agree that it's time to clear a few things up."

"Fine, then, perhaps you'd like to take us back to the beginning. Starting with those two children you shot at the Walsh home. I'd like you to tell us—"

"Tyler," I said, interrupting. "You and me gotta talk."

"I believe I had the floor, Mr. Dahms," Pope said.

"You're gonna be kissing it in a minute," I warned.

"You'll force me to call security."

I smiled at him. "Your Mr. Finch was able to get me my .38 back from the cops today," I told him. "Got it with me right here."

"Is that some kind of veiled threat?" Pope asked, going a bit pale and reaching toward the phone.

"I wouldn't call it *veiled.*"

Finch got quickly to his feet. "You're angry, Dahms," he said. "You got reason to be. But we've got work to do." He crossed behind the desk to stand beside Pope. "And you," he said, nodding at the boss. "We got a situation here. Your attitude isn't helping things, either. Both you guys just cool it."

Pope got his color back. His cheeks flushed bright red. "But, but, but…" he spluttered. "How dare you? You all work for me."

Before Finch could respond, Evelyn shifted in her chair. "Actually," she said, "you all work for me."

Finch nodded. I smiled. Pope's eyes smoldered, but he said nothing.

Evelyn turned to her son. "Mr. Dahms is right, Tyler. It is time to talk. First, I've got to know. Did you have anything to do with your father's death?"

Tyler stared at his mother. His bottom lip trembled ever so slightly. "Is that what you think?"

Evelyn's face was without emotion. "I haven't heard you deny it, Tyler. I think I deserve that much."

"What about what *I* deserve?" he countered. "Do I deserve to be accused of something like that by my mother?"

"I'm not accusing. I'm asking. And you're avoiding the question."

Tyler searched the faces in the room for some support. He didn't find any. He turned back to his mother. "No. I didn't have anything to do with his death."

"Do you know who did?" Evelyn asked.

"Do I, like, *know*, like really *know* who did?' Tyler said, crossing his arms and leaning forward until his head nearly touched his knees. "No. I don't."

Barely checked anger quavered in Evelyn's voice. "Quit playing games, Tyler. Your father was murdered. You owe him. You owe me. You've got to tell us everything you know, right now."

Tyler sat bolt upright in his chair. "What about you?" he wailed. "Goddammit! What about you and Dad? What about what you hid from me? What about that, huh?"

Evelyn blinked several times quite rapidly. "What do you mean? This is about *your father*. Stop trying to make this about you."

Tyler clenched his teeth and stared at his mother. Though his eyes glistened, they were rimmed with fire. The room got very quiet.

"Tyler," I said, "your mom doesn't seem to be getting the answers we need from you. Now, I'm not your mom, or your lawyer, or your friend. I'm going to ask you some questions and if you're not completely honest with me, I'm going to hurt you."

Pope started to say something, but Finch held up a hand. Tyler looked to his mother. Something flickered in her eyes but was quickly gone.

"Do you understand?" I asked him.

Tyler wiped at his eyes and nodded.

"You say your parents hid things from you. Are you talking about Janet Kleiner?" I glanced at Evelyn. "Greg's old girl friend from high school," I told her. "Greg had been seeing her again."

Evelyn blinked again. "I understand."

Tyler snorted. "Like you didn't already know. Like everybody didn't know."

Evelyn turned to study her son's face. His expression was equal parts pride and resentment. "You knew about this?"

"You guys can't hide everything. Sooner or later we always find out."

"*I* didn't know," Evelyn said quietly. There was hurt in her expression but no surprise.

Tyler straightened in his chair. "Come on. It was clear what was going on. Dad was never around anymore. He always had some lame excuse for not being there. How many different excuses was I supposed to swallow? After a while even Dad couldn't keep it up. He just had you make the excuses for him."

"Your dad was a very busy man," Evelyn insisted. "Running a large company is a very—"

"See!" Tyler interrupted. "You're still doing it."

Both mother and son fell silent. After a moment, Evelyn asked, "Is that why you quit football?"

Tyler slumped back down in his chair. "Football's for losers."

"Let's refocus," I said, letting rather more anger slip into my tone than I'd intended. "How'd you find Janet? I know that you and Megan tracked her down."

Tyler's eyes flashed with challenge. "You spying on me?"

"That's what I do," I told him. "That and clean up other people's messes. Now, how'd you track down Janet?"

Tyler paused momentarily before answering. "Dad was pretty sloppy. He'd call her from home sometimes. The phone'll display the last number you call. If you have a phone number, it's not hard getting an address."

I nodded. "Must have hit you pretty hard. Finding out about Janet. And the other thing. Did you confront your dad?"

Tyler eyes steeled. "No. What's it to me?"

"You remember what I said about answering me truthfully."

Tyler shifted uncomfortably in his chair and shrugged.

"So, you confronted him?"

He nodded.

"But you didn't go to your mom."

He nodded again.

"You didn't want to hurt her."

"I just figured she knew anyway."

"About everything?"

"Sure."

I shook my head. "About Ava?"

He glanced at his mother, then back at me. "We don't need to get into that here," he said. His voice was charged with warning.

"She needs to know."

Evelyn broke the silence. "Know what? What do I need to know?"

I turned to her. "Greg and Janet Kleiner had a baby together."

For a moment, she didn't even breathe. Her eyes were unfocused pools of disbelief, but slowly pinpricks of acceptance began to shine through. "A boy or a girl?" she asked.

"A girl. Three years old."

Evelyn turned again to Tyler. "And you met her?"

Tyler sighed, and although he struggled against it,

some of the smugness melted from his expression. "Yeah. After I got the address, me and Megan went over there to…I don't know. To check it out, I guess." He crossed, then uncrossed his legs. "It was completely weird going there. I almost chickened out. Anyway, this Janet was like really happy to see us. She invited us in and she, like, talked to us for a really long time. She even had her roommate take a picture." He shook his head. "It was totally bent."

"And you met the little girl?" Evelyn asked.

"Yeah. Ava. Yeah."

"Your half-sister?"

Tyler put his head down for a moment and when he looked up, a hunger, a need had appeared in his eyes that was volcanic. "Half?" he asked. "You sure you don't have something you want to tell me?"

Evelyn looked at him in bewilderment. Tyler's gaze, however, didn't waver.

"What do you mean, Tyler? What could I have to tell you?"

Tyler seemed to shrink. He lowered his head again. "Nothing," he said. "Not a thing."

Anger swelled within me like an acidic tide. I leaned forward. Tyler pulled back even further. But, before I could vent my rage, something stopped me—a prickling, like a mild electric current running up the back of my neck.

"I've been missing something," I said, sitting back in the chair. I was talking to myself, but my words seemed to have a leaden effect on everyone in the room. Neither Evelyn nor Tyler would look at me. I turned to Pope who was shuffling through papers on his desk. "What haven't you told me?"

Pope didn't raise his eyes.

Finch was staring intently at Tyler. "I think I know," he said. He walked out from behind the desk and sat on the corner facing Tyler. "You're adopted, aren't you, Tyler?"

Evelyn's eyes flashed defensively. "What's that got to do with anything?"

Finch turned to her. "I know this is a sensitive subject."

"It's not a *sensitive* subject," Evelyn insisted. "We've always been completely open about it."

"You didn't mention it to me," I said.

Evelyn clutched her purse a little tighter. "Well, it's not something you bring up in every casual conversation. It's not even something that you think about very much. But Tyler's always known. We've talked about it whenever he wanted." She turned toward her son. "He's always known that it's not important that his father and I aren't his biological parents. We're the ones that raised him, that love him, that will always be there for..." She stopped. "*I'll* always be there for you, Tyler. Remember, it's not important how you come into a family. It's important that you're part of a family."

Tyler grunted. "Some family."

"You're young, Tyler," Evelyn said. "You're at that age when you feel like your parents are from another planet. Everybody goes through it. I was once just like you."

"You're not like me," he replied. "You never woke up one morning to find out that your entire life was a lie."

Her husband murdered and having just been told that he fathered a child with another woman, Evelyn certainly could have argued the point. To her credit, she

301

did not. I, on the other hand, showed no such restraint. "You know," I snapped, "I'm sick of this crap!"

Evelyn whirled around to face me. I shut up.

"Go on, Tyler," she said.

Tyler flashed a glance at me, then focused intently on his mother. "You can't know what it's like to suddenly have no idea who you are anymore."

"Finding out about your dad must have been very hard on you," she said.

Tyler shrugged.

"You were hurt, so you decided to hurt us." Her voice was very gentle, as if she were tucking him in and telling him a bedtime story. "That's why you did the things you did. That's why you were drawn to that…that whole thing. You knew how much that would hurt us."

"They accepted me," he said. "They didn't try to make me into something I'm not."

"Don't you see it, Tyler?" Evelyn said. "That's exactly what they did. They saw the hurt in you and tried to turn it to hate. It was never about you. It was about turning you into one of them."

For a moment, in his eyes, I thought I saw a connection made—a spark and the first whir of something coming to life. But then it was gone, and Tyler slumped back down into his chair.

Evelyn's voice trembled. "Tyler. I'm right here. Please don't shut me out. Let me be here for you. Let me have my son back."

He paused. "I'm not your son," he said. "I'm *her* son."

"What are you saying?"

"I'm that woman's son. That Janet. I'm her son. Hers and Dad's."

Evelyn's eyes went wide.

"She told me," Tyler continued. "That day me and Megan went to see her. She told me. Then I asked Dad about it. He admitted everything. I asked him if you knew, too. He said you didn't, but…but…. How could I trust him?"

Evelyn exhaled deeply. "I don't understand, Tyler. What exactly are you…? Are you saying that your father and this Janet…? That they…?" She didn't finish her question.

Tyler looked at the floor.

Pope stopped shuffling papers. He stood and said, "I think this is something that would be best discussed at another time." His voice was very tight, and his eyes shifted about the room.

"You've been Greg Walsh's lawyer for a long time, right?" I asked him.

"Since the beginning. Since we set up the corporation."

"Then I'm guessing you knew."

Pope raised both eyebrows and looked down at me with disdain. "I'm sure none of us are in the least bit interested in your guesses."

"Yeah, you knew," I said. "You handled it for him. Important client comes to you with a problem, you handle it."

Pope picked up the papers he'd been shuffling. When he looked back up, all eyes were on him. He sighed. "It seemed a prudent solution. The woman was obviously not fit to raise the child. She'd been institutionalized. She was a streetwalker. And Mr. Walsh was not a man to avoid his responsibilities."

I turned to Evelyn. "You and Greg wanted kids?"

"Yes. We'd been trying. We'd even been seeing specialists. Tyler joining our family…it was like a gift, you know." She turned to Tyler. "You've always been a gift. A treasure."

"You see," Pope said. "It was simply a matter of putting the pieces together. It all fit."

"But you didn't tell her," I said. "You lied to her. You and Greg. You lied to her for, like, sixteen years. Was that also the 'prudent' thing to do?"

"That decision was Mr. Walsh's."

"I thought families were supposed to be grounded by trust."

Pope glanced at Evelyn. For an instant I thought that his face betrayed a measure of remorse. "How would you have me respond, Mr. Dahms? I did what I was asked. I did what Greg Walsh thought was right."

"What about Ava?" I asked.

Pope cocked an eyebrow.

"Why didn't you make the same arrangement for Ava? Tyler's sister."

"Situations had changed," he said. "Mr. Walsh felt that, with his financial help, Ms. Kleiner would be an adequate mother. In addition, he was not convinced that Mrs. Walsh would choose to adopt again at this stage in her life."

That was all Evelyn Walsh could take.

"You smug bastards!" she exclaimed. "You sit up here in this goddamned office and make decisions that change my life forever. You don't consult me. You don't tell me the truth. If I'd have known, maybe I could have…I don't know. Maybe Tyler wouldn't have felt so lost. So deceived. Maybe it would have all been different. Maybe Greg would still be…" She stopped, then took a moment to compose herself. "Is the baby…? Ava…? With Greg gone, is Ava being cared for?"

"I, uh…I really don't know Evelyn," Pope said. "I didn't think it was my place to—"

"You really are an asshole, aren't you, Zebulon?" Evelyn interrupted. "It *is* your place. I'm *making* it your place. If Tyler's sister was relying on my husband's support, then it goddamned well is your place."

"I'm sorry you're taking this view of things, Evelyn," Pope said.

Evelyn stared at him.

"I think I might be able to help," I said.

Pope wheeled around to look at me. "You've done quite enough,"

"You don't know the half of it."

"What's that supposed to mean?"

"The kid's been staying with me."

I smiled at Pope's nearly apoplectic reaction, but when I turned to Evelyn I immediately withered. "I didn't know she was Greg's," I told her. "And I didn't know about Tyler. I'd known Greg a long time ago, remember. I'd known Janet, too. She spotted me at the funeral, and she came to see me. She showed up at my house terrified, barely coherent. She said she thought she knew who had killed Greg. She wouldn't tell me who, only that she thought they would try to kill her, too. Then she took off. But she left the kid. Literally on my doorstep."

Evelyn continued to stare.

"I haven't heard from Janet since then, but Ava's been fine. I've got a whole team of…I don't know, I'd guess you'd call them nannies lined up to take care of her."

305

"Where is she right now?" Evelyn asked.

"She's staying with friends. We didn't feel she was safe at my house."

"And I suppose she's safe with your friends?" Pope asked, putting an unpleasant stress on the word *friends*.

I furrowed my brow. "Well, Zebby, he is a district court judge."

"Oh."

"You say you haven't seen the mother since she dropped off the child," Evelyn said. "Do you know where she is?"

"No."

"Are you looking for her?"

"Yeah, but no one's seen her."

Tyler didn't move his head, but he sneaked a glance at me, his eyes darting away when they met mine. "Something to say, Tyler?" I asked.

He shook his head.

Finch, who been sitting on the corner of Pope's desk, pushed to his feet. A single sheet of paper wafted to the floor. His features looked grave. "Tyler," he asked, "after you found out about your father and Ms. Kleiner, who did you talk to about it?"

"What's it to you?"

"Answer me," Finch said.

Tyler shrugged. "Just Dad."

"And your girlfriend."

"Yeah. Dad and Megan."

"Is there anyone she'd have talked to about it? Her friends at school?"

Tyler shook his head vehemently. "No. She promised she wouldn't tell anyone. Particularly at school."

I held up a hand. "Wait a minute. Janet told me that she was worried that the same people who had killed Greg were after her. If they were, how'd they find out about her?"

"Not from me," Tyler insisted. "And not from Megan."

"The trouble with stirring things up, Tyler, is you're never quite sure what's gonna surface."

"What's that supposed to mean?"

"You think Megan would have told her dad?" I asked.

"I don't know. Maybe. They were pretty close. So what?"

Finch looked at me significantly.

Tyler shook his head. "Even if Megan told her dad about Janet, so what? No way he'd tell anyone else. He's a good guy."

"I'm surprised you think so," I said. "Didn't he forbid you to see his daughter after you joined the skinhead brotherhood?"

Tyler glared. "He didn't forbid anything. He still let me come by sometimes. Said maybe Megan would come back around."

"But he spoke to me," Evelyn said. "He was very clear. He came to me and told me that he didn't want you to see Megan anymore. He told me it was because of the people you were spending time with. The things you were saying."

Tyler smirked. "Maybe he told you that, but all I can say is that he's always been a right-thinking guy."

"What's that supposed to mean?" Evelyn asked.

"You figure it out."

I stood. "Let's you and me take a walk, Tyler.

Alone."

I took a step forward. Tyler tried to retreat without bothering to first get to his feet. Both he and his chair spilled over onto the carpet. "Don't let him hurt me!" he cried.

"That's up to you," I reminded him. "You're going to tell me everything I need to know. One way or the other."

"You'd let him hurt me?" he asked, scanning the faces around him.

No one said a word.

"It's game time, pal," I said, reaching down for him.

"Okay!" he shouted. "Okay! Shit! Okay!"

I smiled at fear in his eyes, at the crack in his voice. "Tell me every goddamned thing you know about Charlie Blauer."

Chapter Twenty-seven

The afternoon sun shone brightly into the room through the large window behind Pope's desk. Tyler, sitting opposite the window, had to squint to see us. Pope got up and dropped the blinds, leaving striations of light to slash the room like dozens of razor blades.

I still stood before Tyler, but I'd managed to tamp down some of my anger. "Let me ask again. Did Charlie Blauer know that Janet Kleiner was your birth mother?"

Tyler nodded.

"He spoke to you about it?"

He nodded again.

"Then he knew you were Jewish."

She tried to muffle it, but a slight gasp escaped Evelyn Walsh. I glanced at her, but her eyes did not meet mine. "And he encouraged you to join up with Beam anyway?" I continued.

Tyler nodded yet again, this time combining it with a little rocking motion, like a pigeon on a treadmill.

"Tell me about it," I said.

Tyler stopped rocking and stared at me, his mouth clamped shut, and his heavy breaths whistling through his nostrils.

I turned and went back to my chair. "Tell me," I repeated.

Tyler unclamped his jaw. It trembled, but he managed to get the words out. "Shortly after me and

Megan went to see that woman, I was out at their place and Mr. Blauer called me into his shop. We were all alone. He said that Megan had told him. He asked me how I was doing with it. We talked for a while, then he says it must be weird for me, you know, finding out that the woman was Jewish. I hadn't even thought about it, but Mr. Blauer, he brings it up."

Tyler gave me a tense little smile. I returned it. We were all friends now, right?

"It made me a little nervous, really," he continued. "I mean, he and I hadn't talked about it before, but Megan had, you know? She'd mentioned that her dad didn't have many good things to say about people like that. So, when he brings it up, I was a little, you know…nervous."

"Sure."

"Well, Mr. Blauer he tells me not to let that bother me. He says that it's what's inside a guy that counts." Tyler glanced briefly at Evelyn. "He said that nobody can pick their parents, but they can pick their friends."

"So, Blauer hooked you up with Beam?"

"Not right away, but yeah. We talked a few more times and after a while he said that if I wanted to know more about protecting the white race and doing the right thing for my country, I should talk to the Reverend Beam."

"Did Blauer tell Beam about your heritage?"

"My heritage?"

"About Janet being Jewish?"

"No. He said he'd keep it to himself. That it was between him and me."

I grinned. "It's really nice that you were able to make such a good buddy. You and the Blauers must have been one swell little group. You guys stripping the sheets off the beds, getting all dolled up and heading down to the meeting house. Must have been quite a picture."

Tyler glared. "It wasn't like that," he insisted. "Megan wasn't into it at all and Mr. Blauer…Mr. Blauer didn't really want anyone to know."

"Come again?"

"Mr. Blauer…Nobody was supposed to know about him and Beam."

I grunted. "He tell you why not?"

"People," Tyler said. "People need to be educated. Until they are, they're like, you know, brainwashed by the Jewish-controlled media. When guys like Blauer stand up for what they believe in, people don't understand. He'd have trouble keeping customers. He's got a family to support, you know?"

"So, he lied when he told your mom that he didn't want you dating Megan because of your position on race relations?"

Tyler shrugged.

"And when he told me that he fired Al Grogan because Al was having trouble with a Black coworker?"

Tyler smiled softly.

"So, it's safe to say that Charlie was never an equal opportunity employer," I said.

Tyler smiled more broadly and shook his head.

"Why'd your pals Segulia and Hollenbeck boost Blauer's car that one time?"

"You heard about that?"

"Yeah. I heard about that."

"That was, like, a total misunderstanding," Tyler said. "That's why Mr. Blauer didn't press charges."

"Uh huh. Them killing your old man. You figure

that for another misunderstanding?"

"Who are you saying killed him?"

"Beam, Grogan, Segulia, Hollenbeck, whoever."

"That's bullshit!" he erupted. "If there was evidence, the cops would arrest them."

"Evidence? They carved swastikas into his cheeks, Tyler. I've seen the pictures."

"That don't mean nothing. Anybody coulda done that. Make it look like it was someone from the church."

"Have the Guinness people called you yet, Tyler? Because you gotta be working on some world record for stupidity."

"What's that supposed to mean?"

"Segulia and Hollenbeck. They tried to kill you, remember?"

"That's on *you*, man!" he shouted. "If you guys hadn't kept me locked up. If I coulda got through to them, they'd a never thought I was ratting on them. They just…they were just confused, man."

"Ratting on them?" I repeated. "What do you know that they gotta kill to protect?"

Tyler's jaw clamped shut again. This time there was real panic in his eyes.

"These guys killed your dad," I said. "And you sit there protecting them. Tell me what you know."

"They didn't kill him!" Tyler wailed. "I already told ya. It doesn't make sense. My dad didn't have anything to do with the church."

I don't remember getting to my feet. All at once I was just standing, looking at my balled-up fist, thinking how nice it would feel to beat Tyler's brains in. Pope, Finch, and Evelyn all stood as well. Standing and staring wide-eyed at me.

I took several very deep breaths. "You know what really pisses me off, Tyler?" I asked at last. "That I don't get to give you the hurt you deserve. My life's been turned upside down. I've had to kill people. My old friend Greg is dead. My other friends have been threatened. And I can't go after the person who's really responsible. I'm stuck going after the supporting cast."

"None of that is on me," Tyler said, in a tight, rodent-like squeal.

"It's all on you, son. And you know it. I mean, you found out your family has some secrets. Okay, they're pretty big ones, but what family doesn't have secrets? And let's look at how you handle them. Instead of reaching out and dealing with your problems, you suck yourself into this vortex of selfishness where up is down and wrong is right. You find out your birth mother is Jewish and instead of accepting it, you become super Nazi. You have problems with your dad, and you buddy up with people who go on to kill him. You got a mother who loves you, but you reach out to a group that only cares about how much money they can squeeze out of you."

"I never gave them no money!"

"Your dad did. At least ten grand. He met with Al Grogan down at Sully's Empire Room and tried to buy you out from under them. That's his connection to your so-called church. That's what got him killed."

"You got no proof. That's just what you say. Why should I believe you?"

I'd had enough. "Goddamn you! You still don't get it! He was my friend. And you killed him. I don't care what you believe. I don't care if you live or die. No! Fuck that! That's not true. I wish you were dead. I'd love to see you dead. If they'd carved you up instead of your old man, I'd be dancing with glee."

"I didn't kill my father!"

"The fuck you didn't! Everything comes back to you. To you and the hate you say you believe in. That's all about you, too, isn't it? It's not the Jews or the Blacks or anybody else. You hate yourself. And I don't blame you. I hate you, too."

Evelyn was unsteady as she crossed the room, coming to stand between Tyler and me. She held out both hands, palms upward, as if in supplication, as if a prayer could somehow make it all go away. Her eyes were unfocused and there was a smile on her face. A mirthless, desperate, terrifying smile. The painted-on smile of a clown standing atop a gallows. The smile faded. "It's not all his fault."

Then she turned and placed her arm around her son. "I think I'd like to leave now." She led Tyler toward the door. Then, without looking back, she added, "Lyle, keep me informed about the baby."

I wanted desperately to stop them, to somehow find a way to clear everything up, right there in that room. But I knew it was useless. Still, Pope, Finch, and I all stared at the door for a long time after they'd gone.

Finch offered to give me a ride back to my office where he'd had my car towed. I accepted, grateful to be leaving that room. We were pulling out of the parking lot when he turned to me. "You were pretty hard on the kid."

"Not hard enough."

Finch nodded. "His mother's right."

"About what?"

"About it not being entirely his fault."

"You're not going defend him, are you?"

"No. But I'm not going to let Beam and his people off the hook either. The thing to remember about zealots is that they recruit from the disillusioned and disenfranchised."

"Yeah," I said sourly. "Tyler Walsh. Poster boy for the downtrodden."

"I admit that Tyler's case is a little different. Rich kid. He's always had everything he wanted. That's probably the problem. He's disillusioned because he feels his life has nowhere to go. Since his parents give him everything, he's really got nothing to strive for. He certainly can't expect to better his father in business. With a dad like that, no matter what, Tyler would always feel he was living in his shadow."

"People feel what they want to feel," I said. "You can't go blaming everything on the parents."

Finch smiled sympathetically. "The bottom line is that Tyler was ripe for these guys. Particularly after he found out about the cheating. His perfect dad having an affair? A baby? Being lied to about his parentage? That's all gotta hurt. He'd want to strike back. Blauer. Beam. They gave him the opportunity."

"I hope what hurts is his realizing that he helped get his dad killed."

"You made that pretty clear."

I nodded.

"I gotta say I'm a little worried about Evelyn," Finch said.

I nodded again. "She's taken some pretty good shots. This thing's gotta be messing her up big time. You still Tyler's lawyer?"

Finch nodded.

"Good. You'll be seeing Evelyn then. Be a good

idea to keep an eye on her. Back in that office she looked…Well, she might need…I don't know, counseling or something. Maybe you could mention it to her."

"I'm not sure we have that kind of relationship," Finch said, "but I'll try. What are you going to do?"

I shrugged. "I got people to protect."

I pulled out my cell phone to try my parents again. I noticed that there was a message, but I ignored it, calling them instead. After about the fifth ring, my mom picked up. "Thank goodness you called, Lyle. Are you all right?"

"What'dya hear?"

"I haven't heard anything. What should I have heard?"

"Nothing, Mom. How's Dad?"

"That's why I'm so glad you called. Lyle, I'm afraid you have to come get the dog."

"Dad's having trouble with the dog?"

"No, No. Nothing like that. We're both happy you have the dog. Animals can bring such richness to a person's life. Remember Aunt Agnes and her parrot?"

"Why do I have to get the dog, Mom?"

"Oh. Yes. Well. Uh, you see, your dad and I aren't going to be home for a few days."

"That's good. I was just going to suggest that until things quiet down with these people I'm dealing with, it would be best for you two to maybe be somewhere other than the house. Where are you going? Dad taking you to Bayfield?"

"Uh. No. Actually, uh…we're going to be at St. Francis."

"The hospital?"

"Yeah. They said I could probably stay in the room with him. I just came home to pack a few things. And I'm not sure I can make trips back and forth to take care of little Basil. I'm afraid you're going to have to come get him."

"Why is Dad in the hospital?"

"He's not feeling very well, Lyle."

"What exactly is the matter?"

"Oh, he's had some pain. And you know he hasn't been sleeping well."

"Uh huh."

"And he's gotten worse."

"How much worse?"

"He collapsed. It's okay. They sent an ambulance."

"What's his condition right now?"

"He's sleeping."

"Sleeping or unconscious?"

"It's hard to tell. I'm letting the doctors handle it. They say they are optimistic."

I kept my voice calm. "That doesn't sound good. Them saying 'optimistic.' That doesn't sound good at all."

"I know you're busy. And I wouldn't ask if it wasn't important."

I looked at my watch. It was nearly five o'clock in the afternoon. "I can be there in a little over an hour."

"Good. You'll take him with you then? The dog I mean."

"Sure. First, I'll meet you at the hospital and then I'll swing back to the house and get Basil."

Mom didn't respond right away. "Oh, honey," she said. "Just the dog, please."

"Mom. He collapsed. From the sound of it, he might

be in some sort of coma. I'm coming to the hospital."

"Please, Lyle. Please don't!" she said, her voice rising.

"Why not? Jeez, Mom!"

"You know he doesn't like you to see him when he's…when he's…"

I finished the sentence for her. "Weak? He doesn't like me to see him weak."

"He's a proud man, Lyle."

"Yeah. Too proud to even let people show they care about him."

"He knows you care, Lyle. He knows that."

I couldn't think of a response.

"I gotta go now," she said. "You'll pick up the dog, right?"

"Yeah. You bet, Mom. You need me, give me a call. Okay?"

"Of course, honey. Bye-bye, now."

We both knew she wouldn't call.

Finch dropped me next to my car in my office parking lot. I thanked him and watched him drive away. Standing next to my car in the near empty lot, it hit me. It was too dangerous for me to go back to the Bijou. I was homeless. Homeless and, with my dad off in some hospital and my friends in hiding, utterly alone. I never felt so vulnerable in all my life.

I knew I needed some place to spend the next few days. I decided to go up to the office and check the computer for a place down in Apple Valley. Maybe a motel that took dogs. Failing that, I thought, I could always try to sneak him in somewhere.

Preoccupied with the search for lodging, at first, I ignored the light blinking on my answering machine. I fired up the office computer and took notes on a couple of motels that looked like they might work out. When I picked up the phone to start calling, I checked the message. Wiseman had called. It wasn't good news. It turns out that when the Milkman and Ava had pulled up at Wiseman's after their day together, they were jumped. The Milkman took a pretty brutal blow to the head. His assailants had driven away, leaving him crumpled on the sidewalk.

And they'd taken Ava with them.

Chapter Twenty-eight

Mulligan had been taken by ambulance downtown to the emergency room at Hennepin County Medical Center. When I got there, he was standing at the admitting counter with a large bandage on his head, politely arguing with a young woman in a white coat. Skip stood lookout at the door.

"I cannot stress forcefully enough that it is foolhardy for you to leave the hospital at this time," the woman was saying. "Although your x-rays indicate only a slight concussion, any blow to the head must be treated as a potentially serious injury. Again, I strongly recommend that you allow us to monitor you for at least a couple of hours. After that we can evaluate and determine if there's a need to admit you overnight for further observation."

"I'm sorry, Doctor," Mulligan said, a bit drowsily. "I really am. But I gotta go."

Although Mulligan towered imposingly over the much shorter woman, she stared up at him with an expression of calm, almost parental forbearance. "Whatever you feel you have to do, I'm sure it can keep until tomorrow."

"If I feel worse, I'll come back," he insisted, shuffling before her like an errant child. Knowing that he'd displeased her, Mulligan wore a droopy, *aw shucks* expression.

"Mr. Mulligan, please listen to reason. Falling the

way you did may have caused brain damage. We need to monitor—"

"Again, I'm sorry Doctor," Mulligan interrupted, a placatory smile on his face.

The doctor threw up her hands. "I've done all I can. She turned to a woman behind the desk. "Jennie, have Mr. Mulligan sign an AMA form." That said, she turned back to the Milkman. "That refers to *Against Medical Advice*, Mr. Mulligan. You understand that you may possibly be taking your life in your hands?"

The Milkman nodded. "Yes, ma'am. And I'm really sorry. Thank you for all you've done for me. I really, really, *really* appreciate it."

The doctor gave him a brisk nod and walked away.

"You told them he fell down?" I asked Skip.

"Yep."

"That explains the lack of cops."

"It does."

"We handling this ourselves?"

"We have to."

I raised an eyebrow at him, but he waved me off.

We were still waiting for Mulligan to finish filling out his discharge paperwork, when Edgerton came in. He stopped a few feet in front of the counter. His arms hung limp at his sides, but his eyes frantically searched each of us for information.

"We'll talk outside," I said.

Edgerton's eyes went flinty with anger. "Why the hell can't we—"

I held a finger to my lips. He glanced around at the other people in the waiting area, then glowered at me before nodding his agreement.

The Milkman finished up at the counter and the four

of us wordlessly made our way out of the hospital and up the elevator to the top floor of the parking ramp. Gauzy clouds formed a canopy in the sky overhead, but the late afternoon sun still hung well above the horizon. Great swaths of yellow light sliced across the cement tarmac, knifing away at the comforting shadows that advanced along the walls.

We reached my car and Edgerton immediately began pacing, making short, quick little turns as if dancing an angry jig. "Just what the hell do we do now!" he hissed in a voice as harsh and sharp as a band saw.

"We'll talk inside the car," I said.

"Why inside?"

I stared at him for a moment before surveying the parking lot. I didn't spot another soul, but somehow that made the shadows surrounding us seem markedly less comforting. "It'll make me feel better."

I opened the car door and climbed behind the wheel. The Milkman squeezed into the front passenger's seat, and Edgerton and Skip got in back. With the doors closed, I adjusted the rear-view mirror so I could see Skip. "Where's Wiseman?"

"I told him to stay with his family."

"He call anybody?"

Skip shook his head. "Just me."

I nodded, then turned to the Milkman. He'd been holding up pretty well, but all at once his face folded in on itself. "I'm really sorry, Lyle," he began. His deep voice cracked; his eyes filled with tears. "I didn't see them. I parked in front of the house. Didn't want to park in the driveway in case Max or Vicki or somebody…. Aw, it don't matter. They musta been in the bushes. I was on the ground before I knew what was happening. The guy who hit me was a big fucker, I'll tell you that. Another thing. No hair. The guy had no hair. Probably shaved his head. I saw that before I passed out."

"Harvey Deason," I muttered. "Works for Beam."

Mulligan brightened. "You know him? You know where we can get him?"

I shook my head. "They say anything?"

"Not a thing. They conked me on the noggin, then grabbed up little Ava, and were gone."

"They stuffed a note into his pocket," Skip said, reaching inside his windbreaker.

The note was written on a torn piece of yellow legal paper, printed in capital letters using a blue, fine point marker. *NO COPS. TELL DAHMS WE'LL BE IN TOUCH.*

I read it over several times.

"You think we should call the cops anyway?" Mulligan asked.

I glanced at Skip. He shook his head. "No," I said, "at least not yet."

Edgerton snorted his disapproval.

"You got something you want to say, Stephen?" I askcd.

"Damn right! Ava's going through God knows what and we're fuckin' sitting here. This is bullshit!"

I tried to keep my voice as calm as I could. "We need a plan. We need to talk about this before we do anything. What we don't want to do is go off half-cocked and make things worse."

"Worse! How the hell could things get worse?"

Skip tapped his fingertips lightly on the back of the seat. "Dahms is right, Stephen." Then, turning to me, he asked, "So, you got a plan?"

"Well, no," I admitted. "Not yet. But I don't see sitting around waiting for them to call me."

Skip nodded. "Then again, as you mentioned, that might be better than going off without a clear direction."

I scowled. "We should sit around waiting for the phone to ring?"

"You got a place we can look? You got any ideas where they might be hiding the kid?"

I scowled some more.

"Beam's house?" Skip asked.

I shook my head. "No. Too public. It would have to be someplace out of the way. Trouble is, they could be anywhere. Beam's taken on quite a few followers lately. They could have taken her to somebody's house, an apartment, a trailer. Shit, anywhere."

"Then we're back to waiting for the phone to ring," Skip said.

I turned to stare out the windshield, at the rooftops of some of the surrounding buildings, into the windows of others. Then, slowly, I began to picture the gated driveway leading into Charlie Blauer's place down in St. Helena—the way it cut through the trees, disappearing out of sight, the whole compound ringed in barbed wire. A man who so values his privacy, I thought, likely has a great deal to hide.

"There's one place I'd like to check out," I said. "I can't be sure she's there, but…" I let my voice trail off.

Skip thought for a moment. "Okay. Here's what we do. We set someone up in your office waiting on a phone call while you and I go check out this place you have in mind."

I smiled at him. "You realize that these guys aren't just troublemakers in a bar, Skip. This here's the real deal. These guys are well armed, and they don't mind killing. Especially when it comes to…" I searched momentarily for the words I wanted.

"Especially when it comes to us *darkies*," Skip said. He smiled back at me, but his eyes were as cold and dark as a tomb.

I chuckled defensively. "I was going to say *African Americans*. But whatever you prefer. Anyway, my point is, I don't want you to feel like you have to involve yourself in this."

Skip grunted. "I am involved. One of your people's in trouble, you do what you gotta do."

"One of *your* people?"

"Yeah."

"Ava?"

"Yeah. She means something to me. That makes her one of mine."

I smirked. "That mean I'm one of your people, too?"

Skip stared at me. "I guess."

"This where we join hands and break into a chorus of Kumbaya?"

"No. It's not."

"Damn."

"This is no time for jokes, Lyle," Stephen said.

I nodded. "Okay, here's what I think we do. Milkman, we'll set you up at my office. If these guys call, you can get a hold of me on my cell."

The big man shook his head. "Nope. I'm coming along."

"Irv, you heard the doctor. You're not in any shape to—"

"I lost her. I'll help get her back."

"But—"

Mulligan stared at me. The expression in his eyes left no room for argument. I nodded. "Okay. Stephen, you're on the phones."

"Bullshit!"

"Stephen, someone needs to—"

"I'm going with you."

"Stephen. Somebody's got to be there in case they call."

"Then you do it! You wait for the fuckin' call!"

"It's got to be you. Skip, the Milkman, me. We've done this kind of thing before. You haven't. You couldn't. It's not in you."

"Fuck that! I want to be with you guys."

"This isn't about what any of us wants."

Stephen started to respond but paused. After a moment, he said, "Say I do that. Say I wait by the phone. What happens if they call? What if they call expecting you and get me? What will they think?"

"You tell them you're still tracking me down. They want me pretty bad. They'll wait."

Edgerton stared at me. Anger, sadness, and reason warring across his face like successive images in a flipbook. "I can't just sit around. Not when we don't know what's going on with…" Her name caught in the back of his throat. He shuddered and turned away.

"We're going to get her back, Stephen," I assured him. "But we all have a job to do. Yours is waiting in my office for the call."

Edgerton turned back to me, his eyes burning. "I know what you think. You don't think I can do what needs to be done. Well, you're wrong. They grabbed up my little girl. I'm telling you straight—I could kill them with my bare hands."

I shook my head. "You ain't gonna like hearing this, Stephen. But no. No, you couldn't."

"You don't know, man! This is different. I—"

"I *do* know. I've been there countless times. You're angry. Fiercely, apocalyptically angry. So angry that you're about to bust. And it feels like if you could only unleash it, you could lay waste to the whole goddamned world. But you can't. That's not how it works. If we let you come along, we'd be worried about you. We'd be thinking about you when we should be keeping our heads in the game. You'd be a liability and we can't afford one. I'm sorry, but you're not coming. You want to help? Wait at the office."

"But I—"

I held up a hand. "This one time, just do what I tell you."

Edgerton fell silent.

Skip looked at his watch. "We should get going. I'll drop Stephen. They could have your office staked out and we don't want them spotting you and taking a run at you right there. After that, we'll meet somewhere. You tell me where. By the way, you guys got everything you need? I could stop by my house. I've got most anything."

"What do you mean?" I asked. "Like beer and chips?"

Skip shook his head, then raised his hand and extended the index finger so that it resembled a gun barrel. He cocked his thumb and fired.

I patted the .38 under my jacket. "No, I'm okay."

"You?" Skip asked Mulligan.

The Milkman shook his head. "Don't use one. Thanks anyway."

Skip raised an eyebrow but said nothing. Then he

327

waited while I wrote out the directions to my parents' house. I told him we'd rally there before heading down to St. Helena. I was overjoyed when he didn't ask me why. I really didn't want to try to explain that I'd promised my mommy I'd check in on the dog.

Skip climbed out, nodded at Edgerton to follow, then walked to his own, nearby car. Edgerton had only taken a few steps before he called after Skip to wait for him. Then he returned, coming to stand beside my car. I rolled down the window.

Edgerton put one hand on the top of the Ford as if to steady himself and leaned in close. Most of his anger had drained away, but his eyes retained an anxious wistfulness. "She makes me think of angels," he said. He swallowed hard to fight back a sob. "Like when I was a little kid waking up in the middle of the night, scared after having some dream or hearing some noise. Since my parents didn't believe in God, my sister and I didn't have angels watching over us like other kids. There was just Mom and Dad."

He drummed his fingers lightly on the car. "I'd lie there telling myself that I was safe. That my parents were there for me. That they were enough. But I couldn't help thinking that it would be better if there were angels." He paused. "Having Ava…Taking care of her…I'm supposed to be the one watching over her. But instead, here I am. Still scared. Still wishing for angels."

He turned to gaze out to the horizon. Wisps of clouds were stretching warily out toward the sun, spreading out like the feathers of ghostly wings about to take flight.

"We'll get her back, Stephen," I told him. "I promise."

Chapter Twenty-nine

The first thing I did after Mulligan and I arrived at my parents' house was take Basil outside so that he could take care of his business on my dad's lawn. Ten minutes later when Skip arrived, the dog was still leading me around the yard on a leash, sniffing, darting, stopping, and starting again. Skip stood on the front steps watching for several more minutes before we were ready to come back inside. When we finally approached the house, Skip shook his head dejectedly. "Dog took advantage of me like that, I'd sell him for meat."

Inside, we sat in a circle around the table in my parents' kitchen. Skip appeared calm, his gaze steady, although his eyes smoldered darkly. The Milkman kept glancing about the room. His left hand was balled into a fist while he rubbed his knuckles with his right. But although it was a struggle, he managed to keep his anxiety in check. No one mentioned Ava by name.

St. Helena is just about as far as it can be from downtown Minneapolis and still be included in my trusty Hudson's Twin City Metropolitan Area Street Atlas. I laid it open on the table, staring at a mostly empty grid transected by a black line labeled "County Rd 9." I then traced the few thinner lines that sprouted from the county road—short lines that represented minor roadways that seemed to dead end nowhere. I couldn't help but notice that as I did, my finger trembled ever so slightly. When

I was pretty sure I'd located Blauer's place on the map, I noticed a dotted line that appeared to run adjacent to the property. It was marked "Glickman Trail."

"What's this?" I asked, pointing to the line.

"Looks like a hiking trail," the Milkman said.

"Why would they put a hiking trail out there? It's all farmland. Treeless. Flat. Not exactly one of nature's showcases.

"Probably an old railroad bed," Mulligan suggested. "Besides, I think farm country's kinda pretty."

I nodded. "If this thing runs along Blauer's property, it might be a way in. I remember a cornfield along one side. Can't remember the trail though."

"Good thing you were out there reconnoitering earlier," Skip said. "We might be going in blind."

I ignored him. "We'll be losing the light soon. Best get to it. We'll take my car."

Skip shook his head. "We'll take both cars. The more mobility, the better."

I smiled. "Besides, why ride in my Ford, when you can take your BMW?"

"That, too. You and Mulligan can ride together. You guys check out the trail. I'll go at it another way."

"Don't you think we should stick together?" I asked.

"No."

"But—" I began.

"No," he repeated. "We agree now. You go in from the trail side, I'll find my own way in. When we get there, try and stay out of sight. Search the compound for likely hiding places. If she's there, we get the kid out if we can. Stephen's got my cell phone number. If he calls with new information, I'll get it to you. Otherwise, we give ourselves plenty of time to scope the place out, then rendezvous afterwards at an agreed upon time." Skip glanced at his watch, then pointed at a spot on the map. "How 'bout here at nine o'clock? Here at the trailhead. Sound good?"

"You think we should synchronize watches?" I deadpanned.

"Just watch your ass."

Mulligan and Skip went outside while I turned off the lights and locked up the house. Both appeared dubious when I emerged with the dog.

"Well, it's a hiking trail, isn't it?" I asked. "What could be less suspicious than a guy walking his dog down a trail?"

Mulligan gave me a sheepish little smile. Skip shook his head ruefully.

After the first mile or so, I lost sight of Skip's much speedier car. As Mulligan and I drove toward St. Helena, the tightly packed subdivisions of the suburbs opened up to become farmland, broken up here and there by a country church sitting proudly on a patch of vibrantly green lawn. The sun, though low in the sky, seemed in no hurry to bring on the day's end. It hung poised above the horizon like an indecisive child standing at the edge of a playground, his mother's distant voice calling him in to supper.

As we pulled off the county road and down the dirt road that led to Blauer's place, I began to survey things in earnest. We passed the farmhouse and barn that I remembered were the last structures before we'd reach Blauer's. Just past the farmstead, I spotted the Glickman Trail, a swath cut across the plain that stretched to horizon. The trail was edged on the right side by a cornfield, and on the left by the barbed wire that enclosed

Blauer's compound.

I parked the Ford near the trail, as far off the road as possible. I would have preferred to park it out of sight but couldn't see a spot where it would be both hidden and accessible in case we needed to get away in a hurry. I'd just have to hope that it looked as though it was left there by a couple of guys out for an evening's constitutional. I also had to hope that none of the bad guys on whom we were sneaking up drove by and recognized it as my car. I slipped a flashlight and a pair of wire cutters into the pocket of my jacket, patted the .38 under my arm, and snapped the leash to Basil's collar before the Milkman and I started down the trail. As I took one last glance back, I realized that Skip would have arrived there before us. I didn't see his car.

Mulligan's suggestion that the trail was likely an old railroad bed seemed borne out by its width. It was definitely wide enough to accommodate a locomotive, and—despite a sign posted near the road that declared the trail reserved for hikers and horses—it was clear from the deep, parallel ruts that ran its length that this was largely ignored. The weeds, wildflowers, and prairie grasses along either side were fairly tall, but the few green shoots that pushed up through the hard-packed dirt that surfaced the trail itself stooped close to the ground avoiding the rasp of boot heel, hoof, and truck tire. As we walked in the growing darkness, rosy sunlight flickered through the tall stalks of corn planted to our right, flashing through to the barbed wire on left, which winked back with a sinister glint. I could not help but silently question the wisdom of our plan.

But Basil had no such qualms. He was in dog heaven, sniffing every millimeter of trail, brushing himself as lightly as a whisper against the vegetation that grew along the trail, and beaming wide-mouthed and breathless up at us as we walked along.

We got about a quarter of a mile down the trail, past the point where the clearing that fronted the Blauer property became wooded, when Basil decided it was time to leave some sign that he'd come that way. He went into serious pee spot scouting mode, refusing to continue onward until he'd snuffled out the perfect patch of ground on which to urinate. I tugged uselessly on the leash, interrupting him and making the process take that much longer. Defeated, I rolled my eyes at Mulligan. "We can wait," he said.

But although he thoroughly studied each molecule of earth beneath him, Basil seemed unable to make a decision. I waited. Then waited some more. After what seemed like an eternity, I finally exploded.

"God dammit, Basil!" I shouted. "Just pee, willya!"

The dog, of course, was heartbroken by my outburst. His stumpy tail turned down like a divining rod over a buried reservoir. His shoulders hunched and he stopped dead in his tracks. I turned to Mulligan. There was chastisement in his eyes and, like the dog, my shoulders drooped with shame. That's when I heard it. A low growl down the trail in front of us. I turned around to see a long, dark shadow, close to the ground, emerge from the brush ahead. It was a dog.

Although not a dog the way Basil was a dog. Quite the contrary. This was a great big dog. A dog of Brobdingnagian proportions. A dog with a massive head and even more massive incisors which, at that moment, it was only too happy to display. It glided toward us, the whites of its eyes each a glowing ring highlighting an inky, soulless center. It growled again, eyeing us contemplatively, as if trying to determine which of us would make the better meal. I gulped. It's not enough to say that I was alarmed by the sudden appearance of this animal. I felt suddenly as if an icy hand from beyond the grave had reached out and grasped my inner organs and I was left gasping as the remnants of my heart oozed through its skeletal fingers. I was too scared to move.

Beside me, the Milkman cooed, "Here poochie, poochie."

I whirled around to gape at him. As the spectral hellhound grew ever nearer, the Milkman had squatted down and was extending a hand toward him. The dog responded with a bark as loud as a gunshot accompanied by a snap of his jaws that sent ropes of saliva spinning about his head.

"Probably smells our dog," the Milkman said thoughtfully.

"Let's get the hell out of here," I said.

"If we run, he'll likely come after us."

"If we stay here, he'll likely eat us."

"Now, Lyle, you can't judge a book by its cover. We don't know that this dog would—"

Mulligan was interrupted by another snap of the dog's viselike jaws.

"I know!" I exclaimed, reaching for my gun. "I'll shoot it!"

"Don't do it, Lyle."

I turned to look at him. "Beg pardon?"

"Somebody'd hear," he warned. "They hear us, how we gonna sneak in and find the kid?"

"Shit."

I didn't know what to do. I didn't want to give away

our position, but I also didn't want to be shredded to kibble. I slowly drew my gun from the shoulder holster.

But before I could act, Basil gingerly took a couple of steps forward. The devil dog snarled and reared back, ready to pounce. Basil stopped and splayed out all four legs, prostrating himself before the much larger dog. Then he let go of his bladder. Basil turned his head demurely as a large puddle appeared beneath him, soaking into the firm ground. When he was finished, Basil, head down, inched back toward us, and the big dog moved forward. He sniffed, raised his head to stare malevolently at us, then sniffed again. Finally, he drew himself up and with a regal air, he lifted his leg and peed directly on the spot that Basil had first soaked. One more diffident glance at us and, incredibly, he sauntered away.

"Holy shit!" I breathed.

"Good dog, Basil," Mulligan said, stooping to rub our savior cockapoo behind the ears. Basil glanced uncertainly up at me.

"I owe ya one, bud," I said.

I let my revolver settle back into the shoulder holster. We only got another step or two before something hit the ground in front of us with great force. It skipped away in a puff of dirt before I could make out what it was. But then we heard the crack. The crack of the rifle that had fired at us.

I grabbed Mulligan by the sleeve and twisted indecisively for a moment. Remembering the barbed wire to our left, I clutched tightly onto both the Milkman and Basil's leash and dove toward the cornfield on the right side. "Run!" I hollered.

The Milkman lurched forward, and I slipped behind him, hanging on as he plowed an opening into the field.

Something buzzed past my ear, followed by another crack of gunfire. As we lumbered onward, cornstalks snapped, Basil yowled, and on the trail behind us a peal of barking signaled the return of the demon guard dog.

The Milkman suddenly cut right, and I lost my grip on his sleeve. My foot caught the base of a stalk and I crashed to the ground, losing my grip on Basil's leash as I fell. On the way down, I grazed the edge of a leaf. It traced an icy line across my face. I touched my hand to my cheek, smearing my fingers with blood. I cast wildly about for Basil, but the little guy had vanished. I got my legs under me and managed to stand, but then felt a tug, and a sharp pain ignited inside my tennis shoe. I looked down to see a tear in the leather, extending right down through the rubber sole. I'd been shot. Another bullet whizzed past. I scrambled deeper into the cornfield, my breath now coming in gasps, my heart thudding in my chest. After pushing on several additional feet, I forced myself to slow down, to listen, to be less of a target.

Off to my right, the rustle and snap of cornstalks told me that the Milkman was continuing onward into the field. I, too, sidled in deeper, vainly trying to weave my bulk through the cornstalks without making noise or leaving a trail. After a few minutes of slow retreat, I squatted down and listened again. It was now quiet. I could no longer hear the Milkman moving through the corn, nor did it appear that anyone had followed us in. I thought I heard a plaintive whine somewhere behind me. It might have been Basil. I couldn't be sure.

Cicadas chorused in the distance. A bird joined them, singing shrilly from a perch along the trail. At least I thought it came from the trail. Crouching among the cornstalks, I couldn't be sure. From the road, each row of corn had appeared almost perfectly straight, the space between the rows a path that led directly from one end of the field to the other. But inside, these paths had vanished. Suddenly I was surrounded by a chaotic stand of tough stalks and razor leaves. I remembered stories I'd heard of toddlers wandering out into cornfields, becoming disoriented, unable to find the way to safety although only steps from his or her own yard. I looked up at the tasseled tops of the stalks that surrounded me. If I stood, I might be able to see over them, I told myself. If I stood, they might also shoot my fool head off.

Something gleamed in the failing light. The silken strands of an intricately conceived spider web stretched between two nearby stalks. Although its eight-legged architect was nowhere to be seen, immediately I felt as though something was crawling on me. I willed myself to remain motionless. Although apparently distant, the low growl of the dog seemed to cut through the forest of cornstalks, hugging the ground, weaving precisely toward me. Finally, a man's voice rang out. "Do you think we scared 'em off?"

Another voice, this one tight with anger, replied. "*We*? There ain't no *we*. *We* were supposed to keep our eyes open, ya fuckin' moron. We *weren't* supposed to open up on anybody come walking down the fuckin' trail. That was all yer doing. Now *we* both gotta go back and explain why *you* decided to shoot at them guys. Ya fuckin' moron."

There was a pause before the first man replied. "Well, what was they doing out here anyway? We was told—"

"What were they doing out here?" the second man asked incredulously. "It's a hiking trail. Ya think maybe they coulda been hiking? We'll be lucky we don't have the cops out here now. I ain't taking the heat for this one, I'll tell you that, Hickey. This shit's on you. Now, we better be getting back. Heel, Duke!"

The dog barked a reply.

I stayed low as they crunched their way down the trail. When the sounds of their footsteps had faded, I examined my shoe. My foot stung like hell, but I didn't think I'd lost more than a tiny piece of it. I could tend to it later. I had other things to tend to just then. Obviously, Charlie and Megan Blauer had guests this evening. I didn't know how many guests, but I did know they were armed, on the watch, and really, really jumpy. Something was definitely going on *chez* Blauer. The two that had shot at us were now going back to explain themselves and that was going to stir things up even more. They'd shot at a couple of people without identifying them first and then they'd let them get away. My guess was that the bunch of them would now be out in force, combing the area for us. If we were friendlies, they'd want to apologize or explain away the overzealousness of their sentries. If we weren't, they'd want us out of the way. In either case, they'd find my car. And I had to assume that someone would figure out who'd come a-callin'.

I stood, removed my gun from its holster, and slowly headed in the direction from which I'd heard the voices. On the way, I continued to search for Basil, but had no luck. I'd been crunching onward for some five minutes when I began to doubt that I was actually moving in the direction of the trail. A couple more minutes and an itchy panic began to rise within me.

"That you, Lyle?" Mulligan's throaty whisper sounded several yards away.

I stopped. "Yeah. I'm kinda lost."

"Wait there. I got you."

All at once it was as if the field had been invaded by a panzer division. The stalks in front of me shook violently, then toppled as the big man drove toward me. When finally, he reached me, he turned and briefly admired the wide path he'd created behind him. "This way," he said. Noticing that Basil was no longer with me, he asked, "The dog?"

"Lost him. He's in here somewhere."

The Milkman's eyes flooded with concern, but he said nothing further.

We made our slow way back to the trail, stopping regularly to listen for the sound of approaching bad guys or for some sign of Basil. When we arrived, Mulligan stared at me, waiting for directions. I thought for a moment about heading back to the car, steeled myself, and said, "I think we better go in. I figure most of them will head here to the trail or into the cornfield. We go in, it might throw them." There wasn't much conviction in my voice.

"You think Ava's in there?" Mulligan asked.

"Something's in there."

Mulligan nodded and followed me as I stepped through the grass that edged the trail. Wire cutters in one hand, gun in the other, I approached the barbed wire fence, staring into the woods that screened Blauer's house from view.

It took several attempts to cut through each of the three strands of barbed wire that barred our entrance. By the time I'd managed to etch my way through the last strand, several voices and the whir of an engine sounded on the trail. The Milkman and I were barely out of sight in the woods before a battered pickup bounced down the trail toward us. There were two men in the cab and three more riding in the open bed. The guys in the back were armed; one had a shotgun, the others looked to be carrying rifles. Somehow, although surveying the perimeter as they passed, they missed the opening I'd cut in the fence. They rattled onward, coming to a stop at the spot where Mulligan and I had earlier crashed into the cornfield.

As the search party piled out of the truck, the Milkman and I made our way carefully in through the woods in the opposite direction. It was a shallow stand of mixed, mostly deciduous trees, not providing as much cover as I'd hoped. I felt pretty exposed when we squatted behind a large cottonwood at the very edge of the woods and peered out at the clearing beyond. There was some thirty yards of open, grassy space between where we were and a white, two-story, clapboard house that looked like it dated from the 1930s. A three-season porch fronted the house, lace curtains completely covering the windows, but light shining from within. Next to the house was a much newer building—a long, wide, nearly windowless rectangle—too big to be simply a garage, that likely served as storage for Blauer's construction equipment. There didn't seem to be anyone guarding the outbuilding. But two armed men stood at the front of the house.

"If she's here, I'm bettin' she's in the house," I whispered to Mulligan.

He looked out at all that open space. "How do we get in?"

I rose and motioned for him to follow. We stayed in the woods, which curved around near the back of the house. Although there were no guards back there, there was also no door, and the basement windows were made of impenetrable glass blocks. I didn't see how, outside of a suicidal frontal assault, we were going to get inside. We kept moving under the sparse cover until we got a look at the opposite side of the house. There I spotted a pair of nearly horizontal doors slanting away from the side of the house that looked to lead down into some kind of cellar below. Perhaps, I thought, they'd be a way for us to get in. On the other hand, maybe it provided no access into the house. In that case, if we went under the house and were caught, it'd be like sealing ourselves in a tomb. I pointed to the doors. "What do you think?"

He nodded. "Think we can reach them without being seen?"

"Not really," I admitted. "I think we'd need some kind of diversion."

Mulligan nodded again. "I could do that."

"What do you have in mind?"

"I'll just go back toward the front and make a little noise is all."

"Are you nuts? The guys with the guns would come after you."

"That's the point, Lyle. They come after me, they don't see you sneak in."

I shook my head. "Nope. Too dangerous. We'll find another way."

"The kid may be in there, Lyle," Mulligan said. "I hate to think how scared she must be."

"It won't help Ava none you going off and getting yourself killed."

Mulligan paused, his eyes going a little vacant, before snapping back into determined focus. "Let me live in greatness and courage or here in this hall welcome my death," he quoted.

"We're not in a hall," I pointed out.

Mulligan ignored me. Before I could stop him, he sprang to his feet and began to race through the woods to the front of the house.

"Shit," I muttered.

Moments later, something that resembled a guttural, Indian war whoop rang out. I heard one of the guards up near the front porch exclaim, "What the…?" Then the sound of footfalls moved rapidly away from the house.

I took a deep breath and, keeping low, raced out of the woods and beelined it for the cellar doors. I rounded the corner just as two more men emerged from the house pausing in the yard to stare after their advancing comrades. I ducked back behind the house.

"What are you two doing out here?" one of them asked loudly.

"Shush!" came the reply. "We heard something."

I slipped from behind the house in time to see that all four men were moving into the woods. I dropped and crawled on my belly over to the side cellar doors. My heart sunk when I spotted the hasp and padlock that secured them. I holstered my gun and reached into my trousers pocket for my key chain and the little pick I kept to bypass simple locks. Staying as low as possible, I worked the lock in the waning twilight. After what seemed an impossibly long time, the padlock finally released with a click, and I was able to ease open one of the doors. The shriek of its rusty hinges was like opening a bag of angry screech owls. I slipped into the darkness below the house and closed the door behind me.

Again, I removed my gun from its holster, then

surveyed the room in the circle of dull, yellow glow from the small flashlight that I'd fished from my pocket. It was not a full basement. Rather, it was a small, cramped space with a dirt floor dug out from under only half the width of the house above. Rough pine shelves lined one of the walls, mostly empty except for a couple of dusty jars of ancient, unrecognizable preserves and a coffee can with a masking tape label that read, "Nails."

A burlap bag in one corner bulged with potatoes that smelled strongly of mildew, but in another corner sat an elaborate, handmade doll's house, complete with rooms of tiny furniture, peopled by porcelain dolls no more than three inches long with hinged arms and legs, hand-stitched clothing, and finely painted expressions. Megan's, I figured. Left over from her childhood, now consigned to the cellar, replaced by other toys, other interests.

I walked the length of the cellar and found a narrow wooden staircase—more like a ladder, really—that led up to a trapdoor in the ceiling. I closed my eyes and tried to picture as vividly as I could what I'd guessed about the layout of the house above. As near as I could tell, the trapdoor would open into the enclosed front porch. I snapped off the flashlight and stood listening in the darkness for sounds of activity up in the house. All was silent. Not so much as a footstep creaked on the floorboards above. Clutching my revolver, I climbed the stairs and pushed against the trapdoor. I still heard nothing. I got the door cracked open enough that I could peer into the porch. It was empty. The guards were still outside chasing after the Milkman. I hadn't heard any shots, I thought. He was probably still okay.

I emerged onto the porch, closing the trapdoor

behind me. Now the tricky part: I had to get inside the house without raising the alarm. The front door was oak with three small, beveled glass windows at eye level. I gazed down a short hallway that opened into a living room beyond. I didn't see a soul.

I was turning the doorknob when the screen porch door banged behind me. A young man with a blond buzz cut wearing camouflaged trousers tucked into black combats boots stared at me. His jaw dropped and his eyes lost their focus. For a moment he looked like a cartoon character who's stepped off a cliff, hanging there in disbelief, about to free-fall into the canyon below. I shot him before he could raise his gun.

I glanced out into the yard. Two men positioned near the tree line heard the shot, turned, and began to race back toward the house. Then footsteps sounded from the inside. I dropped to the floor and scooted into a corner with a clear vantage of both doors, hoping I'd be able to drop whoever came into the porch first—the men outside or those within. The porch door and the front door opened at nearly the same instant. Another guy in camouflaged pants entered from the yard, stumbling into the porch over the body of the man I'd shot.

From inside the house, Matty Beam stuck out his head, his right ear heavily bandaged. His eyes went wide as I raised the .38, took aim at him, and pulled the trigger. Beam let out a little yelp, but the bullet merely grazed him below his left armpit. He was able to pull the door closed before I could get off another shot. The soldier on the porch with me was momentarily distracted by the shot I'd got off at Beam, but only momentarily. Before I was able to turn my gun on him, he'd wheeled around and had the muzzle of his rifle centered dead on my chest. It was trigger-happy Hickey. The corner of his mouth curled into a cruel smile as he fingered the trigger.

I sucked in what I was certain would be my last breath.

But a sharp crack sounded outside, followed by the shatter of glass. Hickey spun like a figure skater practicing a triple lutz. When he stopped spinning, I spotted a large bloody hole in his chest. He crumbled to the floor. I exhaled deeply, truly astonished to find myself still alive. Skip, I realized. Mulligan had no weapon. Skip was out there somewhere with a high-powered rifle. He'd saved my life.

Panicked voices sounded close to the house. "Get inside!" someone shouted. "We're sitting ducks out here!"

I lunged for the door into the house. I was just inside as the porch door banged shut, two armed men tripping over the bodies out there. I was able to throw the deadbolt before they'd got back to their feet. I looked down the short hallway that led to the living room. Beam wasn't in sight. The whole house seemed to shudder as the men in the porch booted the front door. A couple of knocks like that, I thought, and they'd be in here with me. I fired a round into the door, more to slow them down than with hope of stopping them. Then I headed down the hallway.

I stayed low, making my way into the living room, holding my revolver in front of me with both hands, ready to shoot anything that moved. In the living room, a sofa upholstered in a pale gold and rose floral pattern took up nearly the entire wall opposite the TV set. Directly ahead of me, a wood-framed archway led into a dining room beyond. To my left, an open staircase led up to the second story. I decided to try the dining room.

All I had was a dim notion that if I could get my hands on Beam, I might be able to barter my way out of there. Behind me, the front doorframe cracked again loudly. I rushed into the dining room, did a hasty survey, then turned toward the narrow entrance to the adjacent kitchen. He'd been hiding just inside the archway. I should have spotted him. There was just no excuse for it. But I hadn't.

Beam hit me hard with something. I couldn't tell what. When I turned to face him, the world had become blurry and unstable. My .38 fell lazily from my fingertips as the floor seemed to lurch me off balance, propelling me directly toward Beam. He took another swing at me, but I got inside and drove my right into his midsection. I really got my weight behind it, so I was surprised that Beam managed to hold on to his club. But he doubled over, and I was able to slip behind him, locking him into a full nelson. Then I stumbled toward the wall, driving the top of his head about two inches into the plaster and lath. He moaned as he dropped his weapon.

The front door finally gave way and two armed men burst into the house. I wasn't able to retrieve my .38 before they reached the dining room. One, I didn't recognize. The other was the guy I'd been calling Dark Eyes. I turned to face them, using Beam as my shield. Both men had handguns, their eyes electric with fear and hate.

I got lucky. They didn't just start shooting. Instead, we all stood for a moment—wordless, staring, Beam going limp in my grasp, my hands clasped behind his neck. Then, from the adjacent kitchen, a man's voice broke the silence. "You know, Dahms," Frank Sullivan said, emerging through the narrow doorway, "you really know how to fuck things up."

I whirled around, clutching Beam in front of me. Sully had a great big old .44 caliber revolver stuck in his waistband. With some difficulty he maneuvered it free, past the substantial roll of flab that hung over his jeans. He grinned sheepishly and shrugged.

"I walk out of here, Sully!" I shouted. "Or I swear I'll snap this asshole's neck!"

"I believe you would at that," Sully said, an affable lilt to his voice. He turned to the two men covering me. "Relax, boys," he told them.

"It's more than just him, Mr. Sullivan," Dark Eyes said, his words rushing forth, tumbling over one another. "There's another one. Out there. He shot Hickey. This one, he shot—"

"Sounds like they need you outside," Sully interrupted. "Get out there and help sort that out, okay?"

Both men wavered, their frightened eyes darting from Sully to me, then to Sully again.

"I mean it. I'll handle this fella. Them guys need you outside."

When they still hesitated, Sully exploded. "Get out there now, you cowardly bastards! Get out there or I'll shoot you myself!"

Dark Eyes stared at the gun in Sully's hand, nudged the other guy with an elbow, and led him outside, closing the front door behind them.

When they'd gone, Sully turned back to me. Keeping me covered with the .44, he strolled across the room to where I'd dropped my .38. He shifted the larger gun to his left hand, then stooped to pick up my gun with his right. He examined it appreciatively for a moment before raising it. He took aim and said softly, "*Auf Wiedersehen.*"

Desperately, I hoisted the unconscious Beam up off the ground, at the same time ducking my head down behind him, praying Sully wouldn't have a clear shot at me. It's difficult to describe the sound. Holding him, it was as if I *felt* the bullet as it struck Beam nearly in the center of his forehead. First there was the crunching of bone, then the muffled slurp as the projectile passed through his gray matter. Then more crunching, followed by the splat/drip of blood and brain bursting wide out the back of Beam's head. And all of this was wrapped in another sound—a shrill cocoon of a scream that I was unable to hold back.

When, at last, my eyes refocused, I found that I had dropped Beam and was standing in the open, staring at Sully.

He took a deep breath. Then another. It was only with difficulty that he was able to regain his self-possession. Finally, the good-natured grin returned to his face, but I thought I detected a nervous quiver in his voice when he spoke. "Now, let's get you reunited with that little girl of yours."

Chapter Thirty

I was mess. I was covered in Beam's blood. It streaked my hair, soaked my T-shirt, and stung my eyes. The room was rank with the smell of burnt gunpowder and an overpowering stench rising from Beam's corpse. Sully's bullet had not only swept away his life but had also voided his bowels.

Sully kept me covered with his .44, as he wriggled my dad's .38 into his waistband. He smiled grimly, pointed across the room with the barrel of the big gun. "She's upstairs." He motioned for me to take the lead. "Prude's watching her."

As we ascended, Sully groaned quietly as he labored up each step. I tried to slow my breathing, hoping to get my jangled nerves under control before I went in to see Ava. Framed photographs hung along the wall leading up to the bedrooms. There was a black and white study of a young man posing proudly beside a pristine coupe that dated from the early 1950's. Then the same man, a few years later, wearing a coal black suit, a stiff collar, and a bow tie standing beside a woman with hollow eyes dressed in a bridal gown. Next came what I took for Charlie Blauer's high school portrait, his hair fashionably long, the wings of his collar wide enough to support a Cessna, his suit coat a remarkable orange-brown plaid. Finally, near the top of the stairs, hung a photograph of Megan, her blonde hair piled high on her head as if styled for a school formal, tendrils falling to frame her delicate features.

I paused at the top of the stairs. Sully's face was puffy, pink, and sweaty. "First door on the right," he prompted.

The door was open. Prude was standing just inside, her back to a wide dresser topped with an oval mirror. When she saw me, she straightened, puffed up her chest, and automatically checked her hair with both hands. As I entered, for an instant, there was an amorous playfulness in her eyes. But when she'd taken the full measure of me, this ardor was replaced by shock. I looked past her at my reflection in the mirror. Suffice it to say that I was no longer anyone's dreamboat.

"My God, Sully!" Prude exclaimed, but then she held her tongue.

Both Megan and Ava were on the floor beside the bed. Lined up next to them was a row of stuffed animals, some sitting upright, others toppled over like plague victims. Megan had a skinny arm around Ava. Both were curled up, knees close to their chests, huddling together. Megan refused to look up. Ava stared at me with wide and, I thought, hopeful eyes.

"You okay, honey?" I asked.

She nodded.

Sully grunted and wiped some of the sweat from his brow. "I gotta admit you kinda caught me off guard. We really didn't expect you to drop by. You don't have many fans here, you know."

"Yeah," I said, "but they love me in France."

Sully grinned and Prude forced out a loud, but mirthless chuckle.

"You know, Dahms," Sully said. "I like you. I really

do. Under other circumstances we coulda got along real good. But we got these circumstances. I just don't quite know what we're gonna do here."

"We could end it. You could just let us all go."

"If only it were that easy."

"Might be that easy," I said. "Beam's dead. We call the cops. They come in here, we pin it all on him, and you and I go back to our lives."

"Wouldn't end like that," Sully said. "Too much has happened. And I ain't going to jail."

"I think we could work something out so that doesn't happen."

There was a small chair in the corner of the room, wood with an embroidered cushion embedded in the seat. Sully pulled it away from the wall and sat down heavily, careful to keep me covered the whole time. He ran his hand over his balding pate and nodded a couple of times, thoughtfully, like a man still considering his options. I was grateful for that. It was the only thing keeping me alive.

"I just don't see any way around it, Dahms," Sully said at last. "Not the way things are. But if you got something to say, I'll listen."

I smiled. "Well, you wouldn't do time for killing Beam. I'd make sure of that. He was trying to kill me. You stopped him. You're a goddamned hero."

Sully chuckled. "You know, I never liked that self-important son-of-a-bitch. Always giving orders like he's goddamned God Almighty. I worked with him, but I didn't like him." Sully shook his head, his eyes focused momentarily on something faraway. "But we had us a good thing going there for a while. St. Helena's been good to me. This is our home, you know, Prude's and mine. Weren't born here. Our people are down in Missouri. *Misery*, we call it now. We've been up here so long, no place else'd seem like home to us. Seen this town go through a lot. Even watched old Matty grow up. Not that we knew him as well as some others. I mean, Prude and me, we go to all the football and basketball games out to the high school, but Matty didn't go out for sports much. A little prissy for that, maybe. And he didn't come round like so many others trying to get me to serve him before he was old enough. Nah, I didn't really get to know him 'til he comes back from law school. Then, I guess, I got to know him too well."

Sully grinned. "Folks'd come into the bar talking about him and how he'd come back with some pretty queer notions. They said he'd made a couple trips down south and out west. He'd gone out and visited with these Christian Identity folks."

He shook his head again. "Personally, I don't have nothing against nobody. I don't care if you're a regular American, or if you're Jewish, or Black, or whatever. Don't see no sense in getting all fired up about this…what they call it, 'maintaining racial purity,' or any of that nonsense. Not really. But after Matty'd set up the website and the first few hard cores come a calling, well, I started to take notice. I heard that Matty was raking it in pretty good. Donations, he called them. Fools sending other fools money, I called it. But it got me to thinking maybe I could get in on some of that action. I cozied up to Matty some, but it wasn't until Al Grogan got here that things really got interesting." Sully chuckled again. "That Grogan was plain crazy, I'll tell ya. He'd cut you up just for looking at him. But it was a useful kind of crazy. He had all kinds of connections. Friends he'd made down in Texas when he was running down there. Friends he'd made in stir. Knew how to get his hands on just about every kinda gun you'd ever want to own. Even the hard-to-find collector's shit that goes for real money. Matty was in. He thought we were arming the faithful for the coming race wars or some such crap. What we were doing was making money. A whole lot more money than old Matty ever knew about. Grogan and me? We cut a deal. Real sweet. We were dealing in goddamned big quantities, too. Big enough we needed a kinda warehouse. Somewhere out of the way where we could come and go without us drawing suspicion. You know what I mean?"

"Sure" I said. "A place like this."

Sully nodded. "Seemed like the perfect spot. I talked to Charlie but at first he wasn't having any of it. He flat out told me to go to hell. But he, uh…See, he owed me money. A while back Charlie'd overextended himself. A couple of big projects went bad on him. When the bank wouldn't give him another loan, he come to me. So that and a little pressure at school convinced him to play along. Kinda what they call a silent partner."

"What kind of pressure at school?"

Sully grimaced and glanced briefly up at Prude, then at the two girls on the floor at his feet. "I shouldn't like to say. Not real proud of myself there. But an awful lot of money was riding on the thing and Grogan said he'd handle it. I let him handle it. Actually, he got them two boys you killed—Segulia and Hollenbeck—he got them to do some stuff. They stole Charlie's truck once. And they made a couple of passes by our little Megan here. Nothing harmful, mind you. Just a little reminder to her daddy that this kind makes a better friend than an enemy."

"You threatened his daughter?" I asked. "And Blauer joined up with you anyway?"

Sully shrugged. "We didn't give him much choice. Like I told ya, that Grogan was plain crazy."

"Where's Charlie now?"

Megan glanced up briefly. Her blue eyes were dark, almost gray, like a summer sky sheathed in clouds.

"Charlie's in the next room," Sully told me. "Deason's in there with him. You know Harvey, don't you Dahms?"

"I've had the pleasure."

Sully smiled. "Doubt it was a pleasure. Anyway, Charlie's pretty mad right now. He ordered us out after Walsh got killed. He's right put out we're still here. When Matty and the boys showed up with the little girl earlier today, he started making all kinds of threats. Figured we'd let him cool off a bit. Also thought keeping Megan away from him might help him with his thinking."

I set my mouth in a soft grin, glancing past Sully at Megan's bedroom window. Night had fallen, but a floodlight at the front of the house cast a bright yellow light into the yard. The window was open, and a light breeze was blowing into the room. The air was fresh with promise. The window was probably big enough for me to get through, I thought. But we were on the second floor. It would be a helluva drop. And besides, there were more guys with guns out there.

Sully caught me looking and winked. "What we need now is to decide what to do with you." He moved the gun barrel in a tight circular motion, as if painting a bull's-eye on my chest.

"You said Charlie's been upset since Walsh got killed," I said. "Charlie have anything to do with the killing?"

Sully chuckled. "Nah, Charlie's a tough old nut but he ain't got no killing in him."

"Unlike you."

His eyes went steely, and he held the .44 absolutely steady. "I'll do what I have to do."

"Why'd you guys kill Walsh?" I asked. "Seems like you'd have wanted to keep him healthy. You'd already touched him for ten grand, right? Seems like there should have been more where that came from."

Sully smiled. "Beam told me you knew about that. Said you tipped him to it before you shot up his ear. Truth is, Matty didn't know about it before you told him. Grogan and me? We didn't exactly share everything with Matty. That Walsh money went into the private account. Grogan's and mine. Coulda milked that cow dry, I was thinking. But things don't always go like you plan."

"What happened?"

Sully leaned back in his chair and sighed. "What happened was this. When little Tyler found out about his daddy's indiscretions, he took it pretty hard. He'd been going out with Megan for a while and was hanging out over here all the time. I asked Charlie if maybe he'd *work* on the boy a bit. Young folks'll listen to somebody's not their own mom or dad. Charlie laid it on long and loud about rich pricks like his old man not giving a damn about regular people. Got Tyler thinking that guys like Charlie and Matty were the only kind that really understood. When Tyler was pretty well in, I had Al Grogan call Greg Walsh. Invite him to sit down to a little chat. Well, Grogan and Walsh get together at my place, and we convince Greg that Matty will…I guess you'd call it *excommunicate* little Tyler. For a price. Couldn't rightly let Matty in on that one. Matty, he was a true believer. Once you're in the fold, as far as he's concerned, you're in. Besides, we wanted to keep things off the books, so to speak."

Something that might have been a moan sounded down the hall. Sully stared out the open door for a moment before continuing. "We hit Walsh up for ten thousand dollars and damned if the guy isn't desperate enough to go for it. We make Walsh promise not to mention it to anyone, not even his wife, or the deal's off, and maybe Tyler gets hurt. So, he gives us the money. A few days go by. Grogan and I figure what the hell? Worked once. We'll try it again. But this time we don't set up the meeting at my roadhouse. This time, Grogan and me, we meet Walsh downtown at night, in the parking lot of his own office building. Supposed to make Walsh feel safe. Anyway, we ask Walsh for more money and the guy goes loony. Says he's going to the cops. Says he won't be blackmailed anymore. He comes after me pushing and punching and yelling. I wasn't expecting that, you know? Anyway, I got this knife with me and…I don't remember exactly it happening, but the next thing I know, Walsh is on the ground whimpering. Grogan, he looks down and says, 'He ain't dead yet.' Then, just like that, he pulls his own knife and shanks him again." Sully paused, spreading both palms out before him. "Walsh stops whimpering."

He swallowed hard. "I didn't know what to do. Grogan wants to just hightail it out of there, but I'm not so sure. I figure the least we can do is give us some time, hide the body so it's not found right away. So, we put it in the trunk of the car and start driving around looking for a place to stash it. But I was scared, you know? I didn't know what the right thing was. And Grogan, he's no help. So, I think of Matty. He's a lawyer. Maybe he'd think of something could help us out. We pull over and I give him a call. I tell him that Walsh is dead. That it's an accident, but he's dead. 'Course Matty wants to know what we were doing with Walsh in the first place. I fudged that a bit. I told him that Walsh called Charlie to talk about Tyler's being involved in Matty's church. I said that Charlie wasn't man enough to face Walsh, so he sent down Grogan and me. Matty didn't put much stock in Charlie, so he believes what I told him. And everyone knows how, whatchacallit, how volatile Grogan is."

Sully chuckled. "*Was* I guess is more like it now. Anyway, I told Matty I was afraid the cops would shut us down for good if they find out. Matty tells us to wait 'til he can get there. One thing I gotta say for Matty, he was pretty cool under pressure. I'm about messing my drawers with that body in the trunk and all, but old Matty's cool as a Frigidaire. He insists we go back to the parking lot to wipe the place down. Good thing, too. Our prints were all over the place, blood on the ground. We go back to driving around, thinking what to do with the body, talking about alibis and all that. And Grogan, he gets this idea. He's worried since he's the only one of us with a record, the only one done real violence before, and since he's the guy that stabbed Walsh last, that we might be thinking he's the one to take the fall if it comes to that. He starts getting agitated. And you didn't want to be around Grogan when he's agitated. Then he gets this idea. He spots that Mex restaurant. Place is closed, streetlight's out so it's pretty dark in back by the dumpster. We figure it's good enough. But when we get Walsh out of the trunk, Grogan hands Matty a knife. I still got mine, and Grogan's got a spare. Grogan tells us to stab the guy."

I shook my head.

Sully shrugged. "I know, I know. It didn't make much sense to me either, but I checked, and the guy's already dead, so I didn't see the harm. Besides, Grogan isn't somebody you cross lightly. So, I do it. Beam said no at first. Probably didn't want to get any more involved than he already was. But Grogan ain't letting him off the hook. Makes him do it over and over. Me too, over and over. And Grogan starts stabbing him again too. Over and over. Then Grogan takes the knives from us. Says they're his insurance policy. Then we drive away."

"What about the swastika's carved into the corpse? Why do that?"

Sully screwed up his face into a vaguely comical squint. "They were Matty's idea. Kinda my fault, but Matty's idea."

"What do you mean?"

Sully grunted. "Well, back when we were driving around, I sorta decided to come clean with Matty about little Tyler's background. If he was gonna help us out the jam, I thought he might need to do some thinking about Walsh and the little sweetie he's had on the side. Matty was as ticked off as I'd ever seen a body. Not about Walsh having some Jew girlfriend but about her being Tyler's momma. You know, how that made the boy a Jew. Kept saying that Tyler'd duped him, how that wasn't right, and how he was gonna get his. Matty'd had plenty of time to stew over this by the time we got rid of the body. We were about to drive away when Matty says *wait*. He goes back over to the body and he's messing around with it in the dark. We don't even see what he's doing. We got no idea about them swastikas 'til we read about it in the paper."

"I don't get it," I said. "The swastikas made it look like Beam or at least someone from your little group was involved. His doing that doesn't make sense."

"I know," Sully said, giving his head a rueful shake. "I asked Beam about that later, but he just gives me this look. I think he was just pissed and decided to send Tyler a message. Calm as he seemed, I don't think Matty was thinking exactly straight. But damned if it didn't look like it'd work out anyway. The cops find the body and everything we read made it sound like they thought Tyler was the killer."

I nodded. "Two of the knives turned up in the Hollenbeck kid's garage. You know how they got there?"

"You know, that's really all your doing," Sully said.

"Yeah, like I'm to blame for any of this."

"There's blame enough for everybody, Dahms. Like I said, things were going pretty well. The paper made it sound like the cops thought Tyler'd killed his dad. Matty'd told everyone not to worry. He said we could expect the cops to come 'round, but since we were innocent and since the good Lord smiles on the righteous and all that, we'd end up all right. And the truth is, for a while there it looked like all we had to do was wait around for Tyler to take the fall. Then you had to rile old Matty up that way. Matty being Matty sends Grogan and Deason after you, but you don't back off. Next thing, you're down here looking for Charlie. Then things go right to hell. Them boys spot you in my place and decide to tail you. You all end up at Walshes and the boys musta decided that with you working for them, you'd be trying to pin this on one of us. Guess they wanted to put an end to it right there. A stupid play, but hell, they were young, right? Being young is all about being stupid."

"Uh huh."

"Of course, Matty drew a particular sort, too," Sully added. "These guys, they'd sit around drinking, puffing themselves up. Talking about killing people. Beating 'em. Having their women. It was all pretty…whatchacallit… pathetic. Anyway, after they died, Beam convinces Grogan to plant the knives. Make it look like it was them that helped Tyler kill his daddy. Grogan gets cute, though. Holds back one of the knives. The one Beam used. Beam goes along saying he only wanted to plant two anyway. But the truth is he wasn't real happy about it."

Something creaked downstairs. Sully paused, sitting bolt upright in the chair. After a few moments of silence, he relaxed.

"Who sent Grogan after me at the zoo?" I asked.

"Grogan sent Grogan," Sully said. "He was plenty riled over you killing those two at the Walsh place."

"And Simpkins? The guy who showed up at my place last night?"

"He was pretty tight with Grogan. I don't think Beam authorized either of them runs at you. You know how it is—hard to keep a lid on things when the fur starts flying."

"How about Janet and Ava? They had nothing to do with any of this. Why involve them?"

Sully sighed. "Like I said, Matty was real mad about

that woman being Tyler's mom. Starts wondering if Walsh told her he'd be meeting with us the night he got killed. That's what Matty said he was worried about anyway. I told him I didn't think Walsh woulda said anything to her. I mean, why would he? But Matty? He says he's taking no chances. I didn't really buy it, though. I think he was just looking for an excuse to go after her. He sends Grogan and Grogan tracks her down." Sully grinned. "She's got herself a millionaire sugar daddy and Grogan finds her doing her skanky business on the street. Takes all kinds, I guess. Anyway, he rattles her cage a bit. But instead of telling him what he wants to hear, the stupid bitch comes right out and says that if Grogan comes near her again, she'll go to the cops. Grogan said he'd a killed her right there, but there's too many people around. 'Course, he weren't one to leave unfinished business." Sully paused. "'Fraid he went back and got her later."

"She hasn't been found," I said.

"Not yet. But then nobody's gonna look too hard for that kind, are they?"

I glared at him, but a small sob drew my attention. I'd been so focused on Sully that I'd forgotten that Ava was still in the room. I turned to find her staring at me with clear, expectant eyes. I couldn't guess how much of the conversation she'd been able to follow. Far too much, I feared.

I forced myself to smile—a gentle smile, like the one my mom gave me sometimes when things crept out of my closet at night or Dad was angry with me. Gazing at Ava, I saw some of her mother in her. Some of Greg, too. Both had asked me for help. Both were now dead. A fearful pressure welled inside of me. "Everything's going to be okay, honey," I told her. "I'm sorry I couldn't keep you out of this."

Her eyes were uncertain, but she returned the smile, and in a voice that cracked as if near bursting with forgiveness, she said, "That's okay, Lyle. I still love you."

True absolution is a fist in the belly. I felt suddenly hollow, barely able to draw breath. Ava waited for me to reply. "I love you too, honey," I said at last. Then hopelessly repeated, "Everything's going to be okay."

I hated myself for lying to her. Nothing was okay.

After a moment, I turned back to Sully. I tried to sound confident, but my voice quavered with helplessness. "Well, if things went down the way you say, I don't see where you've got many problems."

"You don't, do you?" Sully scoffed, his expression clouding, becoming more determined.

"Heck no," I continued. "Think about it. Grogan's to blame—him and Matty. Grogan did the actual killing. Matty was the ringleader. Now, they're both dead. Case solved."

"Bullshit, Dahms!" Sully exclaimed. "*I* stabbed Walsh first. It was an accident, sure, but I did it. I'm supposed to believe you're just gonna forget that? I seen the way you are. No way you let me go knowing what you know. You'd come back. You'd want to get me the way you got Grogan. The way you got them two boys. I don't know as I could get the drop on you again."

"You're wrong," I assured him. "If you let me go— if you let Ava go—I'll owe you our lives. That's a pretty big debt."

Sully brightened, but only for a moment. "Nice try, Dahms," he said. "But no way I could ever trust you. The way I see it, I got one play. I make sure it looks like it was all Grogan and Beam. And I don't leave no one around can testify different."

I held up a hand. "Hold on, Sully. That makes no sense. You got a chance to end this. You start killing now, you're throwing that away. You're throwing your life away."

He wasn't listening to me anymore. He turned to his sister. "I'll call Harvey. He can bring Charlie in here. Watch over things while Dahms and I go back downstairs."

"No, Sully," Prude pleaded. "Isn't there some other way?"

Sully shook his head. "Can't think of one, Prude. I don't want to go to jail, and I don't want to run. We gotta put things back the way they were. We gotta go home with all this behind us." He chuckled lightly. "Besides, Prude, you know there's no way you could get by without me."

"Like you could get along without me, you old slob," Prude chided him, flashing a smile. But the banter was just habit, the smile more like a wince.

Sully turned back to me. "I figure with the slug from your gun in old Matty, I just make sure his fingerprints are on this gun when all's said and done. Cops don't like him anyway. Should look like he did what he did, then you caught up with him, and y'all killed each other."

"And the little girl?" I asked.

"Sorry," Sully told me. "I feel plenty bad about this, but what are you gonna do? I don't see how I can let her out of here. You hadn't a shot up Matty's ear, maybe he'd never have snatched her up. Matty said he wanted to hurt you. He sees you with this girl here and figures messing with her would hurt you most."

I stared at Sully. It took a moment for that to sink in. Their taking Ava had nothing to do with her being Janet and Greg's kid, I realized. They likely hadn't even made the connection. They'd taken Ava solely as payback for my wounding Beam. The danger she was in. It was all on me.

Sully glanced at Ava, then looked back at me with genuine sympathy. "Might help some, you knowing that she'll go after you. It's not like you're gonna have to watch it or anything."

I nodded, even smiled at him. "And the Blauers? What do you do with them?"

"I'm truly sorry about all this, Dahms," Sully said.

As he rose from the chair, my first impulse was to rush him right then and there, but I forced myself to hold back. He'd take me downstairs, I thought. Put me in the same room as Beam, then let me fall where I would. Better to get out of the room, away from Ava, before I made my move.

"Okay," I nodded. "Let's go."

"After you," he said, pointing.

I didn't make it to the doorway. There was a loud, grunting noise in the hall outside and Dark Eyes came into the room. He came in fast. He came in backward. His feet weren't touching the ground. Then he crashed into the far wall, collapsing into a heap on the floor. For a moment, I was too stunned to move. I stood immobile, my mind spinning, trying to process what was happening.

Suddenly, the Milkman was standing in the doorway. I stared at him, but he was looking past me at the girls on the floor. Then I remembered Sully and the gun in his hand. Luckily, Sully had been nearly as startled as I'd been. I dove at him before he could aim properly. He fired, but it was off target. The sound of the shot in the small bedroom swallowed all other noise. Sully seemed strangely silent as I bowled into him, knocking him to the floor. I was able to grab his arm and I bashed it again and again on the floor until his fingers released the gun. I raised myself slightly, reared back, and clocked him on his left cheek. I felt the crackle of his cheekbone as it shattered against my knuckles.

Something hit me from behind as I was reaching over Sully for the gun that he'd dropped. Before I could grasp it, a black low-heeled pump stamped painfully down on my outstretched hand. Prude lifted her foot and tried to kick me in the head before she stooped to pick up the gun. She missed and I was able to grab ahold of her leg, pulling her off balance. She came down directly on top of me. I thought I felt something crack but managed to slip out from under her as she reached for Sully's gun. I pawed for it too, but she was far closer to the gun than I was. I began to push myself to my feet, and as I did, my elbow jabbed into the prostrate Sully, poking equal parts flab and gun handle. My dad's gun, I remembered. It was jammed into Sully's belt. I latched onto it and pulled. I pulled again. I pulled a third time and finally was able to wrestle it free.

Prude stood, Sully's gun in her hand, with her back to the open bedroom window. Still on the floor, I was swinging my gun around toward her when she pulled the trigger. I rolled out of the way, shuddering as the bullet thudded into a floorboard next to me. Frantic, I spun around, hoping to get a shot off before Prude could shoot again. Then I heard what sounded like a cough—a single cough, short with a whistle of phlegm—that seemed simultaneously to come both from just outside the house and from inexplicably far away. I moved to raise my gun, but Prude had the big .44 leveled at me. I stared into her eyes. I saw no trace of anger or even alarm in them. Rather, they were soft, as though with regret. Then, like a baton wielded by a drunken symphony conductor, the gun in her hand began to sway, drawing my gaze away from her face. The front of her housedress was stained with blood. She'd been shot, I realized. Shot from behind through the open window. Skip, I remembered. It took a moment for her to fall, but Prude Johnson was dead before she hit the floor.

Sully groaned but appeared unable to get up. I struggled to rise as the Milkman reached down and grabbed each of the girls by the arm and pulled them to their feet. "Sorry, guys," he said. "But we really gotta get out of here."

Megan just nodded, but Ava burst into tears. She threw herself toward Mulligan, her little arms outstretched. Mulligan let go of Megan and gathered Ava up into his arms. That's when Harvey Deason burst in.

Deason did a quick survey of the room, spotted the gun in my hand, and ducked behind Mulligan and Ava. Seeing the giant skinhead, Megan dived across the room from Deason. The Milkman turned, but with Ava in his arms he was unable to do anything before Deason swung on him. A string of saliva arched across the room as Deason's fist connected with the side of Mulligan's head. Mulligan wavered, then fell to his knees. He was still clutching Ava as Deason booted him savagely in the side. Mulligan rolled, dropping Ava, and Deason bent over to scoop her up. I pulled the trigger. Deason yelped as the bullet thudded into his left shoulder, but it didn't stop him. He grabbed Ava and hoisted her high in front of him.

"You shoot and you hit her!" he shouted at me. "Don't risk it!"

"Fuck you," I replied. Then I shot him in the left shin. His pants leg exploded with blood and flesh.

Incredibly, Deason didn't go down. He was cursing, still holding Ava, when Mulligan reached out an arm, hooked him, and pulled his wobbling legs out from under him. Deason fell on his back and Ava managed to squirm free. She bolted toward me, but Deason held firm to her shirt. Ava stared at me, just out of reach, arcs of fear sparking in her eyes. I was about to take another shot, but something was suddenly in my way. It was Mulligan. He stood, then dropped directly down on Deason, ramming his elbow into Deason's face. Deason's nose burst, splattering the back of Ava's shirt with blood as she broke free. Deason sat up, reaching blindly, but Mulligan hit him again. After that, Deason stopped moving altogether.

As I snatched up the fallen .44, Ava stood for a moment, glancing first at me, then at Mulligan. She was shaking uncontrollably, her hands still at her sides. I reached out to her, but something rustled behind me, and I turned to see Sully sitting up, gazing in horror at his sister's blood-soaked body on the floor next to him. By the time I'd turned back, Ava had run to Mulligan who'd once again gathered her up in his massive arms. Tears streamed down the big man's florid face. Ava went limp in his embrace.

After a moment, she raised her head and her eyes met mine. "I want my mommy."

I nodded at her solemnly. "I know."

She turned away, burying her face into Mulligan's chest.

Sully had crawled over to his sister and was cradling Prude's head in his lap, sobbing uncontrollably.

"I've got to check the rest of the house," I told Mulligan. He was still blubbering but nodded at me in agreement.

I found Charlie Blauer sitting on the edge of the bed in his room. My appearance in the doorway barely registered on him. "Blauer," I called.

He raised his head. He stared at me, but he wasn't really there. "Look what I did," he said. He wasn't talking to me.

"Your daughter needs you," I told him.

"Look what I brought into my house," he said, slurring his words slightly.

"There's blame enough for everyone, Now, go to her. She's in the bedroom."

He stared at me blankly. Then, without another word, without so much as a flicker of emotion, he stood and meekly walked past me.

I checked every room but didn't find any more bad guys in the house. I couldn't go back upstairs. Instead, I called the cops, dimmed the lights, then crouched down in the darkness of the empty living room. The air was suffused with the smell of the dead. I trained my father's gun on the front door against intruders, guarding as much against phantoms as flesh and blood belligerents. Voices from the bedroom drifted down to me. First Megan's voice, then her father's, mingling with Sully's sobs. The minutes slunk by like sullen zombies. I stared down the barrel of the gun, waiting for the cops, careful to avoid the shadows. Greg, Janet, even Prude Johnson, were in the shadows, casting glances, blaming me. And the voices from above—hollow yet filled with mourning and awful realization—were accusatory soundings in the dark.

Chapter Thirty-one

I never did see Skip. Since St. Helena is far too small to have its own police force, the Apple Valley cops handled the cleanup. By the time they arrived, Skip was long gone. But while Skip had made himself scarce, there was a familiar face waiting for me as I stepped off the Blauer porch and was nudged toward a waiting patrol car. Basil rocketed toward us, leaping and striking me so hard I nearly went over. Whether due to greatness of spirit or feeblemindedness I couldn't say, but the dog seemed to hold no grudge against me for dragging him into a war zone and losing him in a cornfield. Instead, he was ecstatic to see me, a whirling, squirming, little, buff ball of forgiveness.

The Milkman and Ava came out of the house behind me. Basil ran to Ava, and she leaned down to let the dog give her a smack. Then she looked up at me with a grim little smile before being led away by a burly patrolman who promised candy and sodas once they got back to the public safety building.

I was taken away separately. The patrolman charged with transporting me was none too happy that I insisted on bringing the dog along. But Dad's pal Davidson was senior officer on the scene and with shake of his head he told the younger patrolman to allow the dog in the car.

At the station, we were herded into separate interview rooms, except Basil, who was allowed to stay with me. The Apple Valley cops questioned me for hours. I told them everything I knew in exquisite detail, except the minor matter of Skip having been a member of our rescue party. Just as they seemed to be winding up with me, Augie Tarkof arrived, and I got to go through it all again. By the time I'd finished, dawn was streaking the sky. My stomach had been growling pretty steadily and when we were done, Augie took pity on me, buying us each a microwavable burrito from the suburban cops' well-stocked vending machine. Augie avoided eye contact as he tucked ferociously into his burrito. When I asked him how the diet was going, he told me to shut up.

When they finally let me go, Davidson cautioned me to be available for the inquest, then strongly urged me to stay out of both Apple Valley and St. Helena until I was needed. Beam had quite a few followers, more than the cops would ever know about, let alone round up. Bringing down Beam left a bunch of guys who viewed beating on people as a normal recreational option with nothing to do in their spare time. Davidson pointed out that these guys would not be happy with me and that the cops couldn't guarantee my safety. I told him I didn't think staying away would be much of a burden.

The Milkman was waiting in the lobby for me. I should have expected it, but nonetheless it came as a blow when he told me that County Child Protection Services had taken Ava away. He'd been assured that she would be well looked after and if they needed us for anything, we'd be contacted.

We all made the next day's paper. They even spelled my name correctly. But for the most part, the story of the fall of Beam's "church" was presented as a kind of morality play, where not man but the hand of God had smitten the heretic, leaving all right with the world. A despondent Sully, it was reported, was now cooperating fully with the police. He'd told them everything, including the spot on the Blauer property where he'd helped bury Janet Kleiner.

Disregarding Davidson's advice, a few days later I returned to Apple Valley and found myself standing beside Mavis Kleiner as Janet's remains were re-interred in a plot that Mavis had purchased for herself. Turnout was light. Just me, Mavis, the rabbi, and, surprisingly, Evelyn Walsh.

After Janet had been lowered into the earth, I walked Mavis back to her car. "I'd hoped that the baby...that Ava, would be here," she said, glancing back toward the grave.

"Me, too," I said.

Mavis raised her palms in a gesture of reluctant resignation, then slowly eased herself into the car. As she drove away, I turned to find Evelyn waiting for me. "I wanted to thank you," she told me. "I mean, there's a check on the way, but..." She paused, unhappy with herself.

"You've nothing to thank me for, Evelyn. If I'd acted differently, so much of this would never have happened."

She smiled thinly, but her brow furrowed. "I've told myself that, too," she said. "I've spent night after night thinking about all the mistakes I've made. I thought I was doing everything that you're supposed to do. I followed the rules. But both Greg and Tyler...Look what happened to them. Tyler became everything I feared for him, and Greg... If I'd been a better wife maybe Greg would never have strayed. Maybe the risk to our marriage would have stopped him. But then, if he hadn't have taken that risk, we'd never have had Tyler." She paused. "Or Ava."

I sighed. "I don't think you have yourself to blame for the thing between Greg and Janet," I said, hoping I sounded wiser than I felt. "No matter what you'd have done, when Janet came knocking, Greg was going to answer the door. He was, uh…He was a guy with a strong sense of responsibility. He'd taken responsibility for Janet back when he was young and at his most impressionable. Time and distance weren't going to change that. Not for him. I don't know what it was about the guy. Not everybody gets over the arrogance of youth, I guess. You know, when you think you're invincible and no challenge is too great, no risk too dear."

Evelyn nodded but made no reply. I shuffled beside her for a few awkward moments.

"Well," she said at last, lowering her eyes, "there are risks that are worth taking. I hope so, anyway. I…I've been thinking. Mostly about the little girl. Mostly about Ava."

I nodded.

Evelyn raised her head. "I've talked to my lawyers. I've decided to see about instituting adoption procedures."

I stared at her. "You're what?"

Her eyes were steely, her voice firm and strong. "She *is* Tyler's sister. And Tyler's my son."

"Yes, but she's not…"

"Mine?" Evelyn interrupted. "I'll tell you one thing I know for sure. One thing that all adoptive mothers know. You don't love your children because you made them. You love them for who they are and because they complete you. I don't love Tyler less because I'm not his birth mother. In fact, it's possible that makes me love him more, treasure him more."

"But her *real* mother..." I began.

Evelyn's eyes flashed.

"Her *birth* mother," I corrected myself. "She was your husband's lover."

"I know what you're thinking. That having her around will only remind me of..." She broke off, shaking her head. "And that may be true. But I keep coming back to the fact that Tyler's sister, my dead husband's child, needs a home. A family. We're her family. Tyler and me. We need to bring her home. Who her birth parents are doesn't preclude Ava from having a good home and a family that loves her."

"Yeah, but—"

Evelyn made a slashing gesture with her hand. "Whatever you're going to say, do you really think it hasn't occurred to me? Do you think there is something in this decision that you understand more than I do?" She paused. "Greg isn't the only one with a strong sense of responsibility."

Evelyn extended her hand. I took it and wished her and her family every happiness.

****

Perhaps a week later, I was driving my dad back from the hospital after one of his weekly chemotherapy appointments. My mom had contrived to force us together, claiming that she'd promised to help out at a church function that day and telling us both that it wasn't too much for her to ask that father and son spend part of one afternoon running an "errand" together. The silence between us was uncomfortable, but I was determined not to let it get me down.

I was finally starting to feel a little better. The bruises on my face were fading nicely. The wound at my side only bothered me when I turned in my sleep, and the slight infection I'd developed from the bullet nick of my foot was responding to antibiotics. I'd had a date with Naomi the night before. We'd had dinner at the Rusty Scupper, a seafood restaurant on Industrial Boulevard in Minneapolis. Landlocked, surrounded by warehouses and freeway, it was notably lacking in salty ambience, but the food wasn't bad. Naomi had a New York strip steak. I'd had the bacon-wrapped sea scallops. We shared a bottle of wine and later she shared my bed. We hadn't spoken directly about it, about how she saw no future in our relationship. Perhaps, I hoped, we never would. Perhaps we'd just go on being together until the future simply sneaked up on us.

Dad and I were only a few blocks from home, winding our way past the ramblers and split-levels of the neighborhood where I'd grown up. When these houses went up in the late 1950s and early '60s, the developer had managed to save many of the old elms that had been growing on the land. But the towering elms that had lined the streets in my youth had since been lost to disease. The young, sturdier maples that had been planted in their stead appeared dwarfish by comparison. Coming home, I was always struck by how everything seemed to have diminished with the passing of the years.

On the sidewalk ahead, underneath one of the maples, I spotted two boys, both about twelve years old. They stood close, leaning toward one another, their jaws jutting forward. One kid was bigger than the other— heavy set, with a shock of unruly, light brown hair that stood nearly upright in the breeze. The other kid was blond with skinny arms and feet so big it looked like he was wearing clown shoes. They were obviously arguing, and the smaller kid was starting to back away when the big kid suddenly decked him. The blond kid collapsed onto the sidewalk in a crumpled heap. I slowed the car and pulled over to the side of the road.

"Jeez!" Dad said, wincing. "Whatcha doing now? This has nothing to do with us."

I ignored him, got out of the car, and approached the two twelve-year-olds. Both stared at me with eyes that alternated curiosity and fear. Behind me, I heard my dad rolling down the car window. "You all right?" I asked the kid on the ground.

Lying there holding a bloody nose, he looked up at me as if this was perhaps the stupidest question he'd ever heard. "No."

The bigger kid shifted back and forth on his feet a couple of times, as if doing a boxer's shuffle. "Never mind him," he said, finding the courage to sneer. "He just wants attention."

I shook my head, bent over, and extended a hand to the kid on the ground. "Let's get you up and see how you're doing?"

He ignored my hand, preferring to stay down. "I'm okay," he said, his voice charged with defiance.

I turned to the kid who'd smacked him. "Was this necessary?"

"Sure was."

I raised an eyebrow. "You know," I told him, "my dad taught me that this kind of thing is never necessary. He taught me that a man that can't hold his temper ain't worth much. But…" I paused and shrugged. "Looks like you've chosen a different path. Good luck with that."

I turned and walked back to the car, careful not to so much as glance back at either of them as I got in and drove away. We were about a block further down the road when my dad shook his head. "I never taught you that."

"I know."

We got home and I helped Dad out of the car and into the house. As I was leaving, he said something about my maybe driving him to another appointment soon. Maybe. If Mom was busy. I told him I'd like that.

When I got back to the Bijou, I knocked on Edgerton's door, but there was no answer. I'd been checking on him regularly since Ava had gone. Rather more often than he was comfortable with. I wasn't really worried about him. When I'd told him about Evelyn Walsh's plan, he'd said only that he was glad that Ava would be going to a good home. Then he quickly changed the subject. Since then, I hadn't mentioned Ava to him but, like I said, I'd taken to checking on him pretty often.

I went to my room, took Basil outside, then returned to watch *Jeopardy* on TV. It was nearly over when Basil, who'd been lying contentedly on the bed next to me, stiffened and began growling at the door. A moment later, there was a knock, the door swung open, and Edgerton entered. He looked around briefly and without apparent interest. The dog refused to settle down. Even after Edgerton had patted him, Basil continued to eye the door, grumbling suspiciously.

"What you doing?" Edgerton asked.

"Final Jeopardy," I said, pointing at the TV.

He nodded and we watched together in silence.

When the program was over, I got up and switched off the TV.

"Want to grab a couple of beers?" I asked. "Maybe some dinner?"

"Okay, but you'll have to front me some cash, though. I'm sorta tapped and rent's due next week."

I shrugged.

He nodded again, but when I turned for the door, he didn't move.

"Something else?"

"Yeah," he said. "I've been thinking about Ava. About her and that Evelyn Walsh? That gonna be all right?"

"Well, it's not a done deal yet. These things take time. Some agency will need to sign off on it. A judge will have to review the case. I gotta think the judge will have some questions. This can't be an everyday thing."

"So, what do you think? You think Ava will end up with her?"

I nodded. "She's got money. Her lawyers are top-drawer. She'll make it happen."

Stephen waited a moment before asking. "You were pretty big buds with her late husband, right?"

"Yeah."

"So, you think maybe after Ava's all settled and they've had a chance to, you know, bond and all...You think, maybe she'd let us come by and see the kid?"

"Maybe. Yeah."

"I'd like to see her. I miss her."

"Me, too."

He cocked his head and smiled crookedly. "Things have been kinda...kinda quiet around here lately. Don't you think?"

"Comparatively. But that's not necessarily a bad thing."

Edgerton stared at me keenly. "Got something I want to show you," he said, his eyes suddenly sparkling with mischief.

"Now, Stephen—"

"Just take a second," he interrupted, darting past me and out the door.

Moments later, he returned, backing in slowly, shielding something from my view. He turned to reveal that he was cradling something small and black. I couldn't make out what it was at first. Then it moved.

Edgerton set a small, black puppy down on my bed. I watched, momentarily speechless, as Basil gingerly approached the intruder, growling and sniffing a couple of times before looking back up at me. His eyes brimmed with disappointment. Basil, who'd patiently accepted his loss of status as perceived head of household while Ava was with us, did not appear at all happy to have his restored place in the hierarchy challenged by this fur ball.

"Isn't he beautiful?" Edgerton asked.

I actually fought back a sob. "What have you done?"

Edgerton beamed. "I bought us a new puppy."

"Stephen, you're…you're kidding right. I mean, there's no way—"

"He's a Lhasapoo," Edgerton broke in. "Half Lhasa apso and half poodle. I thought we'd call him Nigel. You know, after Nigel Bruce—Watson to Basil Rathbone's Sherlock Holmes."

"I know who Nigel Bruce is, Stephen," I said, my voice rising. "And *we're* not going to call him anything. You do what you like, but I want nothing to do with another dog."

Edgerton's expression drooped, but he couldn't quite suppress the smile that played at the corners of his mouth. "Now that's hardly fair, Lyle. I mean, I got the little guy so Basil would have a friend. We're gone so much of the time. Poor Basil is here all alone. I mean, he needs someone. You know, now that Ava's gone."

"We all miss Ava, Stephen. We've been through that. But this is just too—"

"Look!" Edgerton interrupted. "They're already playing together."

The black puppy had been steadily inching toward Basil, who had been forced to retreat to the far side of the bed, where the black puppy had now cornered him. Basil looked first at the floor. Then he looked up to me for rescue as the puppy began to nuzzle him roughly. The puppy blithely went about his business, paying no attention at all to the distressed whimpers issued by his new best friend.

I stared at Edgerton for some time. "Well, at least this one's got a tail," I observed at last.

"Yeah," Edgerton said, his victory smile breaking wide. "It's nice and bushy all right. They tell me Nigel here might shed a little more than Basil. You might want to get yourself a lint brush. You still buying dinner?

"I guess."

Edgerton chuckled. "Tell you what. You put Nigel in the kennel, and I'll buy dinner."

"I'll let you."

As we were locking up, Edgerton once again turned toward me, a thoughtful, even melancholic expression on his face. "Lyle," he said. "About the dog."

"Yes, Stephen."

"You owe me seventy-five dollars."

A word about the author…

Brian is a graduate of the University of Minnesota whose Dinkytown neighborhood provides the setting for his mystery series featuring private investigator Lyle Dahms. The Dahms novels spring from his lifelong love of mystery fiction, especially the works of Dashiell Hammett and Raymond Chandler, as well as more contemporary masters like Robert B. Parker and G.M. Ford. He is a three-time finalist in the Pacific Northwest Writers Association mystery and suspense contest. Brian spent much of his professional career working to alleviate domestic hunger serving as the operations director of the Emergency Feeding Program of Seattle & King County as well as the manager of the Pike Market Food Bank in downtown Seattle. Married with three beautiful daughters, Brian now lives and writes in Ocean Shores, a small city on the Washington coast. www.brianandersonmysteries.com

Thank you for purchasing
this publication of The Wild Rose Press, Inc.

For questions or more information
contact us at
info@thewildrosepress.com.

The Wild Rose Press, Inc.
www.thewildrosepress.com